Mountain Man Daddy Series
Books 1 to 4

S.E. Riley

The Redherring Publishing House

Table of Contents

Mountain Man Sheriff (Book 1)

Blurb

Lauren moved to Willow Town to start afresh, but the first person she met was the town's Sheriff. And he put her in cuffs. Nate liked things to run by the book, but the curvy newcomer to his town was certainly shaking things up.

Lauren

I had spent 10 years with my cop ex, in a marriage that broke me in more ways than one. I had been young and in love...how things have changed. I was grateful I was now out. I wanted a fresh start and picked Willow Town as the perfect escape. But my past caught up to me, and no matter how much I hated it [at first ;)], I needed the Sheriff.

Nate

I shut myself off after getting my heart broken. Now, I lived for my job and Saturday night catchups with my younger sister. That's until Lauren crushed into my life. All sass and wit, the curvy newest bartender sparked something in me. And when she asked for my help keeping her safe from her ex...well, my desire to keep her safe soon ran deeper than just my duty as a Sheriff.

Prologue

Lauren

I couldn't remember the last time I had been in handcuffs. I was certain that I hadn't been in the back of a sheriff's truck back then, either.

Sheriff Hollis, at least that's what he told me his name was. I have trouble trusting law enforcement these days, especially when he kept looking at me as if I was crazy. I might have screamed if that distrusting look passed across his green eyes one more time.

Fortunately, he didn't look at me again after loading me into the back of the truck. Instead, he was busy running the plates again. I thought he was only running them again to placate me. He didn't seem to believe that my ex-husband would ever tamper with documents to change the ownership of my car.

Maybe this was all karma's way of getting back at me.

I had finally packed my meager amount of things and left my controlling cop husband. When I threw a dart at a map, it landed on Willow Town. This was supposed to be my chance at a new beginning, but instead, I was being driven to the local jail.

What a way to make an impression.

Here I am, Willow Town, newly a criminal and ready to terrorize you all by stealing my own car, I thought as the sheriff drove over the bumpy back roads.

"You know, this is all a mistake. I've already told you that once. If you would actually listen to me, you might see that I'm telling the truth."

"Miss, you were trying to break into a car on the side of the road. That car back there was reported as stolen. You are either the thief or may have seen something relevant to this case. We can sort that out when we get back to the station."

"Holy shit," I said, leaning back against the seat and trying to adjust my wrists in the cuffs. "You are a real piece of work, aren't you? No wonder you're the sheriff."

"And what's that supposed to mean?" he asked, his jaw clenching as he looked at me in the rearview mirror. "If anyone in this vehicle is a piece of work, it's you. Do you honestly think I would believe that you weren't trying to break into that car? When I pulled up, you were about to throw a rock through the window."

"Because my keys were locked inside *my* car!"

I never would have been arrested if he hadn't pulled up when I tried to break into my own car. I wouldn't have had to do this if the car hadn't broken down in the first place. I had been in a hurry to get out and find out what was wrong with the engine, slamming the door before I remembered to grab the keys.

"You can't prove that. Facts are the car is reported as stolen, and you were going to break a window. While I can't question you on what I think you were about to do, I can question you concerning the stolen vehicle."

"Lucky me," I muttered, closing my eyes, and hoping it would all be over soon.

By the time the questioning was over, the sun had set in Willow Town. I was still without a car as the police tried to figure out what was happening. Apparently, my story of an ex who happened to be a corrupt cop wasn't good enough for them. I had expected as much. Cops never wanted to believe that one of their own could be corrupt—not even if they were from different counties and had never met.

Still, they had pried open the car and given me back the duffel bags that were in the back seat filled with belongings after sifting through them. My car would be held until they determined whether it was mine or not, despite showing them my insurance.

Go figure!

Rather than argue with them, I slung both bags over my shoulders and walked down Main Street. Main Street was one stretch of road that seemed to house the commercial district of Willow Town. Everything you needed was on this one short stretch of town. I tried to find my new workplace and home while looking around at the small buildings. Most of the buildings were quiet, their lights off, and their curtains were drawn. It was too late at night for anyone to be awake unless they were patrons of the one and only bar in town.

When I entered Taz less than 10 minutes later, there was a woman with bright blue hair behind the bar. She looked up at me and smiled, speaking to one of the other bartenders quickly. She rounded the bar and joined me, wiping her hands on her towel.

"How can I help?"

"Hi. I'm Lauren...I'm looking for Kayleigh."

"Ah, yes, Lauren. Pleasure to meet you." She shook my hand firmly before looking at her watch. "Thought you'd be here earlier? Did you get lost on your way here?"

"Sorry, no. Car trouble." I giggled nervously.

"Happens to the best of us," she said, smiling as she reached into the pocket of her apron and withdrew a key. "You must have had a long trip getting here. Go get some rest. The apartment is upstairs. It's small but cozy. If you need anything, come down here and let me know. I'm usually here from noon onwards."

"Thank you," I said, taking the key.

Kayleigh nodded. "I have a bar to tend to. I'll see you tomorrow night at seven for your first shift. Try not to be late."

"Thank you," I said again, turning the key over in my hand. "You don't know how much I appreciate this."

Kayleigh smiled as she walked around the bar. "You sounded like someone who was looking to start their life over. I've been there before."

Smiling, I nodded and backed away from the bar as more patrons clustered around it. "I'll see you tomorrow night."

"Have a good night, Lauren."

I left the bar and headed to the little apartment above it. She was right; the apartment was small, but it was cozy. It was the first place I could call my own since the divorce. Curtains hung over the window, and a few pieces of furniture spread throughout the apartment. It wasn't much, but it was enough to hold me over until I could start buying my own belongings.

Instead of dwelling on what the apartment wasn't, I smiled at what it was. It was the first place I ever had that belonged to me and only me. There was no ex-husband with his name on the lease.

When my head finally hit the pillow later that night, I got the overwhelming sense of finally being home.

Chapter 1

Nate

Saturdays were beer night. Me and my sister Sarah would abandon all our responsibilities and head to Taz for a few rounds. It was a weekly tradition that we had been carrying on for years. I could count the number of times we had missed our beer night on one hand.

Even though I was avoiding the new bartender like the plague—and had been for the last four Saturdays I came in—she wouldn't keep me from beer night.

Arresting her had been the highlight of my month. The entire drive to the station was filled with her incessant chatter about how she couldn't possibly have stolen a car. I didn't believe her at first, or even when we got to the station, but I had been sure she was telling the truth by the time I had released her from custody.

It had taken longer than I would have liked to verify her story, and even then, the story seemed hazy at best. It was only when calling the dealership and giving them the VIN that it was confirmed the car had been sold to Lauren and not her ex-husband. The plates had still been registered to Jason Guthrie, no matter how many times I ran the plates.

Still, there had been something that told me that this woman hadn't stolen the car. There was something about how her eyes had darted around the station, as if looking for her husband, nearly scared that he would pop out of the shadows.

It was too late at that point to make amends. She was pissed off, and there was nothing I could say to make her believe I was just doing my job.

Not that it mattered. Apart from beer nights, Lauren and I hadn't seen each other since then. It was a small town but living on the outskirts—and spending most of my time at the station—helped me avoid majority of the population. It was sometimes lonely, but it was better than watching my ex-best friend walk around with my ex-girlfriend on his arm.

I nursed my beer far in the back corner of the bar, trying to erase the thoughts of my disastrous last relationship from my mind. Despite my efforts to relax and have a good time, there was a brown-eyed blonde that kept skating around the edges of my vision.

Watching her as she worked was something else. Each time I came in on a Saturday, she was working, and she made sure I wasn't in her section. It had been annoying at first, but now, it was entertaining. She was doing everything in her power to ignore me, but I didn't miss how those brown eyes looked at me every now and then.

"Don't hate me for being late," Sarah said as she slid into the chair across from me. "I promise I tried to be on time this week, but my classes were running late, and getting back to town took longer than I thought."

I laughed and shook my head, taking another sip of my beer. "Sarah, relax. School comes first. It's fine."

Sarah grinned as Kayleigh shoved a cold glass of some craft beer in front of her. Kayleigh was gone as quick as she had come, off to serve more of her patrons.

"So," Sarah said, looking over at the bar to where Lauren was determined to ignore us. I caught her eye for a second, winking at her only to see a scowl cross her face. Lauren turned away, smiling at one of the men in front of her.

"So, what?"

"So, you still interested in that bartender?"

I scoffed and shook my head. "I'm not interested in any bartender."

"I forgot that you've sworn off women," Sarah said, smirking around the rim of her glass as she took a sip of her beer.

In a way, she was right. I didn't have time for women in my life and didn't want to have time for them. Not after my last girlfriend had spent most of our relationship cheating on me with my best friend. While I had moved on from that, I still had no interest in dating anytime soon. I was happy alone.

"It's easier this way. I have more time to focus on my career."

Sarah rolled her eyes, leaning on the table. "You do realize that sounds insanely lonely, right?"

"It's fine, Sarah. It's what works for me right now."

She hummed and drummed her fingers on the table, not bothering to say anything more on the subject, easily switching the topic to her classes. As I listened to her talk, I knew that Sarah would make an amazing lawyer one day. She was passionate about helping people and righting wrongs. She loved a good argument. My heart swelled with pride as she talked about some of her lessons.

"Hey," Kayleigh said, approaching the table with a wary smile nearly an hour later. She was carrying two more beers for Sarah and I. "I hate to ask this, but I have to pick up Bryce early on Saturdays from now on. Lauren is still new at closing the bar. Would you mind waiting with her, Nate? Just for the next few Saturdays? I know I shouldn't worry about something happening to her, but it's still late at night with a bunch of drunks lingering."

"Not a problem, Kay. Tell Bryce I say hello," I said before downing the last of my beer.

Sarah waited until Kayleigh had walked away before smirking at me with a knowing look. I said nothing as I sipped at the new, chilled beer. Sarah drummed her fingers on the table, trying to drive me insane. Her smirk grew as I glanced over at the bar, looking for the curvy blonde before looking away.

"We really aren't going to talk about how attracted you are to Lauren?" Sarah asked, her tone light and teasing as she traced her finger through the condensation on her bottle.

"We aren't going to talk about that because you're wrong."

Sarah's smirk drew as she shook her head. "You keep telling yourself that."

"I will."

***

It was well past midnight when Lauren rounded up the last drunks. She helped them outside to waiting cars driven by their wives or loved ones, before heading back inside to clean up. I watched her the entire time from my place at the table in the corner. Though she looked like she was ignoring me, I could tell from the tension in her shoulders that she was aware of my presence.

Instead of acknowledging me, she went to the stereo in the corner and connected her phone. Moments later, some country song was blasting through the bar, and she sang along to it. She raised her hands above her head, twirling around as she worked at cleaning the bar top and drying the glasses. I tried not to watch her, but the way her thick hips swayed was hypnotic.

Lauren worked in silence, acting as if she was the only one in the room, until she moved to the tables at the far end of the room. Every now and then, she would look up at me and scowl before going back to scrubbing away sticky liquids and crumbs of food. Finally, she turned the music down and sighed.

"What?" I asked, smirking as I took a sip of the beer I had been nursing for the last hour.

"You could help clean up," Lauren said, looking at me over her shoulder as she scrubbed at the last of some congealed nacho cheese on a table. "Instead of sitting there and looking pretty."

"You think I'm pretty?" I watched as a red blush crept across her cheeks. She shook her head and moved to another table.

"I don't think about you at all."

"I think you're lying about that," I said, teasing her. "I think you spend more time thinking about me than you ever want to admit. In fact, I'm sure you're thinking about me right now."

"Thinking about murdering you," she muttered, glaring at me over her shoulder.

"You know, you probably shouldn't admit your homicidal tendencies to the sheriff."

The corner of her mouth turned slightly before she again schooled her face into a blank expression. Lauren finished with another table and started cleaning the last. I watched her, wondering what she was thinking about. For years, I had been good at reading people. Not her, though. Never her. Maybe that was part of the interest I had in her. Even though we'd barely exchanged a word over the past month, something about her reeled me in. She kept me on my toes like nobody else ever had.

"Back to my original comment," she said, tossing a rag at me. I caught the rag before it hit my face, grinning at her scowl. "Get off your ass and start cleaning."

"I don't work here," I said, stretching my legs in front of me and crossing them at the ankles. "In fact, I am a paying customer. You wouldn't ask a paying customer to help clean up, would you?"

If looks could kill, I would be dead already. She would have crossed the room and skinned me alive if she had been given half the chance.

She gritted her teeth and shook her head. "You are such a pain in my ass." She grabbed the half-finished bottle from my hand, wiping rather roughly where my beer had been sitting, and walked away.

"Not on purpose," I said, grinning when she turned back to her cleaning.

"I have a hard time believing that your behavior isn't on purpose."

Lauren said nothing else as she finished cleaning the bar. I could have gotten up to help, but that might have given her the idea that I wanted to help her. I didn't. The less fondly she thought about me, the better. If I even stood a fraction of a chance with her, I would ruin it like I ruined every other relationship in my life.

She shone too bright to have her light smothered by my darkness.

When she was finally finished cleaning, I felt like more of an ass than before for not helping her. I didn't apologize as I watched her grab the keys and take off her apron. She hung the apron over a hook behind the bar before moving to the front door.

"You coming or what, Sheriff?"

I got up from the table, smothering the smile that threatened to appear at her irritation. "I don't know. I thought I might stay here a little longer since your customer service skills are outstanding."

"Get off your ass, put up your chair and get to the door or I'll lock you in here and call the police about a robbery."

"Funny," I said, upturning my chair on the table and following her to the door.

Lauren smiled sweetly and shrugged, unbothered that her threats were falling on deaf ears. Instead, she looked amused as she flipped me the middle finger.

"That's mature."

"I never claimed to be mature," she said.

"Well, I wouldn't expect maturity from a criminal such as yourself."

"Watch it, Hollis. You're starting to sound like you're enjoying my company. Wouldn't want that, considering you're an intolerable bastard on your best day."

Instead of getting to know her like I wanted to—goading her into talking to me some more—I stayed silent. I waited with her outside as she locked the door. She kept her mouth set in a thin line as she looked over her shoulder at me before climbing the stairs to her apartment. I waited as one of the few taxis in town idled in the background, the several beers I had adding a haze to my vision.

Still, my mind was clear enough to briefly consider what would happen if I followed her up those stairs.

Chapter 2

Lauren

The sun was beating down, warming the shores of the riverbank. There was something about late summer that made everything seem better. I laughed as Kayleigh balanced Bryce on her hip while wading into the river. The little boy giggled and leaned over her arm, reaching for the shimmering water.

Movement from the other edge of the river caught my eye. When I looked up, I could see Nate standing on the other side, a fishing pole draped over his shoulder and a tacklebox in his hand. He glanced at me for a moment, his mouth setting into a hard line before he picked up the cooler at his feet and walked further down the river.

I watched as he worked methodically, putting a lure on the line before casting it into the water. For a moment, there was a look of peace on his face. That was before he looked up, and our gazes locked. The serene smile was gone and replaced with another deep frown. I rolled my eyes and looked back at my new friend and her son, determined to enjoy the day despite the grouch across the river.

"What's his problem?" I asked, wading into the water with Kayleigh and Bryce. She looked up, scanning the riverbank before her eyes locked on the sheriff of Willow Town.

"Nothing," Kayleigh said, grinning as she set Bryce in the water and held his hand. "He's a good man, but he's a little reserved. Not that I can blame him. He had to grow up fast."

"He always seems irritated with me whenever I see him."

Kayleigh chuckled and shrugged. "That's just his face. He's a grump most of the time, but he's also the kind of man who would give you the shirt off his back if you asked for it."

None of that lined up with the man that I had seen so far. He seemed determined to push my buttons at every turn. He was annoying and irritating. I couldn't stand him, but at the same time, I wanted to get to know him better. I wanted to know what makes him tick. But I would be lying to myself if I didn't feel like wringing his neck and burying him six feet deep every time I saw him.

To say my emotions regarding the sheriff were complicated was an understatement.

"I find that hard to believe," I said, glancing back at Nate. He scowled, turning his back to me.

"Give him time. He'll come around, eventually."

I snorted and ran a hand through my hair as the wind blew. "I don't know about that. He threw me in jail without considering that my story might be the truth. Besides, why would I even want him to come around?"

"To be fair, you did tell me that you were about to break into a car, and your ex is crazy. And you want him to come around because he is hot as hell, and you two have off-the-charts chemistry."

"Yeah, it's not my fau...wait, what? We do not have chemistry," I said, making a point of not looking at the sheriff. "We could not have less chemistry."

Kayleigh rolled her eyes. "Oh yeah? Then why does he show up at the beginning of your shift on Saturday and stay until the end? Or how about how you look like you're going to jump over the bar at him whenever he orders a beer."

"I do not," I said, my voice tight.

"Yes, you do. You look at him like he is the most attractive man you've ever seen. Hell, you look at him like you would drag him into a closet and have your way with him if you could. Try telling me again how that isn't chemistry."

"I don't even know what chemistry is," I said, trying to find another way out of this conversation. "My ex-husband and I were married at nineteen. Stupidly young, I know. And now I'm twenty-eight, and I have no clue if I even had chemistry with him."

"Oh," Kayleigh said, wiggling her eyebrows at me. "So, you're interested in older men now, then?"

"I'm not."

"I would say that you are. Nate is thirty-five. That's older."

"I'm done with this conversation," I said, wishing the ground would open up and swallow me whole.

"You have chemistry with Nate," Kayleigh said, looking over at the sheriff and giving a small wave. "You should see what would happen if you explored that with him."

"Shut up." I grinned, my cheeks flushing a bright red, as I crouched down to splash a little wave at Bryce. The boy squealed and jumped, water splashing everywhere.

For the rest of the morning, we played in the water as I squelched any thoughts of the sheriff. At some point, he packed up his fishing gear and left, giving me one more scowl before waving amicably at Kayleigh and Bryce.

Well, fuck you too. I snarled in my mind as I turned around to splash around the water some more. As noon approached, thoughts of the sheriff were in the distant past as I had easy fun with Kayleigh and her son.

Kayleigh was a good boss, but she was a better friend. There was a part of me that worried about getting close to her. If my ex found out where I was—and I didn't doubt that he already had—it might put Kayleigh and Bryce at risk.

When I left them that afternoon, I was certain that I would do whatever it took to keep them safe. That meant that I would keep Jason away from them at all costs. I'd keep my distance as much as possible, but I wanted a friend. I needed a friend.

By the time I got home, I was done worrying about Kayleigh and Bryce. My ex had always been crazy and controlling, but he had never been dangerous. They would be safe. It was me he was after and nobody else.

At least, I didn't think he was until I saw the picture taped to my front door. It was a picture taken on the day I was married, my white dress hugging my body as my ex-husband stood behind me with his arms wrapped around my waist. In the picture, we looked happy. There was no sign of what was to come.

My heart was hammering in my chest as I tore the picture down and crumpled it up. For a moment, I hesitated outside. I didn't want to enter the apartment in case he was in there. I reached out and tried the handle, breathing a sigh of relief when I found it was still locked.

"He's just messing with your head," I said softly as I unlocked my door. "He's messing with you, but he isn't here. He can't bring you back."

With that in mind, I entered my apartment and got ready for work.

***

The bar was open, but Kayleigh had given me the early shift. It was only midnight, and the party in Taz would remain open for a few more hours, given that it was another Saturday night in Willow Town. I smiled and waved to some of the regulars as I left for the night, eager for the cool night air to hit my skin.

The wind was blowing softly, easing the heat of the day as I walked outside. I tilted my head back and looked up at the stars littering the sky. Back in the city, I was lucky if I was able to see any stars.

As I climbed the stairs to my apartment above the bar, there was an uneasy twist in my stomach. When I turned the corner of the landing and saw the door to my apartment was wide open, my heart froze in my chest. My knuckles turned white as I gripped the railing and climbed a step higher. Shattered glass coated the mat in front of the door, a picture of me and my friends torn in half among the mess.

Without thinking, I turned and ran down the stairs. I took a deep breath before I entered the bar, trying to remain calm as I scanned the room for the man I knew would still be there. When my eyes locked with the sheriff's, I crossed the room to his table.

"I need help," I said before he could say anything else.

Nate set down his drink, his green eyes searching my face. What he was looking for, I didn't know, but whatever he saw had to have been enough. He stood up, towering over me, and nodded to the door.

When we got outside, he stopped and crossed his arms. "What's happening, Lauren?"

"My apartment was broken into. I think it's my ex. A picture from my wedding was taped to the door the other day when I got home, but I didn't think much of it. I thought that he was only messing with me. I didn't think that he would break in."

"Stay down here," he said as we stopped at the bottom of the stairs. "If you hear anything while I'm up there, run to my truck and get in. Make sure the doors are locked behind you, and then call the station."

"We can just wait for the cops to get here. You don't have to go up alone."

He chuckled and rolled his eyes. "I'm fine, Lauren. Just run for the truck if you hear anything strange."

I nodded, looking to where his truck was parked less than ten feet away. He normally parked in one of the spaces by the stairs to my apartment on Saturday nights. Try as he might, pretending he didn't care, a part of me knew he parked there to make sure I was safely in my apartment before he left.

Now, even my apartment didn't seem safe.

"Nate," I said, my voice catching in my throat as he walked

away. "I'm scared. What if he's down here and waiting for me?"

Nate looked at me for a moment, the look in his eyes softening. "Come with me then, but stay behind me. If I tell you to run, you do it without arguing."

"Fine," I said, glaring at him.

Nate took the stairs two at a time, pushing the door open wider with the toe of his boot. I stood behind him, my arms wrapped around my torso as I tried to hold myself together. My heart was hammering in my chest as Nate turned the living room lights on, and I could see the full damage done.

Clothing was scattered across the room, torn in half. Pictures I had kept framed on the walls were thrown to the ground and destroyed. As we walked down the hall to the bedroom, I could see lotion and perfume bottles shattered in the washroom.

If the living room was bad, my bedroom was worse. The sheets were ripped and torn into pieces. Stuffing from my pillows covered the floor. Drawers had been thrown open, and their belongings spilled throughout the room.

"This is a mess," I whispered, my eyes wide as I looked around. There was a sharp pain in my chest as the room seemed to grow impossibly smaller.

Nate crossed his arms and turned around slowly, taking in the room and its destruction. He sighed, glancing at me.

"Are you okay?"

"No."

"I'll deal with this. Just keep trying to hold on, okay?"

I nodded. "Okay."

Nate's arms dropped, and he pulled out his phone. He paced away from me as he dialed a number and waited for the call to connect. Even as he stood a distance away, he kept his eyes trained on me.

My heart was hammering in my chest as he stared at me. I felt as if I was out in the open and vulnerable. It was as if someone was seeing me for the first time and stripping back the protective layers I kept in place to keep myself safe.

After a few more moments, he tucked the phone into his pocket. Time seemed to move fast from then, my mind a blur. Red and blue lights lit up the night soon after, as one of the officers came around the corner. Nate grabbed me by the shoulders and led me downstairs. He walked me over to the car that had just pulled up. Two officers jumped out. Nate went back up with one of them. I stood there, shivering, even though it was a warm night.

"Lauren, what's happening?" Kayleigh asked, though it was difficult for me to acknowledge her presence. I was experiencing the world around me through a foggy lens.

"I don't know," I said. Kayleigh wrapped a blanket around me, squeezing my arms as the officer who had remained with me started getting my statement, asking me questions to which I was giving one-worded responses.

At some point, Nate returned alone. By this time, patrons from Taz had walked out, trying to figure out what was happening.

After giving my statement, I turned to Nate, my mind clearing up a bit. Instinctually, survival mode began to kick in.

"Is there any way we can go and get my wallet? I need it to rent a motel room for the night."

Nate's eyebrows furrowed. "Why don't you stay with Kayleigh for the night?"

"Yes, you can stay..." Kayleigh began to say, but I interrupted her.

"I can't. If my ex does anything to them, I will never stop blaming myself. A motel is fine for the night."

Kayleigh and Nate both sighed.

"You're not staying at a motel. It's not safe. You'll stay at my house for the night, and then we'll figure out what comes next in the morning." I opened my mouth to argue, but he gave a sharp shake of his head before pulling keys from his pocket. "Let's go. These officers will take care of things here."

"Like hell you're driving," I said, trying to grab his keys. Nate moved quickly, holding the keys high above his head. "You've been drinking."

"I had a few beers, Lauren. I'm fine. Well below the legal limit."

I glared at him. "Give me the damn keys, Copper. You, of all people, should be following the law, don't you think?"

"Lauren."

"Nate."

"Now who's the pain in the ass?" he asked, still holding the keys high above my head. "It's fine, and I'm fine, Lauren. You're the one that's not fit to be driving. Not after finding out that your apartment was broken into."

"Don't pretend you care more than you have to. Just give me the damn keys and stop being stubborn."

"Fine. For tonight, you win. Don't think that this is ever going to happen again, though. Nobody drives my truck."

He tossed them to me before stalking toward his truck, leaving me no room for argument. I scowled at his back, considering tossing the keys into the bushes. Tossing the keys would mean that both of us would have to walk to his house. I wasn't sure I wanted to spend that much time with him right now, especially not in the open, in case Jason was watching.

As much as I wanted to piss him off, I needed a place where Jason couldn't reach me for the night. Nate was offering me that place, and I wasn't about to turn him down. Now that the shock was starting to wear off, I realized that there was only one motel in town; if Jason was staying anywhere, it would be there. I couldn't risk it. Nate was the sheriff, and his house was the safest place I could be. Jason wouldn't do anything with Nate around.

Kayleigh chuckled beside me. I had honestly forgotten she was standing beside me.

"What?" I asked her, fingering Nate's keys in my palm.

"Oh, nothing. Seems you are in safe hands, then." She winked as she walked off towards Taz.

My mind was too jumbled up to read the tone in her voice, so

I followed Nate towards his car.

"About time," Nate said as I got behind the wheel.

"Shut up," I muttered, adjusting the seat and mirrors to accommodate my height. "Where am I even going?"

"Old Mill Road. Head toward the edge of town, and when you see a dirt road, get on it."

"Fantastic."

"You're more than welcome to walk," he said, his tone gruff as he crossed his arms, tilted his head back, and closed his eyes.

"How am I supposed to know where I'm going if you're taking a damn nap?" I asked, as the truck rumbled to life with a twist of the key.

"End of Old Mill Road is another road. Turn left. My house is at the end."

"Great company," I muttered, following his directions.

The corner of his mouth turned slightly, but he said nothing, continuing to sit with his eyes closed.

The drive to his house was bumpy and isolated. Nate's soft snores filled the truck. When I pulled up outside his house, my mouth nearly dropped open. Everything was dark stone, warm-toned wood, and glass. It was modern but set far away from the rest of town. Isolated.

I turned off the engine and stared at the house. "This is where you live?"

"Apparently," Nate said, opening his eyes before getting out of the truck. "It's where you'll be staying tonight, too. Now, hurry up. My night was ruined, and I would like to get some sleep before I have to work tomorrow."

"Ass," I muttered under my breath, following him to the house and wondering how I would survive a night with him.

Chapter 3

Nate

When I woke up to singing in the morning and the sound of a shower running, my first instinct was to grab my gun. The second was to hop in a cold shower of my own and forget who was naked down the hall. The cold shower would shock me out of imagining what would happen if I walked down that hallway and joined her, running my hands up and down her curves.

If I got in the shower with her, that would be the end of the careful boundaries we had drawn between us. The attraction that had been simmering would boil over.

If I let her in, I wouldn't be able to let her go.

Bringing Lauren here had been a bad idea. There were dozens of other places I could have sent her for the night, but instead, I brought her here. The only person besides myself who had ever been here was my sister. That was the way I wanted it. I didn't want people in my space. I wanted to be alone, but I had brought Lauren here. I had taken the first step in letting her into my life. It scared the living hell out of me.

What the hell am I doing?

I got out of bed and ran a hand down my face, wondering what I was supposed to do now. It was clear that Lauren was already awake, and I wouldn't have any time to think about the next step. She would be on my ass about something the second she knew I wasn't sleeping. Honestly, I was amazed that she hadn't woken me up just so she could be on my ass about something.

When my phone started ringing, I was grateful for a few more seconds of delay.

"Hello, Sheriff."

"Lawson, what's the news on the apartment?" I asked, not bothering with the pleasantries.

"Unsure of who was in here, but it seemed too personal to be a stranger. Too targeted. More likely, it was somebody close to her. We've lifted some fingerprints from the scene, but it was only one set, and we suspect they're Lauren Guthrie's."

"Alright, I'll be there shortly to look at the state of things with fresh eyes. Seal the apartment until I get there, and keep an officer stationed by the door."

"Yes, sir."

As soon as the call ended, Lauren came barging into the room. Her wet blonde hair hang down her back in loose waves. She crossed her arms over her ample chest and stood in the doorway like she owned the place. It bothered me. Lauren was too comfortable in my space. I didn't want her to be comfortable. I wanted her to go home and forget that she had ever been brought over here.

Still, I wasn't letting her see that her being in my private space set me on edge. I didn't want her to think that she had the upper hand in any situation. If she was going to invade my space, I wouldn't let it bother me.

"What the hell are you doing?" I asked, standing up and stretching. "This is my room, in case you missed the closed door."

"Didn't miss it, just ignored it." Lauren perched herself on the edge of my dresser. Her long tan legs stretched in front of her as her shorts rode up. She fidgeted with the buttons of her sleeveless blouse, picking at a stray thread.

I looked away, trying not to stare at her. After a few moments, I looked back at her legs, wondering what they would feel like wrapped around my waist. She smirked at me as if she could read my mind. Scowling, I stared at her, daring her to look away. Lauren met my glare with a look of amusement, fire dancing in her eyes. Playing with her was a dangerous game.

"What do you want?" I asked.

"I heard you on the phone."

I cocked an eyebrow at her and crossed my arms. She had to be the most annoying person I had ever met, but that didn't seem to bother her at all. Instead, she kept inserting herself where she didn't belong. Like behind a door listening to private phone calls.

Lauren looked like she was making herself more comfortable as she leaned back against the mirror and propped one foot on the dresser's edge. I wanted to haul her off the dresser and toss her on the bed. However, that wouldn't improve the situation between us.

"And?"

She rolled her pretty brown eyes. "Are we going back to my apartment or what?"

"A normal person would say thank you."

I sighed and ran a hand through my hair. I tried to think of what else I could do with her. Taking her back to her apartment wasn't safe. Leaving her at the only motel in Willow Town alone wasn't safe either. The best way to watch her and make sure her ex-husband stayed away was to keep her at my place.

"Until we have this entire mess figured out, you can stay here. It's a big house with a good security system."

"That won't cause any gossip around town at all," she said, shaking her head. "Not even a little bit. There is no way that Sally down at the beauty parlor would ever start spreading rumors about how the new girl in town broke into her own apartment just to get that attractive sheriff closer to her."

"And once again, we are back to the fact that you think I'm pretty," I said, smirking as she rolled her eyes.

"I'm just telling you what the elderly women of Willow Town think. Personally, your advanced age is more of a deterrent."

I almost would have believed her if I didn't see the lingering glances she was giving me. "You don't seem to mind my advanced age at all. Thirty-five isn't that old."

"You keep telling yourself that, Grandpa. As if we weren't giving the town enough to talk about. Now they are going to talk about how the elderly sheriff is keeping that nice young woman trapped with him."

"Jesus, Lauren," I said, my voice nearly a growl as I shook my head. "Can't you just say thank you and be done with it like a normal person?"

"I was getting there," she said, a pink flush appearing on her cheeks, but the amused smile didn't fall from her face. "Thank you."

"Get out so I can get dressed."

She smirked and crossed her arms, her eyes trailing over me slowly. I hated the way my body reacted to her stare. Before she could notice the way I was straining against my pajama pants, I disappeared into my closet.

"Get the hell out."

Lauren's laugh filled the room before I heard the door close behind her.

I'm fucked, I thought as I got dressed quickly. The sooner I got rid of her, the better.

***

Not long after I dropped Lauren off at her apartment—making sure that there was an officer there with her—I was called away on a wellness check. By the time I finished with that call, it had been an hour and a half. The entire hour and a half was a war between doing my job and wanting to return to her place to investigate for myself. My officers were good, but I needed to see what we were dealing with. I needed to know how far this ex-husband was willing to go to get her back.

If he wanted her half as much as I did, he was willing to do whatever it took. That was the scary part. I was a rational human being with boundaries. He clearly was not. He had already proven that he was willing to cross lines to be in her life with the fake car theft report, and now this?

I couldn't allow that to happen. He was a threat to her. She had run away from him and their lives together.

My phone started ringing as I left the wellness check, an unknown number flashing across the screen.

"Hello?"

"Well, hello there, Hollis," Lauren said, irritation clear in her voice. "When you brought me here, I told you that I would be packing my bags and driving back to your place to drop them off before coming back to work...though I still think living with you isn't a good idea, but oh well." I drew in a slow breath in response to the tone in her voice. God, this woman was infuriating. "Now, Officer Lawson and I are standing out at my car, and it seems as if the battery has been removed and several cables have been ripped out."

"Stay there with Lawson until I get there," I said, jogging back to my truck, and getting in. I slammed the door shut and cranked the key in the ignition.

Before she could respond, I hung up and tucked the phone back into my pocket. I flicked the sirens on, red and blue lights flashing as I took off down the road. The faster I got to Lauren, the better.

When I got back to her apartment, she was leaning against her car with her arms crossed. Her glare could make weaker men run and hide. I stalked across the parking lot to stop in front of her, matching her glare with one of my own. She tilted her chin upward, daring me to speak.

"Well, I guess you're happy now that I have no choice but to depend on you," she said cooly. The accusation in her voice took me aback. I gritted my teeth, taking a moment to breathe before I said something I would regret. When I was sure I was calm, I closed the distance between us, our bodies nearly pressing against each other. Lauren swallowed hard, but the challenging look didn't vanish from her face.

"Let's get one thing straight..." I said, my tone low as I leaned closer to her, "...I am not a controlling bastard, and I never have been. If you ever accuse me of anything like that again, you'll see what I'm really like."

"Is that a threat?" she asked, the corner of her mouth tipping upward and amusement sparking in her eyes.

I saw red, my hands clenching into fists at my sides. She was in danger, and the only thing that seemed to matter was picking a fight with me?

"Lauren, I'm trying to help. You need to stop acting like you know exactly what is happening and let me do my job as the sheriff of this town."

"Oh?" The smile dropped from her face as she crossed her arms. "I don't know what's happening here. Why don't you enlighten me, Sheriff? It seems like the life I thought I was escaping followed me here."

She scoffed and brushed by me, her shoulder hitting my arm just above my elbow. I took a deep breath, trying not to say something I would regret. Lauren was infuriating—so infuriating that I had a hard time imagining she had ever let her ex push her around.

I headed straight for the car and took over from Lawson, assessing the damage. Minutes later, Lauren stood by my side. I didn't tell her to step back. Lauren bit her bottom lip, watching as I took picture after picture and emailed myself my notes. From what I had seen, she liked to pretend that she was alright when she was really freaking out inside. She was terrified that her ex-husband was getting closer to her, and there was nothing I could do to ease her fear.

At that moment, I had never felt more like a failure at my job.

If looking over my shoulder while I worked would make her feel even a little bit better, I would let her.

"You won't be driving anywhere anytime soon," I said.

"I will drive wherever I want."

"No, you will not. You think that detaching the battery is the worst thing your ex-husband did to your car? Lauren, we need to get Mike, the mechanic, over here to haul your car into the shop and look over it."

"That doesn't mean I'm not going to stay locked up in your house."

"It would be safer than going all over town by yourself and not knowing where he is."

She rolled her eyes and leaned back against the side of her car. "He's a cop. He's not stupid. He won't try to pull anything in the middle of town."

"You don't know that," I said, sending a quick text to the town's mechanic. "You don't know what he's going to do if he sees you alone."

"That's my risk to take," she said, her tone sharp as she walked away from me. "Besides, according to you, I'm a criminal anyway. But don't worry too much about me. I can, and will, handle myself."

She took off before I could say anything else, heading into the bar. I considered following after her but causing a scene in the bar would only result in Kayleigh kicking my ass.

With a sigh, I grabbed the packed bags she had left on the ground and tossed them into my truck. I would pick her up later tonight after she was done working. After that, I would start ignoring her and hope it would make living together more tolerable.

Chapter 4

Lauren

When I stepped outside, Nate was sitting on the front porch, staring out at the trees lining his property. I smoothed down my backless dress and kept my head high, not bothering to look at him as I made my way to Kayleigh's car. It had been a long few weeks, and I needed a break from the man I was sharing a home with.

"You look hot," Kayleigh said as she got out of her car to pull me into a tight hug. "Are you ready to drink until the sun comes up?"

I laughed and nodded, stepping back from her hug to eye her gold dress. "You look amazing too."

"Let's go."

A loud slam of a door sounded behind us. I looked over my shoulder to find the porch empty. With a roll of my eyes, I got into Kayleigh's car and leaned back in the seat.

"What was that about?"

I sighed and ran a hand through my hair, loosening the curls that cascaded down my back. "I'd really rather not talk about it until I've got a few drinks in me."

"That can be arranged."

I grinned as she turned the car around and headed away from Nate's house. With every mile she drove, I could feel the weight lifting from my shoulders. The further away I got, the more the tension melted away.

***

At some point during the night, pitchers of beer turned into shots. We had gone a town over to escape spending time with anyone we knew. Actually, it had been at my request. I didn't want the nosy townspeople to overhear anything we said and gossip about it over coffee tomorrow morning. Sarah was the only exception to the rule. Since I began staying with Nate, Sarah had made a point of coming over every few nights to cook dinner and irritate her brother.

When Sarah walked through the door shortly after we started drinking, I invited her to our table while the waitress brought another empty glass for the pitcher of beer.

"So..." Kayleigh said, pouring herself another glass of beer, "...what is going on with you and the sheriff?"

"Please gloss over all the dirtiest details," Sarah said, sipping her beer. "I don't want to know what you and my brother are doing in his house, but I also kind of want to know. It's been a long time since he let a woman in."

I groaned and threw back another shot, twirling the glass on the table as I considered how much to tell her. Kayleigh had known the sheriff her entire life, and Sarah was his sister. They would see Nate from a different angle than I did.

Still, if we were going to get into the dirty details, she needed to know how I had even appeared on the sheriff's radar in the first place. I suspected that Sarah already knew some of the details, but another part of me said she didn't know anything. Nate didn't seem like the type to tell other people my personal business.

"I know," Kayleigh said, grinning at Sarah. "The chemistry the pair of them have is off the charts."

"I've seen it. Nate didn't look at his ex-girlfriends like that. Ever. He didn't have many while we were growing up—he was too busy taking care of everyone else. But now that he's met her, it's like watching him fall hard and fast for the first time in his life."

"You two are ridiculous," I said, rolling my eyes and finishing my beer before pouring another. I would need more than a couple of drinks to get through my story. "Absolutely insane. There is nothing between us."

"Keep telling yourself that," Sarah said, smirking as she crossed one leg over the other. "Now, start telling us about how you and my brother first fell in love."

I rolled my eyes again, knowing better than to try to argue with her. After spending only a few days with Sarah, it was clear that when she made up her mind about something, she wouldn't change it unless absolutely necessary.

"I left my ex the day I finally had enough money. He had always been controlling, and I was never what he thought the wife of a police officer should be. It was just toxic. The love I thought we had sizzled away quickly, replaced by..." I shuddered, remembering the lonely nights and equally terrifying days. "I got tired of being told what to do and how I should look, so I filed for divorce. Days before I moved to town, my divorce was finalized. The last time I saw Jason in the lawyer's office, he said he would never let me go."

"So, why did he sign the papers?" Sarah asked.

"I never thought he would. I just thought that the papers would stall him long enough for me to escape. Complaining to his boss never worked. Neither did calling other stations and trying to get other officers involved. The police are all for protecting their own and would call Jason. They told him what I was doing."

"If reporting him wasn't working, why would he ever bother signing the papers?" Kayleigh asked, leaning forward on the table.

"I caught him on a phone call one night. He didn't know I was there. He thought that I was out with one of the few friends he approved of. I came home early, though. As soon as I heard him talking about drugs going missing from an evidence locker, I started recording out my phone. I don't know why I recorded it, but call it instinct or whatever. But let's just say I had overheard some conversations like that in the past, and I knew this was my chance."

"What did you get?"

"Enough to convince him that I would go to the district attorney and ruin his career. He was on a burner phone talking to one of the officers he was working with. They were talking about when to steal the drugs and how they would resell them."

"And that's how you were able to force him to sign the paperwork?" Kayleigh said, her eyes widening as a small smile crossed her face. "I always knew you were a badass."

"Reporting him wasn't enough. Blackmail had to be."

"Do you still have copies of those recordings?" Sarah asked.

I nodded, taking a long sip of my drink. "Yes. I wasn't going to give him my only copy, and he knows it. I've got several stored in different places. That was what was keeping him from coming after me immediately."

"What changed?"

"The district attorney started looking around at some other cases. There was an article about it online a few weeks ago. A gun in an important cartel case went missing. Jason was one of the officers who made the initial arrest. Though they haven't said as much, they are likely investigating him as well as the other arresting officers. If he has me back, he has all the other recordings."

Kayleigh draped one leg over the other, leaning back in her chair. "Is that why the apartment was trashed?"

I nodded and swallowed hard as a lump rose in my throat. "Yeah. That was Jason. Maybe he was looking for physical copies of the recordings." I scoffed. "He needs to try harder if it was him. At least, we're pretty sure it was him. Nate has me staying at his place until they find Jason."

"And how's that been going?"

"Well," I said, setting the shot glass down on the table. "The door slamming is a daily occurrence. Plus, he doesn't speak much to me."

Kayleigh smirked and took a sip of her beer. "You sound almost sad about that."

"Shut up. I do not." I grinned and shook my head, pouring my own glass of beer and finishing off the pitcher. "It makes living with him a lot easier. We come and go, and neither of us really has anything to do with each other."

Sarah laughed. "Except the nights I come over. Those nights, the sexual tension fills the room. They both glare at each other like they're three seconds away from ripping each other's clothes off."

"We do not," I said, my cheeks turning a dark red. "I told you before. Nothing is going on between me and your brother."

"I think you should stop lying to yourself," Sarah said, her tone light and teasing as she smirked at me. "Nate has let you in more than anyone else. He's letting you see his world. Hell, he talks about you when you're out of the room and makes you sound as if you are too good to be true."

"I don't think I believe that," I said, my cheeks feeling as if they were an inferno that couldn't be controlled. "He barely even talks to me."

"Because he's emotionally stunted," Sarah said, laughing and shaking her head. "I love him, but it's true."

Kayleigh shook her head. "He's always been a stubborn one. No more worrying about it—and don't argue and say that you're not because I know you are—we are going to drink and have some fun."

As the bartenders cranked the music louder, I downed my beer with a smile. Kayleigh got up to dance, her hands above her head as she moved with the beat. Another round of shots appeared on the table in front of us. I drank both of them before she had a chance, the alcohol flowing through my veins. Sarah laughed and ordered another round, getting up to join us.

"Shouldn't you slow down a little?" Kayleigh asked, eyeing the shot glasses in front of me.

"I haven't had a night like this to relax in years. I want to just forget about my ex-husband and the sheriff and just have fun."

"You know, Nate could be good for you. I think you're good for him," Sarah said as she grabbed my hand and spun me around in a circle.

I laughed and shook my head. "I'm better off alone. Besides, the sheriff can't stand me. He's made that pretty clear."

Kayleigh rolled her eyes. "If you say so."

"I do. Now, come on, I love this song," I said, grabbing Kayleigh by the hand and dragging her onto the dance floor. Sarah was close behind us, singing along with the music as she lost herself to the beat.

We danced and drank until I couldn't feel my legs anymore. I was laughing and having fun, the stress from the last few weeks melting away. It wasn't often that Kayleigh and I had the night off together, so I was going to make sure that I made the most of tonight.

The annoyingly attractive sheriff was far from my mind.

***

The ground seemed a thousand miles away as I danced on top of the table. I stopped counting how many drinks I had once the room became hazy. However, the haze was starting to clear, and I was still dancing. Kayleigh was grinning up at me from where she danced beside the table, her phone in hand.

"Did you take a video?" I asked her, smiling as I twirled in a tight circle.

"Yes, and I sent it to someone who might find it very interesting. He should be walking in any moment now."

Kayleigh smirked as I kept dancing, not entirely registering what she had just said. I moved my hips to the beat, feeling like I was back in college and having the time of my life with my friends.

There wasn't a worry in the world that could touch me. I had been waiting for the better part of nine years to be this free. Now, I finally was.

Kayleigh and Sarah had both stopped drinking a while ago, trying to tell me that it was getting late and that we should slow down. Their words had been lost on me as I let myself go. Everything that had been keeping me chained up for years was gone.

I was going to have a fun night if it was the last thing I did.

Nobody was going to ruin that for me. Never again.

"What do you think you're doing?" a deep voice boomed over the music.

I turned around, the smile dropping from my face, when I saw Nate standing there with a deep frown on his face. He bent down to pick up my heels from where they had landed on the floor. The heels dangled from his finger as he looked up at me.

"Hello, Sheriff," I said with a smirk. The song changed as I continued dancing, turning my back on him. He wasn't going to ruin my fun. I wasn't going to let him.

"I haven't been able to get her down," Kayleigh said, pointing at me.

"Traitor," I said, glaring at Kayleigh before I started giggling. "I can't believe you called him. I was having fun. He's no fun. He's going to make me have no fun too."

"Hold these," Nate said, handing Sarah my shoes. She took them as Nate crossed back into my field of vision. I scowled at him, dancing and refusing to let his presence bother me.

In seconds, his big hands wrapped around my waist, his fingers skimming against my bare back as he lifted me down. I froze for a moment before kicking him in the stomach.

"Hell, Lauren," he said, grunting as he put me on the ground. "Can you act like a damn adult and go get into the truck?"

"I'm having fun," I said, crossing my arms over my chest and quirking an eyebrow. "You go home. I'll be home later."

Nate sighed, moving too fast for me to stop him. One moment I was on the ground, and the next, I was slung over his shoulder with his arm wrapped around my bare thighs. I could feel his fingers on my bare skin, setting off a fire inside me. His fingers dug into my thigh, his grip on my body tight.

"Here are her shoes, Nate. Lauren, you sleep well, yeah. See you tomorrow," Sarah said from somewhere to my left.

"Don't think they'll be doing much sleeping tonight," Kayleigh remarked before the two women started chuckling.

I didn't have it in me to reply. In my stupor, all I did was grin and start humming, swaying slightly as Nate carried me out of the bar.

While sober me was perfectly capable of trying to ignore the attraction I felt for the sheriff, drunk me wasn't. I put my hands on his lower back, lifting myself up enough to stare at his ass.

"You have a nice ass," I said, reaching down to smack it lightly.

Nate froze, his shoulders tensing. "Don't do that again."

I laughed. "Why not, Sheriff?"

"Lauren."

"Sheriff," I mimicked, reaching down to smack his ass again. "Very nice ass."

Nate started walking again, not bothering to respond until he was standing beside his truck. He opened the door and tossed my heels onto the back seat before dropping me onto the seat. I brushed my hair out of my eyes to see the frown set even deeper on his face.

"Why are you upset?" I asked.

"What was that in there?" Nate asked, his tone sharp.

I didn't want to listen to any of his yelling. Not tonight. Tonight was supposed to be fun. Tonight was supposed to be about forgetting all the stress. I didn't want to listen to him yell. I didn't want to fight again.

Maybe that was why I wrapped my legs around his hips and pulled him to me. Before he could react, I was leaning forward and kissing him. His arms bracketed me on either side, one hand coming up to grab my hip. Nate's mouth moved against mine, but when I ran the tip of my tongue along his lower lip, he gave a low groan sending heat straight to my core. Nate pushed his hips against me, his hardened cock rubbing against me through the layers of clothing that needed to go. It was as if he could read my mind, his hands pulling down the straps to my dress, my breasts plopped out. His large calloused hands were on them, squeezing. I moaned, tilting my head back, and his mouth landed on my neck.

Nate's hands tweaked my hard nipples as need ran wild through me. My fingers laced through his hair, pulling him closer while his hands traveled back down my body to lift one of my legs and hook it around his hip.

I moaned, my hands sliding down his body. I flicked open the button of his jeans, my hand sliding inside the waistband to grip his shaft. In that instant, it was as if a bucket of ice-cold water had been poured over his head.

Nate ripped himself away from me, putting feet of distance between us. I could feel the imprint of his fingers on my body, even as he stood there looking like he had received the shock of his life.

I knew what he would say before the words ever left his mouth. It still didn't stop the aching in my heart when he shook his head. Before he could start speaking, I was already mentally building the walls back up around my heart.

"That was a bad idea. You're drunk."

"I knew what I was doing," I said, pulling up the straps of my dress. I may have been drinking, but I knew what I was doing. I had wanted to kiss him, and take me right there. I wanted to lose myself in him.

I was building the wall back up around my heart to keep that from happening.

"Fine, that was a bad idea because it was a bad idea. Is that good enough for you?"

He didn't wait for a response before storming around the front of the truck and getting in. I reached up and wiped away a tear before twisting to face the front and closing the door.

"That can never happen again," Nate said, starting the truck and turning in the direction of Willow Town.

Why does he have to sound like that kiss was the worst thing to ever happen to him?

"Got it," I said, wiping away another tear before willing myself not to cry.

He wouldn't get the best of me.

I wouldn't let him.

This kiss had been a mistake, and I wasn't going to make the same one twice.

Chapter 5

Nate

Tossing and turning all night had done nothing but frustrate me more than I already was when we got home. I replayed the kiss a thousand times in my mind, wondering what would have happened if I had given in. If I had let her grab my hard length. It would have been so easy to lean back in, kiss her senseless and consume all of her. I should have allowed the single thread I was holding onto to snap. I should have kissed her until we both forgot our own names.

Would that kiss have gone further than it already did?

Would I be waking up this morning with her in my bed?

It had been a long time since I had allowed a woman to get anywhere close to me. I kept the few women in my life at a distance, ensuring mutually destructive relationships. For a long time since my last relationship, there had been too much going on in my life to let anyone in.

Yet, Lauren seemed to have a way of wiggling herself beneath my skin and staying there. She wouldn't take no for an answer, and she didn't let me get away with any of my shit.

I shouldn't have pulled away from her last night. I should have kissed her deeper before the hurt look had ever appeared on her face. There were a thousand different things that I could have and should have done.

Instead, I told her that it was a mistake that could never

happen again.

I'm an idiot.

I would be amazed if she ever forgave me for what happened last night. I wouldn't if I were in her position. I would hold on to that anger and allow it to drive me further away until there was a safe distance between us.

If I were her, I would allow a single kiss to ruin everything we had.

When I walked onto the back deck with coffee in hand, I was surprised to see Lauren already awake and sitting in one of the giant chairs. She stared out at the lake with a steaming cup of coffee. She had never been a morning person—at least not as long as I had known her.

For a few minutes, I stood back and watched her. She seemed content to stare at the wilderness before her. It was one of the reasons I had purchased this land and built a house on it. The isolation was a welcome comfort. It was peaceful and quiet in a way that town never was.

I wondered what she saw when she looked out at the forest surrounding the area. Did she see the same sense of lonely isolation that my sister did whenever she visited? Or was Lauren more like me? Did she look out at the woods and find a sense of peace that had been missing until that point?

Her blonde hair was piled on top of her head, and her long legs were draped over the arm of the chair. Lauren was beautiful. There was no doubt about that. She was smart and kind and nothing like the person I had thought she was when she first moved to Willow Town.

I had seen all the differences in who she was, and what I had thought within the few weeks I had been watching her interact with the community around her. It was interesting to watch her walk into a new place and make friends with the people there. She did it with an ease that I would never understand. Out of all the people who lived in town, I was the only one who seemed to have a problem with her in the course of knowing her.

I didn't have a problem with her anymore. At least, no problem other than picturing her naked multiple times a day.

"Morning," she said without looking up from whatever it was she was staring at. "You going to sit down and drink your coffee, or are you going to keep staring at me?"

Warmth flooded my face as I took the seat beside her and sipped my coffee. Was I that obvious? Apparently, I was.

"Do you want to talk about what happened last night?" I asked, my tone unsure. I wasn't in the habit of talking about emotions. It made me wildly uncomfortable, but something about her had me stepping out onto a ledge for her.

"Not even a little bit," she said, sipping her coffee. "It happened. I kissed you. You turned me down. It's fine. I'm an adult, and I can handle rejection."

I wanted to tell her that she was wrong, but she wasn't. I rejected her last night and wasn't prepared to explain why. I ruin everything that I touch. Why admit that to her? It would only send her running in the opposite direction faster than she already was. Trying to deny what she said would only do more harm than good.

"So, did you, Kayleigh, and Sarah have a good time? I didn't really think you were the type to go out and drink your problems away." I winced and took another sip of my coffee. "That wasn't supposed to sound as judgmental as it did."

"Glad you cleared that up," she said, her tone flat as she looked at me for the first time that morning. Her eyes were rimmed with red and dark bags circled beneath them.

"Why were you crying?"

"None of your business, quite honestly."

"Fair," I said, ignoring the small stab of pain in my chest. Guilt washed over me in waves. She had been crying, and no matter what she said, I was sure it had to do with me.

"I'm just worried about Jason and whatever happens next. He

was always controlling, but now he's scary. The mechanic called me. Finally got around to looking at my car even though it's been weeks."

"Small town mechanics aren't known for their speed. What did he say?"

"Brake lines were cut."

My hand clenched around my cup. "I didn't know that. I haven't talked to the mechanic yet."

"Well, now you know. You were right."

"I don't take any pleasure in being right about that. Tell me more about this ex-husband. Jason."

She shook her head. "We got married right after high school. For a few years, we were happy. And then the promotions started, and suddenly I had to change. I had to be like the other officers' wives. He liked to control where I went, what I ate, and how I dressed. Everything. Nine years of my life were spent being his doll. Finally, I saved up enough of my own money and filed for divorce."

"Would that be enough to send him after you like this?"

"Absolutely," she said without taking a moment to think about it. "Appearances are everything to him. His wife walking away from their nine-year marriage would embarrass him. He would do anything to maintain his image, especially when I blackmailed him into signing the papers. If that ever got out, there would be more trouble."

My eyebrows shot upwards. "You blackmailed him?" There was something that I wasn't understanding. She didn't seem like the kind of person who would blackmail others into doing what she wanted, but then again, I don't know her as well as I like to pretend I do. "I'm going to need an explanation, Lauren."

"There was nothing else I could do. I found out about something he had done that would put him in jail for years. I recorded it, blackmailed him, and saved my life. He no longer controls me."

"Then why is he coming back around?"

"Did you read the story about the district attorney investigating Crawford City Police for evidence that went missing from a cartel case?" she asked, not looking at me as she spoke.

"Yes."

"He was one of the arresting officers. The district attorney is launching an investigation into the missing gun. It's possible Jason did it. It wouldn't be the first time that he stole evidence and sold it."

"Is that what blackmail you have?" I asked, trying hard to see the situation from her eyes. She was desperate to get out of a controlling marriage. If she had blackmail material, she would and should use it. If I were in her position, I would have done anything I could to escape.

"I have him admitting to stealing and selling drugs. Several copies of it. While he wants me back, he also wants those recordings under his control. Especially now that they're investigating the cartel case."

I nodded and looked down at my coffee. It was a lot to process, and it made Jason incredibly dangerous. "I don't think you should be going anywhere alone until my teams finds him and figures out what to do with him."

She scoffed and shook her head. "No. I'm not hiding from him and his childish games. It isn't happening. I have a life to live, and I'm not going to back down and cower. If he goes down for being a corrupt cop, that's not my problem."

"Lauren, you aren't thinking about this rationally."

She stood up and looked down at me, fire burning in those big brown eyes. "Let me be clear about one thing, Sheriff."

I winced at the way she said sheriff. It wasn't the same playful and teasing tone that she normally used. It was bitter and filled with poison. I wanted her to go back to the playful Lauren, who spent her days lurking around my hallways. I missed the playful Lauren that climbed into my truck every night after work and teased me about the stick up my ass.

"I will not allow you or anyone else to tell me what to do with my life. I lived that way once, and it will never happen again."

"You don't know what you're risking," I said, setting my coffee to the side and standing up. "You have to think about this, Lauren. You need somebody with you. He's less likely to do something if you have someone else with you."

"And I told you!" She stormed closer to me, her chest inches from mine as she tilted her head back to glare at me. "I will not be held under his control again! Not anymore!"

"Lauren!"

"No! Do you hear me? No!"

"I'm not going to let you risk getting hurt," I said, wanting to reach up and run my thumb along her cheek. I had a feeling it would result in coffee being poured all over me.

"Why do you even give a shit?" she asked, her tone sharp as she crossed her arms. "Why now? You didn't give a shit when I told you that my ex-husband was framing me with the car."

I had no good answer. I could tell her I was just doing my job, but that only felt like half the truth. I would have found her somewhere else to stay if I was just doing my job. I would have found her a place that wasn't my own, and I would have only checked in with her when there were updates on the case. It's what I would have done in any other situation.

Instead, I kept the curvy blonde close because I was selfish and stupid. She could protect herself. She didn't need me.

"See?" she said with a nod when I was quiet for too long. "This is exactly what I thought."

"Lauren."

"No. Don't Lauren me. I'm going back to my apartment. It's been weeks without anything happening, and even Jason can't wait around this long. He has a job."

"At least let me drive you back."

She shook her head, her eyes glistening. "I'll call Kayleigh."

"Lauren."

Lauren didn't bother to turn around as she raced into the house and slammed the door shut behind her.

"Shit!" I ran my hands through my hair and looked toward the house. There was no world in which I hadn't made this entire situation worse than it already was.

Chapter 6

Lauren

Three weeks was a long time to deal with a broken heart. At least I had work and cleaning up the apartment back into a livable space to keep me preoccupied. But even with being busy, the time seemed impossibly long. And yet, my heart was still aching each time I thought of the sheriff and how his green eyes had stared helplessly at me. If he had asked me to stay, asked me just once, I would have stayed.

He didn't ask. Not once. He had demanded.

Nate had done the same thing that Jason would have done. He told me what I had to do without asking. It hadn't been about trying to protect me. What had happened with Nate was about control.

I would be damned in hell before I let any man have control over me ever again. I wasn't that woman anymore. I would never be that woman again.

Since that day, I hadn't heard from him once. He had skipped Saturday drinks with his sister, choosing to avoid me instead of carrying on a tradition I suspected was years old. He was a creature of routine, and him avoiding the bar spoke volumes. Even Kayleigh was starting to wonder where he had gone.

Now, I was sitting on my couch for the third weekend in a row, eating ice cream and watching movies. There was a storm raging outside. Thunder rolled every few minutes, and flashes of lightning lit up the sky. The metal staircase outside was making noise as the rain and wind pounded against it.

With a sigh, I got up and checked the door, making sure I had locked it before heading back to the couch and my tub of ice cream. I pulled the blanket over my legs, selecting another movie to watch.

As the wind howled, I heard a knock at the door. My heart was hammering in my chest as another knock soon followed, the dialogue of the movie I was watching fading into the background. A third followed. It had to be something hitting the door. Nobody would be coming over here, especially not this time of night. Something was knocking against the door. There had to be some sort of reasonable explanation for what was happening.

It's just the wind rattling the door, I thought as I leaned back deeper into the couch. *Only the wind. Nothing else is out there. My mind is just playing tricks on me because I stayed up too late.*

There was a bang against the door, too loud to be a knock. My heart was pounding in my chest as I reached for my phone. My hands were shaking as I dialed the only number I could think of. There was no time to think twice about whether calling him was the right move. I crossed my fingers, hoping that he would pick up.

"Lauren," Nate's deep voice said as soon as the call connected.

"Nate, I think someone is trying to get into my apartment."

"Listen to me carefully," he said without missing a beat. "I need you to stay quiet and get to a room with a lock on the door. Get in there and lock it until I get there."

In the background of the call, I could hear shuffling before the truck door slammed. I got up from the couch, grateful I had closed the curtains. There was another thud against the door as I crept to my room and shut the door.

It was getting harder to convince myself that it was my overactive imagination and staying up late to watch horror movies. That's all it could be out there. Nobody was trying to get in. I was irrational and looking for an excuse to get Nate over here.

But what if there is someone out there?

That wasn't a risk I was going to take.

"Nate," I said, twisting the lock. There was another large thump. "I'm scared. Please hurry."

"I'm on my way now, Lauren. I'm just down at the station, so I'll be there in a few minutes. Just lock the door until I get there. Stay on the phone with me. You don't have to say anything. Just stay on the line so I can hear that you're alright."

I twisted the lock and leaned back against the door, sliding until I sat down. On the other end of the line, I could hear Nate's steady breathing, even as my blood rushed to my head. The station was ten minutes away. All I had to do was stay locked in the room for another ten minutes, and Nate would be there. He would help me.

I wish there had been somebody to help me months ago, I thought, thinking about the night I finally left Jason.

Coming home early from a night out with my friend had been dumb luck. I shouldn't have been home early. However, I wouldn't have gotten the recording if I hadn't gone home until I was supposed to. That recording was the one thing I had needed to set myself free.

Seven weeks before I got the recording, I knew the marriage would end. When I looked in the mirror, I was so far from the person I used to be that I didn't recognize the woman staring back at me. The woman in that mirror had been a shell of a person. She was weak.

I had never been weak.

That day, I had walked out of the washroom after staring at the woman I didn't know for far too long. When I had joined Jason by the car, ready to go to an important dinner, he insisted that I had made us late.

That day was the first and last time he left a mark on me.

I took a deep breath, listening to Nate's breathing on the other end of the line. I counted his breaths, trying to calm myself down and forget what had forced me to this point.

"Okay, Lauren, I'm outside right now. There's nobody on the stairs. It's just me, okay? I'm climbing the stairs now."

"Okay. Okay."

"I'm outside your door now. Come let me in." Nate sighed. "There's nobody here, Lauren. It was just the wind. You're safe now. Come let me in."

I took a deep breath and got to my feet, unlocking my bedroom door and crossing the room to the front door. I hung up the call and twisted the lock, opening the door. Before I could say anything, Nate crossed the threshold and pulled me into a tight embrace. He buried his face in my neck, his arms tightening around my waist.

The embrace was unexpected, and I froze in his arms. He stepped back after a moment, his arms dropping to his sides. I felt the loss immediately. Being in his arms had made me feel safe. It was as if I was protected from the world around me. Nothing would have been able to hurt me as long as Nate was near and holding on.

Without his arms wrapped around me, I felt vulnerable and exposed.

At that moment, he was the one person keeping my head above water since I couldn't do it by myself anymore. I needed him by my side. I needed to know that one person in my life would protect me.

"Sorry," he said, his face turning red as he looked down at me. "I shouldn't have done that."

"That's all you have to say? After three weeks, you're sorry for hugging me?" I shook my head and ran a hand through my hair. "You can go now. I'm sorry for ruining your night."

"Lauren, don't start with that shit."

"I'm not starting with any shit. I told you that you could go now."

"Fuck, Lauren, I'm not going anywhere. Would you just stop running your mouth for five minutes and let me talk?"

I crossed my arms, cocking one hip and staring at him. "Fine."

"You're infuriating," he said, moments before closing the small gap between us.

His mouth pressed against mine as his fingers weaved their way through my hair, pulling me closer to him. Our bodies pressed together as he kicked the door shut behind him.

Nate's hands traveled down my body, his finger gripping my hips as I weaved my fingers into his hair. Our mouths slanted against each other, the kiss searching and desperate.

His mouth left mine, trailing down my neck, alternating between kissing and nipping at the skin. I moaned as his fingers slipped beneath my shirt, splaying against the skin there. Heat spread wherever he touched.

I ran my hands down his chest, stopping at the hem of his shirt. His hands left my waist long enough to pull his shirt over his head. Within seconds, his mouth was back on mine. My fingers trailed along his muscled torso, trying to commit him to memory.

"Bedroom?" he asked, his mouth leaving mine to trail down my neck again.

"Yes," I said.

He quickly picked me up, my legs wrapping around his waist as he carried me to the bedroom. Nate groaned as I ground myself against him, trying to relieve some of the tension building at my core.

Nate laid me down on the bed, kneeling between my legs. He looked down at me, his eyes warm as he surveyed my body.

"You are stunning," he said before reaching for my top. I helped him pull it off before taking off my pajama shorts and tossing them to the side.

For a moment, I wanted to cover up. He was the first person I had been naked in front of besides my husband in nearly a decade. Before I could even cover myself, his mouth wrapped around my nipple while his fingers found my clit.

I writhed against him as he nipped at my skin. Nate chuckled lowly, moving to the other breast and showing it the same attention he had shown the first.

"Fuck," he groaned, pressing his erection against me.

I reached between us, opening the button on his pants and trying to shove them off his hips. Nate raised his hips, helping me get his pants and boxers off before kicking them to the floor.

"Much better," I said, leaning forward to kiss his neck. Nate groaned, pressing himself against me again.

My hips bucked against him as he pressed against my clit harder. Nate trailed kisses along my body, nipping and sucking as he plunged two fingers into me. I came apart around him, writhing as he curled his fingers, drawing another orgasm out of me.

"Condom?" he asked.

"Nope. I'm on the pill."

"You're okay with this?"

"Shut up and fuck me already."

Nate chuckled and lined his cock with my core, hesitating for a moment before slowly thrusting. His moan filled the room as I hooked my legs around his waist, moving in time with him. We fell into a steady rhythm, my nails dragging down his back as he picked up speed, moving his hips faster.

I could feel my inner walls closing around him, squeezing him tighter and tighter until stars danced across my vision. I moaned, digging my nails into his back.

"Fuck, you feel good," he said, pulling back as he found his own release.

Nate fell to the bed beside me, rolling onto his side to look at me. I rolled onto my side, tucking an arm beneath my head. He smiled softly, his entire face lighting up in a way I hadn't seen before. His arm wrapped around my waist, pulling me closer before he kissed my temple.

"I'm going to go lock the door," he said, getting out of bed. I watched him walk out of the room, wondering what had just happened.

Why would he just leave like that? Didn't he want this as much as I did?

I thought that he wanted me. I thought that this might have been the beginning of the gap between us closing. Instead, it felt like someone had just rubbed salt into the open wound that was my heart.

There was a part of me that wanted more. That part wanted to run after him and demand answers. That part wanted to know why he was scared of everything we could be.

There was another part that told me to back off.

Maybe it was just sex. Maybe that's all I could let it be.

Emotions were running high, and I was damaged goods. I didn't have time for anything more than just sex, and I certainly didn't want to drag him down with me. No matter how safe he made me feel, we had both lost control.

When he returned, I pushed all the worried thoughts from my mind and enjoyed being wrapped in his embrace, no matter how temporary it might have been.

Chapter 7

Nate

The bed beside me was cold when I woke up and a hazy light filtered through the thin curtains. I sat up and looked around, but Lauren was nowhere to be found. I closed my eyes and opened them again, thinking that it might have been a dream and I would wake up back in my own house.

It was no use. When I opened my eyes again, I was still in her room. The sheets still smelled like the vanilla perfume she used and sex. I groaned and rubbed my face, propping myself up on my elbows and looking around.

"Lauren?"

There was no answer from any of the other rooms. I sighed and fell back into the pillows. She didn't seem like the type to run away the morning after, but I wouldn't put it past her either. Not after all that she had been dealing with these past few months.

I got out of bed and walked around the apartment, but she was long gone. Her shoes weren't by the door, and her keys were missing. My heart was beating quickly as I walked back to the bedroom and grabbed my jeans, tearing my phone out of my pocket. Disappointment flooded through me as I dialed her number.

"Hello, Sheriff," Lauren said when she answered my call.

"Hello, Lauren. Care to tell me where the hell you are so I can stop having a damn heart attack about what is going on right now?"

Every scenario possible was going through my mind. I still wasn't sure that it had only been wind at her door last night, but I wasn't going to tell her that and make her worry. There had been no sign of someone trying to break in, but her ex-husband was a cop. He knew how to cover his tracks if he was up to something.

All I could think of was her ex waiting for her outside the building and taking her when my back was turned.

"Stop being dramatic, Hollis. Everything is fine. I just needed some space."

"You know..." I said, my irritation growing along with the disappointment, "...most people would have woken up the person they were leaving in bed and told them that they were heading out."

"We aren't in a relationship," Lauren said, her tone sharp. She sighed. "Look, I need some space to think about this and what it means. This is new for me. So new. And big. I didn't think I would be with anyone else for a long time after my ex-husband; to be honest, it's scaring me. This was a big step. I need time and space. I will not get that space if I'm in that little apartment with you, trying not to sleep with you for the third time in twelve hours."

"Fourth," I said, smirking when I heard her irritated huff. "Get it right, Lauren."

"Remember the version of you that didn't want to talk to me? Can we go back to that for a few hours?"

"Or you could come back here, and we could talk about whatever is going through your mind like adults. I ruin a lot of things, Lauren. I'm not really interested in ruining this."

She hummed for a minute. I could hear the radio playing in the background. "Look, Nate, I really like you. A lot. And that scares me because up until last night, we hadn't talked to each other for three weeks, and the last time we talked, you were trying to tell me what to do. It reminded me of Jason, and I just can't deal with that."

"Lauren." My heart was sinking to my feet. The last thing I wanted to do was remind her of the man she had run from.

"Don't, please."

"Laur, are you really doing this right now? I thought that last night would have changed things for us. I thought we were finally going to get a chance to talk about whatever this weird thing between us was. And yet, here you are, running away from it. I'm not your ex-husband. I never meant to try to tell you what to do."

"But you did, Nate! You did," she whispered, her breathing hitching. "If you had just asked me to stay, I would have stayed. Instead, you demanded that I stay. You treated me like I'm yours to command."

"I didn't mean to."

"I know." She sighed. "I know."

"Then please come back so we can talk about this, okay? I really don't want this to be another one of those things I ruin."

"Nate, whatever feelings I have for you aren't enough right now, okay? I've got too much going on in my life, and you've got your own shit to deal with. And with Jason running around town the way he is, I don't want to put you at risk either."

"Lauren, I'm a cop. I don't need you to be worried about me. I'm more than capable of looking after myself."

"Nate, so is he." Lauren sniffled, and I immediately pictured tears rolling down her cheeks.

I sighed and ran a hand on my jaw, sitting down on her bed. "I'm not leaving until I know you're alright and we have worked this out. Your ex doesn't scare me. I think you're running scared because you don't know what to make of all this. Neither do I. That's why we should talk."

"Nate, just go home, okay? I'll talk to you when I'm ready."

"Fine."

I hung up and tossed the phone on the bed, falling back to stare at the ceiling. I could feel my chest tightening as I linked my hands behind my head. There was nothing I could do to change her mind, and there was clearly nothing I could say to get her back here. For once, ruining everything wasn't on me. She decided to walk away without figuring out what was happening between us.

For a moment, I was grateful for how the morning was going.

This was a mess, and I didn't know how to fix it. She was running from me, again, and I wasn't sure I wanted her to stop.

"Fuck," I groaned, getting up and pulling my clothes back on.

I liked her. I really liked her and had been suppressing that since we met. And yet, it might not be enough. It wasn't enough if she was right.

After gathering the rest of my things, I walked out of her apartment and closed the door behind me. I reached into the little potted plant beside her door, grabbing the key she had hidden inside. I locked the door before slipping the key into my pocket.

This wouldn't be the end of us if I had anything to say about it. I just needed to figure out how to fix it.

Instead of heading home, I walked into the station and headed straight for my office. I closed the door behind me before taking a seat at my desk and pulling up the search database.

"Jason Guthrie," I muttered, typing the name into the search bar. "Who are you?"

I should have researched about him before now. But it had been incredibly busy the last three weeks dealing with one issue or another in the town. Or maybe that's what I had told myself, trying not to think about Lauren and how much I had fucked that up.

But now, I really needed to find out all I could about her ex if I was going to protect her. I had no evidence that he was the one who had burgled her apartment, and the case had gone cold, the blue file mocking me in my open cases folder.

As records of his time at a police academy came up first—along with articles on awards he had won and cases he had been involved with—I scowled at the grin on his face, wondering what Lauren saw in a man like him in the first place.

Jason Guthrie was young but had worked his way through the ranks quickly. He had one recommendation from a superior after another, and not one of them had flagged how he was treating his wife.

Although maybe they had.

I knew what the city cops were like. They thought they were better than their peers and kept their noses turned up. They thought that their families were a reflection of themselves and kept them on a tight leash.

That was part of why I had chosen to be an officer in a small town instead of the city. I had more freedom to move along at my own pace. There was no pushing for higher ranks as soon as I got the next promotion. There was time for a life without posturing and pretending to be something you weren't.

Lauren had been the wife of a cop who thought appearances were everything. I could see how that would be a problem even after only knowing her for the past few months. She was a spitfire who spoke her mind and didn't give a damn about who she was talking to.

While her attitude pissed me off more often than not, it also kept the chemistry between us. She wouldn't just take whatever I was saying at face value. She challenged me.

Lauren was the kind of woman that made me want to be a better man.

Of course, I could see how much her personality would be a problem for a man trying to build his career. It would irritate a lesser man who only gave a shit about what was going on in his life.

She deserved better than that, and she deserved better than me.

I sighed and pushed back from my desk, running a hand down my face. After seeing how connected her ex-husband was, I wasn't surprised that she was worried. He could pull all kinds of strings without anyone knowing what he was up to.

"Fuck," I said, getting up from my desk and pacing back and

forth in front of the large window that overlooked the town square. My phone started ringing, Sarah's name flashing across the screen. I scowled and considered ignoring her call, but if I did that, she would only march down to the station and make the situation that much more miserable.

"Hello, Sarah."

"You're an idiot, you know that?" she said, her tone cutting deep.

"And why, may I ask?" I asked, even though I knew exactly what we were talking about.

"You know full well what I'm talking about. Why the hell are you letting Lauren just walk out of your life without a fight? You're making a huge mistake."

How did she know?

I had wanted to ask, but it wasn't a surprise to me that Sarah might be privy to what was going on between me and Lauren. Her, Lauren, and Kayleigh were becoming fast friends. At least Lauren had people she could confide in. I sighed, comforted by that.

"She made it perfectly clear that this is all too much for her," I said, sighing as I caught sight of the one person I wanted to see more than anyone else.

Lauren was sitting on one of the benches, her knees drawn to her chest. Kayleigh sat beside her; Bryce settled between them. I watched Lauren play with Bryce, a toy car in his hand, as he drove it up and down her legs. She tilted her head back, laughing as Bryce drove the car off her knee and flipped it through the air.

"Are you even listening to me?" Sarah asked, sounding breathless as if she had gone on a tirade again.

"Not really."

"You need to fix this, Nate. You've never been happier than when you were with her. I love you, and I want to see you happy. Fix this with her."

"I don't know what to do, Sarah."

"I don't know what you're going to do either, but you'll be the biggest idiot to have ever walked the earth if you don't fix this."

"Are you done calling me an idiot yet?" I asked, staring at Lauren through the window.

"Yes. I'll talk to you later."

"Love you, Sarah."

"Love you too, idiot."

After tucking my phone back in my pocket, I stepped back to the window and looked at Lauren. She was standing now, with Bryce in her arms, and spinning in quick circles. She looked as if she didn't have a care in the world.

I wanted to go outside and demand that she talk to me, but that would only put more distance between us. Instead, I closed the curtains and sat back down at my desk.

For now, I would have to sit back and let her have her space. If she wanted to continue whatever was happening between us, she would.

At least, I hoped she would.

Chapter 8

Lauren

I thought telling Nate I needed space and time to think wouldn't feel like ripping my heart from my chest, but it had. Every single day for the last month, it felt like I had ripped my heart out of my chest before starting to stomp all over it. Telling him I needed space was supposed to be easier than this. It wasn't supposed to hurt as much as it did.

The nights that hurt the most were Saturdays. Nate wouldn't show up for his normal drinks with his sister. Instead, he would arrive just as I was closing the bar and wait in his truck without saying a word as I locked the door. His truck would sit in the parking lot, illuminating the staircase to my apartment until I had locked the door and turned on the living room light. Seconds after that, the truck's engine would roar, and Nate would disappear from my life for another week.

I knew it was my fault, but it was surprisingly easy for him to avoid me in a small town. He seemed to have no problem staying hidden away until Saturday nights.

I wish that I could say the same. I spent more time out than ever, walking around town and trying to catch glimpses of him wherever I went.

Though my little adventures were great for meeting new people in Willow Town, they were less than stellar for easing the pain I had put onto my own heart. All those walks around town only made me wonder where he was hiding and who with. He was an attractive man who could find another woman easily.

Why am I even thinking about him finding another woman when I'm the one who pushed him away? I thought as I ran a hand through my hair and took a shaky breath.

Running away from him the morning after we slept together had been a bad idea, but it was the only thing I could think of doing. When I woke up that morning, a note had been sitting on my living room floor. I had picked it up with shaking hands, seeing Jason's familiar writing on the envelope.

Pictures were inside the envelope of me and Nate arguing or leaving the bar together. One picture was taken when he pulled me into a hug that night. In each picture, there were gouge marks where Nate's eyes should have been.

It was a clear warning, so I did what I had to do.

I broke my own heart to keep the man I loved safe.

With a sigh, I leaned back on my couch and closed my eyes, trying to erase the thoughts of the last month from my mind. There was nothing I could do about it now. I had made my choices, and I was stuck with them.

That didn't stop me from opening my eyes and grabbing my phone, scrolling through the contacts to his number. If I called him over now, would he even come?

Don't do it, I thought, tossing the phone across the couch, and reaching for the remote instead. I flipped through the movies, looking for something that would distract me for another night.

When I found nothing, I grabbed my phone again and gave in to the little voice that had been begging me to call him for the last month. I missed him more than I thought I would. I wanted him to come back so we could fix things. I wanted to apologize for what I had done. I wanted to beg him to let me back into his life.

"Lauren," Nate said, his voice deep and raspy. "You know, some people like to sleep when it's two in the morning."

"I thought you might not be one of those people," I said, my heart hammering in my chest. This was a bad idea. Even if I told him what was going on, there was no way he would ever forgive me.

"Lauren, I don't want to be rude."

"That's a pleasant change."

"Laur, stop," he said, sighing. "It's been a month, and now what? Now you want to talk?"

"I have a lot of explaining to do. Will you come over so I can do it?"

There was a long pause on the other end of the line. I could hear his steady breathing hitch before he exhaled.

"Fine, Laur. I'll be over there in twenty."

"Thank you."

"Don't thank me yet. Bye, Lauren."

"Bye, Nate."

After I ended the call, I tossed the phone to the side and pulled my thin blanket up to my chest. The cushions enveloped me as I put on a mindless movie and waited for Nate to arrive.

Barely five minutes after I put the movie on, there was a knock at my door. I frowned, grabbed my phone, and walked to the door. If Nate was coming from his house, it would take him the twenty minutes he had said.

I looked through the peephole, and my heart leaped to my throat. Jason stood on the other side of the door. I slowly backed away from the door, listening to Jason wiggle the handle. I heard a heavier thump against the door as I reached my bathroom.

My palms were sweating as I closed the door and turned the lock. Nate would be here soon. I just had to hope that my front door was enough to keep Jason outside until then. There was another thud against the front door.

"Lauren, let me in. You have been avoiding me for too long, and it's time we talk," Jason yelled, his voice carrying through my apartment and sending a shiver down my spine.

I fumbled with my phone, dialing Nate's number again. It went to voicemail. I sighed and slumped down against the bathroom door, sitting on the cold tile and feeling the tears start to drip down my cheeks. I wiped away the tears and shut my eyes, hoping Nate would drive a little faster.

At that moment, I was glad I had given the spare key to Kayleigh last week after Nate had handed it back instead of returning it to the flower pot.

"Lauren!" Nate's voice called through my apartment. "Laur, I'm here. Open up."

Shaking, I got to my feet, the steady thudding of the door for the last twenty minutes still playing through my mind. I crossed the living room as quickly as I could, pulling open the front door, and throwing myself into Nate's arms.

"Please take me away from here."

"I will," he murmured, holding me tight. "I'll take you somewhere safe."

***

Nate kept his arm around me as we walked inside his house, my bags in hand. As soon as his front door was shut and locked behind us, I turned to him and looped my arms around his neck.

"Lauren," he said, his arms circling my waist. "What are we doing?"

"I need a distraction. Please. Anything. We can talk later, but right now, I just need to feel something other than terrified that my ex is coming after me."

Nate gave me a sad smile and brushed a strand of hair behind my ear. "I don't want to take advantage of you. We have a lot to deal with."

"Not tonight," I said, standing on my toes and kissing his neck. "Please, just not tonight."

He groaned as I nipped at his neck, trailing kisses until I couldn't reach any higher. In one smooth motion, his arms looped beneath me, lifting me up before pressing my back against the nearest wall. His mouth was scorching hot as he sucked and kissed my neck, tearing my shirt off and tossing it to the side. I arched my back as he kissed the tops of my breasts, his hand sliding around my back. The moment my bra fell away, his mouth was on my nipple while his hand tweaked the other one.

I ground against him, heat building in my core as I ran my hands through his hair and wrapped my legs tighter around him. His hardened cock rubbed against me, drawing a groan out of Nate.

Nate's mouth moved to the other nipple as he pulled us away from the wall and walked down the hall to the bedroom. He quickly put me down and pulled off my shorts and panties. Nate grabbed my legs, hooking them over his shoulders before his tongue swirled around my clit. I bucked against him, gripping the sheets as he continued to swirl his tongue, fingers dipping inside me.

My inner walls tightened around him as he thrust his fingers in and out. With a few more strokes of his fingers, I convulsed around him. Nate grinned as he hovered over me, kissing me hard before flipping us over.

"Ride me, baby," he said, running a hand along my hip.

I moved over him, trying to swallow the self-conscious feeling that washed over me. Nate's eyelids were hooded as he watched me, his cock bobbing as he propped himself up on his elbows.

"You're beautiful," he said as I hovered over him, running my hands down his muscled torso. "I love all your curves." His hands trailed over my waist before softly massaging my belly pooch. "I don't think I'll ever get used to how sexy are."

Nate's hands moved lower before grabbing my hips with a smirk and pulling me down onto him. I moaned as he sank deep inside me. He guided me as I rocked back and forth, his fingers digging into my hips as he thrust upward.

"Just like that, baby," he said, one hand weaving into my hair and pulling gently. I arched my back, changing the angle until my inner walls convulsed around him.

He groaned, his own release coming hard and fast as I slumped against him. I rolled to the side, tucking myself against his body.

"I missed you," I said softly, the words hesitant as I looked up at Nate.

Nate's fingers drifted along my side. "I missed you too. We need to talk, though."

"I know," I said, draping an arm across his torso. I took a deep breath and closed my eyes. "I love you."

His hand paused on my side, his body stiffening beside me. "Excuse me?"

"That's what I've spent all this time thinking about. I love you."

His fingers started drifting up and down my side again. "I love you too. Even though it's crazy and we barely know each other. I fell for you the moment we met."

"Say it again. I need to hear you say it again."

He smiled and kissed my temple. "I love you too."

Chapter 9

Nate

Lauren had spent the last three weeks living in my apartment, her belongings cluttering up my space and her early morning singing driving me insane when all I wanted to do was sleep in.

This morning, it was some rendition of a song that I barely recognized. I groaned and rolled over, burying my face in my pillow until I heard the shower running. My dick twitched at the thought of her in my shower. Instead of suppressing my feelings, I got up and walked into the bathroom, stripping my clothing down along the way.

The steam fogged up the mirrors and the glass door, but I could still see the silhouette of the curves I traced my tongue around the night before. I stroked my hard cock as I opened the door, grinning at her little squeal as I stepped inside.

"Morning," Lauren said, a lazy smile on her face as she reached down, her hand replacing mine. My head fell back as I groaned, leaning back against the wall as she toyed with me.

"Morning," I groaned, grabbing her wrist and using it to pin her against the wall.

Lauren smirked, one leg hooking around my hip as she pulled me into her. She moaned as I lined up and slipped inside, the hot water pounding against my back. Lauren's nails raked down my back as I thrust inside her, pushing her body up against the wall and keeping one of her hands pinned against the wall.

"Faster," she said, digging her heel into my back and urging me deeper.

I moved faster, letting go of her hand to rub her clit. Lauren came apart around me, her legs shaking as she gripped my shoulders. Her inner walls squeezed me tight. I kept my grip on her as I thrust deeper and faster. I moaned as I finished, my fingers digging into her soft flesh.

"We should probably get cleaned up," Lauren breathed as I set her back down. She gave me a playful smile and looped her arms around my neck.

"We have other things we need to do today, and if you keep pressing yourself against me like that, we're not going to get them done," I said, frowning down at her.

"Fine," she said, reaching for the soap. "Be boring."

"I will."

I kissed her temple before helping her wash her hair.

We had a long talk a few weeks ago. Lauren had been holding back more than I had known about. We had been sitting on the couch when she pulled out the envelope, showing me the pictures of us. My blood had boiled when I saw the fear on her face. It was then that she had admitted the only reason she pushed me away was to protect me.

At first, it had pissed me off. I didn't need her to protect me. I was supposed to be protecting her. Instead, I had failed her when she needed me the most. When I put myself in her place, I realized that I would have done the same if I were her. She loved me and had done what she thought she needed to. I couldn't fault her for that, even if I was angry with her.

Since then, I had kept my eyes out for her ex, but so far, I hadn't seen Jason around town. The officers at my station were running different daily routes, staying unpredictable, but none of them had seen Jason Guthrie either. Even unannounced checks at the only motel in town didn't lead to anything. He came and went with ease, and that was the part that bothered me the most.

He was comfortable sticking to the shadows and knew how to avoid the officers looking for him. I believed that he was unhinged in some way, though. He wouldn't have come here looking for her if he wasn't. He wouldn't still be lurking around town and trying to break into her apartment.

"What's got you looking so worried?" Lauren asked as we got out of the shower. "You've got that *I'm a scary sheriff* look on your face again."

"I *am* a scary sheriff," I said, my tone teasing as I grabbed two towels and tossed her one of them. "I'm just thinking about your ex."

"While I'm naked," Lauren said, drying herself off. "That's weird. Can't say that it's a turn on."

I laughed and rolled my eyes, heading off to get dressed. Once we were both dressed, we walked to the truck and headed into town. Living with Lauren was an interesting experience. It had been a long time since I had lived with a woman. Candles were starting to appear all over my house, and we were flying through food like crazy. Of course, that was probably my fault. I only bought what I had when I still lived alone. I wasn't used to sharing my meals with someone else.

"Why did you seem so awful when I met you? People only had good things to say about you, but you were cranky as hell," Lauren said as we drove down the dirt road.

"I don't know. Her theory is that I'm stunted emotionally. My sister thinks it's because our dad died when I was young, and I had to be the man of the family before I was even a teenager."

"I'm sorry to hear that. Was it rough?"

"It wasn't a great time. My mom struggled a lot with addiction for a few years after that. She got cleaned up a few years ago, but it was too late, and the damage was already done. She passed away in her sleep one night. Organ failure."

Lauren reached over, taking my hand and lacing her fingers with mine. "Those people are right about you, you know. You are a good man."

"I try to be."

She sat beside me, listening as I told her about my childhood and the years of caring for Sarah and my mother. Her thumb stroked across the back of my hand as she inserted her own stories of growing up with a pair of loving parents. We traded stories back and forth, and the ease between us warmed my heart even more. I grabbed her hand and kissed her knuckles as she told me about her ideal dream house, describing it in such great detail that it merged with what I had been working on for the better part of this year.

"How about I take you somewhere else instead of grocery shopping?"

"I'm up for anything."

I grinned and turned the wheel in the opposite direction. It was nearly an hour's drive to where we were going, but I didn't mind. Lauren connected her phone to the stereo and played all her favorite songs, singing along as loud as she could. I laughed as she danced in her seat, pulling out as many crazy moves as she could think of. We pulled off the road and onto an empty plot of land.

"What is this place?" Lauren asked as she got out of the truck and started walking around.

"It's where I'm going to be building a new house. Construction starts next week."

"You're building it?" she asked, looking up at the tall trees surrounding the property.

"Why not? I built the first one. I was thinking I could rent that property out to one of the families in town. Move into a place a little bit bigger."

"Oh?" Lauren asked, looking over her shoulder at me and arching an eyebrow.

I looped my arms around her waist and pulled her close. "Yes. I was thinking a lot about my future a month or two ago. I saw this cute blonde woman and her friend playing with the friend's child, and it got me thinking."

"Did it?" Lauren asked, turning around to loop her arms over my shoulders. She smirked and ran her fingers on my jaw. "Thinking about what?"

"I want all that one day. I want it with you, so I thought I better start working on our dream home."

"Our dream home?"

"Our dream home," I said, nodding. "Only if you want it, though. If not, I'll just build the coolest house around, and you can visit whenever you'd like."

"I want that too. It already looks so much like what I was telling you earlier on." She turned to me, a sparkle in her eyes. "Funny how life works out."

She laughed as we walked around the small space already cleared, and I showed her where all the rooms would be. Lauren's laughter surrounded us as we danced in the kitchen and ran down the hallway. By the time we came to a stop, we were holding each other and swaying back and forth to music playing in the truck.

"How about we go back home, and I show you the plans that were drawn up? You can make whatever changes you'd like."

"Sounds perfect," she said, smiling as we let go of each other and walked back to the truck.

***

When we got back to my house less than ten minutes later, the front door was wide open, and the glass windowpanes on either side of the door were broken. Shattered glass lay across the porch, and a baseball bat was leaning against the wall.

"What the hell," Lauren whispered, getting out of the truck and slamming the door behind her.

"Laur, stay here, okay?" I got in front of her and took her face in my hands.

"Nate, I'm scared."

"I know, baby. Go back to my truck. Call the station and request backup. I'm going in."

Chapter 10

Lauren

"Like hell you're going in alone, Nate," I said, my hands clenching into fists at my sides as he opened the passenger side door and reached beneath the seat. "Jason's in there. It has to be him."

Nate pulled out a little black box and entered a code before pulling out a gun. He checked the magazine and clicked off the safety. My eyes widened as he kissed my forehead softly before stepping back.

"You can't do this, Nate. Not alone. I won't let you," I said, trying to hold back the tears starting to blur my vision. "Please don't do this."

"Lauren, I'm not going to sit here and argue with you about this. I need you to be safe. You need to get back in the damn truck and call the station."

"Nate," I said. "This is a bad idea. Please. Just wait with me until the officers get here to help. You don't need to go in there."

"I'm not going to let him continue terrorizing you. This ends now."

At that moment, I could only see Nate's lifeless body lying on the ground. I could see Jason above him, already trying to figure out how he would hide what he had done. He would get away with it, and nobody would ever know the truth about what happened to Nate.

I couldn't let it happen. I wasn't going to let it happen. Nate was not going to risk his life to save me from my ex-husband. I was the one Jason wanted. Me and the recordings. I wouldn't let Nate get himself into trouble to protect me.

"You're going to get hurt," I said, my vision going blurry as tears appeared in my eyes. "I don't want anything to happen to you. I can't deal with him hurting you. He won't hurt me. Let me go after him."

"I'm not going to get hurt," Nate said, his hand coming up to cup my face. He kissed me quickly. "I love you. Get in the truck and stay there until the other officers arrive. Please. I can't do my job if I'm worried about you too."

"Please don't do this."

"Get in the truck, lock the doors, and call the station," he said before walking away.

I stared after him for a moment as he walked up the front porch steps, his gun held in front of him. After taking a deep breath, I got back inside the truck and locked the doors. My hands were shaking as I dialed the number for the station.

"Willow Town Police."

"It's Lauren. Get to the sheriff's house as fast as possible," I said, my voice shaking. "There's been a break-in. We think that there's somebody still inside. Sheriff Hollis has gone in on his own."

"We're sending two units there as fast as possible, Lauren. Where are you right now?" the person on the other end of the call asked. I didn't recognize their voice, but I suspected it was one of the few officers I hadn't met yet.

"In the truck. The doors are locked."

"Good. Stay there. Help is on the way. I'm going to hang up now to take another call. If something happens, call the Sheriff's personal line. I'll reroute it through to one of the officer's cell phones."

"Thank you."

When the call ended, I was left alone in the truck. Nate's house was a nearly twenty-minute drive away from town. Twenty minutes was a long time to wait for something to happen. My heart was pounding in my chest, and I could hear my blood rushing in my ears. Nate was in there alone, and there was nothing I could do to help him. I couldn't go charging in there, it would only distract him, and I didn't have a weapon. I would be no help to him. The best I could do was sit in the car.

Unless there was evidence.

There was no car in the driveway, but Jason had to have driven up here. It was a long walk, and there was no way he would have had the energy to walk that far with how hot and humid the day was.

I got out of the truck and walked down the long driveway, looking for tire tracks that didn't match Nate's. Not even my car had been up here. Sure enough, I found tracks that had been hastily swept through. They looked like they were barely visible, but they were there.

After snapping a few pictures, I started following the tracks. We hadn't noticed a car on the way up here, so it wasn't parked down by the road. That had to leave it somewhere on the property unless Jason was long gone. Based on who he was as a person, I suspected he was waiting inside for the perfect moment to strike. He would take what he wanted without any regard for the consequences.

I was halfway around to the back of the house when I heard the gunshots, and my stomach dropped to my feet.

"Nate!"

I ran as fast as I could to the front of the house, my heart pounding. Shattered glass crunched beneath my feet as I took the porch steps two at a time and raced into the house. Another gunshot echoed through the hallway.

"Nate!"

"Lauren! Get out of here!"

I ignored him, desperate to find him, even as I heard glass shattering. Nate shouted and more glass shattered. In the distance,

I could hear sirens shrieking.

"Nate!"

"Lauren, get the hell out of here!"

There was another gunshot before a vase a few feet away from me broke, glass spraying everywhere. I felt pieces scrape against my face, drawing blood as I dropped to the floor.

Jason and Nate appeared at the end of the hall, grappling over the gun. Nate groaned as Jason drove his knee into Nate's torso. Nate was quick to recover, slamming his elbow into Jason and yanking away his gun at the same time.

"Lauren, I just want to talk," Jason said, blood in his teeth as he struggled with Nate. "This would have all been over real quick if you'd have done what I told you to do."

I stood in the corner, pressing myself as far back as possible. Nate glanced at me before gritting his teeth. He turned the safety on before throwing his gun at me. I swore and leaned forward to catch it, the metal fumbling in my hands. Clutching the gun to my chest, I stared at Nate with wide eyes. Terror kept me frozen in place.

"Run! Protect yourself!" he yelled before lunging forward and catching Jason around the waist. The two men fell to the ground, trading punches.

I took one look at the gun in my hands before my fight or flight response kicked in. Jason punched Nate hard, blood spraying onto the floor. I screamed, tears running down my face before I took off running.

The sirens outside were getting louder. I started running back to the truck, trying to yank open the door as Jason came charging out of the house, blood on his hands. My stomach lurched as I looked at him before abandoning my efforts to get in the truck.

I was faster than Jason. I always had been. We had run together all through high school and kept up with it once we had graduated. It used to drive him insane that I could outrun him.

I hope I still can, I thought as I took off down the driveway in the direction of the sirens. All I had to do was run faster than Jason until the other officers arrived.

"Get back here!" Jason shouted, his footsteps pounding against the ground as he followed me. "You bitch! You ruined my life!"

"You ruined it yourself, you corrupt piece of shit!" I yelled back, determined not to let Jason know how scared I was.

Jason laughed, the sound low and dangerous. "When I catch you, I'm going to make you wish that you had never taken that recording in the first place. You don't know what I'm capable of, Lauren, and I think it's about time I showed you."

Nate was shouting from somewhere behind us, but I couldn't look back. I had to keep running. I had to keep the gun away from Jason.

Suddenly, I collided with the ground, and a heavy weight settled on me. I kept a tight hold on the gun, knowing I would be dead when Jason got his hands on it. He flipped me over.

"You think you can blackmail me?" he asked, leaning forward. Blood from his broken nose dripped onto my face. "You think you can threaten to ruin my career, blackmail me, divorce me, and then just get away with it—"

I drove my knee upward, into his balls. His rant was cut off as he fell to the side, clutching himself.

There was no time to waste. I got back to my feet and started running again. Jason was still groaning behind me as I sprinted down the driveway.

"Get back here!" he shouted, his booming voice echoing through the forested area around the house.

Glancing over my shoulder, I saw that he was back on his feet, and Nate was close behind him. I only had to keep running for a little while longer. The police would be here soon, and then we would be okay. We would be safe.

We had to be safe.

I could hear his footsteps getting louder as he got closer to me again. As I pushed myself harder, my chest was heaving, the sirens louder and louder. Cars whipped up the driveway, dirt flying behind them. The first car stopped, the sirens cutting off as two officers climbed out of the car and started running toward me.

"Drop the gun!" one yelled, aiming her gun at me. "Put your hands in the air!"

I stopped running and threw the gun to the ground as the second officer ran forward to grab it.

Arms wrapped around my waist, and I was tackled to the ground, the air knocked out of my lungs. I gasped for air as a heavy weight pressed against the middle of my back. The weight was only there for a matter of seconds before it was lifted off me.

"Lauren, are you okay?" Nate asked, kneeling in front of me with blood pouring from his face and onto his shirt. "Laur, baby, are you okay?"

"I'm fine," I said, panic rising in my chest as Nate helped me get to my feet. "I'm fine."

His arms wrapped around me tightly, holding me close. "You're fine. You're going to be fine."

"We're going to be fine," I said, tears rolling down my cheeks as I pressed my face into his chest.

We held onto each other for a while before he pulled back slightly. "I need to take care of this," Nate said, stepping away from me. "Give me two minutes, okay?"

I nodded, swallowing hard and trying to hold off my tears. "Okay."

Nate kissed my forehead before walking over to Jason. He stood over the other man, listing his Miranda rights. I stole a glance at Jason, saw the vile scowl on his face, and my life flashed before my eyes. How had it come to this? At some point, Jason and I were so stupidly in love, even voted for the couple who would last the longest in high school on top of being Prom King and Queen. That seemed like ages ago. How wrong everyone had been.

But for all the heartache and pain Jason had put me through, I was glad it brought me to the one man I knew deep down would only love me and make me happy.

***

After hours of questioning, I was exhausted. The district attorney and several federal agents had rushed from Crawford City to Willow Town, but it was still a long drive. When they arrived, I was pulled into a little room and asked thousands of questions. While I answered every question they had, my mind was on Nate. He had been whisked away to the clinic to deal with his wounds before he would be questioned.

"Thank you," Agent Rossi said, holding her notepad by her side. "I appreciate the information you have been able to provide us on Jason Guthrie and the recording you have sent. We will be in contact in a few days to discuss the next steps with you, but I suspect he will go away for a very long time."

"Thank you," I said, a weight lifting from my shoulders. It was finally over. My nightmare was finally over. Someone else knew the truth, and they would make sure that Jason could never get to me again.

"Do you need a ride anywhere?"

"Can you take me to the clinic on Main Street?"

Agent Rossi nodded and led the way to her car. She didn't say anything as she drove through Willow Town, and I didn't bother trying to start a conversation. I stared out the window, looking at the people who were staring at the car. In a few hours, they would all know what had happened.

When we arrived at the clinic, one of the nurses took me to Nate's room. I closed the door behind me as he looked at me from the bed.

"Are you okay? I wanted to go to the station with you, but they wouldn't let me," Nate said, getting out of the bed and crossing the room to pull me into his embrace.

"I'm okay," I said, tears slipping down my cheeks. "I'm okay now. I promise."

"I was scared, Lauren. I still am. I don't know what comes next, and I don't know how to keep you safe."

"I can keep myself safe, and Jason will be going to jail," I said, leaning into his hug. Jason was out of my life for good. "I don't know what comes next either. I just know I want to be with you. I was scared for a long time that you would be like Jason. I was worried about getting involved with another cop. I thought that it would be like repeating history."

"And what do you think now?" Nate asked, pulling away slightly.

"I think that you're nothing like him, and I never really knew what it was like to feel loved until I met you."

Nate's fingers weaved through my hair as he pulled me to him for a kiss. He pressed his forehead against mine, our breath mixing as his arms tightened around me.

"You are the only person I've ever been able to see a real future with," Nate said, sounding as if there was a lump in his throat. "I thought I was going to lose you. I don't ever want to feel that way again."

"I don't think this will be easy. You and I have a lot of our own baggage to deal with, but I know I want to spend the rest of my life with you."

"Good," Nate said with a smile, kissing me quickly again. "I wasn't planning on letting you go again. I don't have a ring yet, but I'm going to get you one and do this right."

I leaned back to look at his wounds, running my fingers lightly down his face. "I don't need a ring right now. I have you. I love you."

"I love you too," he said, a smile stretching across his face. "But I'm going to buy you that ring someday."

"Someday is good enough for me."

"Stay with me?"

"Forever."

Epilogue

Nate

One year later

Lauren's hair was shining beneath the sun as she tilted back her head and laughed while our dog rolled around in the grass. We had gotten the dog a few months after moving into the house we built. Lauren thought all the big halls had been too empty and quiet. Her solution had been bringing home the dog one night and insisting that the golden retriever would be staying.

I had been powerless to refuse her like I was with most things these days. All it took was one little flash of that stunning smile, and I was a goner. She had me wrapped around her little finger, and she knew it.

It didn't bother me. She was wrapped around mine too.

"What are you thinking about?" she asked, twisting her engagement ring.

"I'm thinking about the wedding," I said, not bothering to tell her that she had me whipped. She already knew that.

"Oh?" she asked, a smile playing on her lips. "What about the wedding?"

"We should run away and elope tomorrow."

I didn't care when we got married. All I wanted was for Lauren to have the wedding of her dreams. As happy as I would have been to run away and elope, I knew that wasn't what she wanted.

"Sarah would kill me," Lauren said, grinning at the mention of my sister.

In the past year, the two had grown closer than ever. Add Kayleigh into the mix, and most Saturday nights, there was a trio of women gathered around my table drinking wine while Bryce raced his trucks through the house.

"Yes, she would."

"I guess we aren't eloping then," Lauren said, tucking her hands into her sweater pockets while a breeze blew harder, shaking the leaves in the trees.

"Guess not."

I took a sip of my coffee and stared at the line of trees surrounding the property. One day, I wanted to cut down more of the trees and build a pool and pool house. It would last us for years, and the kids we both wanted would love it growing up. We could be the house they brought their friends over to.

It was strange what a year and a half could do. Lauren had waltzed into my life and changed everything. She showed me that a life of isolation was nothing to be content with. She made me want the groups of friends over every week and the laughter that filled my kitchen. Lauren had been the one to change everything for me in a matter of months.

"You've got that look on your face again," Lauren said, smirking as she looked at me.

"What look?"

"The look you get when you're thinking about how much you love me."

I laughed and shook my head. "Maybe I was."

"I knew it." She sighed and twisted in her seat, draping her legs over the arm of her chair. "I love you too."

"I know," I said, sticking my tongue out at her.

Lauren laughed and shook her head, pulling her hand out of her pocket. She handed me a slim box wrapped in black paper. I raised an eyebrow as I looked at her. Lauren shrugged and nibbled on her bottom lip, sticking her hands back in her pockets.

"What is this?"

"Open it."

I set my coffee to the side and unwrapped the box. She stared at me as I lifted the lid, her eyes never leaving mine.

"What's this?" I asked, confused by the black and white picture I was looking at.

"Our baby."

It took me a moment to register what I was holding.

"You're kidding," I said, tossing the box to the side and getting up to pull her into a hug. "You're pregnant?"

"Two months today."

I grinned and held her tight, swinging her around in a circle. "That's amazing! Holy shit. We're going to be parents."

"We're going to be parents," she said, her grin spreading across her face as she laughed. "We're going to have a baby."

I laughed, kissing her, and wiping away the tears running down her cheeks. She hugged me tight, laughing and pressing her face into my chest. It seemed surreal, but it was happening. We were having a baby.

As I held her on the deck, I felt content for the first time in my life. Since Lauren entered my life, there were no more lonely nights. We were starting our own family, in a house we had built.

Life was good.

Mountain Man One Night Stand (Book 2)

Blurb

Naomi was burdened by her family's problems. Things were finally turning for her when she got the opportunity of a lifetime. Tyler lived a secluded life in Paytin Town. He liked it that way until the arrival of a curvy journalist upended his carefully laid-out plans.

Naomi

It started with an undeniable attraction and a one-night stand. I thought we would never meet again. But 6 months later, Tyler was holding all the cards to unlocking my career's full potential. We were stuck together for the next four months, and I couldn't stop thinking about how his hands had felt on my body. Things got complicated quickly, compounded by my family issues and accidentally revealing a secret that wasn't mine to share.

Tyler

I isolated myself for a reason. My only desire was to have my art speak for itself without the farce of the fortune behind my name. Working with a journalist to spread the word about an upcoming auction should have been smooth sailing. Until I saw who the journalist was——a one-night stand that had been plaguing my every waking moment since it had happened. Having Naomi in my space will test every morsel of my control...and desire.

Prologue

Naomi

I saw him from across the club as soon as he walked in. He didn't look like the other men surrounding me. There was something self-assured about how he carried himself that had heat rushing to my core immediately. His gray eyes scanned the room before he made his way to the bar.

"He's gorgeous," Leslie said, leaning closer to me with a mischievous smile. "You should go see if he wants to have a little fun."

My cheeks warmed as I rolled my eyes and kept swaying my hips to the beat of the music. Tonight was about forgetting the horrible afternoon I had had. Dropping Zach off at rehab never got any easier. My baby brother would always promise me that this would be the last trip, and then three months later, he would relapse.

I understood that he was struggling with addiction, but sometimes I wished I wasn't the only one fighting for his sobriety.

"You should go after him," Caroline said as she slithered her body along Leslie's, drawing the attention of a few different men in the club.

"I'm good here," I said.

There were more than a few reasons why a one night stand with a stranger was a bad idea. There was too much going on in my life. I didn't need to risk another potential complication.

We danced together; laughing and moving to the music until our drinks were empty and sweat coated the back of my neck. I held my empty beer bottle up to my friends before nodding to the bar. They grinned at me before moving back into the middle of the dance floor.

I weaved my way through the crowd to the bar. The bartender was leaning against the other end of the bar, talking to a small group of women. I sighed, knowing it would be a long wait, and climbed onto one of the empty stools.

"Hey," the man beside me said. I turned to look at him, shocked to be staring into his piercing gray eyes. "I saw you dancing out there. You're good."

"Thank you," I said, offering him a polite smile. "You should come dance with me."

"Dancing has never really been my thing. I'm better with my hands."

All thoughts of avoiding a one night stand flew from my mind. Seeing him from a distance had been completely different than seeing him up close. He was clean-shaven with a sharp jaw. Everything about him oozed confidence. He was the kind of man I would stay away from if I met him on the street.

Which was exactly why I started considering one night of fun with him.

The bartender came back over and stopped in front of me. "What will it be?"

I looked at the man beside me. "Shots?"

He grinned. "Tequila."

The bartender quickly poured the shots and set them in front of us. I downed the shot before setting the glass back on the bar. The man beside me drank his own before handing the bartender a bill.

"Keep the change," the man said.

"What do you say we get out of here?" I asked, crossing one leg over the other. The hem of my short black dress rose higher, and his gaze immediately dropped to my bare skin.

"One night? The hotel I'm staying at is close by."

"One night."

He got up and offered me his hand. I sent a quick message to my friends, letting them know where I was going before taking his hand. The man led me through the crowd and into a car already waiting by the curb.

A limo? Who is this man?

"What's your name?" he asked as the door closed behind us. "Eric, my hotel, please. And some privacy."

"Of course, sir," Eric, the driver, gave a quick nod before disappearing in front of the divider.

I smirked.

"My name...not important," I said, moving to straddle his lap.

His hands gripped my hips as his mouth met mine. I could feel his cock hardening beneath me. I pressed down against it, rubbing myself against him through his jeans and moaning at the sensation.

I should have probably waited until it was just the two of us, but I wasn't really thinking at the moment. I was trying to go with the flow.

Something I hadn't done in many years.

The man moaned as I tore my mouth from his to start kissing down his neck. His hands slipped below my dress, kneading my ass as he thrust upward. He pulled one hand away from my ass and removed his wallet, finding a condom within a second. Then, he pulled back long enough to reach between us and unzip his jeans, raising his hips high enough to shimmy his clothing down.

I lifted my dress higher as he rolled the condom on. His fingers slipped between my legs, stroking against my clit slowly. I writhed against him, not wanting to wait any longer.

His hand knotted in my hair, tilting my head back as I lowered myself onto his cock. He groaned, kissing the tops of my breasts as I rode him. I could feel the release building, but he quickly flipped us over, pressing my back against the seat.

He kissed down my body, pushing the dress higher. His mouth found my clit, his tongue circling the bundle of nerves until I was bucking against his face. I moaned as his fingers entered me, thrusting deep and fast until my inner walls were clenching around him.

"Come for me," he said, his voice rough.

He continued to work his tongue over my clit as I came, stars dancing across my vision. Before I could catch a breath, he thrusted his cock deep inside me, and I was chasing another release.

The limo came to a stop as he finished. We were quick to rearrange our clothing before getting out. I avoided looking at Eric, knowing we weren't exactly silent back there. Thank God the gray-eyed man led me through the hotel, quickly. My heart thumped with excitement.

Our clothing only stayed on long enough for us to get into the hotel room. We fell into bed together, losing ourselves in each other's bodies.

Chapter 1

Tyler

"I don't want a damn journalist living in my house and following me around," I said as I paced back and forth on the dock. Waves lapped at the shore as I paced, rocking the kayak tied to the dock.

"It's just for four months, Tyler. You said that you wanted to have big publicity for the charity auction. Since you don't want the world knowing who you really are, this is the next best thing."

I sighed and ran a hand down my face. Hillary was right, but that didn't mean I wanted to listen to her. While I was determined to remain anonymous, we had to get creative with marketing if I wanted my paintings to sell. A journalist shadowing my work and writing an article was certainly one way to do that.

"Tyler, she seemed like a nice woman when I met her. She isn't going to name you in the article or take any pictures of you. She's signed a contract and NDA."

"Great," I said, staring out at the water. "And when exactly am I supposed to go pick her up from town?"

"She gets into Paytin around noon. Bus number three-twelve. You shouldn't be able to miss her either. Pretty woman. Blonde hair, brown eyes, a lot of freckles."

"Pigtails and a sippy cup too?" I asked, my nasty mood turning on Hillary.

"Get over yourself, Tyler. You're being an ass. Go into town, pick her up, and try to be as nice as possible."

"I'll pick her up and bring her here. I make no promises about being nice. You know I don't like having my privacy invaded."

"Goodbye, Tyler."

Hillary ended the call before I could continue arguing with her. Instead of calling her back, I looked back toward my house. It was a large enough house with three different wings. I would put her in the one furthest from me. With any luck, she and I would barely cross paths. She could write her article based on what little she did see while staying with me.

I walked back to the house and took a left down a little path to my studio. It was a freestanding building that was made almost entirely of glass. There was a perfect view of the lake down below that had inspired more than one painting.

The current canvas I was working on was only in the early stages of being designed. I stared at it for a moment, wondering what else I would need to add to it. I had never been able to plan my paintings too far in advance. They changed based on my moods and inspiration. Any time that a new feeling struck me, something was added or taken away. It was how I liked to work. It was completely free and unrestrained. There were no rules governing what I could and couldn't do, unlike the life I had left behind.

As much as I wanted to stay and work on the painting, there was no time. It was already eleven, and Paytin town was nearly forty minutes away. I still needed to shower and get coffee.

***

I arrived minutes before the bus pulled into the depot. I kept my baseball hat pulled down low over my eyes, shielding my face in the shadows. People wouldn't notice me unless they stared for a few seconds too long.

When the bus doors opened, and the blonde journalist stepped off, my jaw nearly hit the ground. She was the last person I had been expecting, yet here she was. The one night stand I hadn't been able to get out of my head over the course of the last six months.

"Well, I didn't expect you to be here," I said as I pushed off the post I was leaning on and walked toward her. "You're Naomi Avion?"

"And you're Tyler Garner?" The corners of her mouth turned upward as she shook her head and adjusted the bag draped over her shoulder. "Unbelievable. The story that's supposed to change everything for me is about the man I fucked in the back of a car before I was ditched in the middle of the night."

I froze, staring at her. "You can't publish anything about that. Nothing. Do you understand?"

She scoffed and took off her sunglasses. Then, I noticed the deep and dark circles beneath her eyes. Even though she was as stunning as the night we met, there were hollows in her cheeks, and exhaustion clear in how she carried herself. Naomi looked like life hadn't been kind to her in the last few months.

"Why would I ever publish something about the most humiliating night of my life?" she asked, venom in her voice as she walked over to the pile of luggage the bus driver was making.

I followed her, wondering how the hell this could have happened. If she knew who I was, then everything I had been trying to avoid was about to be blown open. A part of me felt a small shred of guilt about the wrong name that she had been given. Tyler was my first name, but the last name that I worked under wasn't right. It was one of the few ways I had found to protect my identity.

"Look, I don't care what you think about that night, but let's get one thing clear," I said as she picked her suitcase out of the pile. "I have a private life and want it to stay that way. I don't want you to expose me to the public, and I certainly don't want details of what I do in the city."

She rolled her pretty brown eyes and looked around the parking lot. "I signed a contract. I'm not stupid. Your team will approve my article before it ever goes to my editor. Now, can we go to wherever it is we're staying? I've had a long bus trip and an even longer winter. I'm looking forward to spring in the mountains."

"That one's mine," I said, nodding to a black truck parked in the center of the lot. "Do you want me to take your bags?"

Another roll of her eyes. "Don't go pretending that you have manners now, leaving me in the hotel, no note, nothing..." She whispered the last few words. "I'll manage fine by myself."

Naomi marched over to the truck and hefted her suitcase into the bed. There wasn't one hair out of place as she turned to me with a raised eyebrow and crossed arms as if to prove her point.

This is going to be a long four months, I thought as I unlocked the truck. She got in and tossed her tote bag on the backseat before shutting the passenger door. I stared at the truck, wondering exactly what I had just gotten myself into.

The drive back to my home was long and quiet. Naomi read a book, her legs crossed beneath her, and the seat leaned back. It bothered me that she had made herself comfortable in such a short amount of time. I didn't know anybody else who seemed so at ease in a foreign environment, or in front of a stranger.

She's seen me naked. After that, there's nothing left to feel uncomfortable about, I thought as I turned around a sharp bend in the road.

Other than recognizing me as the man she slept with, she didn't seem to think anything else of me. There was no instant recognition in her eyes, just as there hadn't been the first night we met. It was what had drawn me to her when she sat beside me at the bar. She hadn't known who I was then, and it was refreshing.

Based on how she was acting now, she still didn't know who I was, and I don't think she cared to find out either.

When we pulled up to the house, she was out of the truck before the engine was off. I wanted to scold her for jumping out before the truck was completely immobile, but I was pretty sure she would only turn around and kick me in the balls. She didn't seem like the kind of woman who would take shit from anyone.

With a sigh, I turned off the engine and got out, watching as she climbed into the truck's bed and grabbed her suitcase. She didn't bother to look at me as she jumped down. Her gaze scanned the property, landing on the house. Her eyebrow raised, but I couldn't tell if she was impressed or disgusted.

"Where am I staying?"

I scowled and stuffed my hands into the pockets of my jeans. "This way."

I led her around to the southern wing that faced the forest. There was a separate entrance that she would be able to use, but it also connected to the main wing as well. As long as she stayed in those two wings while I was working, we would be just fine. I'd have to send her a schedule with suitable interview times to keep our interactions at a minimum.

"There's a kitchen in the main wing that you can use as you'd like. Stay out of the northern wing, as that is my personal space. While you are here invading my privacy, I would appreciate it if you stayed out of my way."

Naomi looked at the glass walls of the main room and nodded. "Fine. You won't see me unless it has to do with the story I'm writing."

Before I could say anything else, she was inside the house, locking the door behind her. It was a clear message that I received loud and clear.

She would stay out of my way, and I would stay out of hers.

Chapter 2

Naomi

I waited until he had walked back toward the main wing before slumping against one of the walls and sinking to the floor. I clutched my knees to my chest, trying to ignore the tightness in my chest. When I agreed to spend four months away from people and write the article of a lifetime on a reclusive artist, I thought I would be staying with an elderly man. I didn't think I would stay with the man who had given me the best orgasms of my life.

A few articles were written about Tyler in the past, all of which suggested that he was much older than he appeared. None of them said that he was a man in his thirties.

Four months were going to be a lot harder than I thought.

After a few more minutes of trying to collect myself, I got to my feet and walked into the bedroom. There was a massive bed in the middle of the room, and two walls were made entirely of glass. I could see the lake and the forest without ever having to get out of bed.

When I walked into the bathroom, my jaw nearly dropped at the bathtub sunken into the ground. It was seamless against the wall. Where the bathtub stopped, the windows began, overlooking the lake.

It was the kind of place I would never want to leave under normal circumstances.

I returned to the bedroom and put my suitcase on the bed,

ready to settle in for the next few months. There was more than enough closet space for the meager amount of clothing that I had brought with me.

When I was done putting the clothing away and had stationed my laptop and camera on the desk, I pulled out my phone and scrolled through the contacts. I went back and forth about calling my brother a few times before I hit the call button.

There were several long rings, and for a second, I wondered whether or not my brother was curled up in a bathroom, throwing up whatever substance he had just taken. It wouldn't be the first time I had caught him in the middle of that particular act.

"Hi, Zach," I said when the call connected. "How're you doing?"

"Hey," he said, sounding as if he was out of breath. "Just got back from a run. Are you in Paytin? How was the bus ride?"

"It was alright. You didn't answer my question."

He sighed. I heard the sound of a door closing on the other end of the line. If I closed my eyes, I could picture my brother walking to the other end of our childhood home, where his bedroom had been since we were children.

"Mom was rushed to the hospital shortly after you left..."

"Wait, what? Why didn't no one tell me? Where is sh..."

"Hold on, sis. We didn't want to worry you on your long bus ride to the mountains. Mom's home now and resting, but the doctors say the cancer is metastasizing. They think she's got another year left in her at best, but they won't know until they run more tests."

The glass walls around me could have shattered, and I wouldn't have known it at that moment. It felt as if I had left my body and everything around me was just a figment of my imagination.

We had always known that her cancer would come back, and we were unsurprised when it did at the beginning of winter. Mom was a fighter and had been doing chemotherapy and radiation, but now it looked like it wasn't working like it should. She was getting weaker, but when I told her that I would cancel the trip and stay home, she nearly disowned me.

My mom wasn't a woman who wanted people hovering around her when she was sick. She wanted her independence, and I knew she didn't like that I was seeing her fade away in a hospital bed.

"Okay. I'll book a bus back and be there late tonight. Or maybe I might be able to just take a taxi. Only a four-hour drive from here to the city if I take a taxi, no stops."

"Naomi, stop. We're fine. Mom is resting, and I'll take her to the hospital in the morning to get the tests run. There's no need to call a taxi and rush back here."

"Zach, I want this to sound as nice as possible," I said with a sigh as I stared out at the lake. "You're in no position to take care of Mom. You've only been out of rehab for a few weeks. You're not supposed to be dealing with this much stress while you're in recovery."

Zach was quiet for a while. If I hadn't been able to hear the sound of his breathing, I would have thought that he had hung up.

"I'm going to say this as nicely as possible," Zach said, a bitter edge to his voice. "I'm going to be better this time, Naomi. I'm done ruining all of our lives. You've been taking care of our family for a long time. It's my turn now. Stay where you are and work on your story. If she takes a turn for the worst, I'll call you, but Mom wouldn't want you to come back home."

"I know," I said as I wiped away the tears that rolled down my cheeks. "If it gets to be too much for you, call me, and I'll come home, okay? I can't lose you again."

"You won't. I'm going to get better, Naomi. I promise."

"I love you, Zach."

"I love you too, Naomi."

When the call ended, I sat down on the bed and leaned forward, trying to ease the restricting feeling in my chest. I took deep breaths as I tried to focus on where I was and the job at home. Mom wouldn't want me to come home, but Zach wasn't strong enough to deal with her cancer. He needed to focus on getting himself better before he could devote time to her.

I had to give him this chance, though. He needed to know that I believed in him, even if I was sure it was only a matter of time before I would have to return home.

When the shaking in my hands finally subsided, I stood and changed into a pair of leggings and an oversized band shirt. My hair went up into a messy pile on top of my head before I grabbed my denim jacket and took off out the door.

If I was going to be here for a few months, it would be a good idea to get to know the property. From what his manager had told me, Tyler owned sixteen acres surrounding his home. The entire lake sat in the middle of his property, completely secluded.

The birds were chirping as I walked toward the woods. A small path led through the trees that looked like they had been lined with stones. I followed the path until I came to a small ravine that looked as if it fed into the lake. There was a wooden bridge that crossed the ravine, and on the other side, there was a small clearing.

I crossed the bridge, my curiosity getting the best of me. While I hadn't brought my camera, I had brought my phone along with me. Before stepping into the clearing, I snapped a few pictures of the ravine and sent them to Caroline and Leslie.

There was a small fire pit lined with wooden chairs and benches. It looked like the perfect entertaining spot I had difficulty aligning with Tyler. He didn't seem like the type of person who was close to anyone. I couldn't imagine him bringing out his friends and having a party, but he could surprise me.

I trailed my fingers along the smooth wood as I walked in a circle around the pit. I took another picture, wondering if it was something I should include in the article.

The reclusive artist keeps a secret area for entertaining.

It wasn't interesting. If I had read that headline, I wouldn't read the article. I needed something about him that would grab readers' attention and hold them captive. It had to be something that the other articles hadn't done before.

An inside look into his life was sure to drum up attention for his upcoming charity show.

As soon as I heard that he was holding a charity show and auctioning off some of his paintings, I knew I wanted to be involved.

The first time I had seen his work was in a small gallery near my house. It had been a showing during the early days of his career nearly twelve years ago. I had only been fifteen at the time, but something about the dark elements he hid in beautiful landscapes and portraits called to me.

I vividly remembered a painting of a woman's face. She had been beautiful beyond reason, but when you got closer to the painting, you could see a car crash reflected in her eyes.

It had been a shocking discovery, but after that, I had studied the paintings more closely. Each held a tiny secret, some sort of disaster that had happened. There was darkness hidden in every light.

Since then, I had been to galleries showing his work more often than I would admit to him—especially after knowing he was the man from my one night stand.

I looked around the clearing for a while longer before heading back to the house. Tyler was standing beside a barbecue with his hands tucked into the pockets of his flannel jacket.

Even though it was spring, there was still a bite in the air, especially as the sun began to set. I walked over to him, buttoning up my jacket and tucking my own hands into my pockets.

"Hungry?" he asked, opening the barbeque and grabbing the spatula. "Making burgers."

"Sure. Thank you."

He nodded and started flipping the burgers before closing the lid again. Tyler said nothing as he grabbed a beer bottle from a little table nearby and took a sip.

"If you want one, there's more inside the house," he said, tilting his bottle toward the large porch that spanned the length of the north and main wing of the house.

"Thanks," I said, heading inside to grab a beer. If I was going to get through the first night without allowing the awkwardness to consume me, I would need something to take off the edge.

When I returned with my beer, he was flipping the burgers off the grill and onto buns. Cheese was melted over on top, and condiments had appeared on the little table beside the barbecue.

Tyler handed me a plate with a burger before dropping down into one of the chairs nearby with his own dinner. I added ketchup and relish onto my burger before taking my beer and dropping down into the seat beside him.

"So, why sixteen acres of wilderness?" I asked, looking around. "It seems pretty lonely up here."

"That's the point."

I took a bite of the burger and nearly moaned. It was the best burger I had ever had. It only irritated me—this man seemed as if he could do no wrong. I wanted to find a flaw with him, something that would make me feel more like a normal human sitting beside him.

"Where do you paint?"

"All over the property," he said, nodding to the lake in front of us. "By the water a lot. In the studio. There's a pretty nice spot by some mountain foothills at the other end of the property, but it's a lot of work getting everything out there."

He sighed and got up, not saying anything, as he put another burger on his plate and settled back down in his chair. I got the sense that he didn't want to talk about it any longer, and that theory was proven a few minutes later when he excused himself and went inside.

I didn't bother to follow him. I had gotten enough information out of him for one night.

Chapter 3

Tyler

The more I thought about Naomi staying with me for the next few months, the more agitated I got. There was something about Naomi that drove me crazy. She had caught my eye that first night we met, and she had stayed in my head for far too long after. Seeing her again had been a distant hope. It hadn't been a reality that I had ever considered.

Now I was sneaking out of the house early in the morning to avoid being seen by her. I had forgotten several paintbrushes in a cup of water again, and it had destroyed them.

I pulled my jacket closer to my body as the wind blew cold. Winter was still trying to put up a fight even as the flowers started to grow back. When I got to the truck, I stopped in my tracks and stared at Naomi.

"What the hell are you doing here?" I asked, my voice harsh as I unlocked the truck. "Shouldn't you still be sleeping or something?"

Naomi shrugged and reached up to push a strand of her hair behind her ear. "Hillary gave me your schedule. She said that you would try to avoid me as much as possible."

"Remind me to fire Hillary when I get back," I said before I got in the truck and slammed the door shut. The engine roared to life, cold air blowing through the vents.

I wasn't going to fire Hillary, but Naomi didn't need to know that.

As much as I wanted to lock the truck and leave Naomi out in the cold, there was something about the look she gave me as she rounded the truck that had me rooted in place. She got in and slid onto the seat beside me, reaching for the heat to turn it up.

"Won't start heating up until the engine's warm," I said, driving down the driveway and turning towards town.

"Great. Are early mornings always this cold here?"

"We're at the bottom of a mountain range. Winter tends to hang on a little bit longer here. Mornings will be cold, but the afternoons will be better."

She nodded and leaned back in her seat, staring out the window. Naomi sighed as she watched the empty road passing by. My nearest neighbors were a good distance away. I liked keeping people out of my business.

Naomi seemed like the complete opposite. She had on the night we met too. I still remember how she danced as if she didn't have a care in the world. She had seemed carefree and happy when she was dancing unlike the woman who stepped off the train and moved into my home.

Now, she was quiet and withdrawn. She didn't have that air of confidence around her that had been so alluring in the first place. The woman sitting beside me seemed like a shell of the person that I had first met.

As I drove, it left me wondering what had happened in the last six months. The weight of the world didn't seem to be on her shoulders the last time we saw each other.

"Why didn't you want me to come with you?" Naomi asked, glancing over at me.

"I need to buy painting supplies. Standing around in an art store while I take too long to pick out what I want isn't a good time."

She scoffed and rolled her eyes. "You say that like you have an idea of what a good time is. I'm starting to think that the man I met in the club was all an illusion."

"He was a different person," I said, my hands tightening on the wheel. "People are more than one thing. That part of my life is one that I don't explore often. I prefer to live a simple life in the woods."

"You know, writing a story about you would be a lot easier if you would give me something interesting that people haven't heard before."

"You've seen me naked. That's more than most nosey journalists get."

Her face turned a bright shade of pink as she crossed her arms. "I'm not sure writing about a night of sex with a reclusive artist is good for my public image. I'm trying to build a career, not continue chasing around these fluff pieces about reclusive artists."

"Alright," I said, trying to hide my amusement at her irritation. "If you weren't writing fluff pieces, what would you be writing?"

"Stories that mean something."

"So, you would argue that a story about an artist doesn't mean anything to anybody?"

"I would say that it's less important than actual news," she said, another bright pink blush coloring her face. "The articles about artists like you matter to some people, but I want to write articles about war zones and politics."

I drummed my fingers on the wheel, wondering if I should bother pushing her any further. The bags beneath her eyes seemed a bit brighter when she spoke about journalism. It was hard to believe at that moment that journalists were the scum of the earth.

"That article about an artist is what is going to inspire another artist," I said, gripping the wheel tighter as we drove around a sharp bend in the road. "That article could save a child living in extreme poverty with parents who don't support them. It could be the push they need to pursue their dreams and screw what anyone else says."

"I know what it means. It's just not what inspires me. It doesn't feel like I'm making the difference I want to make."

I nodded, deciding to stop pushing her for right now and settle back into the silence I was comfortable with. If I kept talking to her, I would start to tell her things about myself. I didn't want anything personal I told her to end up in the article, and I didn't know if I could trust her. She wanted to advance her career, and people looking to get further in life generally screwed me over.

"Why did you leave that night? I wasn't expecting you to stay or anything, but I thought you would have at least said goodbye before taking off? Or left a note or something..."

In that moment, she looked small and vulnerable. She gave me a hesitant look as she picked at one of her nails. I sighed and drummed on the wheel again, trying to figure out what I could say that wouldn't hurt her more than the truth.

That night, I had seen her, and the rest of the club faded away. If she hadn't approached the bar when she did, I would have been seconds away from going over to her and asking her to dance.

I didn't dance, but I had been willing to make a fool out of myself for her.

It had been a long time since I had felt that way about a woman. Especially once we were in bed and talking before she fell asleep. Moments after she had fallen asleep, I had gotten out of bed and slipped my suit back on, knowing that if I stayed for another moment, I might have let her inside the careful walls I had built around my life.

"Never mind. Forget I asked," she said, twisting in her seat to angle her body away from me. "I don't know why it bothers me. We were just having sex, and that's all it was."

"It's complicated," I said, frowning as the half-truth came out. "I have a lot going on in my life, and I'm not looking for anything serious. I wasn't that night, either. Leaving seemed easier than having to stay and explain all that. The explanation doesn't usually go well."

"So," she said as I pulled into the parking lot outside the art store. "You're a giant chicken shit, and that's why you treat people like shit. Good to know. Maybe that will be the headline."

Naomi got out of the truck and slammed the door shut. I watched as she stalked toward the art store, her hands in her pockets and her shoulders tense. She didn't bother to wait for me as she marched inside and let the door swing shut behind her.

Well, that couldn't have gone any worse.

Maybe it was better this way. Instead of being in my way for the next few months, she would avoid me as much as possible. I would give her whatever she needed for her article, and then she would be on her way, and we would never have to see each other again.

Chapter 4

Naomi

His tongue circled my clit as his fingers plunged in and out of me. I could feel my walls pulsing around him, stars dancing around my vision. Heat flooded my core as he pulled his mouth away from my body and looked up at me.

"Not yet. Don't come yet. Not until I tell you too."

I moaned as his mouth descended on my core again, his fingers moving faster. He twisted his fingers, curling them and rocking them back and forth. My hips bucked off the bed, my release building faster.

"Please," I said, breathless, as he looked up at me again.

"Come," he said before his mouth latched tightly on my clit.

A loud crash woke me before I could finish my dream. I scowled and threw the blankets off my body, trying to ignore the sexual frustration that was building up inside me. If I was smart, I would leave Tyler alone to do whatever he was breaking and finish off what the dream started.

We hadn't spoken to each other in nearly a week since the trip to the art store. I had spent time trying to catch up with him, but he seemed better at avoiding me than I expected. No matter how early I woke up or how late I stayed up, he was already gone. It was getting to the point where I was considering just calling the article a bust and heading back home.

I was halfway back to my bed when I heard a shout from the

other end of the house. With a sigh, I pulled on my black silk robe and made my way into the main wing of the house.

Tyler was sitting in the middle of the living room, shirtless, with a broken vase scattered around him. His torso was covered in streaks of blue paint, and his hands were stained black.

"What the hell?" I asked, looking around at the mess. Not only was the vase shattered, but a glass table had also crashed to the ground. "What happened?"

"None of your business," he said, his voice more like a growl than a person speaking. "Just go away, Naomi."

"And leave you surrounded by a bunch of broken glass so you can start cutting up your feet? As great as that would be to put in the article, I'm not going to do that."

"You and that fucking article," he said, glaring at me as his hands clenched into fists. "I never wanted that article written in the first place. I never asked for you to be here again."

"Listen, be a bitch about this all you want," I said, walking to the closet in the front hall and grabbing a broom. "But I'm going to clean up this mess while you deal with whatever the hell is wrong with you."

He stayed seated on the couch long enough for me to sweep away a pile of glass before he got up and took off to his wing of the house.

"Whatever that was about," I muttered as I finished cleaning up the glass.

I retreated back to my wing of the house and started getting dressed. As tempted as I was to start packing my suitcase and buying a bus ticket out of here, I was stubborn. He wasn't going to scare me off that easily. This article was the chance of a lifetime. Yes, it was what I considered more of a fluff piece, but thousands of eyes would be on it. Tyler Garner was a big name, and the person who wrote an article after spending months with him would be a name that other publications would remember.

After I was dressed, I grabbed a book and took off outside.

Sitting by the lake and reading was just what I needed to recharge and decide how I would deal with Tyler.

To my surprise, he hadn't taken off after the glass incident. Instead, he was standing by the edge of the lake painting. My mouth nearly dropped open when I saw his continued half-nakedness. His skin shone in the sunlight, and it was hard not to remember how I traced my tongue along his flexing abs only months ago.

Play it cool, I thought as I dropped down into one of the chairs a few feet away from him and cracked open my book.

"Go away," he said without lifting his eyes from the canvas.

"Nope. You said I was free to go anywhere I wanted as long as it wasn't the north wing. That means that I can sit here and read. If you don't like it, you can go away."

He sighed, setting his paintbrush on the easel's edge in the glass jar. "Naomi, I'm not asking. I don't like people watching me while I work."

"Those mountains are so pretty," I said, looking out over the lake. On the horizon, the tops of the mountains rose high. "Do you think you could take me to the other end of the property so I can see them before I have to go in a few months?"

"I can't focus with you here," he said, ignoring my request.

"That's a shame," I said, smirking as I flipped the page in my book and started reading. "I can focus perfectly fine. If you don't want to work in silence, we can talk about whatever the hell that was back there."

"I tripped over the rug, knocked over the vase, and sent the table flying when I crash-landed on the couch."

"That doesn't seem likely."

"Fine. I was pissed off at my mother. She's the one who bought the vase and the table, so I smashed them both."

"Are you always violent?" I asked, my heartbeat speeding up as I shifted away from him slightly.

"No. Just when it comes to her. Breaking the table and the vase was oddly cathartic." He sighed and ran a hand through his hair. "She called me. I answered, and I don't normally do. She told me again that I was a disappointment to the family and that I wouldn't be a miserable man living in the woods if I had just done what she wanted. It started with throwing the vase, flipping the coffee table, and breaking the glass."

"So, I don't need to worry about you then?" I asked, not knowing what else I could or should say about his mother. By the sounds of it, he didn't want to talk about her, and I wasn't prepared to push.

I could understand the need to break something, though. When my mom was first diagnosed, Caroline and Leslie had taken me to a rage room. I had smashed everything in sight and then asked for more. It had mildly helped with processing some of the anger I felt at the world.

He snorted and picked up his paintbrush again. "You shouldn't even consider worrying about me, Naomi. I'm not the kind of man you ever worry about. Just keep to yourself, or better yet, go home. I'll send you some facts that you can put in your article that nobody else knows, and then you can be on your way."

"Oh, Tyler," I said, my tone patronizing as I closed my book and set it to the side. "I'm not going anywhere. The contract I signed said I would be here for four months. Half a month is already over, and you haven't given me anything good for the article."

"Just make something up."

"Tyler Garner: The Life and Times of Erectile Dysfunction."

His laughter sent a shiver down my spine. "Catchy. Still. Go away."

"Not happening."

"Naomi."

I hummed and twisted in the chair, kicking my legs over one arm and leaning back against the other. "If you don't want to give me something good for my article, let's talk about your mommy issues."

"My mommy issues are not fodder for your story."

He put the brush to the canvas and painted a pale gray streak across half of it. Below the gray streak was a wash of dark shadow and some trees. When I looked at it, I had no clue what he was painting, but he seemed to see something beyond the paint and the colors.

"So, you admit you have mommy issues then?"

"Are you going to be annoying the entire time you're sitting out here?" he asked, painting dripping from his raised brush and down his torso. I resisted the urge to get up from the chair and wipe away the paint. My hands on his body would only lead to another mistake.

"That's really dependent on whether you're going to give me anything interesting for my article or not. What's your process when you first start a painting?"

I took my phone out of my pocket and opened up a new document as he swirled another line of color onto the canvas. He didn't say anything as he dipped his brush onto a palette sitting on a table beside him. A bright red slash appeared through the dark colors as his jaw set in a hard line.

"I don't know. I grab a canvas and start painting."

"You don't plan anything before you begin painting?" I asked, typing away on the small screen. "Nothing that you think that you should paint and draw before you begin painting?"

"Not even a little bit. Sitting down and sketching out a painting before it's done doesn't bring any real emotion or thought to the canvas for me."

"What about—"

"Nope," he said, cutting me off as he painted another red streak across the page. "You've asked more than enough questions. I need a break and silence."

"Not what you said before," I said under my breath, grinning when I saw a red tinge on his cheeks.

"That was a very different situation."

I chuckled and opened my book again. If I was going to spend the next few months bothering him, he deserved a break every now and then. I read a few chapters, flipping through the pages even though my mind was far from the book. As much as I wanted to lose myself in a good story, all I could think about was the shirtless man in front of me.

He glanced at me every now and then, a strange look on his face. Tyler stared at me for a few moments before turning the canvas, so his back was to me. I watched the muscles moving in his back, wondering if my nails had left marks when we were together.

"When did you get that tattoo?" I asked, seeing the script on his ribs when he moved his arm. "What does it say?"

Tyler lifted his arm and twisted, looking down at the tattoo as if he had forgotten it was there. "Running out of time."

"That's morbid."

"Yeah, well, I got it about a month or so after you and I slept together. My life was going more to shit than it currently was, and a few too many drinks made me think it was a good idea."

"Do you regret it?" I asked, though I wasn't sure if I was talking about our night together or the tattoo.

"No," he said, and, at that moment, I knew he wasn't talking about the tattoo.

Chapter 5

Tyler

"She is driving me insane," I said, pacing back and forth across my studio. "I don't know what to do to get her to leave. Every time I turn around, she is there."

"Well, maybe you need to fuck her again and get over it," Jack said from the other end of the phone. "Or just talk to her and get to know her. I don't know what answer you're looking for."

I had my best friend on speakerphone in the middle of the studio while I paced. He was the only one who would understand what was going on in my life.

"I don't know. It's more than just a quick fuck and forgetting she exists. What if she figures out who I am? What if she uses that to get ahead?" I asked, running my hand through my hair. "Jack, I'm freaking the fuck out right now."

"Well, what heir to a massive fortune pretending to be a reclusive painter wouldn't be freaking out? You have a woman you don't know who has been in your personal space for what, a month now. She's signed contracts, but you can't trust that she isn't going to break them to get ahead in life."

I sighed and leaned against the wall. He was voicing exactly what I feared. I wanted to trust her with the truth, but I couldn't trust that she wouldn't put it into an article. My mother was the only member of my family who knew where I was and who I was pretending to be. I didn't want the rest of them to know. My life ran best when they remained far away from me.

"Look, I don't know what to do. You're thirty-four. Isn't it time you stopped caring about hiding from your family's fame?" Jack asked. "You've been in front of the cameras your entire life. People know who you are. Running away to the woods hasn't made them forget."

"And you know I want nothing to do with that lifestyle or my family's money. None of that is for me. Not with the kind of expectations that they set. Until my family changes their narrow-minded view of the world, I don't want any part of their insanity."

I stopped pacing and looked out the window at the lake. Naomi was sitting on the end of the dock with her legs dangling just above the water. Her hair was blowing in the breeze, and she looked as if she didn't have a single care in the world.

For once, I found myself wishing that she would march herself up to my studio and start bothering me again. Arguing with her was entertaining, even if it was infuriating at the same time.

"You're going to inherit the money when your grandfather dies. You know it, and everybody else within the business world knows it. You need to start figuring out a plan beyond hiding in the woods."

I understood Jack's perspective. He had been hiding from his family fortune for years. When his grandmother passed away last year, he inherited an entire fortune he never wanted. He had gone from living a simple life on the beach to being in front of the cameras and being torn apart on social media.

"How do you handle all of it?" I asked, taking a seat on one of my stools near the window and continuing to watch Naomi.

"I take a few pictures, and then I go on with my life. It isn't worth letting them get to you. By the time whatever story they post about you has gone viral, another story is already on its way to being viral."

Sighing, I scrubbed a hand along my jaw. "Thanks, Jack. I've got to go talk to my resident pain in the ass about what she is and isn't including in the article."

And about what I've been putting off for too long.

"Good luck," Jack said before he ended the call.

I got up and grabbed my phone, tucking it into my pocket. There were several things that I wanted to talk to Naomi about, and the night we shared months ago was one of them.

Naomi got up and looked toward the studio as if she could read my mind. Our eyes met, and her mouth curved upward into a smirk. There was mischief in her eyes as she dusted off her jeans and made her way up the slight hill that led to the studio.

When the door opened, I turned to face her with a thousand different thoughts running through my mind. I didn't know where to start with her. She leaned against one of the walls and crossed her arms, that mischievous smile still on her face.

"So," she said, drawing out the word. "I have an article to write, and you are being incredibly difficult to get along with."

I was tired of hearing about that damn article, but I was glad it had brought her back to me. I hadn't been able to stop thinking about her since that night in the bar, and it was time I did something about it.

I rolled my eyes and crossed the room to stand in front of her. The smile dropped as I invaded her space. I could hear her breathing hitch as she looked up at me.

"Let me be clear," I said, leaning close enough to kiss her. "You are getting under my skin with your damn article. You're the most irritating person I've ever met, and every time I look at you, all I can see is you spread out on that hotel bed, begging me for more."

Her cheeks flushed a bright pink, and she was speechless for the first time since we met.

"I'm tired of fighting the attraction to you, Naomi. I think you're tired of it too," I said as I took a step back, needing some space between us if I was going to continue this conversation. "You're here for three more months. I'm not in the position for anything serious, but I am open to casual sex."

I didn't know what was going through her head as she looked at me. There were no emotions on her face as she worked through what I said. For a moment, I wished I could turn back time and pretend as if I had never said anything to her.

"I haven't been able to get you out of my head either. And to be honest, I need a way to relax and forget about everything going on in my life right now."

I looked at her, noting the dark shadows still beneath her eyes. They had paled slightly since she first arrived, and the color was coming back to her skin. She was gorgeous, but she looked exhausted with life.

"What's going on in your life?" I asked, wanting to see a little more of the woman standing in front of me.

Naomi chuckled and shook her head, stepping around me. "Casual sex means that we don't discuss our baggage."

I nodded, feeling heat rise to my face as she started walking around the studio and looking at the blank canvases scattered around the room.

"What are you working on?" she asked when she stopped in front of the painting I had been working on over the last couple of days. "This doesn't look like the one you were working on last week."

"That one is in the drying room," I said, pointing to a small door to the back of the studio. "This is a new one."

"What is it going to be?"

I shrugged and walked over to the painting in question, looking at the swirls and slashes of dark paint on the beige canvas. It was in the beginning stages of an underpainting, but I wasn't sure what the finished product would become.

"I was driving through one of the towns nearby the other day...I'm not sure which one, so don't bother asking...and I saw an abandoned, covered bridge. Thought it was interesting, so I wanted to paint it."

Naomi nodded, pulling out her phone and typing down what I

had said. I wanted to snatch the phone from her and throw it across the room. I didn't want my every word and inner thought recorded, especially when I was trying to get to know her as a person. However, she was here to do a job—that was the only thing that kept my temper under control.

"In your article, I don't want any pictures of myself or anything too personal."

"What's too personal for you?" Naomi asked, still staring at the underpainting.

"A lot of things."

"The article will go to your team before it's even considered for publication."

I held back the sigh of relief and settled for a nod. "Good. I don't want to be a public spectacle."

"And yet you create art that is made a public spectacle for a living," she said, finally looking away from the painting and fixing me with a curious gaze. "You're an interesting person, Tyler. I'm going to spend the next couple of months figuring you out."

"I wish you wouldn't," I said, my chest tightening as a small wave of panic crested.

She smiled and shrugged. "I know."

My hands were aching for a paintbrush as she left the studio, off on whatever adventure she had decided on for the day.

As soon as the door closed behind her, I stalked over to one of the blank canvases staged around the room. Within moments, I had a palette of paint ready to go and was putting brush to canvas. Streaks of beige and brown appeared on the canvas as I tried to force Naomi out of my mind. I dropped the palette to the side and pulled my shirt off, not wanting to ruin another one, before tossing it to the side. I grabbed the palette again and dipped my brush in the darkest shade of brown, getting to work again.

All I needed was Naomi out of my mind and life. After she was gone, I could go back to the life I loved. At least, that's what I kept trying to tell myself.

Chapter 6

Naomi

Hot water bubbled around me as I took another sip from my glass of white wine. The night was colder than the ones before it, and the hot tub had been calling my name after another tense phone call with my brother.

Our mother was getting worse, but Zach insisted he had it under control. When I spoke to my mom for a few moments, she said that Zach was still sober and doing better. I wasn't sure that I believed her, though. She was always good at pretending there was nothing wrong with her son. I think it was her way of coping with the truth, but it didn't help anybody.

A large part of me wanted to run back home and handle everything like I always do. I wanted to make sure that Zach wasn't at risk of breaking his sobriety again, and that my mom wasn't fading faster than either of them was telling me.

I *needed* some control of the situation but had none, which bothered me the most.

And then there was the email I had just gotten a few moments ago.

I looked at the phone sitting on the edge of the hot tub and considered ignoring it all. I could pretend that I had never received the email, but that would only leave everything in a bigger mess than it already was. Everything would spiral further out of control, and I would still be left picking up all the broken pieces.

More so than ever, I needed this article. I needed it to do well and launch my career forward. The money would help my family more than I could imagine. It would mean that I could pay for my mother's treatment and ensure that Zach could get back on his feet properly without worrying about how he would pay for food and rent. He could continue to live in our family home with our mother for free, and I would keep their fridge stocked with food. He could keep working as a web developer and save up enough money to move out and start his life properly.

In my head, it had been the perfect plan until I got the email.

With a sigh, I grabbed my phone and set the wine to the side. I took a long pause, trying to ensure I was calm before calling my brother.

"Hey," Zach said, answering the call on the second ring. "How's the trip going?"

"It's good," I said, my voice tight. "When were you going to tell me about the house foreclosure?"

There was a long pause. I wondered if he was running around and trying to come up with a story that would explain this all away. Lying was one of the things he was best at.

"How do you know about that?" he asked, his tone defensive.

"Don't worry about that, Zach. We're going to lose the house? Where the hell is all the money you're making going? I thought you were getting back on your feet and making enough to pay the mortgage?"

"Look, Naomi. Stop worrying. I have everything handled here; you don't need to worry about it. I have it under control."

I wanted to scream. "Zach, you have never had anything under your control in your entire life. I've got two and a half months left before I have to finish the article. I need you to take care of Mom and make sure that the bills are paid. After that, you can go back to being irresponsible and letting me handle everything."

"The fucking bills are paid," he said, his tone venomous. "Don't you pretend that you actually give a shit, either. You only called to bitch at me because, for once, someone has to rely on me and not you. How's it feel being the failure this time, Naomi?"

After a long pause, I heard loud music in the background of his call. A person was shouting his name, and another was screaming about something else. A siren shrieked somewhere in the distance, but it was getting louder. More people started shouting about an overdose as the music cut out.

Before I could say anything else, Zach ended the call.

My heart plummeted to the ground and broke into a thousand little pieces as I put the phone back on the side of the hot tub. Zach promised me that he was going to stay sober. He had promised me that he would be able to handle staying home with our mom.

Maybe it was my fault. I knew better than to trust him. It was the same cycle repeating itself over and over again. He had been doing better, and I had trusted him. I had asked Caroline and Leslie to check in on him. They reported back to me every week. They took turns bringing meals over every couple of nights to make sure that everyone was fed. None of them had seen the signs.

That meant that Zach was hiding his fall off the wagon better than he ever had before.

I ran a hand down my face, looking up at the ceiling and trying to blink the tears out of my eyes. I had done this to him. Letting him take on this much responsibility so soon after rehab was a bad idea.

A lump rose in my throat as I grabbed the wine glass and downed it.

"Need a refill?"

I chuckled and held out the glass as Tyler appeared. He took the glass from me, his fingers brushing against mine. Tyler opened the wine fridge that sat on the desk in a cupboard and grabbed the open bottle. He filled the glass higher than I normally would before handing it back.

"Thank you," I said before taking a sip.

"You looked like you could use it," he said, folding his arms and leaning against the edge of the hot tub.

I didn't miss how his eyes trailed down my body as the bubbles dissipated and the water stilled. He looked back up at me, a fire in his eyes.

"Want to join me?" I asked, splashing a little water his way.

"I'm not sure if that's a good idea right now," he said with a pointed look toward my phone. "You didn't sound happy from what very little I could hear."

"I wasn't."

As I took another long sip of my wine, he looked like he was at war with himself. He drummed his fingers on the edge of the hot tub as the wind rustled the leaves in the trees. I sank lower into the water at the cool breeze and closed my eyes.

"Are you okay?" he asked.

"Not even a little bit, but that's not my problem."

Tyler gave a heavy sigh before I heard the rustle of clothes. When I opened my eyes, Tyler kicked off his shoes and stepped out of his jeans. I watched as he pulled his shirt over his head, revealing his toned torso. Heat shot between my legs as he stood in front of me. It was the most of his body I had seen in months, and I could feel my excitement growing rapidly.

He had mentioned something casual between us nearly two weeks ago, but nothing had come of it. There'd been teasing and stolen glances, but nothing more. It seemed neither of us wanted to go there just yet.

Until now.

"Do you want me to take your mind off of it?" he asked as he got into the water, his boxer briefs hiding nothing.

"Yes."

One second, I was across the hot tub from him, and the next, I was straddling his lap. His hands settled on my hips, gripping them hard as his cock hardened beneath me. He had barely touched me, yet I felt as if my entire body was on fire.

"Fuck," he muttered, his fingers digging into my flesh. "I didn't bring any protection out here. I was just going for a walk."

"It's fine," I said, running my hands over his chest and down the ridged plane of his stomach. "I've got an IUD, and I'm clean."

"Me too."

It was all the convincing he needed. His lips found mine in an instant. Our mouths slanted together as I rocked against him, trying to relieve the pressure already building between my legs.

I ran my hands through Tyler's hair as his hands ran up my body. His fingers worked against the strings of my bikini top until both knots were undone, and the fabric was falling away from my body. My nipples pebbled the moment the cold air hit them.

Tyler pulled back to look down at me before he took a nipple in his mouth. The other he rolled between his fingers until I was rocking faster against him, my release already building. When he moved his mouth to the other side, still toying with both nipples at the same time, my orgasm crested.

"Already?" he asked, his voice low and filled with amusement as he pulled back.

"What did you expect? You've been teasing and taunting me for the last two weeks...scratch that, more like 7 months."

A deep rumble escaped his throat. "Should we keep track of how many orgasms I can give you tonight?"

I couldn't think clearly enough to give him an answer. It didn't matter, though. His mouth was already on my neck, nipping and kissing the skin there as he stood up. My legs wrapped around his waist as his hands traveled down my body, leaving a tingling trail wherever he touched.

My bikini bottoms fell away before Tyler put me down on the edge of the hot tub. He kneeled between my legs, his fingers drifting up and down my thighs.

"I've thought about this a lot since that night," he said, his fingers grazing against my clit.

I moaned, and my head fell back as his tongue followed the trail of his fingers. My hips rocked against his face as he looped one arm around my back. I gripped the edge of the hot tub, my head falling back and my eyes closing as his fingers entered me.

"You like that?" Tyler asked, moving his fingers faster. "You going to come again?"

"Yes," I said, nearly breathless, as he twisted his fingers and his tongue circled around my clit before he sucked hard.

My hands flew off the edge of the hot tub as he continued to lick and suck, his fingers still rocking inside of me. Stars started to dance at the edges of my eyes as my core clenched around him. With one more hard suck on my clit, I fell apart around him again.

"That's two," he said, standing up and removing his underwear. He tossed them to the side before sitting back down in the water across the hot tub from me. "Get over here and ride my cock."

I didn't need to be told twice. His hands dug into my hips as I positioned myself above him. He lifted his hips as I sank down onto his cock. Our moans mingled together in the night air as his hands ran up my body to massage my breasts.

When he tweaked my nipple hard, I rocked against him a little, teasing him. Tyler grinned, one hand slipping down to grab my ass. He thrust harder into me, sinking himself fully.

The last of my restraint snapped as I moved faster, chasing after another orgasm. We moved together, our thrusts matching as his hand fisted in my hair. He pulled gently, changing the position of my body before thrusting harder. My inner walls clenched around him, and his cock pulsed as he gave another thrust.

We fell apart together, waves of our orgasms washing over us. I slumped against Tyler's chest, my breathing shaky and my legs numb.

This feels so good. So perfect...me and him...
No!

I couldn't go there. With a sigh, I got up and pushed myself off of him.

"Where are you going?" he asked as I climbed out of the hot tub and grabbed my towel.

"For a shower."

"Stay for a little while," he said, something unreadable on his face as he looked at me.

I shook my head and wrapped the towel tighter around my body. "That's a bad idea. This is just sex, remember?"

He swallowed hard and nodded. "I remember. Have a good night, Naomi."

"Good night, Tyler."

I turned and fled from the backyard, heading toward my wing of the house. If I didn't have space from him, I was going to make a mistake. I was going to tell him that I didn't want this to be just a casual thing.

I needed that space, and I needed it now, even if it hurt me to walk away from him.

Chapter 7

Tyler

The sun was barely beginning to creep over the horizon as I finished loading the bed of my truck with everything I needed to spend a day painting. It had been a long winter, and few trips had been made to the foothills of the mountains. Now that the snow was gone and the water was starting to warm up, it would be the perfect time to go to the waterfall.

"Where are you going?" Naomi asked as she appeared beside me with a tote bag over her shoulder and a travel mug of coffee in her hand. "You wouldn't be trying to sneak away without me again, would you? I thought we were over that."

I looked at her, mixed emotions flowing through my body. Things between us had been tense since we fucked in the hot tub. She had kept her distance over the past week, and I hadn't bothered going to seek her out. I was the one who instigated a casual relationship. I shouldn't have been surprised when she walked away the other night.

And yet, I had been hoping that she would stay and finish that bottle of wine with me.

Now, I didn't know how to feel. Naomi sipped her coffee as if nothing had ever happened, but I could see how her fingers drummed against the strap of her canvas tote as she kept it close to her body. She was on edge about something.

"Are you alright?" I asked, wondering for the millionth time what was happening in her life.

"I'm fine. It's just family bullshit," she said as she walked around to the passenger side of my truck. "Don't worry about it."

I got the feeling that there was a lot more going on in her life than she would ever be willing to tell me about. Still, I wanted to know. Maybe I could help her with whatever it was.

But instead of pressing her, I got in the truck and started driving along the dirt roads that led through my property to the foothills. Every now and then, I glanced over at her to find her with a book in her hand. The sun shone in the window, illuminating the golden strands of her hair.

When I stopped the truck at the bottom of a path, she was quick to get out and grab her tote. I followed suit, moving to the back of the truck and pulling out my painting backpack and a canvas.

"Do you paint up here often?" Naomi asked as she grabbed the easel I had pushed to one side. When I tried to take it from her, she rolled her eyes and started marching up the path.

"Stubborn ass," I said.

"You still didn't answer my question," she said, looking over her shoulder at me. "Do you paint here a lot?"

"Mostly in the summer. There're some flowers still left in bloom, but the water is a lot warmer."

"Can I still swim in it now?"

I laughed as I followed her along the path I had worn on the ground. "It's going to be cold, but if you want to try it, go ahead."

Naomi grinned as the roar of rushing water could be heard rising above the silence. She walked quickly, nearly jogging as we rounded the corner that led to the bottom of the waterfall.

A wide clearing at the bottom of the waterfall and a lake fed into a small river. Wildflowers were starting to bloom near the rocky cliff that led to the top of the waterfall. Off in the distance, a couple of deer disappeared into the bushes when they saw us.

"So," I asked as I took the easel from her and set it up at the angle I wanted. "Why don't you tell me about this family bullshit?"

Naomi sighed and dropped her bag to the ground before sitting down beside it. She stretched her legs in front of her and leaned back on her forearms, staring up at the sky.

"I think that's a bad idea."

"Why? Once this article is written, you and I are both going to be out of each other's lives. I'm the perfect person to tell."

As much as it bothered me to say it, it was the truth. Once this article was written, she and I would be going our separate ways. She would return to her life, and I would return to my solitude.

Although it was getting harder to imagine the house without her. I could hear her listening to music every morning while she got her coffee ready. I could hear her singing to herself, and a few times, I had walked in while she was dancing around the kitchen.

A house without her would be quiet and sleepy. There wouldn't be a breath of life breathed into the atmosphere each morning. I would be alone.

It bothered me more than it should.

Naomi looked over at me and rolled her eyes. "Fine. My mother has cancer, my brother is a drug addict who is trying to hide the fact that he's fallen off the wagon for the millionth time, and my family home is heading into foreclosure. And apparently, I'm the family failure this time around."

For a minute, I didn't know what to say. I couldn't think of a single appropriate thing to say in this situation. All the etiquette classes my mother had forced me through as a young kid had done nothing to prepare me for this moment.

"Are you okay?" I asked, thinking that it was the best response I could give.

She chuckled and sat up to grab her coffee and take a sip. "Define okay."

"If you need to go back home, we can finish this over the phone. I'll even let you annoy me over the phone every day."

Naomi sighed, looking guilty as she turned to fully face me. "Is it wrong to say that I don't want to go home just yet and deal with that mess? I don't want to have to charge back into the inferno and fix everything like I always do. Zach told me that he had it handled. I fucked up, and I believed him."

I sat down beside her, reaching for her coffee and taking a sip. She glared at me as she snatched the travel mug back and set it out of my reach.

"You didn't fuck up," I said, still trying to figure out what the right response in this situation was. "You didn't do anything wrong. Your brother told you he would be able to handle it and then let you down. I don't see how that's your fault."

"It is. I should have seen it coming. I thought that things would be better with my friends checking on him and my mom every few days. He had just finished his longest stint in rehab before I came here. I thought that it would be fine, and he was ready to keep at it."

"You couldn't have known that it wouldn't be," I said, looping an arm around her waist as tears appeared in her eyes. She leaned into my side and sighed. "You thought that you were doing everything right."

"I don't know what to do anymore. I need this article to do well. I need to make my name as a journalist to fix everything that has broken again."

"I don't think that it's your responsibility to fix everything. Your brother is a grown man, isn't he?"

"Yes."

"Well then," I said, brushing her hair out of her face. "He can take care of himself. As for the family home, it's just a place. Focus your attention on your mom, and don't worry about the rest."

"You make it sound so easy. As if I can leave my brother out in the world helpless."

"Naomi, I mean this in the nicest way possible, but his decisions are not your problem."

She pulled away from me and took a deep breath. "I know. I

think I'm going to go swimming."

It was a clear end to the conversation. I watched as she grabbed her bikini out of her bag before hiding behind a tree to change. When she emerged, she didn't bother to look at me before diving into the cold water.

"It's not warm," she said as she swam closer to the waterfall. "It's not as bad as I thought, though."

"Enjoy that. I'll be up here."

I took off my shirt and hung it on a branch before setting up my palette for a new painting. I didn't miss how her eyes slid over my body, but I wasn't going to go after her right now, either. As much as I wanted to have her screaming my name on the banks of a waterfall, she looked like she wanted to be alone.

As I painted, I glanced at her every now and then. She stopped swimming after a few minutes to bundle herself up in a blanket and start flipping through a book.

When I was done painting, I stepped back to look at it. I had captured the waterfall on the canvas, but I had chosen the focal point of where the water met the lake. A woman was swimming in the water, but beneath the lake, there was a shadowy monster with its arms wrapped around her waist, dragging her down to the depths.

Before Naomi could see it, I grabbed the canvas and wrapped it gently in a linen sheet I kept in my painting bag. The paint was still a little wet, but it was set enough that loosely wrapped fabric wouldn't disturb it.

"What do you say we go get some dinner?" I asked as I wiped the paint off my torso.

Naomi closed her book and got up, gathering her belongings and keeping the blanket wrapped around her body. "Sure, but I need a shower and something to wear first."

***

"Okay, Tyler," Naomi said as we sat down across from each other.

"Tell me about yourself. I feel like after exposing my family to you this afternoon, I should know something about you."

"I'm not talking about my family," I said, my tone sharp. "It's not a good story, and to be quite honest, I don't know what you're planning on putting in your article."

"And here I thought we were getting along pretty well," she said, picking up her menu and opening it. She was stiff in her seat as she scanned the options for dinner at a local diner in town.

"I'm sorry," I said, picking up my own menu. "I'll talk about a thousand other things but not my family."

"I didn't ask you to tell me about your family. I asked you to tell me about yourself. If you'd stop jumping to conclusions about what kind of person I am, maybe you would have realized that this conversation is entirely off the record."

I studied her for a moment, wondering if she was telling me the truth. Yes, I was attracted to her, but I still didn't trust her beyond what I needed to for her to live in my home. I had no way of knowing what she would put in that article.

After she finds out you're lying to her, the cruel voice in the back of my head said.

I didn't know how she would react when she found out the truth.

"I like living alone," I said after we had ordered and the waiter had dropped off our drinks. "I like the peace and quiet of not having someone else in my space. I like working alone and being free to come and go as I please. It's freeing."

Naomi leaned forward and clasped her hands together. "It sounds lonely."

"Why would it be lonely when it's what I want?"

"I don't know. There's nobody around to share those special moments that happen every day with. Do you really like watching sunsets alone? Or sitting in that big hot tub and staring out at a lake with nobody to enjoy it with?"

"It's nice. It's peaceful."

Naomi hummed and sat back in her seat, grabbing her drink and taking a long sip. "I think you have no idea how lonely you actually are."

"And what would you base that opinion on?"

"You hated the thought of having me around, but you make breakfast for both of us every morning when I'm getting ready, and you make dinner every night. You may disappear before I come to get some, but the food is always waiting."

"Common courtesy. You've been living in my home, meaning I should feed you," I said, not wanting to let her know that I only did those things for her. The few times Jack and his wife had been to my house, I never made them food. We usually ordered out, or if they were staying a long time, Jack did most of the cooking.

"You could just admit that you're lonely," she said as the plates of food were set in front of us. "I won't judge you for it."

"How about you ask me questions for your article?"

She nodded, and I could see the walls going back up around her. I couldn't blame her. I had done the same thing. Naomi was getting too close to the truth, and I needed her to back away. I needed to maintain the small semblance of control I had over my emotions. When she left, I couldn't be sitting at home and feeling her absence.

We fell into an easy conversation about painting and when I had first picked up a brush. Every few minutes, she would enter another note in her phone, and I wondered what she was thinking about me. I wondered what would be in that article and whether it would draw my family and the limelight back into my life.

I hoped it didn't.

As we talked, the food on our plates slowly diminished before we ordered dessert. With each minute that passed, I felt more and more like I was in over my head. She was out of my league in every way, yet she still looked at me as if she wouldn't want to be anywhere else.

When I left her outside her wing of the house that night, I

considered pushing her against the wall and kissing her until both of our heads were spinning.

Instead, I forced myself to remember that this was a casual relationship and went back to my own wing.

Chapter 8

Naomi

Tyler had just stepped out of the shower when I entered the north wing of the house. We had spent days trapped inside as the rain poured down outside. I was tired of pacing around this house and not exploring the one part of the house I had been told I couldn't go into.

As it turned out, the north wing of the house wasn't as exciting as the rest of it. There was a huge office and library with a bedroom and bathroom. Nothing else. Tyler stood in the middle of it all with a towel slung low around his hips and water dripping down his body.

Instead of dragging him to the bed, I turned to one of the large windows that overlooked the trees.

"What are you doing in here?" Tyler asked.

I could hear drawers opening and closing. In the window's reflection, I could see him moving around his bedroom.

"It's sunny out today. I thought that we could go somewhere. I know there are a bunch of old towns in this area. I thought that we could go see the oldest one."

"We could, but you still didn't answer my question. I thought that I told you not to come in here."

I shrugged and turned around to look at him as he finished pulling on his jeans. "It's been nearly two months since I came here...you should have already noticed that I don't listen to you much."

He rolled his eyes and pulled his shirt on. "I did notice that. I should have known that sooner or later, you would find your way in here."

"So," I said, walking to the hallway. "How about that really old town?"

"Whatever you want," he said as he grabbed his wallet and keys.

***

Old buildings rose up around us. While some of them had been painted with bright colors, there were others that had the original brick. Tyler led me down Main Street and along a few of the side streets before we came to a street with several abandoned buildings. Tyler grabbed the camera he had draped around his neck before we left and started taking pictures.

"How's your brother and mom doing?" Tyler asked as he turned and took more pictures of another building.

I sighed and pulled out my phone, taking a picture of one of the buildings in front of us. I zoomed in slightly on the broken glass, enjoying the way it reflected the buildings behind us. As I thought about how much to tell him, I snapped a few more pictures before sending them to Caroline and Leslie.

"I don't know. I talked to him again last night, and he sounds worse. I hung up on him, actually, and then felt a bunch of guilt, so I called him back."

"Why'd you feel guilty?" Tyler asked, lowering the camera and looking at me.

"He could overdose and die, and the last thing I did was hang up on him."

It was a thought that bothered me all the time. Talking to Zach was like walking on eggshells. I never knew what the last thing I said to him would be. How could I live with myself if he overdosed after a fight? Rationally, I knew that I couldn't control him, and I couldn't control whether or not he overdosed. I knew his decisions were on him, but it kept me up at night.

"He could get hit by a bus or struck by lightning or any other number of things," Tyler said. "You don't know when anybody is going to die, Naomi. You can't sit here and worry about what you said to him before it happens."

"I know. I'm coming to that realization too. I feel awful, but I want to back away and let him figure it out on his own. For the last several years, I've always been the one who has picked him up and put him back on his feet. I'm twenty-seven now. He started pulling this shit when I was seventeen."

"How old is he?"

"About your age," I said, looking him over. "Thirty-one."

"Three years younger, but still. You were taking care of your older brother when you were supposed to focus on starting your life. Do you resent him for that?"

I bit my lip, holding back the tears that blurred my vision. "Every single day of my life."

Tyler wrapped his arms around me, holding me tight. I could feel his chin resting on top of my head as I wrapped my arms around his waist and clung to him like he was the only thing keeping me afloat.

"It's okay to resent him for that," Tyler said softly. He ran his fingers through my hair. "It's okay to be upset with him for derailing your life. Nobody is going to blame you for that."

"I know," I said as I pulled back from him and wiped my eyes. "I know that. But then I feel guilty for not dealing with it because Mom is sick, and she doesn't need the stress of dealing with him."

"You're handling more than your fair share of the stress," Tyler said. "It's okay to be upset at the world for that."

"Zach needs to start figuring this shit out on his own. I can't keep lifting him up, and I know that I can't. That's part of what this trip was supposed to be about. It was about leaving Zach to figure it out while I tried to make something of myself."

"Then why are you worrying so much?"

"Mom could die. Her cancer isn't getting any better, and Zach isn't around to deal with it. More than ever, Mom needs a stable and relaxing environment. How can she have that when Zach is snorting everything that he sees and the bank is threatening to take our house?"

Tyler looked at me for a moment, and it seemed as if a million things were going through his head. It looked like he had several things he wanted to say, but each time he opened his mouth, whatever it was he wanted to say died on his tongue.

"This isn't your problem," I said, running a hand through my hair. "I shouldn't have unloaded all of that on you. It's not your place to listen to me whine."

He shook his head. "No, that's not what this is. I'm just trying to figure out what I can say or do to help you."

"Don't worry about it," I said.

I crossed the street to another abandoned building and took a few pictures of the graffiti and the broken glass. These buildings had been standing on their own for a very long time, and they would continue to stand no matter what storms beat against them.

Tyler appeared behind me, his hand grazing my waist for a moment before he moved on down the street.

"You deserve to be happy, Naomi," he said after a few moments as he pointed the camera at me. "Even if you are a pain in my ass."

As I laughed, I heard the sound of the camera shutter clicking.

"Let's get some more pictures for your paintings and then head back home."

***

When we got home, Tyler parked the truck outside the studio. He opened the door and let me inside before dragging some of his painting supplies out of his truck. Tyler shuffled off to the drying room with several paintings wrapped in linen.

I walked around the room, looking at the blank canvases he

had stationed around the room again. Since I've been here, I have seen him sneaking out late at night to sit in here and paint. I had watched from the deck as the lights came on in his studio and his shirt came off. Watching him paint was a work of art on its own.

Tyler got a look of concentration met with peace when he painted. He moved with a brush in his hand as if there was a song playing a tune only he knew.

In the entire time I had been with him, though, I still hadn't seen a completed painting. He would work on a piece and hide it behind the locked door of the drying room before I could even sneak a peek at what he was doing.

Sometimes, it frustrated me to no end. Part of writing the article was getting to see how the paintings had come to life. It was hard to describe his process if he never let me see the final result. I wanted to see how paintings similar to the ones I already loved came to life. I wanted to see what the end product of the peaceful concentration was.

"Teach me something," I said, looking over my shoulder as the drying room door opened.

Tyler walked up behind me and opened a cupboard, pulling out a paintbrush and a bottle of pale gray paint. He said nothing as he poured some of the paint onto a small plastic tray before setting the tray on the edge of one of the easels.

"This is an underpainting. Sometimes I do one to block out the shapes of what I want to paint," he said as he stood behind me and put the paintbrush in my hand. "Other times, I just want a smooth base layer before I start painting."

Tyler's hand clasped mine, and he guided the paintbrush into the paint. His body was pressed against mine as his hand dropped from mine. I took a deep breath, trying to still my shaking hand as I lifted the brush to the canvas and stroked downward.

"Good," he said softly, his breath fanning over my ear and sending a shiver down my spine. "Now, keep doing that."

It was hard to focus as his hands slid beneath my shirt and

flattened against my stomach. His touch sent heat straight between my legs. His hands slid higher on my body as I painted another line on the canvas. His thumbs teased the skin beneath my bra, skimming the edges of my breasts.

"You okay?" he asked, his lips descending on my neck. I tilted my head to the side, giving him more access as I put the brush back in the paint. "Don't stop. Finish the painting."

As he spoke, his hands slipped beneath my bra and started their assault on my breasts. He pinched my nipples between my fingers, twisting them hard before strumming his thumb on them. The paintbrush fell to the ground as I lost the last piece of self-control I had.

Tyler chuckled, and his hands left my breasts as I turned around. He pressed closer to me, forcing me to take steps back until my back was pressed against the line of cupboards that spanned one wall.

"There's something I've always wanted to try," he said softly as he undid my jeans.

"Then why haven't you?" I asked as he slipped the denim down my body, helping me step out of the jeans before kissing his way back up my leg. Every touch of his lips to my skin lit a fire. I was soaked and needy, desperate for more of him.

"Because you're the only person I've ever felt comfortable letting in my studio."

I was left shell-shocked as he stepped back and turned to one of the other cupboards. He reemerged from the cupboard with a rolled up white canvas. Tyler said nothing as he spread it out in the open space of the huge room.

Bright colors from the sun setting over the water streamed through the window as Tyler opened small containers of paint and placed them on one of the tables. He grabbed a handful of new paintbrushes and dumped them onto the table beside the paint.

"Come here," he said as he took off his shirt and tossed it to the side. I could already see the bulge straining against his jeans as he picked up a paintbrush and dipped it in the white paint.

Before I could ask what he was doing, he bent down and pulled one of my nipples into his mouth. I moaned, my head falling back as he switched sides. His mouth left my body again but was replaced with the cold paint. My nipple pebbled harder as he kissed his way down my body, the paintbrush following along behind him. I heard the soft clung of the paintbrush as it fell to the ground as he kneeled between my legs seconds later. He dipped his hands in the paint before gripping my ass.

His tongue found my clit, circling slowly as he held me in place. I moaned as he toyed with me, his hands sliding up and down my legs. Every nerve was standing on end as he pulled back and dipped his fingers into another jar of paint.

Tyler splashed the paint onto the canvas as I got on my knees in front of him. He stilled as I helped him out of his jeans before licking from the head of his cock to the base. As I took him in my mouth, he splattered handfuls of paint onto the canvas.

My mouth slowly moved up and down his cock, teasing him as his hands weaved through my hair. His hips moved faster as my nails dug into his thighs.

"Not yet," he said, pulling out of my mouth before kneeling with me. "On your back."

I laid down, and in moments his body was over mine. My legs wrapped around his waist, and his cock ground against my clit. When I moaned, he ground against me harder, his head dropping down to my neck as he sucked hard.

"You're going to leave a mark," I said breathlessly as he pulled back and kissed the parts of my breasts that weren't covered in paint.

"That's the point," he said, his mouth moving down my body before he latched on my clit again.

His hands gripped my hips as he licked and sucked until I saw stars. I was still writhing from the orgasm as he slid inside me and flipped us over. I rocked against him, feeling my inner walls clenching around him hard.

Before I could find my release, he was sliding out of me. His hands ran down my back, leaving a trail of tingles before he swatted my thigh.

"On your hands and knees," he said, waiting until I was in position before moving behind me.

His cock thrust into me from behind at the same time that his fingers found my clit. I clenched the canvas in my hands, arching my back and deepening the angle as he thrust faster. His other hand came down on my ass as I yelled his name, grateful that nobody could hear us.

"Come for me," he said, smacking my ass again.

I did as he said, orgasming around his cock. He continued to thrust as I rode out my orgasm, his own following.

We fell together in a sweaty, paint-covered mess, curling up beside each other as our chests heaved. Tyler rolled onto his side and tucked his arm beneath his head. I did the same, facing him as the night stars lit up the studio. His fingers traced my jaw as he stared at me with something I couldn't quite understand in his eyes.

"What?" I asked, reaching up to wipe whatever he saw off my face.

"Nothing," he said, smiling as he stopped touching my jaw to drape his arm over my waist. "I'm just happy that I got to experience that with you."

At that moment, I knew that leaving the grumpy recluse was going to break my heart.

Chapter 9

Tyler

Naomi poked at her sandwich at a local café in Paytin town, but she didn't take a bite. The iced coffee to her right was nearly empty, but she didn't seem to be able to stomach any food.

I didn't blame her. She was going through a lot. If I had to deal with the same things she was dealing with, I wouldn't have an appetite either. After all that she had told me, I wanted to swoop in and solve all of her problems for her. I would be able to fix everything in the blink of an eye with the trust fund I had access to. I rarely touched it, but for her, I would. For her, I would go back to my family and fall back into the life they wanted for me so she wouldn't have to worry anymore.

"What's on your mind?" I asked.

She took out a small notebook and a pen from the bag at her feet. "Not a whole lot of anything, honestly. I'm trying not to think about everything that is going on. Now, tell me some things about this article. Juicy bits for your fangirls."

I laughed and shook my head. "Juicy bits for the fangirls aren't what you want to write."

"You're right," she said, scribbling something in her notebook. "I want to travel the world and write stories about the places that I've been to. I want to head into war zones and write stories exposing what is happening. I want to change the world with my writing."

I was then if I wasn't in love with her before that moment. In that second, I saw a passion that matched my own. I saw a woman who would stop at nothing to be the person she wanted and fight like hell to ensure she got it.

"I have to call Hillary and talk to her about a contract I have to sign today. Are you alright on your own for a few minutes?" I asked, standing up and pushing my chair back in.

I didn't think she would ever accept my help, even if I offered it to her and she got over me lying to her about a large part of my life. She wanted to do this on her own and wouldn't let anyone else get involved.

"Go ahead," she said, scribbling again in her notebook. "I'm not going anywhere."

"Try to eat something while writing that viral article, okay?"

She laughed and rolled her eyes. When her head bent closer to her notebook, I walked out of the café and paced down the street. I looked at the café as I called Hillary, hoping she wasn't busy and would pick up immediately.

"You never call me," Hillary said as soon as the call connected.

"That's not right," I said, smiling as I rolled my eyes. She was one of my few friends, even if she was my manager. "I do call you when I'm upset with you."

"So, why are you upset with me now?"

Through the window of the café, I could see Naomi shifting around in her seat. She turned her back to the window, leaning against it as she pulled her knees to her chest and kept writing.

"The journalist that's here, Naomi Avion. Her childhood home is about to be foreclosed on. I need you to stop that from happening, and I need you to keep it off the books."

Hillary was speechless for a few moments before she cleared her throat. "Are you sure about that? It's going to take a lot of money."

"Pull from the trust fund," I said, saying the words I never thought I would say. "Take whatever is needed out of the trust fund and then pay for the best care money can buy for her mother. Keep it all off the books, though. I don't want her to know about my involvement in any of this."

"Are you sure?" Hillary asked, her voice hesitant even as I heard her typing in the background. "Your family is going to know the second I start pulling funds out of it."

"Do it. I'll deal with them if they have anything to say."

"She sounds like she is something special," Hillary said, gently prying for more information.

As much as I trusted Hillary, I wanted to keep whatever was happening between Naomi and myself private for a little while longer. If she was going to leave soon, it was best that as few people knew about what had happened here and how I felt about her. Sharing that intimate moment with paint nearly a week ago had been enough to cement my feelings for her.

"She is. I've got to go."

"I'll have everything taken care of by the end of the week."

"Thank you."

I ended the call and slid the phone back into my pocket before staring at Naomi again. She was looking out the window now, her head in her hand and her notebook forgotten beside her.

When I walked back into the café, her head lifted, and a smile spread across her face. Naomi finished off half of her sandwich before getting rid of the rest and joining me at the door.

"Call go okay? It didn't seem that long."

"It wasn't, but it went great. Do you mind walking around town so I can get a few more pictures?"

"Sure. My friends love the ones I've been sending them since I've been here. I'm sure they can't wait for more."

"Have you told them about me?" I asked, half-curious.

"Little bits and pieces. They know that you're not an old man like everybody thought, and they know I like you a lot."

She said the last part with a sly look in my direction. If this was supposed to be a casual relationship, she had just washed away the line we had been tiptoeing around.

"Probably a good thing," I said, trying to smother the waves of guilt rolling over me. "I think I like you a lot too."

She blushed and rolled her eyes, hurrying down the street to take a few more pictures. As she took her pictures, I took ones of my own. She was the star in every single one of them.

The longer I walked through town with her, the more I considered telling her who I was. I thought about telling her my entire past behind being a recluse and what I was avoiding if I stepped out into the world now.

When she turned around and gave me that stunning smile, I knew I couldn't keep who I was hidden from her any longer. I wanted to enjoy the rest of the night, and tomorrow I would potentially ruin the fun we were having.

***

We were walking back to the truck when I saw the bright lights shining above the abandoned buildings. Carnival music filled the streets, and children were screaming and laughing. I hadn't seen any sign of an amusement park when we entered Paytin earlier today, but I also hadn't driven us anywhere near the center of town.

"Can we go check that out?" Naomi asked, her eyes shining bright. She was nearly standing on her toes as she looked at the lights. "Unless you want to paint early in the morning."

How could I tell her I wanted to go home and sleep when she was looking at me like I hung the moon?

"Let's go."

The look of childlike wonder on her face when we walked into the carnival was more than worth the hours of sleep I would be losing. I would never sleep again if I got to see that look on her face one more time. There was something extraordinary about the way she appreciated the little things in life.

Since I couldn't grab a canvas and a brush to paint her

expression, I lifted my camera and took a picture. She turned to me after, the smile growing wider as she shook her head.

"Why did you just take a picture of me?"

"You're beautiful," I said simply, letting the camera dangle by the strap that hung around my neck. "I don't want to forget you when you're gone."

"I don't think that walking away from this is happening anymore," she said, gesturing between us. "I thought that was clear when I told you that I really liked you. I mean, I understand if your feelings don't go that far since we had only ever agreed to casual sex."

"Naomi, I don't want this to end either, but I don't know how we're going to make it work. You live several hours away in a city I despise."

She looked around at the small town and the people laughing as their children dragged them on rides. "Maybe it's time for a move. I've heard small town life is nice. I'd be closer."

"And what about everything you want to do with your life? What about traveling and entering war zones and writing stories that change lives?"

I could feel the panic rising in my chest as I thought more about what she was saying. My mind started to spiral. I had only known her for less than three months, which was all too fast. She was talking about uprooting her life for me, and I wasn't sure that I wanted her to do that.

Yes, I wanted to be with her but not at the cost of her happiness.

She laughed and shook her head. "Tyler, calm down. I'm not putting my life on hold to be with you. I'll still do everything I want to do, and you could come with me or stay at home and wait for me to get back."

"Naomi, that's a lot."

"And nobody is asking either of us to talk about it right now," she said, turning away from me.

A band started playing on a stage in the middle of the carnival. The music rose above the sounds of the rides and the laughter. Naomi watched the couples dancing with a small smile as she swayed to the music.

I decided to push all the invasive thoughts from my mind as I closed the distance between us and took her hand. Naomi laughed as I spun her in a tight circle before bringing her to me. We moved to the slow music, one hand on her waist and the other clutching her head. Naomi pressed closer to me, her head on my chest as we danced.

One night with her at the carnival would never be enough, but for now, it was everything that I had ever wanted.

Chapter 10

Naomi

The sound of my phone buzzing was the noise that first pierced the early morning. Tyler was already up and in the washroom, getting ready for the day of hiking the mountains that he had planned for us. When we had gotten home from the carnival the night before, we had packed a picnic bag and stayed up late talking about our walk to the top of the waterfall.

I couldn't wait to hike up to the waterfall and spend time with him after the change in our relationship last night. He and I would start getting to know each other properly. There would be no more shutting down when the other person got too close.

This was our chance, and I wasn't going to let anything ruin it for me.

"What the hell is that?" Tyler said, his voice muffled by the bathroom door and the running shower.

"My phone!"

I rolled over, the sheets falling down around my waist, and reached for my phone. It was still early in the morning—the sun wasn't even streaming in the windows—but nearly two dozen messages were flashing across my phone.

"What the hell," I muttered, unlocking the phone and bringing up my messages.

There was one from my boss, insisting I find a way to renegotiate the contract before the news got out. More messages were filtering in from other people back home asking how I knew *him*, whoever him was.

I rubbed my eyes and yawned, wondering if everyone in my life had simultaneously had a fever dream. None of their messages made sense. Some were congratulatory, and others were critical. I couldn't find a clear theme in any of them.

I opened my feed with another yawn and looked at the pictures flooding in. There were dark pictures of broken glass that I had taken. Leslie and Caroline had posted them, talking about missing me while I was away on a journalism assignment.

I scrolled further, wondering if the answer to the crazy was buried in the messages. The more I scrolled, the more confused I became until finally, I came to a single picture with a red circle around one part of it.

When I zoomed in on the picture, I saw Tyler in the background, smiling as he looked at me. My eyebrows furrowed as I looked at the picture. I could understand why my boss was worried about the contract. I had agreed that there would be no pictures of him and nobody would know who I was with. Other than that, I didn't see why the pictures my friends had posted were circulating around.

"What did you do?" Tyler asked as he came running back into the bedroom, his phone in hand and a towel clutched around his waist. "Naomi, what did you do?"

"I'm not sure, honestly. There's a picture I took that my friends posted saying they missed me. Apparently, some people care that you're in it."

"Yeah, I know that," he said, his mouth in a thin line and his stare as cold as ice.

"I didn't know you were in that picture when I sent it to them. I'm sorry," I said, feeling awful as my stomach plummeted to my feet. "I'm so sorry. I thought that I had checked all the pictures carefully."

"You don't even understand what you've done," Tyler said,

dropping his phone to the bed and running his hands through his hair. "That's the worst part. I'm so angry with you, and you don't even understand what you've done."

"Tyler, I don't get this. What's happening? Please talk to me?"

"I trusted you. I asked you not to take pictures of me," he said, his voice rising as he paced back and forth across the room. "I thought that I could trust you. Fuck, Naomi, I let you in! I fell in love with you!"

I didn't know what to say. My mouth fell open as I stared at him. There was no way that I could understand where any of this was coming from. I knew he wanted his identity kept a secret, but I didn't understand why he was blowing up the way he was.

"Tyler, can you explain what the hell is going on? I don't understand."

He scoffed and rolled his eyes. "Figure it out yourself."

Tyler unlocked his phone and tossed it to me, showing me the picture he had settled on. It was the one I had taken and collaged with a man in a suit. The man looked vaguely like Tyler, but there was a harshness to his features that didn't align with the man in front of me.

"Is this you?" I asked, looking down at the caption. "Heir to a multi-billion dollar fortune, Tyler Brown, is slumming it in some abandoned town out in the mountains."

"Why do you think I asked you not to take any pictures of me?"

"I didn't! I took a picture of the damn broken glass. I checked the picture. I didn't see you in it. If I had, I wouldn't have sent it to my friends."

"I don't care," Tyler said, shaking his head. "You did the one thing I asked you not to do. I saw you taking pictures, but I thought that it would be alright. I didn't think that you and your friends would expose me."

"How about we talk about the fact that you lied to me about who you were?" I asked, my own voice raising as I tossed his phone onto the bed. "I've been here for three months, Tyler! In all that time, you didn't once think that maybe I should know something real about you? Was everything a fucking lie?"

Tyler froze in place, his entire body stiffening as he stopped his pacing to glare at me. "Nothing was a fucking lie except my last name."

"Sure doesn't feel like it! How am I supposed to trust you after this?"

"*You* trust *me*? How the hell am I supposed to trust you after you've exposed me? I was hiding from my family and their wealth for a reason, Naomi. I didn't want anything to do with any of them or their money. Tyler Brown died a long time ago, and Tyler Garner has been living in his place."

"I don't know if I can believe that," I said, getting out of the bed and letting my anger fuel me. If I had known he was in the picture, I never would have sent it out. Him hiding his identity from me was a choice.

"I can't believe you. Pack your shit and leave. I don't know what to think about any of this anymore. I love you, Naomi, and I don't know what the hell to do with that anymore. Please just leave."

I dropped the sheet and held my head high as I walked out of his room. I wasn't going to give anybody the satisfaction of seeing me look weak.

I made my way through the house and walked into the south wing. After changing into a fresh pair of jeans and a tank top, I called a cab. While I was waiting, I shoved everything into the bags that had been sitting at the bottom of the closet for the last three months.

There was nothing that I could do to change his mind, and I wasn't going to beg him to listen to me. He had made up his mind about me the moment he heard that a journalist was coming to stay with him. From the moment I walked in the door, he was prepared not to trust me. He was looking for a reason to get me to leave, and he had finally found it.

Tyler got his wish. After everything that had happened

between us in the last few months, after everything that I had told him, he still didn't trust me. I wasn't about to stay there and beg him to trust me either.

I was going to go back home, write my article, and try to turn around my mess of a life.

With the last of my belongings packed away, I started the walk down the long driveway to wait for the cab by the side of the road.

My nerves were frayed, and I kept checking my watch. All the while, four words consumed my thoughts.

I love you, Naomi.

My heart cracked. What was I supposed to do with that now?

When the cab showed up, I didn't bother to look back as I left Tyler and his secrets far behind.

Chapter 11

Tyler

The hotel was filled with people who had arrived for the charity auction. There was a good turnout, and I suspected that Naomi's article had done the job. Pair the article with my exposed identity on social media; it was one shitstorm after the other over the last three months.

Three months without Naomi driving me insane had felt like a punishment instead of the reward I thought it would have been when she first stepped off that bus.

In those three months, family members called me at all hours of the day. They didn't care if it was the middle of the night or if I was working. They all wanted to know when I would be coming back to the city and what my plans would be once I was there.

Others were wondering what I was planning on doing with my inheritance when I finally got it. It was a polite way of saying that they hoped grandfather would die soon so they could have access to all his money. The ones that weren't in the will were hoping for handouts from the inheritance.

My mother had been the most concerned with the woman I was with. She wanted to know who Naomi was and whether her family came from money. When I told my mother that Naomi wasn't from such a family, she immediately started running through her list of eligible young women who came from her idea of a so-called good family.

It was code for people who would only add to my family's wealth.

That's all that any of them cared about. They wanted to know who had the most money and who would help them make more money. They had no interest in anyone who fell below a certain tax bracket.

And then there were the photographers who plagued my every waking minute.

Paparazzi had shown up at my house in the woods, looking for the next story to write about me. After I called the cops, they took to sitting at the end of my property and waiting for me to emerge from my house. More calls to the police still didn't deter them. If they could invade my privacy, they would.

It was everything that I didn't want to happen, and it did.

If Naomi had taken a closer look at the picture, she would have seen my reflection. She never would have sent it out to her friends.

I knew I had reacted without considering the kind of person she was the moment she was gone. I had jumped the gun and forced her away from me. I told myself that she had betrayed me and that she had done it on purpose.

In the days after she had left, I tried to tell myself everything I could to avoid the feeling of being in love with her. I tried to distance myself as much as I possibly could from her. I didn't want to think about her.

And yet, every time I closed my eyes, all I could see was the broken look on her face when I told her to leave.

"You're going to hurt yourself if you keep thinking that hard," Jack said as he stepped into my hotel room and slammed the door shut. "There are more cameras than you can count waiting for you downstairs."

"I guess the secret really is out," I said, turning to the mirror and adjusting my bowtie. "Where's Hillary?"

"Here!" she shouted as she came flying into the room with bags hanging from her arms. "And what the hell do you think you're doing still in here? You're supposed to be downstairs, shaking hands with all of the people who want to buy your art."

"I would rather light myself on fire," I said, facing her and holding my arms out. "How do I look?"

"Like shit," Jack said, smacking the back of my head. "You've been stressing yourself out about Naomi, haven't you?"

"Shut up," I muttered, fixing my hair before heading to the door. "Let's get this fucking nightmare over with, shall we?"

***

As soon as I entered the ballroom, I wanted to go find Naomi and share this moment with her. More than that, I wanted to start apologizing for everything that had happened between us. I wanted to fix everything that had gone wrong. If I had listened to her or told her the truth sooner, none of this would have ever happened. We would still be exploring a new relationship together.

Not once in three months had I grown the balls it would take to go after her and admit that I had made a mistake. I couldn't. Every time I got in my truck and drove to the city, I started thinking about what she would say to me.

I was a confident man, I always have been, but knowing I hurt her made me weak. I had hurt the one person I had felt comfortable letting inside my life. She hadn't told anyone about me, yet I had kicked her out as if she meant nothing to me.

I have never hated myself more.

"You need to go to her," Hillary said as she materialized at my side. "You made a mistake, and you need to fix it."

"Aren't you supposed to say something helpful in times like these?" I asked her, offering her a small smile as she handed me a glass of champagne. "I thought that managers were supposed to handle things."

"I tried handling things when I picked a journalist I knew you would fall in love with," Hillary said before taking a sip of her champagne and smirking at me over the rim of her glass. "Naomi walked into your life that day because I found out she was that girl from the bar you kept talking about with Jack. You would go on and on, and I knew there was something there. I'm paid to know such things."

I stared at her for a moment, wondering how she had managed to make it all happen. As much as I wanted to ask her, I didn't want to keep rubbing salt in the wound. I had been given a second chance with the woman of my dreams, and I had ruined it.

"How about we go look at some of your paintings and make sure the minimum prices are right before the auction begins?"

I downed the champagne and nodded. "Anything to get out of this room as soon as possible. I feel like I'm suffocating."

Hillary led me to the back room where the paintings were being kept. Security guards stepped to the side as we entered the room. I looked around at the paintings hanging on the walls and sitting on easels. Each one of them had been hours spent on a canvas blending beauty and pain.

"They are stunning, aren't they?" Hillary asked as she looked at one of the paintings in the far corner. It was my favorite one—the one I had painted by the waterfall when I was with Naomi.

"Do me a favor and pull that one from the program," I said, nodding to the painting at the waterfall. "It's too personal to go to just anyone. Have it packaged up and shipped to Naomi."

"Are you sure?" Hillary asked with a raised eyebrow. "How do you know she won't set it on fire after everything that's happened between you two?"

"I don't know whether she will set it on fire, but I can only hope that she won't," I said, stepping closer to the painting to run my fingers over the frame.

Hillary nodded and patted my back. "I'll get it packaged up. You check the pricing on the rest of the paintings."

We worked together in silence until it was time for the auction to begin. Hillary worked swiftly to pad the painting and wrap it up before having a courier pick it up. The painting would be delivered to Naomi in the morning, and I could only hope that she wouldn't destroy it.

The rest of the auction passed in relative peace. I spoke to a few people about upcoming shows I was planning at some of the galleries in the city. Each piece sold for well over the asking price and raised tens of thousands of dollars for several different charities.

"That was a great show," Jack said as he walked with me to my car after the auction a few hours later. "You do some amazing work. I can see why staying in the woods with a beautiful journalist appealed to you."

"Yeah," I said. "She is something else."

"Do you think she knew all those paintings were about her?"

I shrugged and unlocked my car. It was a rental for while I was in the city since the truck was too bulky to be comfortable in the traffic. Even as I got in the car, I longed to be home in the woods with my truck and my lake. I hated the city.

Jack grinned and waved as I started the car and peeled away from my parking space. I didn't feel like going back upstairs to my hotel room. Instead, I turned the car in the direction of the highway and started heading home.

Jack's question played on my mind the entire drive. Did Naomi know that she was in all my paintings? The color of her hair when it was wet, the glimmer in her eyes, the small white scars that laced her palms from the time she had climbed over razor wire with her friends when she was younger. It was all there, captured as a moment in time in each one of the paintings I had shown at the auction.

There wasn't a moment in the last year—since the moment she and I met at the club—that she hadn't been on my mind. There wasn't a single painting done that didn't have an imprint of

Naomi. She was my muse.

As I pulled into my driveway hours later, I knew that the rest of my life would have elements of Naomi lingering in the shadows.

Chapter 12

Naomi

Two months was a long time to be without a traditional job.

When I returned from Tyler's house, I had gone to see my editor immediately. She had been racing around and trying to do damage control while I kept insisting that I would only write the article. She'd agreed to it, and we'd published the article according to the contract I had signed. The focus was on Tyler, his art, and the charity function—nothing personal or news-bite worthy in the way things are these days. But my editor went back on her word a month later and asked me to write about my time with Tyler. That was the last time I worked for that paper as each time I tried to speak, she would cut me off and insist that I hadn't ruined everything by being a complete idiot.

I walked out after the second time she called me an idiot.

Of course, that news had gotten around to several of the other newspapers in the city. Each day I had publications calling me and begging for the Tyler Brown story. They wanted the exclusive rights to my experience in the woods with him. Every time I got a call, I ended it feeling worse than the last.

Nobody was getting the story of what happened between Tyler and I. Nobody but us needed to know the story of what happened when we spent months together. I refused them each time they called. I wouldn't put his life on display more than I already had.

I had already ruined enough for him.

Even if this was the article of a lifetime, it wasn't worth it. Losing him forever had already happened, but putting his life out there still wasn't worth it. A career wasn't worth all the stress that it would bring him.

Instead, I started trying to build the career that I wanted.

With the refusal to sell Tyler's story came the knowledge that I likely wouldn't be headed into any war zones anytime soon. Publications didn't want a journalist who had a code of ethics. They wanted someone who was willing to expose the truth no matter how it hurt.

If Tyler had taught me anything, it was that nobody deserved to have their lives thrust out for everyone to see and judge.

Even being known as the girl who had taken the pictures was miserable. Men with big cameras lived on my lawn. They took pictures every time I appeared in their line of sight.

It had taken them two weeks to discover the goldmine of gossip that was Zach. As soon as I started seeing his face splashed across my social media feeds, I sent him to the other side of the country.

When I sent him, I made it clear that this was his last chance with me. The program would last nearly a year; if that didn't work, he was on his own. I couldn't keep putting my life on hold or keep delaying my career to deal with him.

As soon as Zach was on a plane, I turned my attention to my mom and my blog. Most days, I spent time sitting in her hospital room and working on the latest travel article I wanted to post. So far, the articles were about the little towns that surrounded the city. I wrote about the places that Tyler and I had visited together, each time feeling a stronger ache in my chest.

Even now, trying to write an article about the carnival left a tight pull in my chest.

"What are you looking so lost in thought about?" my mom asked from her position on the bed. Tubes and wires connected her monitors and medications. Her hair had fallen out while I was gone, but there was color to her skin that hadn't been there last week.

"I don't know. I didn't sleep well last night, and this article seems impossible to write. I had a great time at the carnival, but there doesn't seem to be enough words in the world to write about it."

My mom laughed and shook her head. "Darling, you need to go back to your apartment and get some sleep. Come back in the morning with a fresh set of eyes, and then you might be able to see where that mental block is."

I looked at the laptop again, and the words on the screen started to blur. With a sigh, I closed my laptop and got up from my cramped position on the chair.

"I think you're right," I said, walking to the bed and kissing her forehead. "Call me if you need anything, and I'll come back over right away."

"I'll be fine," she said, patting my arm. "Go get some sleep, and if you want to stay at your apartment for a night or two instead of hovering over me like I'm some invalid, that would be good too."

I laughed and rolled my eyes. "Message received. Unless you call, I will stay away for a few days."

It was hard to leave her at the hospital, but the moment I arrived at my apartment, I felt a weight lifting off my shoulders. There was no longer the need to pretend that everything was alright. I could feel as horrible as I wanted and wouldn't have to put on a brave face for my mom.

There was a large brown package leaning against my door. My name was scrawled across the front, and there was a note tucked beneath the large blue bow. I took out the note and stared at the writing on the card.

Naomi,

Tyler had me send this piece to you. He said that it felt too personal for anyone else to have. I thought you should know that he's been miserable, and there have been some strings pulled that you should probably know about.

After you first met him at the club, all he would talk about for nearly two weeks was trying to go back and find you again. I think he went back to that club every night. That's when I decided to track you down and reunite you.

I've never seen him happier and more at peace than he was with you. As you've probably guessed—and I hope you have since you seem like an intelligent woman—Tyler is paying for your mother's medical care. I have also attached the deed to your childhood home. Tyler insists that it has been paid and signed over to you to do with as you please. You no longer need to worry.

Wish you all the best,
Hillary

Tears welled in my eyes as I read the note again. My heart raced in my chest as I grabbed the wrapped painting and dragged it inside. When I unwrapped it, my breath caught in my throat.

Everything about the painting was beautiful but sad. The waterfall crashed down to the lake as the girl was dragged away by the monster beneath the water. I ran my fingers over the ridges of the dried paint, remembering the concentration on his face when we were at the waterfall. If I had known what he was painting then, I would have demanded that he get rid of it.

Now, looking at the painting and knowing that the monster was no longer dragging me down, I felt better. I could appreciate the painting for its beauty and the message behind it without feeling angry at him.

At least, I wasn't angry with him until I thought about the money he spent on the house and Mom's medical bills.

Both amounts were considerable. Even hauling us out of debt from her previous round of cancer treatments would have been expensive beyond belief.

I wanted to scream at him for paying the bills, but I didn't want to do it over the phone.

I moved the painting to lean against one wall and saw another note flutter to the floor. Grabbing the piece of paper, I tried to mentally prepare myself for whatever other news I was about to have shoved at me.

Naomi,

The house is yours. Do what you want with it, and don't be mad at me for paying for it. I didn't want to see everything you love slip away because of your brother.

Love,
Tyler

I sighed and ran a hand through my hair before putting the note on my kitchen counter. After scooping up my car keys, I stormed out of the apartment, prepared for hours of driving and a conversation that may pulverize my heart.

***

When the door opened, I wasn't expecting Tyler to be in a suit with an untied bowtie hanging loosely around his neck. There were dark circles under his eyes, and he looked exhausted. He looked at me warily as he held the door open wider and waited for me to step inside.

I had a lot of time to think during the drive to his house. Too much time. My anger had started to dissipate after the first hour, and all I was left with was a nervous feeling that wouldn't go away. I thought that I would have used the drive up to figure out what I was going to say to him, but I hadn't been able to come up with anything good.

"Why did you do it?" I asked as I stepped inside his home and made my way to the living room. A new coffee table had replaced the glass one he had broken. "Why did you spend that much money? I had everything figured out. I didn't need your help, and I sure as hell didn't want it."

Tyler's eyebrow arched as he crossed his arms. "You were miserable when you got here, and don't even try to say that you weren't. I could see it on your face the moment you walked through my door. You were looking for a way out, and you found it here. How could I let the woman I love go back to a life of misery when I had the power to do something about it?"

"You can't go around throwing out love like it's something either of us are in any position to say right now," I said, feeling the last of the fight leave my body as I slumped down onto his couch.

Tyler sat on the chair across from me and leaned forward, his forearms resting on his knees. "Naomi, I love you, and I was an idiot. I knew you would have never sent out those pictures on purpose, but I was terrified of what would happen once the news about where I was got out."

"Even after everything I had shared with you and all the time we spent together, you still didn't trust me," I said, my chest tightening as I crossed one leg over the other. "You thought I only cared about getting the best story possible. You should have trusted me."

"I know I should have," Tyler said. "As soon as you walked out that door, I knew that I had made the biggest mistake of my life."

"When did you pay all those bills?" I asked.

"Does it matter?"

I nodded. "It matters, and decides whether I walk out of here right now or stay and we try to fix this."

He sighed and ran a hand down his face. My heart started to

race as I waited for the answer. I couldn't stay with him if he had paid the bills to bring me back. I wouldn't be in debt to him and wouldn't stay with him out of a sense of obligation. I needed to know that he wasn't using his money as a manipulation tactic.

"Remember the day we were at the carnival when I stepped away to talk about a contract?" he asked, his gaze meeting mine. "That day, I told Hillary to deal with it all and keep it a secret. Since you know about it, I'm guessing she ratted me out."

"She might have," I said with a small smile. "I thought that the bank and the hospital were just busy and forgot about us for a couple of weeks in the shuffle of paperwork."

He nodded, lips pinched into a thin line.

The air around us was tense with the unasked question.

"So, are you leaving?"

I shook my head. "No. I'm not going anywhere. You and I have a lot of shit to work through, though. I'm sorry I missed your auction yesterday."

"It's okay. There'll be more of that in our future." He smiled wide, a twinkle in his eye. "You know what...how about we start over?" Tyler asked as he stood up and smoothed out his suit. "Come on, stand up and pretend."

"You're ridiculous," I said, standing up and staring at him.

Tyler gave me a bright smile as he held out his hand. "Hello, my name is Tyler Brown. I'm heir to a multi-billion-dollar fortune and your future husband."

I laughed and clasped his hand, giving it a firm shake. "Nice to meet you, Tyler. I'm Naomi Avion, and I would love to move to a small town and settle down with the grumpiest person I have ever met. And oh, I love you."

At that moment, as he stepped over the table and kissed me like it was our last, I knew that we were going to be alright.

Epilogue

Tyler

Two years later

Autumn was the perfect time for a wedding in the mountains. The leaves were changing colors, and the flowers were in their last bloom. It was still a little strange to see the place where I had spent years in isolation, filled with family and friends. Even my family had come to the wedding, though they turned their noses up at nearly everything.

And then there was my wife.

Naomi had never looked more beautiful than she did when she walked down the aisle on her mother's arm and promised to love me forever. She was stunning as she and I said our vows, promising to love each other forever.

Before her, there was no future in which I saw a family. I never pictured myself having a wife and agreeing to love her for the rest of my life.

Sitting at our reception, I couldn't wait until the music stopped and the people left to go home and begin spending the rest of my life with her. Some of the people would be staying at some of the small cabins Naomi and I had built on the far edges of the property. She insisted that we needed places for people to stay when they came to see us.

As I looked at her now, I wondered how I had managed to get so lucky.

"What?" Naomi asked, smiling as she lifted a hand to her face. "Do I have something on my face?"

"No, I just can't believe that we're finally married," I said, taking her hand and kissing the back of it. "And I can't wait for Caroline and Leslie to leave. They've been driving me insane all week."

She laughed, her eyes sparkling beneath the lights strung through the trees. "You were the one who waited until the last minute to hire a photographer. Can you blame them for being up your ass about it?"

With a grin, I pulled her into a tight hug and kissed her forehead. "I have something to show you."

"Oh?" she asked, pulling back from me to take my hand. "And what would that be?"

"This way, Mrs. Brown."

I led her away from the reception and to the studio. On the way, she was stopped by Jack and her mother. Zach was in the corner, nursing a glass of water and flirting with Leslie. He had been doing better, but I still couldn't trust him. I wasn't sure he wouldn't break his sister's heart again. I would be there to pick up all the pieces if he did. She wasn't alone in her struggles anymore.

Jack winked at me as we excused ourselves. He was the only one who knew what I had been working on over the last several weeks.

I was nervous as I held a hand over Naomi's eyes and opened the door to the studio. Carefully, I helped her inside and turned on the lights. With a deep breath, I took my hand off her eyes and waited.

Tears welled as she looked at the painting of the sonogram. We had only found out two weeks ago that we were expecting a baby. Naomi had wanted to keep it a secret until the wedding was over, but we had told Jack together last week.

"This is amazing," she said, walking over to the painting and crouching down to get a good look at the jungle animals I had hidden within the dark areas of the sonogram. "It's going to look so good in the nursery."

"I'm glad you like it," I said, standing behind her and wrapping my arms around her waist. "I know it's only the first scan, but I was thinking I could do one for every month."

The tears that had been building in her eyes slipped down her cheeks. "I love you so much."

"I love you too."

She turned in my embrace, her arms wrapping around my waist. "It's hard to believe that this all nearly ended two years ago. In a weird way, I'm grateful for all that we've gone through."

"Everything we went through brought us to this moment," I said, combing my fingers through the loose curls that hung down her back. "And there's no place I'd rather be."

She smiled and stood on her toes to press her lips to mine.

Happiness flooded over me as I looked down at her and knew this was the start of forever.

Mountain Man Doctor (Book 3)

TRIGGER WARNING
This book contains mentions of alcohol addiction, relapse, and recovery.

Blurb

Divorced and looking for a fresh start, Addie goes back home to Blopton Town, and finds one refreshing addition to the small mountain town. Zane's past was filled with skeletons that threatened to dip him back into his old habits until a curvy distraction ignited a fire that had long been dormant.

Addie

I went back home after spending 8 years away. Nothing about Blopton Town had changed except a charming doctor who gave me butterflies from the moment he touched me. I had vowed to keep away from relationships, but a certain mountain man was making it harder with his patience, kindness, and care. Plus, my parents loved Zane! Letting him in was easy. He was nothing like my ex, Sam. Or so I thought.

Zane

I have a secret. It's easy to forget how one swing of the hand can plunge you back into old habits. I had been doing fine, working on myself and caring for the residents of Blopton Town. Until the first crack appeared. And then I lied. And then I was in denial. It's funny how one lie can lead to much more. Falling and losing Addie before we even had the chance to be something amazing would be the final nail. It should have been until I realized something.

Prologue

Addie

Ten years away from home had never felt so awful.

When I was seventeen, I moved away from Blopton Town and never looked back. Back then, life in a small town had seemed overrated. I was young and wanted to live in a city where nobody knew my name or my parents. I wanted to build a life far away from the sleepy little mountain town.

Now that I was back, I have no clue why I had left.

As I ran, I inhaled the scent of the forest and felt the tension leave my body. The carnage that had become my life started to fade away with each new twist in the trail I took.

My footsteps were steady, and my heart was racing as I came to a stop in front of one of the giant redwoods. The trees towered over me, their leaves littering the ground as fall ravaged the forest.

The trail split into two just ahead of me. To the right was a path I had run a thousand times as a teenager. To the left was a newer path that hadn't been filled with woodchips yet.

I stretched out my legs for a second before I took off towards the new path, eager to explore the new section of the forest. More leaves coated the ground, hiding the path from sight. I kept running in a relatively straight line, dodging rocks and jumping over roots.

Lately, running was the only thing that cleared my mind.

Suddenly, the ground was falling out beneath my feet. I screamed as I fell. A root caught my crop top, ripping it as I plummeted to the bottom of the hole. My ankle twisted as I landed, jerking hard and sending me to my knees.

Tears blurred my vision as I looked around.

Why the hell is there a trap in the middle of a fucking running path? I thought as I tried to stand.

The pain that shot through my ankle was unbearable. I screamed and fell back down, clutching my ankle. Even in the relative darkness of the hole, I could see that my ankle was swollen.

"Help!" I shouted, wishing that I had brought my phone.

The phone was sitting on the dining table in my parents' house, waiting for me to come back. I hadn't wanted anything in the tiny pocket of my shorts while I ran, but apparently, that had been a mistake.

"Help!"

Without being able to put any weight on my ankle, I couldn't climb out of the hole. I scowled and glared up at the leaves falling on me. There was nothing I could do now but shout and hope that somebody would run through this trail like I did.

I shouted until my voice was hoarse before I heard the crunching of leaves near the hole. When I shouted again, the crunching grew louder until it stopped, and a man was looking down at me.

"Please help," I said. "My ankle's hurt, and I can't get out of here."

His lips twitched slightly at my predicament. "Can you move to one side? I'm going to jump down and lift you out."

I scrambled to press myself as close to one side of the hole as possible. The man landed beside me and grinned. That smile knocked the air from my lungs as I stared at him, his eyes the color of sea glass regarding me warmly.

"Hey," he said, crouching down to scoop me up.

He was careful not to hit my ankle as he lifted me higher, placing me on the edge of the hole. I scrambled backward using my hands and good ankle while he lifted himself out of the hole.

"Thank you," I said, staring up at him and trying to ignore how his hands on my body filled my stomach with butterflies.

"I can take you down to the clinic and fix up your ankle," he said. He crouched down and held out his hand. "Dr. Zane Morrin."

"Addie Manning."

"You're okay with me carrying you, right? It's going to be the fastest way to get you to my truck."

"If it means I can have pain meds sooner, go for it."

He laughed and picked me up again, avoiding my ankle. I didn't know what to do with my arms while he carried me, so I settled for looping one around his shoulders and trying to keep myself upright as he walked over the bumpy trail.

The drive from the trailhead to the clinic was short and slightly awkward. Zane made small talk about nothing in particular while I gritted my teeth against the pain. He had given me some pain medication when he got to his truck and wrapped my ankle, but it still wasn't enough to kill the dull ache.

When he carried me into the clinic, I could feel the eyes on us. The man sitting behind the desk smirked as he answered a phone call. My cheeks were burning as he carried me into one of the exam rooms and shut the door behind us.

"Do you have anyone who can come and get you?" he asked.

"Yeah. I can call my mom if you have a phone I can borrow."

"We'll get you one," he said as he took off the wrapping. "Now, let's take a look at that ankle."

He made quick work of the exam, his fingers skating over my skin and sending shivers down my spine. I kept ignoring the butterflies in my stomach as he worked, trying to remind myself that he was just doing his job.

Once my ankle was wrapped, and I was given a pair of crutches, he escorted me out of the office with strict instructions to stay off my ankle. When my mom's car came speeding around the corner, I grinned.

"That's her. Thank you for all your help."

"Addie, what happened?" my mom asked as soon as she put the car in park and walked around to the passenger side. "Is it anything serious, Zane?"

Zane? Did they know each other?

"Nothing lots of rest won't fix..." he said as he helped me into the car.

"Zane, you're needed..." the man who had been behind the desk called out from the door before disappearing back inside.

"Oh, thank God," Mom said as she buckled my seat.

"Gosh, Mom, it's just a sprain...I'll be fine." Mom kissed my forehead before closing the door and rounding the car to the driver's side.

"Keep off the ankle, Addie," he said as he opened the door to the clinic, ready to head back inside. "And call the office later to make a follow-up appointment. I need to make sure that you're taking care of yourself and not doing any more damage."

When the door closed behind him, I finally let out the breath I had been holding. Trying to forget the feeling of his hands on my body would be impossible.

Chapter 1

Zane

I ran a hand through my hair as I finished filling out the notes on my patient's chart. There was no shortage of elderly people coming in, searching for some sort of new medication they could try for a problem they had made up. Though the visits were always long, they kept my day moving. I couldn't fault any of them for looking for something to do.

Hell, I was lonely too. I wanted someone to talk to, and the never-ending line of the elderly provided me with the companionship of some form, even if it was in a completely professional capacity.

There was a knock at the door before my office administrator, Van, stuck his head in the door with a grin. I waved him in and set my notes to the side.

"What's going on?" I asked as his grin grew wider.

"So," Van said, dropping into one of the leather chairs on the other side of my desk. "I noticed that you haven't made a follow-up appointment with Addie Manning yet. Aren't you worried about how her ankle is healing?"

I rolled my eyes and leaned back in the chair. Van was young, and hiring him had been more because of his mother's begging than his actual qualifications—though he had gone to school to be a medical office administrator. However, he kept me on my toes and kept me entertained. He was one of the few people in town who treated me like a normal person instead of someone to talk about.

Still, I didn't like that he was asking about Addie. It meant that he had seen the way I stared at her for a few seconds too long as she left the clinic after every visit.

"And since when do you keep tabs on who's been in the office recently and who hasn't?" I asked. "I've seen her a few times in the last three weeks to check on her ankle, but they've been brief appointments. You would know that if you kept on top of the filing."

Van waved a hand and smirked. "That's a job for another day. Why don't we talk about how irritated you are that she rushes in here and rushes out without giving you the time of day? I've heard it's hard on an aging man's ego."

"I'm only thirty-seven," I said, gritting my teeth as I sat up and started working on my notes again. Thirty-seven wasn't old, but it wasn't young anymore, either. He didn't need to remind me about my age.

With everything that I had been through in my life, thirty-seven felt ancient some days.

"You ignored what I said about Addie, though. That's interesting. If you want, I can go find her file and get her address so you can make a house call."

"That's a massive violation of patient privacy," I said, looking up from my paperwork and fixing him with a stern look. "Please tell me that you aren't doing that."

"Are you kidding me? Mom would have my head." Van shuddered. "She's making you all kinds of fruit preserves for Christmas."

"She really doesn't have to do that," I said, wondering what I would do with fruit preserves. I lived alone, and there was no need to have multiple jars.

"You don't understand. She really does have to. You splinted the cat's leg and gave her baby boy a job. She talks about you all the time."

I groaned and ran a hand down my face. I knew that even after five years in Blopton, I was still a gossip topic among the townspeople. Lately, it had more to do with my relationship status than anything else. It seemed like most of the mothers thought that the only doctor in a small town would be the perfect husband for their daughter.

They didn't know the skeletons that liked to live in my closet. Otherwise, they might have thought differently.

Not a week went by where there wasn't a well-meaning woman who offered me her daughter's number or who gave me their own. All those numbers ended up in the garbage as soon as I got home. I wasn't interested in settling down with anybody.

They wouldn't understand me.

I was uninterested in finding a relationship, at least until I saw Addie. There was something about her that drew me in and held me captive. I wanted to know more about her. I wanted her to be the first person I let into my life in a long time.

It scared the hell out of me.

"Honestly," Van said, shaking his head. "If I have to hear one more story about you, I'm going to go insane."

The phone started ringing before Van could tell me exactly what his mother had been saying about me lately. I glanced at him, but he made no move to go answer the phone.

With a sigh, I picked up the receiver. "Hello, Morrin Medical. Dr. Morrin speaking."

"Hi, Zane," Fleur Manning said, her soft French accent lilting. "Would you mind going to Addie's apartment? She just called me and said that she fell in the shower and her ankle hurts too much to get up. I've tried to lift her, but with the way my back's been hurting lately, I can't."

As much as I wanted to say no, Fleur was my neighbor. She and her husband, Alex, had welcomed me with open arms when I moved to town and caught me up on everything I might need to know while living in Blopton. They invited me over for weekly dinners, and it wasn't uncommon for Fleur to show up on my doorstep with leftovers from their dinner.

"I'll be over as soon as I can, Fleur. Where does Addie live?"

"Those apartments on Main Street. Number five. I'll meet you at the door and let you in."

In the background, I could hear Addie ask her mother who she was talking to. Fleur said something in French before ending the call. I sighed and got up, grabbing a bag filled with supplies.

"And where might you be going in such a hurry?" Van asked, a smirk already forming. "You look like you're off on an important mission. A house call, maybe?"

"Get back to work, and don't worry about what I'm doing," I said before leaving the office.

As much as Van liked to tease me, I knew he wouldn't say anything to anyone about where I was going or what I was doing. He might have only been twenty-six, but he had enough sense to know that some things in this town didn't need repeating.

I loaded my bag into the backseat of the truck and got in. My clinic sat just outside of town by the forest. It was the perfect location for someone who loved the woods but didn't want the townspeople dropping in to chat on their way by. I had work to get down on and couldn't spend much time chatting.

Packing my bags and moving to Blopton five years ago had been an impulsive decision at best. It was exactly the kind of decision that I had been told to avoid making. But I didn't regret making that move, especially when I didn't have that many options to begin with. Getting this clinic had been a welcome surprise. The location was the main reason why I purchased it. I didn't think I would get back into practicing medicine after taking an extended break. I thought I was done with that, but then I saw the little clinic for sale nearly three years ago, and everything fell into place.

Heading into town always left an uneasy feeling. It felt like people were watching me and waiting for me to make a mistake. Living on the outskirts of town and avoiding the drama was easier.

As I drove, I drummed my fingers on the wheel and tried not to think about what I was headed to do. There was a good chance that Addie was still going to be naked when I was there. I had seen plenty of naked patients in my career but being attracted to the patient was entirely new for me.

I won't be acting like a horny teenage boy, no matter how long it's been since I've been with someone, I thought as I turned off the dirt road that led to the clinic and onto the only paved road that led to town from the clinic.

I was going to get to Addie's, and I was going to be professional. I would pretend that I wasn't attracted to her, and everything would be alright. It would only take a few minutes to get her out of the tub, check her ankle, and leave again.

Neither of us would be more uncomfortable than we had to be.

At least, I hoped that we wouldn't be.

Chapter 2

Addie

"I can't believe you called the doctor," I said as I glared at my mom from where I was sitting in the tub. "That isn't necessary. I would have been able to get myself out of here eventually."

"Well, it was either the doctor or your father since you don't have any male friends in town, and I couldn't lift you. I thought that I picked the best option given the situation," Mom said with a slight shrug and a sly smile before murmuring something in French and walking away.

It was then that I wished I had learned more French when I was younger so I could keep up with her whispering under her breath. She had wanted us to speak English at home so she could improve, but it meant that French was barely spoken.

"I don't know why you're so opposed to the doctor," Mom said as she walked back into the bathroom with my black silk robe. "Here."

"Thanks," I said, taking the robe and struggling my way into it. The back of the robe got slightly wet from the tiny pool of water I was still sitting in. "As for the doctor, I'd rather crawl my way out of the tub."

"Don't be dramatic," she said as she sat on the closed toilet seat lid. "He's a nice man. Your dad and I like him very much. He shovels our driveway in the winter, and he comes over for Saturday dinner every week. You've been back in town for five weeks, and you still haven't come for a Saturday dinner with us."

"Well, to be fair, I haven't been able to drive myself anywhere in close to a month which means that even if I wanted to come to the dinners, I can't right now."

She sighed. "I don't know why you don't want to come to the dinners. It's a nice tradition. It's the one point of the week when we can sit down together and spend some time talking about our week."

I had been avoiding the dinners because I didn't want to listen to my father rage about my gambling-addicted ex-husband. He still thought that I had made a mistake in not demanding any spousal support, but I didn't want any of my ex's money. Even if he did have any, I didn't think that I would see any of it.

Saturday dinners would just be another chance for my dad to remind me that my life had self-combusted around me, and I wasn't fighting back.

He still couldn't understand that I didn't want to fight. I just wanted to start my life over without the reminder of everything that had gone wrong.

"I'll think about it," I said finally, knowing that I wouldn't give much more thought to it until my ankle was healed.

A knock on the door ended our conversation for the time being as Mom stood to go answer it. Mom would bring it up over and over again until I finally broke down and went to a Saturday dinner. It would probably be better to do it sooner rather than later. That way, she would back off and give me some time to myself.

There were a thousand other things that I needed to get done, including finding a job. I had worked as a kindergarten teacher for the last six years, but when my divorce was finalized three months ago, I left the job I loved and started packing my bags.

With the school year starting this month, I didn't have much hope of finding a job at the local elementary school, but I had applied to the local school board and was waiting to see what came back.

Right now, getting out of the damn bathtub and finding a job was more important than a Saturday dinner.

"Be careful when you go in," Mom said, her voice traveling down the hallway. "Addie's in a bit of a foul mood."

"I wonder why," I said, tying the belt of my robe a little bit tighter. "Maybe it's because you're inviting strange men over to come to see me naked. Hell, why don't we call the fire department in here, too, while we're at it?"

"I see what you mean about the foul mood," Zane said as he stopped at the door and looked down at me with a smile. "Sorry about this."

"It's fine," I said, looking away from him as my cheeks flamed. "I don't think I'm getting out of here any other way."

Zane moved quickly, crossing the bathroom and lifting me out of the tub. He carried me to the living room and set me on the couch.

"How's the ankle feeling?" he asked as he grabbed a bag from beside the door and brought it over. He got down on one knee in front of me and gingerly took my ankle, placing my foot on his knee.

"Like it would be easier to just cut it off at this point," I said, wiggling my toes.

He laughed, his fingers on my skin sending shivers up my body. I considered asking my mother to leave so the doctor and I could get a little closer.

Damn it. You're a grown woman. Get it together.

I was twenty-nine. Being this worked up over an attractive man holding my ankle was ridiculous. It didn't matter that he was looking at me with those pretty green eyes while his dark hair fell in waves across his forehead. He was the kind of handsome that would send girls running straight for him.

"You're going to be at dinner this Saturday, right?" Mom asked as she perched herself on the edge of my coffee table. "We're having steaks on the grill."

"I'll be there," Zane said, shooting her a smile that I swear made my mother swoon. "Do you want me to bring anything?"

Mom looked at me with a smirk. I wanted to lunge off the couch and clamp a hand over her mouth before she could say anything. With my ankle still being inspected, there was nothing I could do to stop her, and she knew it.

"Actually, would you mind bringing Addie? With her ankle the way it is right now, she can't drive, but her dad and I would really like to have her over for dinner."

I scowled at her before looking down at Zane and subtly shaking my head. I could see the hesitation on his face as he weighed his options. When I shook my head again, he grinned and nodded.

"Sure, Fleur. I'll bring her to dinner."

"Excellent," Mom said as she got up and grabbed her purse. "I've got to get going now, but let me know how your ankle is."

She left as if she hadn't just manipulated me into going to the weekly dinner. I stared at the door for a few seconds after she left, trying not to focus on the absence of Zane's touch as he lowered my foot and stood up.

"Your ankle is looking good. You've slightly twisted it again, but after another week or so, you should be good to start running again."

"Are you sure?" I asked, looking down at the ankle. "I don't want to rush into it too soon."

He gave me a flat look, but the corner of his mouth twitched. "If anybody's going to know, it's going to be me."

"Fair enough," I said, standing up and trying to put weight on my ankle.

As I stumbled, he reached out and caught me, helping me balance again. He took a step back, his hands still holding mine as I stood up.

"See?" he said, grinning as I stepped forward. "It's going to hurt again from your fall, but in a week, you should be walking without problem."

"I hope so. I miss running."

"Well, if you want somebody to run or walk with, I'm always looking for some company. You'd have somebody around to help you if you didn't feel comfortable alone with your ankle still weak."

My cheeks flushed a bright red. I hadn't anticipated his offer, and I wasn't sure what to make of it. It was a kind offer, but I didn't know how to spend time with him without telling him how attractive he was. I was sure that it was something he had heard often enough. He didn't need me telling him as well.

And then there was the fact that I didn't want a man in my life yet. My divorce had only been finalized a few months ago after being with my ex-husband, Sam, for five years, married for three years. It didn't seem right to start dating yet.

Dating. All he offered was a running partner. He didn't ask you on a date. Stop getting ahead of yourself.

"Thanks," I said, limping away from him and to the kitchen. "I appreciate it, but I don't think I'm ready for that yet."

I'm not ready to deal with this crush I have on you.

"Take your time. Just remember that you need to keep your ankle moving."

"I will," I said, turning away from him to pour myself a glass of water. I knew that I was being rude, but I didn't want to encourage him to stay any longer.

"Well, I've got to get back to the office. I've got another appointment in half an hour so I should be there on time if I leave now. You're going to be okay by yourself?"

"Yes," I said, limping back over to him and walking with him to the door. "I'll be fine. And about Saturday, you really don't have to come pick me up for dinner."

"Do you think you'll be comfortable driving in three days?" he asked, those bright green eyes giving me a stare I couldn't read.

"No," I said. "Probably not."

"Then I'll pick you up at five on Saturday."

He left, closing the door behind him, and I was left wondering what I had just agreed to. I didn't want to go to a Saturday dinner or spend more time with him, but somehow, I had agreed to both.

I took my glass of water back to the couch and sat down, sipping it and wondering what excuse I could use to get out of an awkward family gathering now.

Chapter 3

Zane

I looked at myself in the mirror, wondering why I was bothering to wear a nice shirt and my cleanest pair of jeans when Addie wasn't planning on being at dinner. She had called me earlier in the day and told me that she wasn't feeling well and was going to call her parents and cancel.

All morning I had been looking forward to seeing her. I thought that it would be a chance to get to know her without her running away from me like she always did.

Her parents had talked about her over the last five years, but I hadn't thought that I would ever meet the woman behind the stories. They said she hated small town life and would never return. When I found Addie in that hole, I realized that the woman my neighbors had been telling stories about was far more interesting than they made her seem.

After running a comb through my hair and still not being satisfied with the way it fell, I gave up.

When my phone started ringing, I groaned and hoped it wasn't Van calling to tell me about another problem someone had cornered him with. Last week he had called me from his brother's hockey game about a woman with a canker sore. I had been in the middle of making dinner, and everything he described over the phone had made my appetite fly out the window.

I loved helping people, but I needed to draw the line

somewhere.

"Hello?"

"Hi," Addie said, her voice soft. "I thought that maybe I would like to go to dinner with the family after all. I've been away for so many years, and I miss them. I know I'm being annoying changing my mind again, but..." She laughed nervously. "Will you please come and pick me up?"

I smiled and grabbed my keys and wallet, tucking them both in my pockets. "I'll be there soon."

"Thank you," she said. "I'll see you when you get here."

"See you soon, Addie."

I was still smiling as I walked to the truck and headed into town. The drive was long, and I might have taken it a little too fast, eager to see Addie. It had been a long time since I had talked to anyone I was this interested in, but something about her drew me in.

Maybe it was the fact that she suggested we invited the fire department to see her nearly naked when Fleur was escorting me in. She had a sense of humor that I found refreshing. She wasn't like the women who ran in my old circle—at least, I didn't think she was, but I wouldn't know until I talked to her more.

When I pulled up outside her apartment, she was standing on the curb. Her auburn hair was hanging in loose curls down her back, blowing with the breeze as she shrank deeper into her denim jacket.

"You look nice," I said as I rounded the front of the truck to help her in. I looked at her black dress and the plain white sneakers she wore. "How's the ankle feeling today?"

"Pretty good," she said as she stepped up into the truck. "It doesn't hurt to walk on it anymore."

"Do you think that you'll be ready to go for that run sometime soon?"

She laughed, her cheeks turning a pretty shade of pink. "Yeah. I think I could be."

"Good. You let me know what day you want to go, and I'll clear my schedule." I glanced over at her as I started the drive to her parents' house. She had an uneasy look on her face as she played with a loose thread on the hem of her dress.

"You don't have to do that for me. I'll be fine."

I chuckled. "Addie, the last time you went running on your own, you fell into an old hunter's trap. I'm going with you, and that's the end of the story."

She sighed and ran her hand through her hair. "I really don't need that."

"And I told you that it's happening," I said, casting another glance her way. "I don't want to see you get hurt again."

Her cheeks turned a darker shade of red. "If you're sure."

"I am. Now, I want to get to know you better. Why did you move back to Blopton?"

Her hands stilled, and her shoulders tensed. I kept my eyes on the road, not saying anything. She would talk when she was ready, and I was not going to push her to say anything before then. The music played softly in the background as she sighed.

"I guess it's going to come out sooner or later since you live beside my parents. Hell, it's probably going to come out tonight."

"You don't have to tell me if you don't want to."

She shook her head. "It's not that. It's just not easy to talk about. My ex-husband, Sam...he was...or is, I really don't know...Sam is addicted to gambling. It took a massive toll on our relationship, and we were broke more often than not. He wouldn't go to treatment, no matter how many times I offered to support him through it. When we lost the house, I decided that I was done."

"That must have been hard."

"It was," she said. "I promised myself that I wouldn't get involved with an addict again."

Her statement had my heart sinking in my chest. My hands tightened on the wheel. If she had sworn off all addicts, we had no hope. Though I was in recovery and had been for four years, I would always be an addict.

Based on what she said, I didn't think she knew about my alcoholism addiction, and it had me wondering if she knew her mother was the one who dragged me to meetings and helped me get clean after I moved to town.

I don't know if I would have gotten through all those long nights without Fleur by my side. I didn't know where I would be without her, but I didn't think I'd still be alive.

I couldn't tell Addie that, though. If she didn't know I was an addict, I didn't want to be the one to break the news to her, even though I knew I had to. That conversation would be difficult. It would draw out all the other demons I had been hiding for so long.

That conversation would rip me to pieces.

It didn't have to be done tonight, though.

As we drove to her parents' house, Addie was more than comfortable carrying on the conversation. She chatted about applying for a teaching job before launching into stories about the children she had taught over the last couple of years.

When we pulled into her parents' driveway, her mom and dad were racing outside before I had even turned the engine off. Addie jumped out of the car and ambled to her parents, hugging them tightly. I sat in the truck for a few minutes longer, letting them have their moment before I went over.

They separated as I walked over to them, tears tracking down Fleur's cheeks. She wiped them away before her daughter could see them, but, at that moment, I saw how hard Addie's divorce had hit all of them.

"What do you say we go inside and start eating? I've been working on a pot roast all day that is going to make your mouths water," Fleur said, linking her arm through her husband's. "Zane, escort Addie to the table, won't you?"

Addie rolled her eyes at her mother's back before leaning into my side to whisper. "You don't have to do that. I can walk myself to the table."

I held out my arm and bowed low, grinning when she laughed. "Your mother is never going to let you walk to the table, so you may as well let me escort you."

"Well, it's hard to argue with that," Addie said as she looped her arm through mine. "Escort away."

I walked with her through the house to the dining room. Fleur enjoyed throwing dinner parties, not just her Saturday night dinners.

"This looks delicious, Mama," Addie said as she looked at the roast on a platter in the center of the table. "Did you make those good little roasted potatoes?"

"Of course," Fleur said as she disappeared into the kitchen before she brought out a tray of potatoes. "The rest of you can sit while I get the water."

"No wine?" Addie asked, her eyebrows furrowing. "When have you ever made a roast without wine?"

Fleur shrugged, purposefully looking away from me. "Your father needs to watch his waistline."

Alex laughed and took his seat, shaking his head. Fleur glanced at me as she left the room, giving me a slight smile. I led Addie to one side of the table before removing my arm from hers and pulling out her chair. She smiled as she sat down.

"Thank you," she said as I pushed into her chair before taking my own beside her.

"Anytime," I said.

Fleur brought the pitcher of water and a few more side dishes to the table before taking her seat. As the food was dished out, she launched into a story from when Addie was a teenager. Addie blushed and laughed, adding her own arguments to the conversation. Alex watched his daughter and wife go back and forth, smiling as he sipped his water.

I couldn't take my eyes off Addie as she laughed with her mother. It was hard to believe that they had spent years apart when they seemed so close.

Addie turned to me, laughing as she grabbed my arm and argued about something her mother had said. I grinned at her, losing myself in her excitement as she spoke. Being around her was simple.

I didn't want to think about how that would change once she found out I was an addict in recovery.

"Are you alright?" Addie whispered later that evening as the dinner dishes were whisked away and dessert was brought out. "You're looking a little green."

"I'm good," I said, looking down at the hand she had placed on my arm. "I'm just a little overwhelmed. You really are a chatterbox when you get going, aren't you?"

She rolled her eyes. "Oh please, you haven't seen anything yet."

I leaned closer to her, lowering my voice so her parents wouldn't hear me. "I'd like to see a hell of a lot more."

Her cheeks flamed as she rolled her eyes away and withdrew her hand. I didn't miss the way her gaze drifted down to my mouth before snapping back up.

"Play your cards right, and you just might," she whispered back before her dessert was placed in front of her.

Her words sent a rush of blood straight from my head to my dick. I cleared my throat and dug into my dessert, ignoring the gleeful look Fleur gave me. Addie snickered beside me before sipping her coffee.

We spent another couple of hours talking to her parents before we left. Addie was smiling from ear to ear as I drove her home.

When I stopped outside her apartment, she leaned across the seat and hugged me tightly. It took me by surprise, but after a second, I wrapped my arms around her and pulled her closer to me. She smelled like an intoxicating blend of vanilla and orange. It was my new favorite smell.

"Thank you for coming to get me tonight," Addie said as she pulled back. "I'll let you know when I plan on going for that run."

"Have a goodnight, Addie," I said, already missing her the moment she was out of my arms.

I sat outside her apartment until I saw her lights come on. When I was sure she was safe, I pulled away from the curb to head home and figure out what I was going to do about my feelings for her.

Chapter 4

Addie

In the last week, I had been restless as my job interview got closer. The kindergarten teacher position came open at the elementary school, and the principal had been very interested in my resume. I had spent the entire week trying to prepare for all the questions he would ask.

I took a deep breath as I pulled down my pencil skirt and adjusted my silk blouse. It was the only outfit I had nice enough and appropriate enough for interviews. I needed to make a good impression. I couldn't keep sitting in my apartment thinking about the doctor who was driving me crazy.

Though I hadn't seen Zane in the week since the dinner at my parents' house, I couldn't get him out of my mind. It didn't help that my mother kept asking about him, even though they lived a few feet from one another. She liked to bring up what she deemed 'our chemistry' at every other turn. It didn't matter that I told her nothing was going on between us. She still had it twisted in her mind that we would be the perfect couple if I wasn't so closed off to love.

It wasn't that I was closed off to love. Some day, I would find somebody to share my life with again. She just didn't understand why I didn't want that time to be right now and with the doctor.

I took one more breath, pushing all thoughts of the overly attractive doctor out of my mind before entering the school.

The office was small and cozy, with a man and woman working the phones. There was a small nurse's office in the back beside the guidance counselor. The principal's office was just beyond that in a small alcove.

"Hello, I'm here for an interview with Principal Rafferty," I said, approaching the man behind the desk with a smile. "Addie Manning."

I changed my name after my divorce, but it still felt weird to say it out loud. It hadn't happened much since the divorce, but it didn't seem to get any easier.

"One moment," he said, disappearing into the little alcove. When he returned, he nodded to me. "This way."

He led me to the principal's office in the back. I stepped inside, and the man behind the desk rose. He held out his hand, and I grasped it, giving it a firm shake before sitting down.

"Addie Manning, correct?" Principal Rafferty asked as he opened my teaching portfolio. "I have to say, I'm impressed."

"Thank you," I said, crossing my legs at the ankles and leaning forward. "I've spent my time trying to build a well-rounded portfolio that properly conveys the passion I have for teaching and helping young people learn."

"What brought you to teaching?"

"I knew I wanted to be a teacher while I was still in middle school. I had some amazing teachers who inspired me and made me believe that I was going to be able to do anything I wanted in the world. I want to be that person for as many children as possible. I believe that they need somebody in their life to believe in them, especially if they aren't getting that in their home lives."

Principal Rafferty nodded and flipped to another section of my portfolio. "I see that you put a focus on reading and writing. It's more of a focus than we tend to put on it here."

"Being able to read and write are the foundations of school. While I still teach the curriculum for science and math, I make sure reading and writing are largely incorporated into those subjects."

He nodded again. "Very good. I have to be honest...this interview is going to be very short. I need a teacher, and you're highly qualified. When I called your references, they all had wonderful things to say about you and had been heartbroken when you moved away. Since school is in session, there's already a classroom set up for you."

"Am I allowed to come in on a weekend and redo it?" I asked.

"Absolutely. Do whatever you want with the classroom as long as it falls within fire code." He shut my portfolio and pushed it to the side. "What do you say we go get you some contracts to read over and give you a tour of the school?"

"I can't wait."

***

When I got home, I was feeling better than I had in weeks. It felt like I was finally starting to build a life for myself after a couple of months of not knowing who I was or where I was going. Now, I had a job and was starting to settle down in the town that raised me. Everything felt like it was slowly starting to fall back into place.

I changed out of my interview outfit and pulled on a pair of shorts and a sports bra. I grabbed a sweater and my sneakers, lacing them up before heading out the door.

Stretching out, my muscles felt better than they had in weeks. The autumn air was crisp and fresh as the leaves fell to the ground. I pulled my hair up into a high ponytail, sliding the elastic off my wrist to tie it up. After taking a deep breath, I ran around the back of my apartment to the trail that began there.

My footsteps were steady and sure as I hit the trail. It didn't take long for the pain to start creeping back into my ankle. I slowed to a walk, taking my time to stretch and roll my ankle. The pain disappeared after a few minutes, and I started running again.

"Shit," I said as I slowed down again. There was a dull

throbbing in my ankle that wouldn't go away.

For the next few minutes, I rotated between jogging and walking, trying to move like I wasn't in pain. Finally, I had to admit defeat. I sat down on a nearby bench and kicked off my shoe, trying to massage the pain out of my ankle.

Once I was sure that I could start running again, I put my shoe on and took off running. I didn't make it very far, needing to lean against a tree when the pain nearly leveled me to the ground.

"You were supposed to call me when you were ready to go running again."

I looked to my right and saw Zane at the top of a small hill. He jogged down it and stopped beside me, kneeling on the ground.

"Give me your foot."

"I'm fine. It's just a little bit of pain. Nothing that I can't handle."

"Addie, give me your damn foot and stop pretending that you don't need somebody to help you."

I lifted my foot and put it on his knee. Zane took off the shoe and started running his fingers along my ankle. Shivers ran up my spine at the feeling of his hands on my body again. I shoved the shivers away, reminding myself that he was a medical professional looking at my injury.

"It's swollen again. Did you twist it at all while running?"

"No," I said as he helped me put my shoe back on but tied it looser. "I was running, but I stretched first. I didn't think that there was anything wrong."

"You should have called me before you went out running. I would have met you and been able to help you sooner."

"Don't lecture me," I said as he stood up and dusted the dirt off his clothing. "I don't need you to always come to my rescue."

He scoffed and picked me up, tossing me over his shoulder. "From this angle, it looks like you do."

"What the hell do you think you're doing?" I asked, staring at his ass.

"Since you won't cooperate, we're doing things my way."

I glared at his back, hating how attractive I found him at that moment, even though I wasn't a fan of being manhandled back to my apartment.

"Who said I wouldn't cooperate?"

He chuckled. "I don't think you've ever cooperated with anyone a day in your life."

"I resent that."

"But am I wrong?" he asked, shifting me slightly as he neared my apartment building. At my silence, he laughed. "I didn't think so."

"You can't just go around carrying people and acting like you can tell them what to do."

Zane hummed. "Actually, I'm a doctor. It's kind of in my job description."

"Apparently so is a god complex."

Zane laughed and put me on the ground as he stopped outside my building. "You need to alternate ice and heat on that ankle. Next time you decide to go for a run, call me first."

"Fine," I said, crossing my arms and glaring at him, trying to fight the smile that threatened to spread across my face.

After so long being the person that cared for others, it was nice to have someone looking out for me.

"I'm going to go shower and then get straight to that heat and ice," I said, pulling my key out of my bra. Zane's gaze darted to his chest before he gave me that heated stare.

"Do you want someone there in case you fall again?" he asked, his tone teasing despite the heat in his eyes.

"Fine, but you keep your hands to yourself, and your ass planted on my couch. This isn't a free show."

He laughed and followed me inside the building. "I'll be sitting on the couch and keeping my eyes to myself."

I rolled my eyes at him before disappearing into my bathroom. If I was being honest, it was nice to know he was sitting out there waiting to help me in case I did fall again. I wasn't sure that my ankle wouldn't give out while I was showering. Even now, while limping on it, I felt like I was going to fall down.

Once showered and dressed, I walked back into the living room to find Zane scrolling through his phone. He looked up when I entered the room, smiling.

"How's the ankle feel?" he asked.

"Not great," I said, sitting on the couch beside him. He reached down and pulled my foot into his lap, massaging my sore ankle. "That feels amazing."

He chuckled and pressed his thumbs harder into my skin. "See what happens when you let people help you?"

"Nobody likes a know-it-all," I said, wiggling my toes at him. My stomach growled, and I was reminded that I hadn't had food since breakfast. "How about I order a pizza, and you stay to have a slice or two since you've saved me twice now?"

He gave me a smile that had my heart skipping a beat. "I would like that very much."

I got up and ordered the pizza before sitting back down with him. Zane said nothing as he started massaging my ankle again while I turned on a movie. By the time the pizza arrived, my ankle was feeling a million times better, and my entire body was on fire.

"So," I said as I pulled a slice out of the box and nearly burned my mouth on the hot cheese. "Why come to run a solo practice in a small town?"

Zane sighed as he grabbed his own slice and shrugged. "A lot of horrible things have happened in my life, and after a while, I got tired of having reminders everywhere. Moving out here seemed like the right choice. I was away from the reminders, and I got to slow down."

"What's it like being a doctor?" I asked, getting the sense that he didn't want to talk about the demons of his past.

"I love it. I love being able to help people. I never thought when I was younger that it's what I'd do, but once I started medical school, I couldn't think of doing anything else."

Zane's hands moved quickly as he talked about being a doctor. I could see the passion on his face as he spoke. The more he talked, the more I was sucked in. I don't know how long we talked, but by the time he left, the stars were out, and the moon shone bright.

For the first time in a long time, I slept through the night and dreamed of the future.

Chapter 5

Zane

The last person I thought I'd see when I walked out of my Alcoholics Anonymous meeting a few days later was Addie. Yet, there she was across the street with groceries balanced on her hips. She shuffled the bags, stumbling slightly as she walked across the uneven sidewalk.

I ducked my head and crossed the street, pretending like I hadn't just come from an addiction meeting. While I knew that I needed help and wanted others to get help when they needed it, I didn't want her to know about my struggles yet. She had said that she would never get involved with an addict again. Addie had made that very clear, and I wasn't sure how to tell her. I didn't want to ruin my chances with her.

How do you think it's going to go when she finds out you lied to her? the nasty voice in the back of my head asked.

"Hey, Addie," I said, emerging from the opposite side of where the meeting was held. I took long strides until I was at her side. I took the bags from her. "The sidewalk is shit, and with your ankle still hurting, you're only going to make it worse."

"I thought I told you that I could take care of myself," she said, reaching for the bags.

I held them out of her reach with a smile. "I know you can. It's just not a good idea to be walking home on that ankle with all these groceries."

Addie rolled her eyes as though she was smiling. "I guess you're right."

"Can you repeat that? Or maybe write it down? It could be the first and only time you ever say it."

Addie laughed, and the sound was music to my ears. She led the way down Main Street, heading toward her apartment. As we walked, she told me about her lesson plans for her new students. She was nearly bouncing as she turned to tell me everything she planned to do on her first day at school.

"Alright," she said, turning to me as we reached her apartment a few minutes later. "Tell me what's new at the clinic."

"I'm thinking of repainting, and somehow Van invited himself over for dinner tonight."

Addie laughed. "When I first came to the clinic, I couldn't remember him, but it came back to me slowly. He's a character that one. I remember him when he was younger. He didn't care if people wanted him around or not. He was always determined to be exactly where he wanted to be, and nobody could change his mind."

"Good to know that nothing has ever changed with him, then."

She gave me that stunning smile again. "You're going to have a great dinner, even if he is years younger than you."

I looked at her, knowing from her patient file that she was a few years younger than me. "Age is just a number. Van's a good kid, and I think he'll go far in life."

"He's always done everything that he puts his mind to, so I don't doubt it." She glanced down at her watch. "I should let you get going then."

"Addie, do you want to join us?"

Addie shook her head and took the bags from me. "Thanks for the offer, but I'd hate to ruin your night."

"You wouldn't be ruining it," I said.

"I would. Have a good time, Zane. Maybe we could go out for that run sometime soon?"

"Just tell me the time and what trail," I said.

Addie nodded and went inside. I stood outside and stared at the door for a minute before beginning my walk back to the grocery store. With Van coming over, I needed something to make for dinner, and I suspected that I would need a lot of it. After seeing what he packed for himself for lunch, I didn't think a burger and a fistful of chips was going to cut it.

I was going to need to start keeping more food in my house, especially if people started coming over more. If Addie came over, I didn't want to look like that adult who couldn't take care of himself and lived off a bottle of ketchup, cheese, and something questionable in the back of the fridge.

With that in mind, I headed into the grocery store with no clue what to make for dinner tonight.

***

"So," Van said as he took another hot dog off the grill. "You've been spending a lot of time around town with Addie."

"How do you even know that?" I asked, nearly choking on my drink.

"After five years you still have no clue how gossip spreads in this town." Van grinned and put more mustard on his hot dog than any human should. "That's cute. I heard it at the barbershop. One of the guys there heard it from his wife."

"And who else knows about the amount of time I've been spending around Addie?"

Van shrugged. "Most of town. Fleur's giddy about it."

I groaned and ran a hand down my face. "Perfect."

"Don't worry," Van said, a shit-eating grin on his face. "Nobody has started talking about the wedding yet, but I suspect that it's only a matter of time."

I rolled my eyes and took a long sip of my drink. "We're not even dating. Don't get ahead of yourself."

"You want to date her, though, which means that there's hope for a marriage. Do I get to be your best man?"

Van's grin was infectious, even as I sighed. I had a few friends in town, but even after years of living among the locals, Van was my closest friend. If I did have a wedding, he would be the best man without a doubt.

"You drive me insane," I said, not bothering to answer him. "I'm not getting married anytime soon."

"Because you haven't even asked Addie yet."

"What makes you think I'm going to ask Addie?"

Van shrugged. "I don't know. Why do you keep trying to lie to yourself?"

"I'm not lying to myself at all. I know how I feel about her but with my alcoholism, getting involved with her is a bad idea. She doesn't want to have anything to do with addicts."

"You're in recovery," Van said. "You're in recovery and have been in recovery for a few years. You work hard to stay sober, and to be honest, I don't know how you do it with all that you've been through."

"It's not easy," I said. "It takes a lot of work, and there're days when I still feel like drinking, so I don't have to think about everything that happened."

"I think if you're honest with Addie about it, she'll have all the information she needs to make a decision. Who knows, she might just surprise you."

I sighed and ran a hand through my hair. I would tell her the truth one day; I just didn't know when that day would be.

"Why don't you just go over there and tell her how you feel? I've been watching you stare after her for weeks, and honestly, it's getting to the point where you either need to do something about it or let it go."

He was right, and I knew he was right. Sitting around and pining after she wasn't doing me any good. Van made it sound easier than it was. He made it sound like she would find out about the skeletons I kept buried deep in my closet and would not care.

That she would accept me for who I was.

Alcoholism was just the beginning, though. I couldn't imagine anyone who would look past all the other things I had done.

"You look like you're starting to spiral," Van said as I grabbed another bottle of water from the cooler I had brought outside earlier in the evening. "Stop looking like you're spiraling. It's going to be fine."

"I'm a grown man. It shouldn't be this hard."

"You're a grown man who doesn't believe he's worthy of love due to a couple of mistakes he made in his life." Van smirked and leaned back in his chair. "One of those TV doctors taught me that."

I laughed and shook my head, the tension of the conversation easing. As he got another hot dog, Van grinned and settled back in his chair with the bottle of mustard.

"I'm serious. You want her. Go get her. Stop acting like she's going to turn you away when she doesn't even know the truth."

"You're acting like it's your job to get us together."

"She likes you. You like her. I don't see the problem. If you need to send her one of those check yes or no love notes, I'm excellent at drawing boxes."

I rolled my eyes at him, my lips twitching. If I smiled again, it would only encourage him to keep talking. Instead, I got up, turned off the grill, and closed the lid to keep the last few hot dogs warm. I had no doubt that Van would finish them off before he left. He seemed to have a hollow leg.

"All I'm saying is that you don't want to wait until it's too late. Now that her ankle's better and she's going out, somebody else is going to notice her."

I scowled at him. "Why do you keep trying to get me worked up?"

Van shrugged. "Why do you keep letting it work? You're the one that's interested in her. Do something about it."

"Fine," I said, getting up and heading for the house. "Lock up before you leave. You know where the spare key is."

"Where are you going?" Van called after me, sounding amused.

"You said I should do something about it," I said, looking over my shoulder at him. "So, I'm going to go do something about it."

***

During the drive to Addie's house, I nearly talked myself into turning around and driving home half a dozen times. Van would be waiting until I got back, even though I told him to lock up when he left. There was no way he would go home before he knew what had happened.

Having to admit that I was a coward was the only reason I didn't back out and left talking to Addie for another day. Of course, I didn't know when that other day would come.

I parked along the curb beside her apartment and drummed my fingers on the wheel.

The worst that can happen is that she already knows about the alcoholism and wants nothing to do with you.

I pushed the thought as far away from me as I could and got out of the truck. With a deep breath, I walked to her door and rang the bell, hoping that she was home.

Addie opened the door with a grin. "What are you doing here? I thought you had that dinner with Van tonight."

"I did," I said, swallowing hard as my heart hammered in my chest. "But there's been something on my mind lately."

Addie raised an eyebrow and crossed her arms as she leaned against the doorframe. "You came all the way over here to tell me that you couldn't get something out of your mind?"

"No. I came over here to tell you that I can't get you out of my head since we met a couple of weeks ago."

She gave me a blinding smile, and what little resolve and hesitation I had left faded into the background. I closed the distance between us as she reached for me. As my arms went around her, her mouth slanted against mine. The kiss was soft and sweet, and when she pulled away, I wanted to pull her back.

"Well," she said as she looked at me, her cheeks flushed and her eyes bright. "I just opened a bottle of wine. Do you want to come in and have a drink?"

"Do you have coffee? It's been a long day, and I could use a hot drink."

She stepped aside and held the door open. "Do I have coffee? Zane, I love coffee more than I love most things in life."

I followed her inside, all thoughts of telling her about my addiction gone as I tried to figure out where I would take her on our first date.

Chapter 6

Addie

Zane and I spent most evenings together after work for the last two weeks. There was nothing more relaxing than coming home from being mauled by kindergarteners all day long and having Zane show up with groceries to make dinner. Most of the time, he sat on the couch and entertained me while I ate dinner.

It had only taken him one attempt at making burgers for dinner for me to decide that I would do the cooking when we ate in. I wasn't risking food poisoning or eating a brick of charcoal.

And then there were the morning runs. Zane knew all the new trails in town and was more than happy to wake up before the sun and run with me. Every morning he picked me up with coffee in hand and drove me to a trailhead. This morning was no exception.

When I left my apartment, he was already sitting in his truck. As soon as I got in, he handed me a coffee and grinned.

"Rough morning?" he asked, playing with the end of my ponytail.

"How could you tell?" I asked.

"You look like you didn't sleep at all."

"That's a nice way of saying I look like shit," I said, my tone teasing. I took a long sip of coffee, moaning when the coffee hit my tired soul. "This is the best coffee yet."

"You say that every morning," he said, his hand resting on my thigh as he drove out of town. His fingers drifted along my thigh, lighting a fire wherever he touched.

"You keep doing that, and we're going to have a problem," I said, looking pointedly down at his hand.

Zane laughed and squeezed my thigh, his hand drifting higher before he put both hands on the wheel. "That better?"

"Nope."

"Good."

It didn't take long to reach the trailhead. We ran together until the sun came up before turning and heading back to the truck. Running always left me feeling better than when I woke up.

"I haven't seen your house yet," I said as we got back in the truck. "It's closer to here than my place, and I'm starving."

Zane chuckled. "Inviting yourself over for breakfast?"

I shrugged and leaned back in my seat, sipping what was left of my cold coffee. His laughter made my heart skip a beat. It had been a long time since a man made me feel the way that he did. How he looked at me sent liquid heat flooding my body to my core. It had only been nearly two months, but I wanted him more than I had ever wanted anybody else.

Zane turned up the music as he drove to his house. When we reached his driveway, I turned my face away from the window, hoping my mother wasn't outside. I didn't want her to see me and start getting all kinds of ideas in her head, especially when the relationship was so new.

"I think we're in the clear," Zane said, amusement in his voice as he parked the truck. "Your mom is out front, and your dad's car is gone, so I doubt he's home. If we make a run for the back door, Fleur won't see you."

I blushed and looked over at him. "I just don't want her to get excited until we know where this is going, and we've been together a bit longer."

He nodded and opened his door. "I understand. Now come on, I bet I can beat you to the back door."

"You're on," I said with a grin as I got out.

He took off running before I even reached the front of the truck. I smothered my laughter, not wanting my mom to hear me, and followed after him. Even though I knew I wasn't going to beat him, I still tried. When we got to his back porch, he grabbed me around the waist and tossed me over his shoulder.

I was laughing as he walked into the house and tossed me onto the couch. Zane was quick to follow, hovering over me as we kissed. My fingers threaded through his hair as he leaned into me. I pulled him closer, his tongue tangling with mine as I hooked a leg around his hip.

Zane pulled back and looked down at me, heat in his eyes. "As much as I want to continue this, I'm sweaty and gross from running."

"Your point?" I asked, both legs around his waist.

"We're going for a shower."

"Sounds good to me."

Zane chuckled and wrapped his arms around me, lifting me from the couch and walking with me down the hall, his mouth trailing up and down my neck. I moaned as he held me up against a wall, pulling my shirt off and tossing it to one side.

His hands massaged my breasts, pulling my bra out of the way before he dipped his head to suck a nipple into his mouth. I moaned, writhing against his hardened length and trying to relieve some of the tension building between my legs.

We reached the bathroom, and Zane set me on the counter. I watched him as he stripped out of his clothes before turning on the massive shower. The walls of the shower were made entirely of glass, and there was more than enough room for two people inside. Steam fogged up the glass almost immediately.

I hopped down from the counter and stripped out of my clothes, tossing my hair tie on the counter before stepping into the shower with an added sway to my hips. I heard Zane's groan moments before he followed me into the shower, his chest against my back as his hands ran up my body.

Zane toyed with my nipples as the hot water hit my skin. I moaned, leaning back into him as one of his hands drifted down my stomach. His fingers found my clit, circling it slowly and driving me insane.

"Faster," I said breathlessly as he nipped and sucked at my neck.

"You want more?" he asked, his voice raspy as he withdrew his hand. "Not yet."

He spun me around and got on his knees, lifting one of my legs over his shoulder. Zane pressed one finger slowly inside me while he flattened his tongue against my clit. I moaned as he swirled his tongue at the same time he started thrusting his finger faster.

"Yes," I moaned, leaning back against the wall. My fingers threaded through his hair as my inner walls clenched around him. I ground against him, aching for relief as he added another finger.

When he hooked his fingers, rocking them harder, I came apart around him.

"Yes, baby," he said, still rocking his fingers as the last of my orgasm flooded through me. He stood up and claimed my mouth in a scorching kiss when I finally stopped shuddering.

He stepped out of the shower for a moment before he came back, sliding a condom down his cock. My tongue darted out, licking my lower lip before he kissed me again. I hooked one of my legs around his hip, leaning back against the glass. Water rained down over us as he slipped inside me. My inner walls clenched around him as he took a nipple in his mouth, sucking hard as he thrust deeper inside of me. I moaned, rocking my hips in time with his thrusts.

Zane wrapped my hair around his hand, pulling my head back. With the other, he held the soft flesh around my waist. I arched my back, the angle shifting as he thrust harder. His fingers dropped to my hips, gripping the soft flesh so hard I knew I was going to have bruises later on. The thought of his marks on my body only made my orgasm come that much harder.

"Fuck, that feels good," he said, giving one final thrust before he fell apart. He grinned as he looked down at me. "I don't know how I'm going to look your father in the eye after that."

"Good thing we have all day before Saturday dinner. We can give you some more reasons not to look him in the eye."

Zane laughed and grabbed the soap, motioning for me to turn around. "Sounds good to me."

***

When we walked into my parents' house, Zane and I were back to being friends and nothing more—at least until we could get back to his house later that evening. It was hard to pretend that I didn't want to drag him into a room and have my way with him again.

"Stop looking at me like you've seen me naked," I hissed when my parents left the room to start bringing the food in.

"That's because I have," he said under his breath.

My cheeks felt like they were on fire as my parents walked back into the room carrying platters of food. I reached for my water and took a long sip, squeezing my thighs together.

I was thankful I was wearing underwear—even when Zane suggested I shouldn't—but I didn't think they were going to survive beyond dinner. Not with how he was looking at me and rubbed my thigh beneath the table.

Grabbing his hand, I shoved it off my leg. I needed to focus on not being a couple, especially with my mom glancing between us like she knew something was happening. It wouldn't surprise me if she did.

"So," Mom asked, her gaze still darting between us as I scooped stew into my bowl. "Is there anything new and exciting going on in your life?"

Zane saved me from having to lie to her more by launching into a story about one of the patients from the clinic. Dad laughed and joked with him while I kept avoiding glances from my mom.

After dinner, I was sure that she was going to pull me to the side and demand to know what was going on, but she didn't. She stopped looking at us during dessert, a smirk on her face. My heart was hammering as I wondered how much she had pieced together.

"You know," Mom said as she walked into the living room carrying a tray with cups of coffee. "You two would make a cute couple. You look good together."

It was at that moment that I knew she had figured it out. I had never been good at keeping secrets from her. My cheeks flamed as I took a cup of coffee. I stared down at it, avoiding the way her gaze lingered on me before she moved on.

"Addie doesn't need to find anyone else yet," Dad said before sipping on his coffee. "Not after that last idiot she was with. I'd still like to bury him so deep they'll never find him."

"Dad, that's unnecessary," I said, wishing that the ground would open me up and swallow me whole. "That part of my life is over, and I'll start dating again whenever I feel ready."

Mom chuckled as she took her seat. "And who might that lucky man be?"

"I don't know. I didn't say that I was ready to date yet."

Mom smirked, humming as she leaned back in her chair. Zane stepped in and started talking with my dad about football, but the damage was already done. If Mom wasn't sure before, she was now.

There would be no more denying it the next time I was over, but for now, I was going to live in my ignorant bliss and pretend that nothing had happened. I wanted to keep the relationship to myself for a little while longer.

Chapter 7

Zane

The dozen tables that occupied the bar were filled with people watching sports. It was a typical night at the bar, and I only knew that because I had been sitting at the bar for the last four nights after I left Addie's house.

It's been almost six years since I lost my first patient, and the pain hasn't eased. I lost two years of my life to alcoholism after that death. Other doctors had said that time would make it easier, but it didn't.

What was supposed to have been a routine appendix removal for a child went wrong. Even now, what happened in that operating room still haunted my dreams. The appendix burst after we had barely gotten the little girl on the table open. Toxins spilled into her body before I knew what was happening.

I couldn't save her. I had to call time of death and then tell her parents that it was my fault their daughter had died. I hadn't been fast enough. I hadn't gotten to her in time. I hadn't known what to do to save her.

Her blood was on my hands, and no matter how many times I tried to wash them clean, I couldn't.

"Do you want anything to drink?" the bartender asked, approaching me and breaking me out of my spiral.

"Water, please," I said though I was craving something a lot stronger than water.

It was near the anniversary when I considered drinking the most. The memories of that day came flooding back to me as if they were happening in real-time. The mother's screams still echoed in my ears each time I had to tell a patient bad news.

That one loss had been enough to make me give up surgery forever. That, and after the Chief of General Surgery found out about my drinking problem, I was told that I could either quit and move on, or I could be fired and ruin my life. The day I was given the ultimatum, I had been sober enough to make a smart decision.

"Are you sure you don't want something else?" the bartender asked, looking at the still-full glass of water in my hand nearly a half an hour later.

I looked at the bottles lining the back wall, my hand clenched tight around my glass. For a moment, I was worried it was going to break. I released my grip and shook my head.

"Water's fine. Thanks."

"Anything to eat then? Kitchen's still open for a few more hours."

My stomach growled, and it was only then that I realized I hadn't eaten anything since yesterday. "Maybe a burger."

He nodded and walked to the register. "Maybe a burger coming up."

I drummed my fingers on the table, glancing up every now and then at the football game on the TV. I had no clue what was happening—football was never a sport I followed, but it was better than staring at the bottles in the back row.

"I didn't know you'd be here."

My spine stiffened at the sound of Addie's voice. When I had left her apartment earlier, she said that she was going out with a few of the other teachers from school. I hadn't expected her to come here. The bar was a bit of a dive, but there was another one in town that had live music and a better atmosphere.

If I had thought that she would have come to this bar, I would have gone to the other one to wallow in my misery.

I plastered on a grin and turned to face her. "Hey, I didn't know you guys would be coming here."

She wrapped me in a tight hug and kissed my cheek before wiping away the lipstick stain. "Yeah. One of the girls said she likes the food here better. Do you want to join us?"

"Nope," I said, grinning at her. "You have your night with your friends. I'm just picking up some food to go so I don't have to go hungry at home."

She stared at me for a moment, and her smile turned into a frown. "Are you okay?"

"I'm fine. It's just been a long day."

Her eyebrows pulled closer together, a fine line appearing between them. "Okay. If you're sure, you're okay."

"I'm sure. Go have fun, and I'll see you later."

She grinned again, and I kissed her before she disappeared into the crowd to join her friends. As soon as she was gone, I flagged the bartender down and asked him to make my burger to-go.

***

I drove around for hours, not wanting to go home but not sure where else I could go. Fleur had made it clear that I needed to come over whenever I was struggling, but it was late, and I was sure she was asleep.

When I finally got home, Addie was sitting on my front porch with the blanket she kept in the back of her car wrapped around her shoulders. She was looking down at the phone in her hands, as if she was ready to throw it across the yard.

"Hey," I said as I got out of the truck and crossed the yard. "I didn't think you'd be coming over tonight."

She looked up at me with red-rimmed eyes and clutched the phone tighter. "What are you lying to me about?"

My heart stopped in my chest. A million different lies and excuses flashed through my mind. I should have told her before now. I could have told her dozens of times leading up to now.

"And don't try to tell me that you're not lying about anything. I'm not going to be putting up with another man lying to me, so if you have something to come clean about, you better do it now."

I wanted to ask her what would happen if I didn't, but I already knew based on the look on her face. If I didn't tell her what was going on in my life, she would walk out of it forever.

Hell, she still might, even after I told her everything.

It was a risk that I had to take.

"I'm struggling," I said as I sat down beside her. The words nearly got caught in my throat. It wasn't the first time I had said them, but they still felt nearly impossible to say.

"Struggling with what?"

"A lot of things. Alcoholism being the worst one."

She froze beside me, her shoulders tensing as she looked at me. The hurt in her eyes nearly tore me in half.

"I should have told you about it before I ever kissed you. I know I should have. I was a coward. I thought you would never give me a chance if you knew I'm an addict."

"I've never seen you drink," she says, her words sounding choked as if there's a lump caught in her throat.

"I'm in recovery. Have been for the last four years. Still an addict, though."

She nodded, her phone dropping into her lap before she ran her hands down her face. "So, you're struggling."

"Tomorrow is the anniversary of the death of one of my patients during surgery."

"You're not a surgeon," Addie said, clutching the blanket tighter around her body. She held onto it as if it was the only thing keeping her afloat. "How could you kill a patient?"

"I was a general surgeon. A little girl came in with pain near her appendix. We knew that it was about to burst, but the hospital was busy that night. The trauma surgeons were busy, the emergency room was packed, and I overlooked her for a long time."

I paused and blinked away the tears in my eyes. It felt like my chest was closing in on itself as I looked away from her.

"By the time we got to the operating room and got her open, it was too late. Toxins were spilling into her body, and there was nothing that we could do to save her."

"I'm so sorry," Addie said, reaching for my hand. She laced her fingers through mine and squeezed it tight.

"After I told her parents that I killed their daughter, I started drinking. Heavily. It only got worse until I was told that I could either quit or be fired. I quit and kept drinking. I moved here after a year of drinking and took another year to get clean."

"And now the anniversary date has brought it all back." Addie ran her hand through her hair. "You should have told me about this."

"I was scared that you were going to want nothing to do with me if you knew I was an addict. You made it pretty clear that you wanted nothing to do with addicts ever again."

She sighed and squeezed my hand again before dropping it. "You still should have told me. That was my decision to make, not yours."

"And you can still make whatever decision you want," I said, shuffling a few inches away from her. The physical distance between us didn't make me feel any better, but if she was going to walk away, she could.

"Are you sober now?"

"I don't want to be," I said, hating the truth. I wanted to drink. I wanted to lose myself in the alcohol and numb all the pain for the next few days. "But yes. I haven't had a drink in the last four years."

Those few days would turn into a few weeks, which would turn into a few months. Hell, it could turn into a few years. I wanted to lose myself, but I couldn't. I didn't know if I would ever find myself again.

"Call your sponsor," she said as she stood up. "I'm going to go borrow a shirt and go put on a movie. If you want to talk after, I'll be there."

"You're not leaving?" I asked, feeling hope for the first time when thinking about her and my addiction.

Addie shook her head. "I'm disappointed that you hid that from me, especially knowing what I've been through, but it's your problem to share."

"You're not leaving then?" I asked again, needing to make sure that this wasn't a dream.

"I'm not leaving." She bent down and kissed my cheek. "I'm not leaving you to deal with this alone. Just don't ever lie to me again."

"I won't."

"Thank you."

Even as she spoke, I could hear the lump that was caught in her throat. I hoped that she would be okay on her own for a few hours, but she was right. I needed to call my sponsor and talk about everything going through my head. I needed someone who understood what it was like to talk me down from the ledge.

I watched her go inside and waited until I knew she was nowhere near the door before I pulled out my phone and called Fleur.

Chapter 8

Addie

When I woke up the next morning, it felt like I had been hit by a truck. The sleep I had gotten the night before was fitful at best. Everything that Zane told me while we were sitting on his porch kept running through my mind.

He was an addict. He had kept that from me. I had no right to be angry—we had just started dating a few weeks ago—but I was. I was so angry that he didn't tell me when he knew what had happened with my ex-husband.

I looked at him as he slept beside me and wondered if I would have done anything differently if he had told me months ago. He was snoring, rolling over onto his side. I looked at the peaceful expression on his face and knew that if he had told me before we started dating, I wouldn't have even entertained a date.

I never would've given him a chance.

As he slept, I slid out of bed and made my way to the living room. I needed a few minutes by myself before he woke up to think about what I was going to do.

Last night, I told him that I wasn't going to let him go through this alone, and I wasn't. I refused to let him suffer alone, but it was hard. Each time I thought about his addiction, I thought about my ex-husband's addiction.

Unlike Sam, Zane was working on keeping himself clean. He was working on avoiding his addiction, and he was looking for help. He didn't want to live in his addiction. He had known that there was something wrong, and he got help.

I kept reminding myself of that as I walked out to my car and got the bag of clothing from the back.

After I got changed, I started stretching. A run was what I needed to clear my head. I needed to get some fresh air, and hopefully, the chilly air would be enough to shock my system.

"Going for a run?" Zane asked as he walked into the living room.

"Yeah. You coming?"

The words sounded hollow even to me. I wanted him to come with me and pretend that everything was normal, even if it was for a short time. When we got back from the run, we were going to have some talking to do.

"Yeah, just let me get changed," he said before disappearing back into the bedroom.

When he came out, we didn't say anything to each other. I didn't know what I could say to him at that moment. If we were running, it would be easier to pretend that nothing was wrong.

Sitting in the truck next to each other as he drove us to our favorite trailhead was tense and awkward. There was more left unsaid between us that still needed to come out. There was hurt on both sides, and neither of us knew what to say.

"You know, I started running when the urge to drink was bad." Zane sighed and drummed his fingers on the wheel. "It was the only thing that could force me to have a clear head. Mainly because I was so out of shape that running hurt."

"Is that still why you run?"

"No. It just became a habit. After that, I started to enjoy running."

"Well, at least you found something that worked for you," I said. I cringed when I heard how it came out, but nothing else could be said.

We fell silent again as he drove farther away from town. Zane sighed and rolled the window down, letting the cold air into the car before he turned the radio up. I was glad for the distraction.

When we got to the trailhead, we stretched before we took off running. The weight that had been placed on my shoulders over the last day started to lift. Every ounce of panic that I had been feeling started to fade away. I wanted to do something fun. I wanted to have fun before we had to go back and start dealing with the ocean of shit we'd have to wade through.

"You're it," I said, tapping Zane on the shoulder before taking a sharp turn and running in the opposite direction.

I heard Zane's laugh far behind me as I ran as fast as I could. I knew it was only a matter of time before he caught me, but I was going to give him one hell of a chase before then.

As I heard him approaching, I ducked behind one of the trees. He ran by, calling my name as I kept myself hidden from him. I thought he had disappeared until arms wrapped around my waist and hauled me back against a hard body.

"You're it," he said, his voice husky in my ear. I could feel his erection pressing against my ample backside as his lips trailed up and down my neck.

As our clothes started falling off, I only grew more excited. We were only a few feet from the trail. Anybody could walk by and see us at any moment.

"Mmm, you're wet," he said as his fingers circled my clit before dipping inside me.

I moaned, writhing against his hand as he pushed me back against a tree. The bark was rough as it bit into my back, the pain bringing more pleasure.

"Fuck," he groaned. "I didn't bring anything."

"I've got an IUD, and I'm clean."

His clothes were off as soon as the words were out of my mouth.

"I'm clean, too," he said.

I embraced him before kissing my way down his body until I

was on my knees in front of him. The rocks and sticks dug into my knees, sending another shiver of pleasure up my spine.

I gripped his cock, smoothing my thumb over the silky head before I licked my way down his shaft. His hands knotted in my hair when I licked my way back up the other side. His eyes rolled back as I took his cock in my mouth, flattening my tongue against the underside as I took him as deep as possible.

He moaned as I sucked his cock, working the head with my tongue. His hips moved in time with my sucking, pushing himself deeper and deeper. When I felt him tensing, he pulled back.

"Get up, turn around, and bend over."

Heat pooled between my legs as I did what he said, bracing myself against a log. He entered me from behind in one swift move. As he was thrusting, he reached around my body, tweaking my nipples as he pulled me upright against him. I moaned as my inner walls squeezed him, my hand drifting down to my clit.

I rubbed my clit as he was thrusting. His hands traced heat down my body, swirling softly along the soft pooch of my belly, waist, across my hips before moving up to my breasts, massaging them. When my walls started clamping down on him again, he stopped playing with my nipples and clamped a hand over my mouth.

"You wouldn't want anyone to hear you scream my name while I'm fucking you," he whispered, nipping at my earlobe. "Or come see the way you're touching yourself while I'm buried inside you."

His words were all it took to send me over the edge, screaming his name against his hand. He thrust faster, groaning as he finished.

We stepped away from each other, panting and searching for our clothes. Once I was dressed, I wrapped my arms around him.

"We should probably go get cleaned up," Zane said, kissing my forehead.

"Let's go home."

***

After a shower that turned into another round of sex and avoiding the discussion we needed to have, I walked into the kitchen to make a cup of coffee. Zane was still in the shower, singing along with a song I didn't know.

When I opened the cupboard where he normally kept the coffee, it wasn't there. I sighed and looked around the kitchen, wondering where he would have put it. Not once in the time that I had been dating him had he ever put groceries away in the same spot twice. It seemed like he thrived on the chaos.

After opening a few of the cabinets, I was getting ready to drive into town to just pick up the coffee. Searching for the grinds was becoming an endless failure. I opened another cupboard and felt the world fall out from beneath me.

Zane came whistling into the kitchen, but the whistling cut out when I turned around with a bottle of bourbon and a glass in my hand. There was a splash of liquid still left in the glass that stank of bourbon. Behind that bottle, there had been three other empty ones. He had downed three other bottles in an effort to numb the pain, and I had been blind to all of it.

I felt like such an idiot.

I kept falling for men who lied to me about their demons. Who kept their addictions going strong because they refused to get help. They couldn't get help. They needed help. I couldn't do anything about it.

"What the hell is this?" I asked, my voice hollow as I set the open bottle and the glass down on the counter. "You told me that the last time you had a drink was four years ago! You told me that you were sober! You fucking lied to me!"

Guilt flashed across his face, but it was quickly replaced by anger. He crossed his arms, and, at that moment, I saw the ugly beast that addiction brought out in people.

"Who said that I have to tell you everything? I slipped once, Addie! Once! You're going to stand there and act like I'm throwing away everything because I had one drink?"

I scoffed and shook my head. "You're an addict, Zane. And not one who's been in recovery long-term. You've been in a few years, and that's great, but you were feeling low, and you turned to drinking again."

"I can have one drink without it being a massive problem!"

"You drank half the damn bottle!" I said, gesturing at the bottle on the counter. "Half! When did you even do this? When I was sleeping last night? What did you do? Get off the phone with your sponsor and decide, hey, let's do the one thing I shouldn't be doing right now?"

"It's not like that, Addie," he said, pinching the bridge of his nose. When he looked back up at me, there was barely contained fury in his eyes.

"Then enlighten me!"

"Get out."

"You know what, I could have dealt with the addiction. I told you that I was going to go through this with you, but you lied to me again."

"I thought I told you to get out!" he yelled.

"Done," I said, trying to hold back the tears that blurred my vision. "I hope you get help, and I hope you can get right with yourself again, Zane. If you do or you want help, call me. I'll be there for you."

"I don't care. Just get out of my house and stop trying to fix me!"

I walked out of the house, not bothering to gather the things I had left there over the course of our relationship. I would get them later when both of us could be in the same room together without yelling at each other.

As I got in my car, I let the first tears fall. Once they started falling, they wouldn't stop. I hit the wheel as hard as I could, trying to drive some of the frustration out of my body.

When the tears stopped falling, I started the car and drove

away.

I couldn't let him drag me down with him.

Chapter 9

Zane

Two weeks was a long time to go without drinking. It was miserable.

I had been drinking for a week before Addie had found the evidence of my self-destruction. It had started off as one drink late at night, and then it had started spiraling out of control. Before I realized what was happening, the first bottle was gone. Then the fifth bottle was gone. Then the seventh.

It was only when she walked out and left me behind that I realized what I had done.

With one drink, I had managed to ruin my life again.

The day she walked out was the day I dumped the bourbon down the sink. I went to work and then home again, not stopping at the bar or anywhere that served alcohol—other than the grocery store where I bought a new bottle every day.

I don't know why, but I would head into town after finishing at the clinic just to buy a bottle of whatever I found first before heading home. I would then line up the unopened bottle on the counter with the several others I had bought and convince myself that I didn't need to drink them.

It was my favorite form of torture, apparently.

When I got home from work, I added the fourteenth bottle to the line. I didn't even like tequila, but somehow, I purchased three bottles of it.

"Fuck," I muttered as I looked at the bottles. I wanted to crack their seals and start drinking, but I couldn't.

Every day I thought about calling Fleur or going over to her home a few feet away from me and admit I was struggling. I thought about telling her that I had fallen for her daughter before I ruined everything. And then I thought about the look that would be on her face when I told her that.

I grabbed one of the bottles and grabbed the top, ready to twist the seal. When I looked across the kitchen at where Addie had last stood, all I could see was her disappointed face. I could see the hurt on her face when I told her to get out of my house.

When I put the bottle back down, I could hear the addiction calling my name again. I took a deep breath before taking several steps away from the counter. I had thrown away four years of sobriety. Instead of going to the meetings and talking to Fleur, I drowned my sorrows in alcohol and hoped that nobody would notice.

I had known from the beginning that I would ruin everything between Addie and me. As it turned out, I was a self-fulfilling prophecy.

"What the hell are you doing wallowing in your own pity?" Fleur said as she stormed into my house, looking like the hounds of hell were on her heels. "Is this really going to help anything?"

"Go away, Fleur. I didn't give you the key so you could barge your way in here and tell me what to do."

"And I didn't sponsor your ass through sobriety and watch my daughter fall for you to let you throw everything away like this. Now get your ass over to the couch. We're going to talk about this whether you like it or not."

"Get out!" I shouted, feeling the panic rising in my chest.

Fleur snorted and sat down on the couch. "Don't try the angry addict shit with me, young man. I've been there and done that. Now, get your ass on the couch and start talking!"

I scowled at her but stalked over to the couch across from her and sat down. When I kicked my feet up on the coffee table, Fleur sent me a withering look. I dropped my feet from the table and sat up straighter.

"You're acting like a petulant child," Fleur said as she crossed one leg over the other.

"I feel like a petulant child," I said with a sigh, running a hand through my hair. "I don't know what to do, Fleur. I've screwed up everything. I started drinking because I couldn't deal with the anniversary date, and then it just started spiraling from there."

"The anniversary date is the only reason you started drinking again?" Fleur asked, her soft accent soothing as she spoke. "Zane, I've watched you make it through other years without even considering picking up a bottle."

"I don't know. There's been a lot going on in my life the last few months."

"You hid your addiction from someone you cared about," Fleur said. "That takes a toll on you. It puts more stress on you, and you end up in an endless loop of what happens when they find out, and you can't tell them because they will be so hurt and disappointed and maybe angry."

"I really ruined things with her," I said, swallowing the lump in my throat.

"You did. But there's a quality about my daughter that I find amazing. She forgives people. Too often, sometimes. But no matter how bad you think you've ruined things with her, I can pretty much promise you that you haven't."

"I don't even know how to apologize to her."

"Don't worry about apologizing to her yet. We do not get sober for other people. It doesn't last. You have to want to get sober again for yourself. Do you want to?"

"It isn't that easy," I said, running my hands down my face. I didn't know what I was supposed to do. Drinking numbed the pain. I wanted the pain to keep being numb.

"You do know what to do," Fleur said. "You know that it's a

choice you have to make for yourself and nobody else. No matter what you choose, you know you're going to have my support."

"I appreciate that."

"I'm going to be honest with you," Fleur said, shifting on the couch and crossing her legs beneath her. "I want to see you want to get sober again, Zane. It wasn't easy the first time, and it isn't going to be easy this time."

"I haven't had a drink in two weeks."

"Good." Fleur nodded and pulled her phone out of her pocket, looking at something. She looked up at me with a small smile. "There's a meeting tonight."

"I don't know if I'm ready for that."

Fleur tucked her phone back in her pocket. "You don't have to go, but I think it would be a good idea even if you don't talk. Hearing how other people are struggling will make you feel like you're less alone in this battle."

I looked down at my hands, clenching and unclenching my fists. Part of me wanted to go to the meeting, and part of me didn't. I didn't want to hear how other people had it worse than I did, and I didn't want to talk about my own life. All I wanted to do was crawl back into my hole and start drinking again.

"Can we go now?" I asked, knowing that if she gave me more time to think about it, I wouldn't go.

"Go get ready, and we'll go for dinner before we go to the meeting."

Not for the first time, I was grateful that Fleur was in my life. She wasn't going to let me slip through the cracks, even if I wanted to head dive into them.

***

The morning after a meeting was easier for me than other mornings. I felt better after talking to the others and listening to them talk about going through the same struggles I was going through.

However, by the time it came time to head home from work, I was feeling horrible. Two patients needed an oncologist referral. Giving the news to someone that they needed to see a specialist and that I couldn't help them always hit me hard.

"Time to call it a day?" Van asked as he looked up from his filing. "You look like you've been having a horrible time."

"I'm fine," I said, gritting my teeth and putting the last of my files from the day on his desk.

"Are you?" Van asked, quirking one eyebrow. "Because based on the bottle of vodka I saw in your garbage the other day, you're not doing okay at all. Do you want to lose your practice?"

"It was a bottle from a few weeks ago. I haven't had a drink in fifteen days, and it's driving me insane, but I'm doing it."

"Good," Van said, his face brightening into a smile. "I'm glad you're taking care of yourself. You let me know if you need anything."

"Will do," I said, knowing that I wouldn't call him if I needed anything.

Van smiled and nodded, turning back to his work as I made my way to the door.

What I wanted to do after my shift was head to the bar and have a drink. Or go see Addie and beg for her forgiveness. Ask for her help. Fleur was right, though. I have to do this for me. I can't get sober again and have it all fall apart the moment she and I had another problem in our relationship.

If I'm doing this, it has to be for me. It has to be to save my own life.

On the way home, I stopped at the grocery store, craving something to drink. I walked up and down the two aisles filled with alcohol, looking for something that would suit my mood.

This is only a stage of life you're going through. Get your shit together and get out of here.

I sighed and ran my hand through my hair. I picked up a bottle and read the label, pretending that I cared about where the alcohol came from before putting it back on the shelf.

I can do this. Walk away.

After taking a deep breath, I turned and walked back to my truck. I got in and stared at the grocery store for a long time, considering going back in. I wanted to go back in. Everything in me was screaming at me to go back inside, pick a bottle of anything, and head home.

Instead, I started the engine and headed home. I wasn't going to give in to the cravings today. I had to be stronger than the cravings.

I'm doing this for me.

When I got home, I took the first bottle out of the lineup and poured it down the drain. Once I looked at the other bottles, I sank to the floor with my head in my hands. I wanted to pour out the rest of the bottles, but I couldn't get myself up off the floor to do it.

I need those bottles. I can't get rid of them yet. I need them. What if I need a drink?

I hated myself at that moment. I hated myself for needing to keep the alcohol and not being strong enough to dump them all.

After taking a deep breath, I pulled out my phone and sent Fleur a message.

She burst through my door a few moments later, sinking to the ground and pulling me into her arms. "It's okay. You're okay. You're not weak. You're so strong, Zane. You were able to pour out one of the bottles. That's more than you could have done yesterday. I'm so proud of you."

"I've never felt weaker," I said, a lump catching in my throat. I swallowed hard and took a deep breath. "Why couldn't I pour out all the bottles? Why do I feel like I still need them?"

"Because they gave you comfort when nothing else could, but you have so much more to live for now. You don't need those bottles sitting around and cluttering up your life, but you don't have to get rid of them until you're ready."

"That's okay?"

"Honey," Fleur said, holding me closer as tears dripped down my cheeks. "Whatever you need to do to heal is okay."

I nodded and took a deep breath. "Will you help me pour the rest of the bottles out? I don't think I can do it by myself."

"Absolutely," she said, getting up and helping me to my feet.

Together we poured out the bottles, watching as the liquid disappeared down the drain. I felt one step closer to my sobriety with every bottle we poured out. I was one step closer to getting better, and that's all it took.

Baby steps.

I could do this.

Chapter 10

Addie

Three weeks passed without a single word from Zane. I hadn't expected to hear anything from him, although I had hoped. I thought that he might reach out and say something once he started feeling better, but he didn't. There was no word from him. To be fair, I didn't reach out to him either.

I was busy sorting through classroom decorations when my mother walked into my apartment like it was her own home. I grinned at her and got up, wrapping her in a hug.

"You finally have time to decorate your classroom?" Mom asked as she took a seat on the floor and started picking through some of the decorations.

"In another week or two, I'm going in on one of the weekends. I just have to figure out what theme I want to have."

"Have you thought any more about going to see him?" Mom asked, picking up a drawing one of my students had done for me years ago.

"I've thought about it over and over again, Mom. I don't want to butt into his life, and I don't want to be around him if he's still drinking."

"You know, I've been in recovery for the last ten years, and it still doesn't get any easier."

The world fell out from beneath me as I looked at my mother. "I didn't know."

"It was easy to hide from you. Your last couple years of high school weren't spent at home much, and once you got into university, you barely came home. There was plenty of time to fight the alcohol addiction and get into recovery without ever having to have that conversation with me."

I ran my hand through my hair and stared up at my mother. It was a lot to take in all at once. I hadn't known that she was struggling with alcohol when I was in high school. I had been completely oblivious to it. There was no way that I should have missed that, but I did.

"I'm sorry I didn't know," I said, blinking back the tears that blurred my vision.

"I didn't want you to know," Mom said. "I hid it from you, but I got sober. I've been in recovery for the last ten years. I've turned my life around, but it wasn't easy. I almost screwed it up a few times. Don't be so hard on him. He's struggling in a way that I hope you will never fully understand."

"He lied to me, Mom."

"Addicts lie," she said, reaching out to brush a strand of hair back from my face. "He's been sober for twenty-one days. He's going to meetings every day. He's working hard to get himself okay again."

"Why are you telling me that?" I shook my head. "He doesn't want me around. He told me to get out."

"Addie, the way you look at him tells me all I need to know about how you feel about him. And he told you to get out because he's ashamed."

I crossed my legs and stared down at the mess of decorations in front of me. It seemed easier to look at them than to try and look at my mother while I processed everything.

The way I felt for Zane *was* unlike anything I had ever felt for anybody else, but I didn't know that it had been that obvious.

"How's he doing other than trying to stay sober?" I asked, looking up at her.

"He's not doing great. He misses you just as much as you miss him. He knows that you have to do what's best for you, though."

I nodded and changed the subject, talking about possible classroom things with her instead of talking about Zane. Talking about him hurt too much. I didn't give him a chance before walking out on him. I knew what addicts were like, and I still walked away when he was screaming for help.

Guilt twisted and turned my stomach. I kept a hold of my emotions until my mom left, and I was finally alone. As soon as she was gone, I raced to my room and got changed.

I should have been helping Zane when he needed me the most. Instead, I had let him push me away, thinking his addiction would turn him into a monster like my ex-husband. I had closed my eyes to everything I knew about Zane and pretended that he was a different person entirely.

I left him on his own to fight.

As soon as I was dressed, I grabbed my keys and drove to his place. The entire drive, I drummed my fingers on the wheel, trying to think of what I was going to say to him when I got there. An apology seemed like a good place to start, but I didn't know what would come after that.

Would I ask him to forgive me for leaving him when he needed me?

Would I send him spiraling into a drinking binge that would ruin his sobriety?

Would we decide that there was no saving what we had already lost?

There was no way to know what would happen unless I got out of the car, marched myself up to his door, and demanded that he talk to me no matter what the outcome might be. He and I both needed some sort of future or closure. No matter how our conversation went, we couldn't just leave things hanging in the air and wait for whatever came next.

After I took a deep breath and tried to convince myself that this wouldn't be the worst conversation of the year, I walked to the door and rang the bell. I could hear movement on the other side of the door, and I was sure that Zane was looking at me through the peephole. I shifted my weight from one side to the other.

When the door opened, my breath caught in my throat. Zane's cheeks were hollow, and there were dark bags beneath his eyes. I looked him over, looking at the way his clothes hung loosely off his body.

"How are you doing?" I asked, looking over him again. He was paler than he was before, and he looked exhausted.

"Better than I was."

I nodded, my mouth going dry as my heart raced. "I'm sorry."

"I don't think you have any reason to be sorry," he said, giving me a small smile. "I'm the one who kicked you out and lied to you."

"And I'm the one who didn't ask you what was wrong or offer to help you. I think we've both got things to apologize for right now."

"I'm sorry, Addie."

"Well, now that we've both said we're sorry, I want to know how to help you. Can you explain everything to me?" I rubbed the back of my neck and shifted my weight again, feeling my cheeks warm up. "If you're comfortable talking about it."

"Come in," he said, opening the door wider.

When he opened the door, I saw a box of my belongings sitting on the entryway table. A sharp pain radiated through my chest as I looked at everything I had left with him condensed into a small box. It seemed so final, like nothing that I could say or do at this point would help us recover.

"I didn't know when you would come to get those things," Zane said, his voice a little more than a whisper as he looked down at me. "You didn't come and get them for so long that I thought there was still some hope, but now you're here."

"I'm not here to leave you again," I said, looking up at him. "I'm here to be with you in whatever way you need right now."

He nodded, his jaw tense as he led the way to the couches. He sat down on one, leaving the other for me. I sat down and tried to calm my racing heart as I waited for him to say something first. The indecision was clear on his face. His mouth opened and closed several times without anything coming out.

"Whatever you need to say to me about what happened or what will happen, just say it. I want everything out in the open, so we can start working through it."

"I need a partner, Addie. Someone who isn't going to run when I start struggling with my alcohol addiction."

"And I need a partner who isn't going to lie to me or hide things from me when they're struggling. I want to be there for you, Zane, but I can't be there if you don't let me know what's happening."

"We've both made a mess of things between us, haven't we?"

"Yes, we have," I said, pulling my legs up to sit cross-legged on the couch. "That's why I'm asking you what you need me to do to help you get through this."

Zane didn't meet my eyes once as he looked around the room. He twisted his hands in his lap. I held my breath, waiting for him to speak. I needed him to tell me that there was a way we could work through this.

"This is new ground for both of us," he said before wincing. "Well, maybe not you."

"It is new," I said. "Your addiction and your problems are not the same as somebody else's."

Zane took a deep breath and nodded. "Well then, you should probably know more about why I broke my sobriety."

"Whatever you're willing to tell me."

He got up and sat on the couch beside me, twisting slightly in his seat to face me. I shifted my own position, leaning back against the arm of the couch and looking at him.

"The anniversary is always hard for me, but most years, I can handle it. I do everything I can to stay busy, so I don't have time to think about the bottle. This year, I got an email from the girl's father. I'm not going to go into all the details about it, but he was basically blaming me for the loss of his daughter and telling me about the other ways I destroyed his family."

"It was an accident, though. Surgeries go wrong, and patients die," I said, reaching out to put my hand on his knee. "You couldn't have controlled the situation."

"There's a lot I could have done differently."

"There's a lot anybody could have done differently in any given situation. It doesn't mean that it's going to change the outcome."

His lips twitched. "You sound like my sponsor."

"Well, my mom is a smart woman."

"She told you."

I nodded. "She told me."

Zane sighed and put his hand over mine, squeezing it lightly. "After getting that email, I started to spiral even more out of control. At night I was restless. I couldn't sleep, and even if I managed to fall asleep for a few hours, all I could see was Lily's face after the life drained out of her. All I could hear were her parents' screams as I told them that their daughter had died."

"How are you feeling right now?" I asked, flipping my hand over and lacing my fingers through his. "Are you alright talking about this?"

"I want to go get a drink, but it's nothing that I can't handle right now."

"What do you need from me?"

He looked hesitant as he squeezed my hand again. "Will you come with me to a meeting tonight?"

"Of course," I said as I kneeled in front of him and pulled him into a tight hug.

Zane held onto me, his arms tight around my waist as I heard his first sob. He buried his face in my neck and fell apart. I stayed in his embrace, willing to hold him together until he could hold himself together.

"I'm here for you. We're going to get through this, and I'm going to support you through it all."

Chapter 11

Zane

I flipped the sixty-day sobriety chip over in my hand. It wasn't the first time that I had earned the chip, but it didn't make it any less important. I had made it sixty days without taking a single drink. I had done the impossible, and I was coming out on the other side.

Even as I looked at the chip, I knew that I could only take it one day at a time. I wanted to get better, but thinking about anything more than tomorrow made my stomach toss and turn.

All I had to do was make it one more day sober and then another day after that.

It was going to take time, as Fleur liked to constantly remind me when we talked. She offered her time and supported me the same way she had when she helped me get sober the first time.

Addie had gone with me to every single meeting since we reconnected. Even on the nights I didn't want her to come in with me, she sat in the truck or her car and waited for me to come back out. She showed up at my house early in the mornings. She had stayed over to go running. When she said she was going to be there for me, she meant it.

"Congratulations," Addie said as she met me outside. Snow started falling down around us as she hugged me tightly.

I dipped my head down to kiss her before we walked back to the truck. She had been asking me about the blankets and pillows in the back of the truck for the better part of the day, but I hadn't told her. It had taken me a few days to plan the surprise for her, and I wasn't going to let her ruin that surprise by asking a million questions.

"Let's go to dinner to celebrate," Addie said as we got in the truck. "My treat."

"We don't have to do that," I said as I started the engine.

I smiled despite what I said. I was happy that she wanted to celebrate the little things, but it didn't feel like that big of an accomplishment. I was only sixty days sober after having four years of sobriety under my belt.

It was bittersweet.

"I want to if you want to. We should celebrate your successes."

She was right, even if I had mixed feelings about it.

"It's only sixty days sober."

"And it's an accomplishment that you fought for. Now, stop arguing with me and take me to wherever you want to eat for dinner."

I laughed as I shook my head, warmth spreading through my body as I drove down to my favorite diner. Addie sang along with the radio, drumming her fingers on the armrest and bobbing her head. As I glanced at her, I knew that I was head over heels for her.

When we got to the diner, Addie stood in the parking lot for a few minutes, tilting her head back and looking up at the falling snow. I stood behind her, wrapping my arms around her and kissing her cheek.

"Come on, I'm starving, and I have a surprise for you that we can't miss."

"Oh, really?" Addie asked, smiling at me as she wriggled her way out of my embrace and took my hand. "Let's go eat then."

"Well," I said, pulling her back to me. She wrapped her arms around my neck, pressing herself closer to me. "There's something you should know first."

"And what might that be?"

"I love you," I said, brushing a strand of hair behind her ear. "I know we've only known each other for a few months, but I love you so damn much."

"I love you too," Addie said, standing up on her toes and pressing her lips against mine.

I kissed her back, pulling her as close to my body as she could get. When we pulled apart, she looked like she was floating on air as we walked into the diner. As I watched her enter the diner, I could imagine walking into the diner with her every week for the rest of our lives.

***

"Are you finally going to tell me what we're doing out here?" Addie asked as I parked at a lookoff.

It was dark out, but the snow had stopped falling. We were in the mountains at one of my favorite places in the world. The lookoff was a safe place for me. Somewhere I came whenever I needed some time alone to think about major decisions in my life.

"You can see so much of the valley from here," Addie said, walking toward the edge of the lookoff. She leaned against the railing and looked down. "Come over here with me. You have to see this view."

"In a minute," I said, reaching into the back of the truck and digging out the blankets and pillows. I tossed them onto the bed of the truck, spreading them out before joining her at the railing.

"So, why are we up here?"

"There's a meteor shower that should be happening soon. We will cuddle in the back of my truck to make some wishes on shooting stars."

"They're not really shooting stars, though."

"Shush, woman," I said, picking her up and tossing her over my shoulder. I smacked her ass as I carried her to the truck. Addie laughed as I lowered her onto the tailgate and stood between her legs.

"I love you," she whispered.

I grinned and kissed her. Our mouths slanted together as her legs circled my waist. I moaned as she pressed herself against the erection straining against my jeans. She rolled her hips, pressing harder against me.

"The meteor shower is about to start," she said, pulling away from me to point at the sky. I looked up and saw the first few meteors begin to fall.

"Good," I said as she drew away from me and crawled further into the bed of the truck, leaning into the pillows. I crawled after her, hovering over her body.

Heat burned bright in her eyes as she reached for the zipper on my jacket. Snow started falling around us as we shed our clothes. When she was naked, I kissed my way down her body until I got to her breasts. I took one nipple in my mouth, tweaking the other as her nails raked down my back. I groaned as her fingers threaded through my hair, pulling my face up to hers.

I reached between us, toying with her clit as I kissed her, our tongues tangling. She nipped at my lips, smoothing her tongue over the stinging sensation before working her way down to my neck.

As she kissed my neck, she gripped my cock. I nearly came in her hand as she stroked me, smoothing her thumb over the head. She stroked me in time with me thrusting my fingers in her wetness, wriggling as her orgasm started to build. When I looked down at her, seeing the expression on her face, it only made me harder.

"Fuck, baby," I moaned, pulling back from her slightly. I grabbed her hands and pinned them above her head, the head of my cock against her entrance.

As I slid inside her, she arched her back. I grabbed a pillow and lifted her hips, stuffing it beneath them before thrusting. When I let go of her hands, she held onto me, her nails raking down my back again.

I kissed my way back down to her breasts as I was thrusting. She writhed against me as I nipped at her nipples before taking one into my mouth. As I sucked and nipped her, she bucked against me.

When I slipped one hand between us to play with her clit, she came apart again, my name on her lips. I groaned, grabbing her hip, and thrusting harder until I came.

"I missed that," she said as I lay beside her.

"Me too," I said.

I pulled the blankets over us before pulling her against my body. Addie sighed as she nestled against me, looking up at the night sky.

Meteors were falling all around us, bright streaks against the sky. I kissed Addie's temple, holding her against me tighter.

"I can't believe you brought me up here to watch meteors," Addie said, kissing my shoulder. "I love it. Nobody has ever done anything like this for me before."

"We can come up here and stare at the stars as much as you like."

"Promise," she asked, looking up at me.

"I promise."

Addie snuggled against me again, her hand moving softly up and down the planes of my stomach. I wrapped my arms tighter around her, holding her closer. She was everything that I had ever wanted and more. Everything would be alright if I kept her safe in my arms. We would be alright, even after all that we had gone through at the beginning of our relationship.

"Make a wish," Addie whispered, her voice soft.

I could make a million different wishes, but all of them had something to do with her. Everything that had to do with our future together flashed through my mind. They were all wishes that I hoped would come true, but I couldn't settle on any of those ideas.

Instead, I settled on what was true at that moment.

"I wish that this night would never end."

Addie smiled and propped herself up on one arm to look down at me. "We're going to have thousands of nights even better than this one."

Chapter 12

Addie

It had taken several weeks, but I finally had a time when I could drag in all my classroom decorations. Of course, it was while the students were all on Christmas break, but that didn't matter to me. I would have a new classroom by the time they came back after the new year. We would be able to start entirely fresh. It would be new and exciting for the kindergarteners, and I couldn't wait.

Tearing down the old decorations had taken most of the morning, even with Zane helping me. He gathered the pieces of paper and broken supplies, tossing them into the garbage as I sorted through the things I didn't want that could be given to other teachers.

"So," Zane said as he carried the last garbage bag to the door. "What is the theme going to be?"

"I'm thinking jungle safari," I said, abandoning my donation pile to rifle through the decorations I had brought with me. "Look at how cute this is."

Zane looked at the cut-out of a tiger and chuckled. "That thing is massive. Where are you even going to put it?"

I grinned and took the tiger over to the wall beneath the whiteboard. It stood as tall as an actual tiger, and I had spent more money on it than I was willing to admit. The money didn't matter, though. I loved seeing the smiles on the kids' faces. I could already see the smiles on their faces as we picked a name for the tiger together.

"Right here," I said, holding it up against the wall. "They're going to go insane when they see it."

Zane grabbed the stapler I had tossed on one of the tables. He handed it to me and took my place, holding the front half of the tiger against the wall. I started stapling it in place, laughing as Zane pretended that he was trying to hold a wild tiger back.

"You're crazy," I said after I put the last staple into the tiger.

Zane wrapped his arms around me and pulled me to him. "Crazy about you."

I stood on my toes and kissed him, shaking my head when his hands slipped into my back pockets. "You know, once the new year comes, I'm about to get busier teaching. I'll have to work on lesson plans more at night."

"You can work on lesson plans all you want," he said. "I might even learn how to cook something other than boxed mac and cheese, so you don't have to worry about feeding us every night."

Laughing, I pulled away from him. "You don't have to do that. I like cooking."

"I want to do that, Addie. We're partners, remember? You're going to support me, and I'm going to support you. Either way, at my age, I should know how to cook something other than meat on a grill and mac and cheese."

"Alright," I said, going back to my donation pile. "I'll teach you how to cook if you agree to help me move once I find a new place."

"When are you moving?" he asked.

"My lease ends next month. It was only a short one since I didn't know whether I was going to buy a house or not."

"Well, if you're looking for somewhere to live, I know a place. It's beautiful. Backs right onto the woods. It's about a forty-minute drive away from town, though."

"It sounds nice," I said. "But I don't know if I could afford the mortgage on a house right now on my own."

"Who said you would be on your own?" Zane asked as he wrapped his arm around me. "Do you want to go see the place?"

"Can we go after we're done setting everything up? I really want to get the room done today so we can enjoy the rest of Christmas break together."

"Of course," he said, digging into the donation pile and helping me sort through it. "Let's get everything done, and then we can go."

He and I worked through the pile of decorations, stapling them to the walls until my classroom looked like it had been turned into a jungle safari. Toucans and monkeys were placed up high, spreading their wings and flying through the tree cut-outs.

"It looks amazing," I said, grinning as I pulled Zane into a tight hug. "Thank you so much for helping me."

"Addie, I'd do anything for you. You know that, right?"

I smiled up at him and ran my fingers along his jaw. "I'm starting to see that."

"Why don't we go take a look at that house I was telling you about?"

I nodded and took his hand, pulling him to the door. Even if I couldn't afford the house, it wouldn't hurt to start getting ideas about what I wanted when I searched for another place.

Besides, his excitement was contagious.

***

My mouth dropped when Zane turned off the highway and into a driveway. The entire front of the property was lined with trees, as was the winding driveway that worked its way toward the house.

As the house came into view, I started falling in love. The front of the house was almost entirely made of glass and white stone. It was stunning. The house looked like it had been designed specifically for this property.

"Want to go inside?" Zane asked as he stopped the truck and pulled a key out of his pocket.

"How did you get a key to this place?"

"Well, I might have bought it and finished building it a few months ago. I wasn't quite ready to move into it yet, but if your lease is ending and you want to, you could come live here with me."

"You want me to move in with you?" I asked, not quite believing what he was saying.

"Of course," he said, getting out of the truck. He rounded the front of the truck and opened my door, helping me out. "I would love if you came to live with me."

I grinned and kissed him. "I would love to live with you."

"Then let me show you the rest of our new house."

Zane took me by the hand and led me to the backyard. There was a pool, a hot tub, a massive patio, and a deck, both filled with patio furniture and meant for entertaining. The property backed onto the woods, a trail starting at the treeline.

When we went inside, I nearly squealed. The floors were pale, and the walls were dark and moody. The walls were almost entirely glass. The kitchen was huge, and it overlooked the backyard.

Zane led me to the master bedroom, and I fell in love with the bathroom attached to it. The large tub sat beside a wall made of windows that overlooked the forest.

"Do you want to see the other bedrooms?" he asked as he laced his fingers through mine.

"There's more?"

He nodded. "Of course, there is. I want to have children someday. I want a big family with kids and dogs and any other animal you want."

Tears blurred my vision as I smiled at him. "Kids, dogs, cats, and maybe a couple of chickens."

Zane laughed and pulled me into a tight hug. "I'll call around tomorrow and find out if Van knows anyone that makes a good chicken coop. Knowing him, he probably does."

"We're really going to do this?" I asked, looking at him and wondering how long he had been thinking about this.

"We're really going to do this," Zane said. He stepped out of the hug and took my hand again. "I have something else to show you out back on that little trail."

We walked across the property to the trailhead. Zane led the way down the trailhead, talking about the furniture shopping we were going to need to do. Between the two of us, we could fill some of the rooms but not all of them. I grinned, already picturing how I was going to decorate the nursery.

Zane stopped along the path and led me several feet off the trail and into a small clearing. Flower petals were scattered across the snow, and there was a pair of benches with a fire pit in the middle.

"This is ours too?" I asked, looking around at the little clearing. I could already see lights draped through the surrounding trees and nights spent out here falling more in love with each other than we already were.

"Yeah, it is." He kissed my cheek. "Now close your eyes and wait until I tell you to open them again."

"There's more?" I asked, my eyes wide.

"Close your eyes, Addie."

I laughed and did as he said, waiting as the cold air seeped through my jacket. I shifted my weight from side to side, trying to keep warm as I heard rustling behind me.

"Open your eyes," he said. "And then turn around."

I opened my eyes and turned around, my hands flying to cover my mouth as I looked down at him. Zane was on one knee with a little velvet box open in his hand. There was a ring nestled inside the box, gleaming in the last rays of sunlight.

"Addie Manning, I fell in love with you a thousand times since the day I found you in that hole. I knew months ago that I would never love another woman the way I loved you. Hell, I couldn't picture my life without you. I know this is soon, but when you know, you know. I've never been any more certain of anything in my life."

"Yes!" I squealed, nearly knocking him into the snow as I hugged and kissed him tightly.

Zane was laughing when I pulled away. "You didn't even let me ask the question."

"Doesn't matter," I said before kissing him again. "I knew I wanted to spend the rest of my life with you months ago."

"Still," he said, brushing a strand of hair behind my ear. "I want to do this properly."

"Then ask," I said, cupping his face in my hands. "I've never loved someone the way I love you."

"Addie, will you marry me?"

"Yes!"

Zane's grin could have lit up the darkest corners of the world as he smiled and slipped the ring on my finger. I looked down at it, smiling before I kissed him again.

"Can we get out of the cold now and go home?" I asked as we stood up.

"Or," he said, his hot breath grazing across my ear as he hugged me from behind. "We could go start christening the new house. I was thinking we could start with the kitchen."

I grinned and leaned back into him. "Race you there?"

"You're on."

We took off running through the snow, laughing and shouting like we were children again. I had never been happier in my life.

When we got back to the house, he swept me into his arms and carried me to the kitchen, ready to start the rest of our lives together.

Epilogue

Zane

Two and a half years later

Smoke from the barbecue scented the warm summer air. Music was playing softly in the background as our family and friends celebrated the end of summer and the start of a new little life in the town.

"That smells delicious," Addie said as she walked over to me, nestling into my side. Her hand drifted down to her stomach. I grinned as I kissed her temple. "I could eat a dozen of them."

"Should I make another dozen of them for the baby too?"

Addie laughed and elbowed my side. "Funny. As much as I could eat twelve burgers, I don't think I'm going to. My stomach is in knots."

"It's only a gender reveal," I said, running my fingers through her hair. "We're going to find out whether we're having a little boy or girl."

"Your mom is going to lose her mind if we have a boy," Addie said, glancing over at my mother, who was wandering around my backyard and telling everyone who would listen that we had to be having a son.

"I'll be happy as long as we have a healthy baby."

She nodded and leaned closer to my side, her head leaning into my chest. I ran my fingers along her hip, the feeling of her dress silky and smooth. As I stood there with her, I knew that life had worked out exactly how it was meant to be.

"How do you feel with the anniversary coming up in a few months?" Addie asked.

"I'm doing okay. It's getting easier. We'll see three years sober."

Addie smiled and reached up to run her fingers along my jaw. I leaned into her touch as I smiled down at her.

"I'm so proud of you and all you've accomplished," Addie said. "I don't know how we wouldn't have gotten this far otherwise."

"I'm just happy that you came back and stuck around."

"I'm happy that you let me in and let me love you. And that we only have four more months until we get to meet our little baby."

"Speaking of the baby," Fleur said as she appeared out of nowhere. "Why don't we go cut the cake and see what the baby's going to be now?"

"Can't hold back, can you?" Addie asked, her tone teasing as she left me to loop her arm through her mother's. "Lead the way to the cake!"

I followed my wife of nearly a year and a half to the cake, grinning at how she waddled with her pregnant belly. Together we stood beside the cake. People were laughing and talking as they all made predictions about the baby.

"Are you ready?" I asked, wrapping my arm around Addie's waist as she picked up the knife.

"Not even a little bit," Addie said, a line appearing between her eyebrows. "What if I'm not a good mother?"

"You're going to be an amazing mother. Now, cut the cake and tell me that I was right about having a girl."

Addie rolled her eyes, but her smile grew. She cut a thick slice out of the white cake and pulled it out, revealing a pink interior.

"I was right," I whispered as tears started rolling down her cheeks.

"It's a girl!" she yelled, grinning from ear to ear.

Our families and friends cheered as Addie put down the piece of cake and the knife. She turned to kiss me, tears still streaming down her face. My vision was blurry as we pulled apart to a sea of people rushing to congratulate us.

I had never felt surrounded by more love.

If anybody had told me three years ago that I would meet and marry the woman of my dreams, I wouldn't have believed them. I thought I was destined to be alone for everything I had done. My life had only been getting worse before she walked in and changed everything for me.

Now, as I held her in my arms with our baby on the way, I knew that life could only get better.

Mountain Man Handyman (Book 4)

Blurb
Della left Kipsty Little Town searching for something more, breaking her first love's heart. Greer had finally found a rhythm in life that worked for him until a curvy reminder of the past swept back in.

Della
I made my dream come true in the Big Apple, carving out a career that I loved. I had even found love and was moving on. Until it all started unraveling. Realization struck. My Nanna passed away. My fiancé betrayed me. And I was spiraling. I needed to find my center, and I knew the small mountain town that could help me get through it. Home. But now that I was back, I wondered why I left in the first place and whether a certain mountain man would ever forgive me.

Greer
Della left because of me. I was sure of it. I did what I could and tried to move on. Even got married. Then that failed. And now I know why. When I saw Della in her grandma's cabin after more than a decade apart, memories of us together flooded back. The cabin was unliveable, and her only option was to move in with me for a few days. Which turned into weeks. Then months. Alone with her. I've been dreaming about this for years. But I could never go there with her. Not if she was planning on up and leaving me again. Could I be wrong?

Prologue

Della

"I can't do this anymore," I whispered, my eyes wet. I looked at Greer, his expression marred by a frown. He was just as upset. I could see it in the redness rimming his eyes. He was angry, too, and I couldn't really blame him.

"Do what?" he asked, throwing his arms up in defeat. "Be with me?"

It'd been a year since his parents died, and while I helped him through it as best I could, I could no longer pretend I was happy. But he wouldn't understand. He already thought my decision had something to do with him when it didn't. Not really.

I licked my lips. They were wet and salty from my tears. I was trying my hardest to stem them, not when it felt like my heart was shattering inside my chest. I attempted to inhale a full breath, but I couldn't manage that either.

Greer pulled his hand through his hair, visibly confused and frustrated, and I couldn't, in any way, blame him for how he was feeling.

"I need more, Greer. This..." I waved my hand around my grandmother's cabin, "...isn't enough anymore." Nanna's cabin was a metaphor, though, for Kipsty Little Town itself, the small town we called home.

Greer expelled an angry sigh, looking between me and my

luggage. I was planning on leaving before he came home, which I realized may have been cowardly, but I wanted to spare us this pain. I didn't have the courage to face Greer before I left, and had written him a note instead, but he surprised me by coming home early for the weekend. He was studying Landscape Architecture at Colorado University and could only manage to come home on a Friday afternoon and stay for the weekend. It was another reason I couldn't keep doing this and why I needed to leave. He was at school all week, and it felt as though all I really did was wait for him to come so we could spend a morsel of time together.

"Is it me?" he asked. His voice cracked, making me feel worse than I already did. I wasn't only breaking my 18-year-old heart. I was breaking his too. And as much as it killed me, I couldn't keep lying to myself anymore.

Kipsty Little Town had become too small.

I'd lived here my whole life, and all I'd ever really wanted was to leave and find something bigger. And, to some degree, something better, I guess. I felt trapped here, stuck on a hamster wheel that kept spinning without going anywhere. If I tried to explain to Greer the restlessness that had resided under my skin, and in my veins, for the last year, he wouldn't understand.

I took a step toward him, and he matched it by taking a step away from me. The physical distance between us hurt. I loved him with every part of me, but our emotional distance was fraught with tightly bound tension on the verge of snapping us in two. And that, I realized, was what hurt the most. I had loved this boy from the time I was fifteen, he'd been my first everything, and it brought me no pleasure at all to inflict any kind of hurt on him.

But three years later, I had to do what was best for me, and this town, staying here, was not it. But Greer wasn't listening to me. This had almost nothing to do with him, yet in his eyes, I was leaving because of him. That couldn't be further from the cold, hard truth.

"It's not about you," I replied, swiping at the tears sliding down my cheeks. I had to find a way to pull myself together and stay strong in my own conviction. "I love you," I told him fervently. "I'm in love with you. But I can't stay here, Greer. I'm unhappy, and I'm not like you. I can't see my future in this godforsaken podunk town. I want more for my life than being stuck here and living the same life my grandmother has lived."

My life in Kipsty wasn't bad. It had never been. I was raised by a very strong woman who profoundly influenced the woman I'd become. And as much as it hurt my grandmother to see me leave, she understood, better than anyone, why I was doing it. My mother did the same thing when she was my age, except she showed up back here a year later with me in tow and dropped me off on my grandmother's porch. She never stuck around after that. And as much as I hated to admit it, the same restiveness that filled her spirit, existed in me, and it was about the only thing she gave me, besides my blonde hair, blue eyes, and curvy build.

Greer winced, and I watched him withdraw from me. It was like experiencing the loss of air in your lungs. And I was cold without him. Chilled to my marrow. He unknowingly took my air and heat and stepped away. The withdrawal was acute, and I felt it in every cell in my body. But I wouldn't cave. I wouldn't change my mind, and I think he was starting to realize that.

"Then I guess there's not much left for me to say," he told me quietly. For the briefest moment, he closed the gaping space between us, held my head between his strong and steady hands, kissed my forehead, and inhaled my scent one last time. I reveled in that affection, knowing it would most likely be the last.

"I hope you find what you're looking for, Del. I really do."

He stepped back and gave me one last look, his green eyes red and filled with so much I couldn't quite put a name to. He shook his head and walked towards the front door of the cabin I'd lived in my whole life. It was filled to the brim with memories. Memories I'd also have to leave behind once I was gone. It wouldn't serve me to hold on to anything if I wanted to move forward. The memories I'd keep were those of Nanna and me because they'd get me through the hard times ahead.

Greer glanced at me from over his shoulder and opened his mouth as if he had something else to say, but instead, he walked out and shut the door. I collapsed against the back of the sofa, and a sob escaped from between my lips. I slapped my hand over my mouth to smother the sound, but it was difficult when it felt like my lungs weren't working.

The pain in my chest intensified, and I looked up just in time to see my grandmother, Delia, stop between the living room and the kitchen. Without uttering a word, she opened her arms, and I rushed to her, seeking the kind of comfort only she could give me.

"I think I broke my own heart, Nanna," I cried, my head on her shoulder. She wrapped her arms around me, rubbing her hand over my back. "He'll never forgive me."

"Hush now," she replied. "You knew this was the hard part, Della." She pushed me back, hands on my shoulders. "You know in your heart of hearts that you won't be happy if you stay, and you'll only end up resenting that boy if you stay for him. You understand, baby girl?"

I nodded and swallowed the knot of tangled emotions clogging my throat. "Leaving you is hard, too," I told her. And it was. She raised me, gave me a beautiful life, and made sure I turned out to be a decent human being. Everyone in town loved her, but I was so damn lucky she was my family. I was who I was because she made me.

"I know," she replied gently. "But I want you to be happy, Della. You've been a dreamer your whole life, and I'd never stand in the way of those big dreams just to keep you here with me." Her eyes glossed over, and she sniffled. "I love you more than life itself, Della Marie, and I'm so proud of who you are." She dropped a kiss on my cheek. "The bus will be here soon," she reminded me. "Promise me you'll call when you get there, okay?"

"I promise." I threw my arms around her delicate frame and

held her close, breathing in the scent of cinnamon and sugar. "I love you."

"I love you more," she whispered. We parted, and she helped me carry my luggage to the car before she drove me to the bus stop outside town. I didn't look back when I boarded that bus.

I wish I had.

Chapter 1

Della

Mid-December, 11 years later

I shivered next to my car and held my phone up in an attempt to get some decent cell reception. But I was in the Colorado mountains, and it was snowing. The flurry of white snowflakes whirled around me, and I glanced at my car. I was driving up the mountain when I swerved for a squirrel, *a squirrel*, and now my poor Lexus was in a ditch on the edge of a curve in the road.

Sigh.

You'd think a Lexus SUV could handle a wet road and some snow, but it turns out that even the flashiest of vehicles eventually succumbed to bad weather. The worst part was there was no traffic on this road, not this deep into the mountains. I huffed out a frustrated breath, the hot air coming out in a puff. There was little I could do at this point except hope that someone would be coming up this road.

I tried getting my car out of the ditch, but the wheels spun on the wet ground, making it worse. I was capable in many ways but getting a car out of a ditch was beyond what I could do. I climbed back into my car, holding my useless phone in my hands as I tried to stay warm. I didn't want to leave the car idling for long, so I'd turned the ignition off an hour ago. My only option was to wait.

My head hit the headrest, and I squeezed my eyes closed. It was a freak accident, but it was easy to assume it would only happen to me because I was making my way to my hometown after eleven years. Though I was here just over a year ago for Nanna's funeral, but I didn't stay long. And now her cabin was mine. Along with the diner she owned on Main Street.

The whirr of an engine rose above the sound of the wind, and when I glanced in my rearview mirror, I saw a navy-blue Ford Ranger pickup truck rounding the corner. I scrambled to get out of my car and wave down whoever was driving. I couldn't see a face through the falling snow, but I needed help, and this was the first vehicle I'd seen since my car enthusiastically went nose-first into the ditch.

The pickup slowed to stop in front of me, and I exhaled a breath of relief. I waited for the driver to climb out, and I sucked in a breath when he did—shock black hair, muscular build, and brown eyes with sharp brows when he faced me.

"Della Marie, is that you?" he asked, the pitch of his voice high.

"Kyle?" I asked, brows furrowed. "You know I don't like being called that."

"Well I'll be damned," he murmured under his breath. "Same old sass, I see." He walked closer and surprised me when he picked me up and spun me around. I surprised myself when a laugh broke free from between my lips. He put me down and looked me up and down.

"Damn, you look good," he remarked, his lips tilted in a friendly smile. My lips were stiff, but I did my best to return it. He was my first blast from the past, yet another person I'd hurt the day I left. He was Greer's best friend, but we were just as close growing up seeing as we were in the same age group. He'd since grown into his muscular build and had that whole lumberjack thing going on.

He glanced between me and my car. "You need some help?"

"I, uh, got myself stuck in a ditch," I replied. "Forgot how tricky this stretch of road can be."

When he took a proper look at my car, he whistled. "With a car like that, you shouldn't have a hard time on these roads." I was too embarrassed to explain how I landed myself in this situation, so I didn't.

"Think you can get me out?" I asked instead. He scratched the side of his face and blew out a breath while checking my car. "Doesn't look like there's any damage, but I don't have a tow kit in my car. You headed into Kipsty?"

Like I'd be going anywhere else if I was on this damn road.

"Yeah." I sighed. "I've been stuck here for an hour, though. You're the first person I've seen."

"Well…" he looked between me and my car again, "…I can take you into town myself, and come back for your car. That work for you?" I knew the chances of my car being stolen around here were next to nil, but I was still hesitant. However, I was wholly aware that I had no other choice.

"If you won't mind, I'd appreciate it."

Kyle nodded once, and I popped open the back of my car. He looked at my luggage with raised brows. "You moving back or something?"

"Or something," I muttered under my breath.

He chuckled. "I know a whole lot of people who will be surprised to see you, Della. That's for sure."

Rather than respond—I didn't want to think about how *anyone* was going to react when they saw me pull in—I started lifting my suitcases out of my car and wheeling them over to Kyle's pickup. Between the two of us, it took about ten minutes. I grabbed my purse and locked my car before climbing into the passenger side of Kyle's pickup. He turned the key and drove back onto the slick roads. Unlike me, Kyle had chains on his tires, dramatically improving his grip on snow-covered tar.

Not one to sit in silence, Kyle gave me a sidelong look. "So, you never answered my question. You moving back to Kipsty or what?"

There was no getting around this. I blew out a hard breath. "Yeah," I replied quietly. "I'm taking Nanna's cabin."

He chortled and shook his head. "Never thought I'd see the day that you would come back to Kipsty Little Town. And for good, too." I didn't bother correcting his assumption about how long I'd be staying. I was still deciding.

After my life in New York fell apart at the seams, I just needed a place I could run away to, and Nanna's cabin seemed an obvious choice.

"We've all been waiting for a *for sale* sign to pop up," Kyle continued. I looked at his profile, noting how much he had changed. But I supposed time does that to all of us. Life experience too. We all had to grow up eventually. "Most of us were sure you'd sell it."

The thought of selling Nanna's cabin had a band tightening around my chest. I may have left Kipsty when I was eighteen with no intention of ever coming back, but, "I'd never *ever* sell Nanna's cabin." Which was now *my* cabin.

He huffed out a laugh. "You might feel differently when you see it."

"What does that mean?"

Kyle rested his elbow on the door and looked over. "We've had a few nasty storms over the past few weeks. Last I checked, Nanna Delia's cabin had a tree fall on the roof, and you now have a hole in the living room. Not sure you'd actually be able to stay there until it's fixed." My heart plummeted into my stomach.

"Is it bad?" I asked, a lilt to my voice that sounded a whole lot like panic. I had no one in town who could have let me know in advance about the state of the cabin. "Can I stay at the inn?" I asked. The last time I was in town, the inn was still there.

Kyle shook his head just as we rounded another bend and turned left onto the road that led straight into Kipsty. "Inn's full," he replied. "Wedding party, I think."

It wasn't unheard of to have weddings here. It was actually

quite beautiful, especially for a winter wedding. I fiddled with my fingers, partly because I was worried about where I was going to stay. I was suddenly nervous being back here after so long.

Kyle drove down Main Street and headed towards the cabins. He stopped his truck outside mine and climbed out to help with my luggage. While he unloaded my suitcases, I walked up the porch steps and yelped when the wood beneath my feet gave way. I slipped and fell on my ass, my foot stuck between where the wood had splintered. Kyle rushed over and helped me stand.

"You okay?" I rotated my ankle and gave him a nod.

"Fine," I sighed. "You weren't kidding about the state of this place."

I unlocked the front door, and the faint smell of pine, cinnamon, and sugar tickled my nose. Even though it had been over a year since my grandmother had passed away, it still smelled like her. "You weren't kidding about the roof," I murmured under my breath.

Kyle walked in, wheeling my suitcases in behind him, and stopped next to me. "We've been trying to fix all the cabins that the storms have hit, but it's a lot for just me and..." He stopped talking and cleared his throat, rubbing the back of his neck.

"You and?" I prodded.

His expression was reticent, as if he didn't want to say more. I stared at him expectantly. "Say it, Kyle, how bad could—"

"Me and Greer," he interrupted, his expression changing to one of concern. My heart flopped around at the sound of his name, and I had to admit that the other reason I was nervous about coming back was seeing Greer.

"We run a small construction company together," he explained, and I lifted my hand.

"It's okay, Kyle. No explanation needed." Kyle was Greer's best friend, had been since they were in diapers, and it was inevitable that I'd not only hear about Greer but see him too. I just wasn't ready for the latter. My phone started going off in my purse now

266

that I had reception, and when I saw it was my ex, Alex, I sent it to voicemail. He'd been trying to reach me for hours, but I had little doubt that what he had to say wasn't all that important. I had something bigger to worry about, like where I was going to stay.

"You sure the inn is full?" I asked, turning around. The hole in the roof was substantial, and with the wind came the snow and other debris. It was uninhabitable. Which meant I was basically homeless. Just what I needed.

"I can call my mom and confirm," Kyle replied. "But when I spoke to her this morning, she was already complaining about having her hands full with the guests."

I exhaled a heavy breath, hands on my hips. "Then I'll just have to make it work," I told him. "Thanks for your help. You'll, uh, let me know what I owe you for towing my car?"

He gave me a look and dryly replied, "I'm not making you pay shit, Della. I'll go fetch your car now and leave it out front for you."

I thanked him, handing him my keys, and only once he'd left did I fall onto the old, worn sofa. Dust puffed up around me, and I sneezed. Obviously, the place needed some work, but perhaps if I could fix it up, piece by piece, I could fix myself up the same way.

Chapter 2

Della

Kyle towed my car to the driveway less than an hour later, finding me in the same spot I had slumped into. My mind had been consumed with where to start to make the cabin a little livable. He handed me the car keys, reassuring me that the car was fine before confirming that he had called his mother and the inn was full for the next week. He only left minutes later after asking if I was sure about staying in the cabin. I stood by the door and watched him drive away before I quickly kicked into action. I couldn't stay idle for long.

I went into the kitchen, looking for a broom and dustpan. They were exactly where Nanna had left them. I started in the bedrooms, moving around the debris in the living room. There were only two rooms and a small bathroom. Nanna had one of the smaller cabins. The larger two-story cabins were a row up from here. I wasn't surprised to see that my childhood bedroom had stayed the same. The small double bed was pushed against the far wall, and beside the door stood a simple white dresser covered in glitter stickers from when I was younger. In the corner stood the small closet that once kept all my clothes, most of which came from Goodwill in town.

I removed all the bedding and changed it, swept the floor as best I could, and then moved on to Nanna's room. It was slightly bigger than mine, and I would probably take it now that the cabin belonged to me.

I was halfway through mopping the floors—and ignoring the growl in my stomach—when there was a knock on the front door. I rested the mop against the wall and opened it, not entirely prepared for who I'd see. It could have been anyone, really.

People in Kipsty were nosey, and I was sure the town would be abuzz with news of my arrival soon enough—if it wasn't already. It was possibly the only thing I wasn't looking forward to.

Greer stood tall and imposing on my porch, having grown into his muscular form. His blonde hair was messy, and his green eyes clouded over beneath sharp brows. His jaw was sharp, like his cheekbones, and his lips were full and round. I sucked in a hard breath. Okay, maybe seeing Greer was something else I wasn't looking forward to, and now he was here, dressed in dark denim, work boots, a flannel shirt, and a black hooded jacket.

He's really embraced the whole mountain man vibe.

"Greer." His name left my mouth on an exhale.

"I didn't believe Kyle..." he said, his tone hard, "...when he said you're back."

My throat worked as I tried to swallow, but it was no use. It felt as though someone had stuffed a wooly sock in my mouth.

"What are you doing here?" He barked. I flinched at how harshly he'd posed such a simple question. I blinked and remembered myself. We weren't kids anymore, and he didn't get to speak to me like my arrival was inconvenient. I straightened my spine, swallowed around the emotion in my throat, and met his gaze.

"I'm moving in," I said, keeping my tone firm but conversational. It wouldn't do me any good to meet his confrontational countenance with the same.

"You hate Kipsty," he stated, unabashed by his own lack of diplomacy.

I cocked my head and *really* looked at him. At how he'd changed. He was no longer a boy but a 30-year-old man. An

269

attractive one at that. Then again, he was always attractive to me. He *was* my first love. And I never did see him when I came back for Nanna's funeral. I didn't look very hard, though. I was grieving the only family I had left, and Greer was the last person on my mind that day.

"Thanks for the reminder." I huffed. "You come here for a reason other than to confirm that I'm really here?"

He licked his top lip, resting his hands on his hips. Even his stance was hostile and imposing. And for what? Because I dared show my face in my hometown? That wasn't going to fly with me. I had every right to be here, whether he liked it or not. "Was it to ask why I'm here?" I guessed.

He gritted his teeth, a muscle popping in his angular jaw, and like a pro, he evaded my question with one of his own. "Kyle tell you you can't stay here?"

I looked behind me and tried to hide my grimace. When I faced him again, I smoothed my expression. "The rooms aren't damaged," I told him. "It's just the living room."

I stumbled back when Greer stepped forward and into my personal space. He was taller than I remembered. And a whole lot bigger, too. Menacing. He eyed the hole in the roof and the mess on the floor.

"You can't stay here," he said, his voice low. "You'll freeze or worse, Della." It was the first time since he'd shown up that he'd bothered to say my name, and hearing it from his mouth made my skin shiver and my bones shake. He didn't say it with any kind of reverence. In fact, he said it with irritation lacing his tone. But in that deep timbre of his voice. I still felt it down to my toes, which curled in my boots. The truth is, he was right, but on principle alone, I wasn't about to allow him to tell me what I could or couldn't do.

"Pretty sure I'll be just fine, *Greer*. Besides, where am I supposed to stay? Kyle said the inn is full."

"Your car is a better option than this," he replied, jutting a thumb back towards my truck. "You know you'll freeze your ass off in here. It's as cold as a witch's tit outside, and the snowfall is just getting worse. Thought you'd remember what the seasons were like here." His dig was subtle, but I felt it nonetheless.

"I'm not sleeping in my car," I replied incredulously. "I'll freeze in there too! At least here I have a fireplace."

Greer quirked a stubborn brow.

"The fireplace is blocked, Della. No one has lived here since Nanna Delia, and it's been empty for over a year."

"This place is all I have," I told him, folding my arms across my chest when a strong gust of wind came in behind Greer. "I'm not sleeping in my damn car."

"Then you'd best make a plan," he replied. "Because you can't. Stay. Here."

I threw my arms up in defeat, already tired of arguing with this brute of a man. "I have nowhere else to go! I packed up my entire damn life to come here, okay? That what you want to hear? I'm here because my life fell apart in New York!" I didn't mean to say so much, or reveal why I came back, but something about the way he kept *barking* at me made me want to explode. It's not like I expected a red carpet welcome or anything, but *this*? He had no damn right. Asshole.

I rubbed at my temples, feeling the exhaustion of the day creep up on me from behind. When I opened my eyes, Greer was watching me, his gaze hot on my cool skin. His face was taut, skin stretched over sharp bone, and I could see the anger flashing in his eyes.

I sighed, suddenly very tired. "Just go, Greer. I can take care of myself." I'd been doing that for eleven years, and it wasn't about to change. I no longer had any family who could help me navigate this next part of my life. Only God knew where my mother was, but I'd been doing fine without her all my life.

Greer muttered something I didn't catch under his breath, but his hands were on his hips again. He passed me and stopped beneath the hole in my roof, peering up past the tree that had made the hole to begin with. He shook his head.

"We have a few places that need fixing. You see this..." He pointed at an exposed wooden beam. "...is one strong gust of air away from snapping into two and causing this..." He pointed to another, "...to give way and the tree to fully collapse into the house." He took a step forward, swiping his large hand from the tree to the ground. "If the tree falls, the bedrooms will have no access to this other side of the house, and you'll be trapped." He glanced back at me, a flash of worry crossing his face for only a second. "Until we can fix this, you can't stay here, Della. There's no way around it."

My frustration grew, forming a tight knot in my chest. What was I supposed to do now? The inn was at capacity with a wedding party, and our little town didn't have a hotel. And because I no longer had friends here, I couldn't shack up with someone else until my cabin was fixed. I was about to explain this to Greer, whether he listened was another story, but he spoke first.

"You'll have to stay with me if you have nowhere else to go."

My eyes widened. "That's not happening." What a ludicrous suggestion. He'd obviously lost his ever-loving mind.

"It's either my house or your car, and we've established you'll freeze in your car."

"I *really* can't stay here?" I asked incredulously.

Greer shook his head, his blonde hair falling over his forehead. "Nope." He popped the *p* and started for the open front door. His stride was confident, eating up the space in seconds.

Well, shit.

Of all the things I'd thought might happen when I finally arrived, this was not one of them. It was a terrible idea, but Greer had pointed out just how many options I *didn't* have. Leaving me with only one. Without saying anything else, he started wheeling my suitcases that were still by the door outside.

He packed his Jeep while I stood frozen to the floor. I brushed my fingers over my lips, my throat dry and my stomach twisting with discomfort. Greer came back for my last suitcase, and before he could walk out, I asked, "Are you even sure about this?" *This* being him having me stay with him.

He gave me a look, and I felt it *everywhere*. In the pitter-patter of my heart, the hollow of my belly. His green eyes full of so much of what he wasn't saying.

"I'm not thrilled you're back..." he admitted bluntly. The admission was like a sucker punch to the gut with a tire iron. "...but I'm not an asshole..." that was debatable at this point, "...and I'm not about to let you stay here and freeze to death either, Della. You can stay with me before Kyle and I get to fixing your cabin." He turned and walked out, and for a beat, I hesitated. Was I supposed to foll—

"You coming?" he hollered. "I don't have all afternoon to wait for you. We'll fetch your car later."

I blew out a harsh breath, resigning myself to this new turn of events. I grabbed my purse and followed him, not bothering to lock up. In a town like this, we never worried about locking our homes. It was pointless. Even more so because there was nothing of real value. And, well, I had a hole in my roof—locking up seemed redundant. By the time I slid into the passenger seat of Greer's Jeep, he'd already started the car and shifted it into drive.

Chapter 3

Greer

I shifted in my seat as I drove towards my cabin. I was only two roads up from her, where all the two-story cabins were located. It was the same cabin I'd grown up in, spent my whole life in, and now I'd told Della she could stay with me until Kyle and I managed to fix her cabin.

It wasn't the smartest thing I could have done, but Della was out of options. I was still reeling from the news of her arrival if I was honest with myself.

It'd been eleven years since she left, and I never thought she'd set foot in Kipsty again after she made it clear it wasn't enough for her. I recall the day she left like it was yesterday, and the old wound it had left behind was smarting because she was sitting beside me.

"Not much has changed," she remarked, looking out the passenger window before turning her big, blue eyes to me. Her gaze was hot on the side of my face, but I refused to look at her. I wanted to reply but came up short as to what to say.

I couldn't conjure up a single word in response, so I didn't even bother trying.

I turned up the steep road where my cabin was located at the very top. Della was right, though. Not much about the town had changed. The same could be said for the people, but Della would learn that soon enough.

I got to the top of the hill where my cabin sat on the border of the mountains surrounding Kipsty and stopped in the single parking bay on the side. It was semi-private, sitting on almost seven acres of land. The lights shone through the large windows, lighting the cabin from the inside. Without a word, I hopped out and started unpacking Della's suitcases. She came up beside me and took the smaller suitcases from the Jeep.

I carried them up the long staircase leading to the wrap-around porch, unlocked the heavy, solid wood front door, and dropped her bags in the foyer. She took tentative steps when she followed me inside, her gaze flitting around. I'd made many changes and idly wondered if she'd notice, or if she remembered what my home looked like when she'd spent so much time here as a teenager.

We were best friends once upon a time, and then we became more. Now though, we were practically strangers, and what? I was trying to be valiant by inviting her to stay with me? Idiot. It was a terrible idea, but it felt as though I suggested it on autopilot.

The words just came out of my mouth, unlike when I demanded what she was doing here. I knew exactly what I was saying *then*.

"You've made some upgrades," Della said quietly, and when I looked at her, it was like a haze had lifted. I noticed the changes, too. Dressed in dark denim jeans, beige riding boots, and a cream-colored puffer jacket, her blonde hair hung down her back in loose curls from beneath her beanie. She was always curvy, even when we were kids, but now, her hips flared, and her butt was fuller, muscular. I skirted past her ample chest, not wanting to gawk— I'd always had a particular obsession with her breasts.

I shook my head, berating myself for taking note of all things like they mattered. They didn't.

"Yeah," I sighed. "My ex-wife wanted to make it seem bigger," I replied, referring to how I'd raised the ceiling in the living room and added more windows overlooking the valley below that surrounded the cabins all the way down the road to Main Street.

Della's head whipped in my direction. "Ex-wife?" She exhaled. "You got married?"

I grunted in response. I didn't want to talk about Maisy and doubted Della wanted to either. I needed to get her settled in my guest room.

I trudged up the stairs and looked behind me to see if Della was following. I raised my brows at her when she wasn't, and it got her moving.

"You can stay in here," I told her, dropping her bags at the foot of the king size bed. "Sure you remember where everything is?"

She stood on the threshold and swallowed. "Your old room," she half-whispered. Her memory was good because we had four bedrooms upstairs, and this room had been mine. Though I wasn't sure how she'd remembered because none of my high school or college memorabilia adorned the walls anymore.

I couldn't help myself when I asked, "How'd you know?"

Her lips tilted in a half-smile, and she pointed to a spot beside the door. "Our initials." Huh. I'd forgotten about that. We'd carved out initials in the wood when Della was thirteen, and I was fourteen. It was before we started dating, too.

"Right." I cleared my throat. "Then I don't need to explain where everything is." I turned to leave, but Della stopped me, a delicate hand resting on my bicep. She blinked and looked up at me. In that moment, all I could focus on was the blue in her eyes that held so much of my past that it scared me.

"Thank you," she said softly. "For letting me stay here." I stared at her, gritting my teeth. "Can I, uh, make you some dinner?" she asked. I hadn't eaten, but I was planning to head into town to grab a bite to eat with Kyle. The thought of Della in my kitchen rankled me.

"I have plans with Kyle," I replied. I wasn't going to ask if she wanted to join us. "But help yourself to what you want in the refrigerator." I brushed past her, ignoring how her expression fell and walked back downstairs. I was ready to grab my keys and leave when I heard Della's phone ring from upstairs. Her voice was low and hard when she answered, and my curiosity got the better of me. I inched closer to the staircase and perked my ear.

"No, Alex, I'm not coming back," she hissed. The way her voice traveled, I could tell she was walking in a circle. Old habits die hard. It was a nervous tick.

"You *cheated* on me," she continued, her voice rising. "I'd skin myself alive before I even consider getting back together, so stop asking. Stop calling. I'm not coming back." There was a beat of silence and then a final, "We're *done*, Alex. There's nothing you can say or do to fix this, and honestly, I'm glad we're over. You wouldn't have made me happy, and if I made *you* happy, you wouldn't have cheated. So you can stop calling me."

I felt a little guilty for eavesdropping, and knew it was wrong, but I'd take any insight I could get as to why she'd come back. I just wasn't expecting it to be because her relationship had gone south. The irony wasn't lost on me, since Maisy had done the same thing.

Before I could hear anything else, I grabbed my keys and left, taking a quick drive down to Main Street and stopping curbside in front of *The Weary Traveler*—the lone bar-slash-restaurant in Kipsty. I spotted Kyle's pickup before walking in. It was busy, but that was nothing new. People either ate here or at the dinner down the road. I greeted a few people on my way to the bar, giving them a stiff smile. I'd known most of them my whole life, others I'd gotten to know when they moved here a few years back. People rarely ever left Kipsty, but over the last few years, we'd had to build more cabins to accommodate the people who decided they wanted to live here.

It was the Kipsty charm, as I called it.

We had tourists come in, fall in love with the place, and months later, they'd be here permanently.

He was sitting at the bar talking to Hayward, the owner. I sat down with a huff, removing my jacket and slipping it across the back of my chair.

"You're late," Kyle remarked, sipping his beer.

"Your usual?" Hayward the bartender asked. I nodded and turned to Kyle, his expression one of apprehension and expectation.

"So?" he asked without preamble.

I rolled my eyes. "I saw her," I told him. "Don't know why she's back, though."

"You were a dick, weren't you?" He surmised. He knew me better than anyone.

"I might have been," I admitted. "But she was stubborn as hell when I told her she couldn't stay in Nanna's cabin." I knew the cabin now belonged to Della, but the whole town knew that cabin as Nanna Delia's, and it would take a lot for that to change. "So, I told her she can stay with me until we get it fixed."

Kyle choked on a sip of beer, and I slapped his back. "You did what?" He wheezed. Hayward slid my Sam Adams in front of me and leaned on the counter with his forearms.

"We talking about Della Marie?" he asked.

Kyle pointed at me with his thumb. "Dumbass over here said she can stay with him until we fix Nanna's cabin."

Hayward hummed. "So, she's really back then?"

"In the flesh," Kyle replied, saving me from having to answer. "Anyone's guess as to why, though."

I didn't tell them about the conversation I'd overheard. Wasn't my place. Or my business.

"We'll have to fix her cabin sooner than scheduled," I told Kyle. "Can't have her in my house for too long."

"Not sure about that. We've got some emergency fixes scheduled over the next few weeks. And now that she isn't staying there and is safe at yours, fixing Nanna's cabin isn't quite an emergency, now is it?" Kyle said, smirking.

"You are loving this, aren't you?"

"Hey, I'm not the one who invited her to stay over. Why'd you do that again?" he asked.

"She can't stay in that cabin, and you know that," I reminded him. "It was either she freezes in the cabin, or she freezes in her car. Do you have any other suggestions other than her living with me?"

He was shaking his head when Daisy-May, the unofficial town matriarch, and diner manager, sidled up to us. She was dressed in a wildly colored kaftan; her firetruck red hair tied up in a beehive style straight from the 60s.

"Boys," she greeted in that airy voice, smiling wide at Hayward. "Greer, honey, how are you?"

I quirked a brow. I loved Daisy-May as much as anyone—she became Mamma Bear to all of us when Nanna Delia died—but the inflection in her tone gave her away.

"Fine," I replied, taking another sip of my beer. "Does *everyone* expect me to, like, fall apart or something?"

"We're just as shocked as you are that Della Marie is back," she replied warmly. "But we also know it'll hit a little differently for you." Ugh. I loved this town, but I hated how involved everyone was in each other's lives. It was a hazard of being such a small community, and nothing would change that. Everyone's life was up for public consumption, and tonight it was my turn, it seemed.

"It's no big deal," I lied. "Technically speaking, this is her home. Why she's back isn't anyone's business." I gave Daisy-May a look, and she *tsked,* waving me off.

"Leave it to me, honey. I'll find out why she's here." She winked and sashayed back to where all the old biddies were playing poker. Della had been in town for less than four hours, and I did not doubt in my mind that she was already the topic of *many* a conversation. And now I had no way of escaping her at all.

Chapter 4

Della

Snuggled in my navy-blue padded jacket, I slipped the faux fur hood over my head and walked down the road from Greer's cabin. I had been cooped up there for a few days and decided it was time to venture out.

The cabins were nestled in a valley, the trees covered in snow. My truck was safely packed in his driveway after he'd driven it over yesterday evening. I took a deep breath, reacquainting myself with the surroundings. It was still early, and if memory served me right, residents only surfaced around 9 a.m. I didn't sleep much the past few nights. I was in a somewhat strange place, and every sound woke me up.

Greer and I had been avoiding each other since he left me alone to figure out my way around his home. I had managed to entertain myself, and every morning, the fridge was freshly stocked with items I had used the previous day. Much as Greer was ignoring me, he wasn't going to let me starve. It was weird being in his cabin though, not only because of its sheer size but because, like Nanna's cabin, it held so many memories, good and bad.

As I walked, my breath came out in white puffs, and I tucked my mitten-covered hands in my pocket. I strolled until I hit Main Street and found myself in front of the diner. I looked at the sign and expelled a heavy breath.

Nanna had been gone over a year, and yet I could never bring myself to sell the diner either. Or change the name from *Delia's Diner* to something else. Though I wasn't here as the owner. I was here as a patron.

The bell chimed above my head when I walked in, and all heads turned to me. There weren't many people in yet, but hushed whispers filled the space all the same. I couldn't remember anyone inside, but they obviously remembered me. Daisy-May I remembered. She was running the diner in my stead and had taken over when Nanna died. Dressed in a bright yellow long-sleeve romper with ruffles around her neck and her red hair tied up in a side ponytail and yellow scrunchie, she glided over from behind the cash register. Her smile was wide, her arms outstretched.

"As I live and breathe," she said, her voice a light tinkle. Just as I remembered. She wrapped me in a warm hug and squeezed ever so tightly.

"You really are here, Della Marie." She pulled back and held me at arm's length, giving me a once-over.

"You're too skinny," she remarked, and I raised my brows. "But we can fix that."

She touched my cheek and led me to the empty booth, signaling a waitress to bring us some coffee. I sat down, and she followed, eagle-like eyes affixed to my face.

"How are you?" she asked. A young waitress stopped at our table and poured us both a cup of coffee before scuttling away.

I held the warm mug between my cold hands and blew over the top. "That's not what you *really* want to know, now is it, Daisy-May?" I smirked. "If I recall, you were never one to beat around the bush." Daisy-May was the kind of woman who called a spade a spade and had no problem speaking her mind. Nanna was much the same, and they were two women I'd always aspired to be like. I'd succeeded too, which is what made me so successful in my career. However, this was personal.

"Of course I want to know how you are," she replied airily. "It's been eleven years, Della Marie."

"Della," I corrected. "Just Della." I took a sip of my coffee and savored the hit of caffeine to my system. "You saw me at Nanna's funeral."

She huffed—a delicate sound compared to what I would have sounded like—and rolled her pretty blue eyes. "I hardly spoke to you that day, honey. You didn't want to know anyone that day." She wasn't wrong. Nanna's funeral was a haze. "Not that we blamed you, sweetheart," she added. "Losing Nanna Delia was hard on us all, but for you..." She trailed off with a shake of her head, making her 80s style ponytail swish from side-to-side.

"So..." I hedged, "...am I the talk of the town yet?" I glanced around and felt like I was an animal in a zoo exhibit.

Her gaze was soft but discerning. "You had to know you would be," she replied gently. "But everyone's curious as to why you'd come back after all this time?" It was a question I wasn't going to escape. I could evade it all I wanted, but at some point, it would come out, whether I liked it or not. Whether I wanted it to or not. It was also pointless trying to keep it a secret. Everything had a way of coming out in this town.

"I decided to take Nanna's cabin," I said, casting my gaze downward. "I needed a change of scenery, and when I decided to run away from my problems, this was the only place I could think of." I looked back up, and Daisy-May's expression was soft with compassion and understanding. She rested her hand on mine.

"You made the right decision, Della," she said, her tone as gentle as her countenance. "This was always home." I bristled but hoped she didn't see it. I hadn't thought of Kipsty Little Town as home in a long time.

As if remembering something, Daisy-May frowned and sat back the slightest bit. "Last I heard, Nanna's cabin was quite badly damaged after the last storm we had. Were Greer and Kyle finally able to fix it?"

I sucked my lips between my teeth and replied, "No." I sighed.

"I'm staying with Greer until they can fix it."

Her blue eyes widened, and her mouth made an O before she started forward and under her breath, murmured, "That Greer has grown up real nice, hasn't he?"

I walked into that one, and I knew it. But I wasn't going to lie about where I was living. They would find out soon enough anyway when people stopped by Nanna's cabin and wondered where I was.

I chuckled and tilted my head. "I suppose he has," I replied, laughing lightly. "He wasn't very happy to see me, though, so I was surprised when he offered to have me stay in his house until the cabin is fixed."

"Still has a good heart, even as a man," Daisy-May replied easily. "Can't imagine seeing you was easy for him." I hummed into my mug, taking a bigger sip of my coffee before replying, "That goes both ways, I guess."

"You know..." Daisy-May leaned forward, "...none of us were all that surprised that you left. You were always destined to do something big with your life." She cocked her head. "Did you? End up doing something big?" I gave it some thought.

"I suppose so, but I think it became too big, and too much. So, I quit, and left it all behind, kind of like I did with Kipsty when I was eighteen."

It was Daisy-May's turn to hum. "Funny how you ended up right back where you started, huh. All things come full circle eventually."

"The great, big circle of life," I remarked. "Have I missed much since I've been gone?"

Daisy-May laughed. "Not much has changed..." which I'd already guessed, "...the young ones have all grown up, and gotten married, and us oldies are just getting older."

I sucked my top lip into my mouth, latching onto the *married* part. Greer had an ex-wife. But I couldn't exactly press him for details.

"Greer mentioned he got married," I hedged, lifting my gaze to Daisy-May's. She wasn't smirking, not with her lips but with her eyes. "Said he has an *ex-wife*?"

"Right. He didn't tell you anything else?"

I shook my head. "He wasn't very talkative when he mentioned her," I shrug. "And I didn't want to pry."

"Well..." Daisy-May sighed, "...I may as well tell you since his *ex-wife* was a friend of yours and still lives in town with her *new* husband. Best you hear it from me, honey." She looked around as if to make sure no one else was listening, but we both knew they were. "Greer married Maisy Roberts, though she goes by Maisy Finch now."

I felt my eyes widen. My heart skipped a beat. Maisy was my best friend, and if I was honest, I always thought she liked Greer. It was always me, Greer, Kyle, and Maisy, though Maisy and Kyle never dated. But we were thick as thieves growing up. Maisy was the first person I called when Greer kissed me for the first time, asked me to be his girlfriend, and when I lost my virginity to him. And I had no right to feel any kind of way *now*, hearing that Greer had married her. But it still left a bitter taste in my mouth.

"Didn't last long," Daisy-May added. "Two years, maybe. And all they did was fight. She wanted babies a year after they got married, and he just wasn't interested. No one was surprised when they finally got divorced. Rumor has it he never really got over *you*, miss Della, and Maisy couldn't deal with it anymore."

"I hardly think that was it," I replied, finishing my coffee. "The Greer I knew would have married her because he loved her."

Daisy-May gave me a look. "Honey, that man changed the day you left, and he may tell you otherwise eventually, but he was just never the same. Seems you took his heart with you when you got on that bus and never looked back."

I huffed. "I highly doubt that Daisy-May. He must have gotten over me eventually."

She quirked a perfectly shaped brow. "Did you ever get over

him?"

I opened my mouth and then closed it. Had I gotten over Greer? I suppose feelings for Greer waned over time, but if I looked closely enough and examined how my heart broke when I left and how it stayed broken when I started my life in New York, I never did get over Greer. Not really. Daisy-May clucked her tongue as if she knew what I was thinking.

"You've probably fallen in love a hundred times over the years, Della, but our hearts..." she tapped her hand over her chest where her heart sat, "...they never get over that first time."

I hadn't fallen in love a hundred times since I left, but it was a nice idea. Preferable to the notion that I never got over Greer or that he never got over me. Did I love Alex? I wasn't even sure I could answer that. Things with him were still so convoluted. I couldn't bear to deal with that *and* being back in Kipsty Little Town.

Sensing my unease, Daisy-May switched topics and instead asked, "Have you had a chance to think about what you want to do with the diner?" No, the diner had fallen to the wayside, but before I could say that, Daisy-May sat forward again and added, "Because I have a business proposal."

The change of topic was what I needed to stop thinking about the whole Greer situation, and by the time I left, Daisy-May and I had agreed to be partners, though I was going to be the silent one. She'd buy fifty percent, and we agreed the name would stay. It wasn't what I intended to happen when I showed up this morning, but I was relieved to have it off my plate. Now I could focus on something else, like adjusting to small town living.

Rather than go back to Greer's house, I walked towards the cemetery and stopped in front of Nanna's headstone. The cemetery wasn't very big, so her spot was easy to find. I exhaled a heavy breath, wondering what Nanna would have said had I come home sooner before she had passed.

"Hi, Nanna," I started. "I guess you were right. I did eventually come back." I crossed my legs at my ankle, and tucked my hands in my jacket. "I'm not sure what I'm doing here yet, but I'm hoping the answer will come." My breath left my mouth in white puffs. "I miss you so much." My nose burned, but I didn't stem the tears that started. "And Greer wasn't too happy about me coming back, but I can't really blame him, huh?" I looked around, hoping no one could see me talking to a slap of stone like it held the answers to everything that had gone wrong in my life.

"Anyway, Kyle and Greer will fix up the cabin, but until then, I'm staying with Greer. Awkward, right? It was nice of him to offer, but I'm not sure he really wants me there. Hopefully, it won't be for long." I wiped my nose and tapped the top of the headstone. "I wish you were here." And I did. I needed her, even now, but I also knew she'd raised me to be strong and independent, and it's because of that that I knew I'd be okay here in Kipsty.

Chapter 5

Greer

The house was quiet when I walked in. I had no idea where Della had been all day, but Kyle and I had finally managed to assess the damage to Nanna's cabin a week after Della had arrived. The roof had collapsed into the living room courtesy of a large fir tree, which we needed to remove to see how much work the cabin needed before it was habitable again. It was going to be a bigger job than we'd anticipated, and I needed to talk to Della about the cost if I could find her.

What I did notice was that Della had cooked. She'd covered the food with a dishcloth and left a roast chicken in the oven at a low temperature to keep it warm, I assumed. I looked around, my stomach grumbling from the delicious smell wafting from the kitchen, but I couldn't see Della anywhere. I trudged up the stairs, and as I approached her room, I heard sniveling.

I raised my hand to knock but hesitated. I didn't want to see her tear-stained face. Even as a teenager, I couldn't handle seeing Della cry. I wondered if the game was true now, eleven years later, when we were both adults who had lives that were no longer entwined.

I heard another snivel.

Resting my hand on the door handle, I raised my hand again, and knocked.

"Della? You in there?"

There was a beat of silence, and then a muffled, "Yes. Dinner is downstairs if you're hungry." I wanted to be angry with her, keep pushing her away, but I wasn't going to let her stay in her room if she was crying.

"I'm going to open the door, okay?"

When she didn't respond, I pressed down on the door handle and slowly opened the door, poking my head in. Della was sitting on the floor at the foot of her bed, wearing a terrycloth robe with her wet hair piled atop her head and clothes strewn on the floor around her. She'd obviously been unpacking, and I surmised it wasn't the clothes or the unpacking that had her in such a state.

Splotchy skin, red, puffy eyes. It looked like she'd been biting her lip, too. It was swollen and irritated. She swallowed when her blue eyes landed on me, and I saw her chest heave with a deep inhale.

"You okay?" I asked. Whatever the circumstances around her return, I wasn't heartless. Something had upset her, and based on past experience, it took a lot to make Della cry.

"I'll be fine," she said, wiping her face with the sleeve of her robe. "You can go ahead and eat without me. I'm not hungry."

"You have to eat something." I sighed. "Besides, we need to talk about Nanna's cabin. Kyle and I assessed it today."

She blinked and looked around at her clothes. "I'm busy unpacking..." she trailed off and shook her head.

From where I was standing, it looked like she'd started unpacking but was interrupted. I had two choices. I could either leave her here and let her stay upset, or I could coax her into having something to eat and get her to calm down just a bit.

I stepped closer to where she was sitting on the floor and reached for her hand.

"C'mon, you need to eat, and we need to talk about Nanna's cabin."

She looked up at me again and placed her hand in mine so I could pull her up. The innate urge to pull her into my arms hummed under the surface of my skin, but I shook away the feeling and let go of her hand. She followed me out of her room and back downstairs to the kitchen. She took plates out, knives and forks, and I couldn't help but raise my brows when I saw she'd put together a fresh green salad and baked some bread rolls to go with the roast chicken in the oven. She took the chicken out, and I pushed her aside so I could carve it.

I cleared my throat. "Thanks for making dinner. You didn't have to."

"Figured you'd be hungry after working all day." She shrugged. "And it's the least I can do since you're letting me stay here." Her voice was flat, and the need to know what had her so deflated pulled at me. I was still curious as to why she was back, but I also couldn't bring myself to pry, no matter how badly I wanted to.

I set the table while Della dished up, and I didn't even wait for her to sit beside me before I started shoveling food into my mouth. I groaned appreciatively, trying to remember the last time I had a decent home-cooked meal.

"This is good," I mumbled around my food. I glanced over at her and noticed how she pecked at her own food. She caught me looking, and her expression turned sheepish.

"I can't eat when I'm upset."

Without thinking it through, I replied, "I remember." I finished my food and pushed my plate away, wiping my mouth with a napkin. "You want to talk about it?"

Della looked at me out of the corner of her eye, brows furrowed. "You really want to know?"

I lifted my shoulder. "If it'll make you feel better." I knew I'd done an about-face after showing up at her cabin a week ago like a raging bull, but I'd since realized I couldn't hold a grudge against her, no matter how hard I tried to. It felt unnatural after so much time had passed. I'd stayed angry long enough after she left, and did my best to move on and let it go. And for the most part, I had. Obviously seeing her again conjured up some kind of feelings but staying angry was like waiting for rain during a drought. Useless and disappointing.

Della pushed her plate away, her food only half-eaten, and slumped in her chair. "My ex won't leave me alone," she started, fiddling with a napkin and tearing it into tiny pieces before laying them on the marble countertop in front of her. "I sold my event coordinating business, too, when I decided to come back." She shook her head. "Selling my business was the easy part, if I'm honest..." Her voice cracked, and she lifted her hand, wiping under her eyes. "Alex, my ex, cheated on me with his secretary." She turned her blue eyes to me. "Talk about a cliché, huh. And now she's p-pregnant." Her voice cracked, and seconds later, her face crumbled.

She covered her mouth to smother her sob, and my instincts took over when I wrapped an arm around her delicate shoulders and pulled her in for a hug. I even kissed the top of her head, and held her while her body shook.

Della was still kryptonite to me in so many ways, and I'd only come to that realization now that she was back. I hated seeing her upset. I wanted to comfort her, hold her, and promise her it would all work out—like I'd always done. Those same instincts came as naturally to me as breathing, and it didn't matter that I was angry with her for what she'd done years ago. She pulled away and grabbed a new napkin to blow her nose before looking at me. "You said you assessed the cabin. What's the damage?"

I lifted my hand from her back and crossed my arms on the marble countertop. "There's a hole in the roof, as you saw, and the roof in the kitchen has a crack." I sighed. "We can fix it, but it will take some time. We have other urgent cabins that need to be fixed too. Some families are shucked up together, and we need to get to those in order of priority."

"How long will that take?" she asked, her voice scratchy from crying.

I blew out a breath and twisted so I was facing her. "Couple of weeks. We need to source some logs and a few other things, too."

Della sighed, her entire body slumping forward as she rubbed her hands down her face. "Couple of weeks," she muttered. "Shit. Okay, I can move into the inn. The wedding should be done by—"

"No!" I said abruptly, shocking the both of us. I cleared my voice before adding, "I mean, you can stay here until we're done. I'm okay with it…if you are," I told her. I didn't want her to worry about where she'd be staying while we fixed Nanna's cabin. I wasn't about to put her out on the street. "The cost is another thing we need to talk about."

Della nodded, looking straight at me. "And?"

I scratched the side of my face, worried about how she'd react when I told her. But she had to know. "A few thousand, at the very least. Our estimate from start to finish is about ten thousand dollars."

She didn't even blink when she replied, "That's fine. I made a whole lot more than that when I sold my business, and Daisy-May offered to buy half the diner a few days back." I felt my brows rise.

"You sold the diner?" It had belonged to Nanna Delia and was left to Della when Nanna passed. Daisy-May had been running it while Della was gone. The diner had been around since before Della and I were born, and it was a fixture in Kipsty.

"Half of it," Della replies. "We're partners, but she'll keep running it. I'm still trying to figure out what I'm going to do with myself."

I sucked my top lip into my mouth, contemplating how much I *could* ask without it seeming like I was digging for information. "You said you sold your business," I hedged, waiting to see if she'd share some more with me. She wasn't obligated to, but I knew Della. At least I used to. Whenever she got upset, she needed a moment to gather herself, and her thoughts, before she spoke about it. She was a talker, and didn't like keeping things bottled up. I wondered if that had changed.

"And I thought you hated me," she countered, a half-smile edging up one side of her mouth. It seemed she was ignoring the direction the conversation was taking.

I huffed out a brusque laugh in spite of myself. "You know how I feel about surprises, Della." I hated them. It was a wound from my childhood, from when my parents were unexpectedly taken from me while I was 18. "And you are one hell of a surprise." Never in a million years did I think she'd come back. She was set on leaving, and she had stayed away for long that it was easy to assume she was never coming back.

"You might not believe me..." she started, "...but I came back because this was the only place I could come to. It was the first and *only* place I thought of when..." She looked down, swallowed, and shook her head. I gave her a minute to gather her thoughts.

"I couldn't cope anymore," she continued. She was opening up, and I could stop her and tell her I didn't care what her story was. But I did care and denying it was purposeless.

I was about to ask about the business she'd owned and sold to alleviate the tension between her shoulders when she said, "I was an event coordinator in New York. Had a very successful firm of my own after interning for a few years. And I don't know, my clients became more demanding, and I was working long hours even though I employed six people who worked for me. Then Alex, my ex, cheated on me with his secretary. We've been together for five years, but he started talking about marriage and kids and..." she shrugged a shoulder, "...it freaked me out. I couldn't picture my future with him."

She huffed out a breath and turned to face me, her eyes bright blue from shed tears. She wasn't crying anymore, though. "You asked me why I came back, and now you know."

I pulled my hands through my hair. "I'm sorry, Della. I really am. That's a lot for one person."

She let out a harsh burst of laughter. "I guess so. I keep asking myself if it's my punishment for leaving Kipsty in the first place," she said. "But then I think it's punishment for leaving you too."

Chapter 6

Della

I expected Greer to say something in response to my last statement, but he didn't. He regarded me, the look in his eyes indiscernible, and then looked away, clearing his throat.

"You should get some rest," he said. "I'll take you to the cabin when I can and show you what we intend to do." It was on the tip of my tongue to ask him about Maisy, but I bit back the urge and stood. I quickly packed the dishwasher and leftovers from dinner for Greer to take for lunch the following day. He disappeared upstairs at some point, presumable to take a shower and go to bed. I felt alone in his cavernous home, even though he was there.

Part of me regretted allowing myself to be vulnerable around him, but the other part, the larger part, felt safe enough to do it. If I could be vulnerable with anyone, it was Greer. Even after years apart, I still saw glimpses of the boy I'd left behind. Or maybe the young girl in me sought those parts out just to see if they still existed.

I went upstairs and back to the guest bedroom, sighing heavily when I saw the clothes on the floor that still needed to be packed away. I was staying here a few more weeks, so I might as well get comfortable and store away everything.

I shut the door, and leaned against it, counting my breaths until they evened out. Until I no longer felt frayed at the edges. I packed away my clothes, and zipped up my suitcases, placing

294

them at the bottom of the wide cupboard that took up half the wall beside the bathroom door. After changing into my pajamas, I stared at the bed. I was exhausted but felt too listless to sleep. I hadn't brought a book to read, and my kindle wasn't charged. But I doubted I could concentrate enough to read anyway. My mind was jumbled after speaking to Alex an hour before Greer came home, after listening to him explain his indiscretion and indirectly trying to pin it on me. After speaking to Greer, and unintentionally spilling my guts, it all left me drained. I crawled into bed, and tried to sleep, tossing and turning.

At about 2 a.m., I heard a noise coming from downstairs, and after slipping my robe on, I opened my bedroom door. I padded my way down each step and rounded the corner to the sunken living room. A shirtless Greer was watching *Sports Center,* the Colts versus the Patriots. I leaned against the wall and watched him for a while, not saying anything.

His dream was always to play in the NFL, but he tore his ACL in high school. It wasn't long after that his parents died, and I remembered how much he'd changed after that. Sensing my presence, he turned his head, his gaze catching mine.

"Did I wake you?" he asked quietly. "I couldn't sleep."

I pushed off the wall and lowered myself onto the buttery leather sofa beside him. "Couldn't sleep either," I replied, tucking a strand of hair behind my ear. I pulled my robe around me tighter. "You mind if I just..." I hesitated, "...sit here for a bit?"

Greer's gaze was intense as his eyes tracked my features. But he shook his head and turned his attention back to the television. We watched silently, but I was content to just sit beside him.

Warmth radiated from his body, and I soaked it up. It was familiar but also new. Still comforting, though. But I didn't want to think too much about that. I looked around, thinking back to my conversation with Daisy-May, about Greer and Maisy, and tried, in vain, to find anything that would allude to a woman ever having lived here. There was nothing.

Greer caught me looking, and when I glanced in his direction, my cheeks warming from being caught, his brows were furrowed. "You looking for something?"

I bit the corner of my bottom lip and swallowed. "Signs that you were married," I replied softly.

Greer drew in a deep breath and let out on a sigh. "She took all her things when she moved out," he replied, looking at the television. I was waiting for more but that too was in vain because it became obvious he wasn't in a sharing mood. And I was far too curious for my own good. I contemplated just coming out with it, telling him I knew more, but then he'd know Daisy-May had spoken to me. And it felt like a gross invasion of his privacy.

"I can hear you thinking," he said dryly, making me snicker. He used to say just that when we were younger, when I had something on my mind but not the courage to say it out loud.

So, I went with it. "How'd you end up marrying Maisy?" I asked, waiting for some kind of reaction.

All I got was a droll look, and an almost imperceptible shake of his head. "People in this town talk too much," he muttered. He let out a breath. "'Spose you would have found out eventually," he continued. "Lasted almost two years, but we should never have gotten married." He cleared his throat. "I'd just graduated from college when we started dating, and I don't know, I guess proposing felt like the next right step. So, I proposed, and we got married." He shrugged. "Turns out she wanted more than I could give, and when the fighting became constant, she left." It sounded so simple when he put it like that. But knowing Greer, that's probably exactly how he remembered it. No frills or graces. It was so Greer.

"You must've loved her," I stated gently. "If you married her." I was in no position to judge or be jealous in any way. He had every right to move on, and I'd never begrudged him that. I was, however, shocked that it was with Maisy.

"I thought I did," Greer admitted. "But I was lonely after you left, and she was always there. Made a difference that we were at the same school and friend circle."

I nodded, a knot in my throat comprised of many emotions, but I didn't press for more information. I curled up on my side of the sofa and leaned my head on my hand. My eyes started drifting closed, and what I was sure was an hour or so later, I felt strong arms lift me and carry me up the stairs. I burrowed my face into Greer's bare chest, breathing in his clean, crisp scent. I felt weightless when he lowered me onto the bed and tucked me in. I thought I felt his lips brush my forehead, and I was sure I'd reached for him and asked him to stay. But it was all fuzzy in my state of sleepiness. I rolled over onto my side and snuggled into the warmth of the duvet.

***

Things between Greer and me became better. We would catch up over breakfast before he went to work or during dinner. Greer would tell me stories about the town and the people we went to school with—laughing at the happier moments and feeling a smidge of guilt at the sad times. It was great to hear what happened around Kiptsy Little Town when I was away. When I wasn't with Greer, I would explore the area or head over to the diner to speak with Daisy-May. I was slowly getting acquainted with my hometown, and more than once, I asked myself what would have happened if I hadn't left eleven years ago—a question I would pose to Nanna's grave when I visited to clean it up or replace the flowers with fresh ones.

Greer and Kyle were still pretty busy tending to the other cabins, but Greer would always take the time to pass by Nanna's cabin and let me know what else would be needed. Over the past two weeks, we had slowly built up a list of things that needed to be worked on when my cabin was next up.

I was looking out the window at the dreary, snowy weather one morning when I heard some movement from downstairs. I felt a warmth fill me, wanting to catch up with him before he left. It wasn't lost on me how I was beginning to enjoy this routine we'd found ourselves in. Then I heard voices, realizing he wasn't alone. The second voice, however, was female. My brows furrowed. I couldn't pinpoint who the voice belonged to, so I quickly changed into some warm clothes and made my way downstairs.

"I don't know what you're doing here, Maisy," Greer said harshly. I froze. Maisy was here?

"Wanted to see for myself that it was true," she replied haughtily.

Greer sighed. "See if what is true? Be specific. You know I hate word games." He was irritated, that much I could discern from the tone of his voice. I sucked in a breath and walked downstairs. Maisy's head whipped to the side when she saw me, her expression a mix of surprise and disdain.

She gave Greer an incredulous look. "So it's true she's *staying* with you?" She huffed.

"Hi, Maisy," I greeted, stepping towards Greer. I stood beside him, and without thinking about it too hard, I wrapped my hand around his bicep. I knew it was a possessive gesture, but it was obvious to me that Greer wanted Maisy to leave, and if I still knew Maisy in any way at all, it would make her mighty uncomfortable to see me show Greer affection. It always had.

She looked at me, her eyes ablaze with indignation. Though I didn't know why. She was married to someone else. She even had the obnoxious diamond on her left hand to prove it.

"Didn't take you long," she replied, lifting her nose in the air. She was shorter than me by a few inches and had to look up the slightest bit to meet my eyes. "Been here less than a month and you're already shacking up together?"

I quirked a brow.

"I hardly think it's any of your business where I'm staying."

Greer straightened beside me and folded his arms but didn't brush my hand away from his bicep. "You're wasting your time,"

Greer told her. "Della is staying here until we can get her cabin fixed, not that I owe you an explanation. You don't live here anymore."

Maisy made a noise in the back of her throat, her cheeks a ruddy red. Her eyes traced my features, and I knew that I was a threat to her at that moment. We were best friends once upon a time, so it wasn't a stretch to assume I still knew her tells. Her nostrils flared; cheeks puffed a little. Eyes widened.

"You have a lot of nerve showing up here," she told me. "We were all better off after Kipsty's Golden Girl left."

"You mean *you* were better off because you had a shot with Greer?" I replied coolly. I felt Greer's gaze on the side of my face, but I kept my eyes on Maisy. "Too bad you fucked it up."

She laughed derisively. "And now you think you can have him back? Is that it?"

"Not at all," I replied evenly. "Greer was just kind enough to offer me a place to stay for a while. I'll be out of here as soon as my cabin is done."

Before Maisy could offer up a pithy response, Greer continued, "Anything else I can do for you? Or are you just here to stick your nose where it doesn't belong?"

"I hardly think my return warrants a visit," I added, looking at Greer. He honed his gaze on Maisy.

I looked back at her. "You'll have to excuse us," I said lightly. "We have somewhere to be this morning, and I'm afraid we're going to be late."

I was lying, I had no idea what mine or Greer's plans were for the day, but Greer's disposition was clear to me. He didn't want Maisy here. And neither did I if I was being honest with myself. I knew I'd bump into her eventually, but not like this. And I certainly wasn't expecting to be met with such hostility when I'd done nothing to her.

"You should never have come back," she told me, her tone brazen with an undertone of bitterness.

I expelled a calm breath, using Greer as an anchor. "Well, I did, and I'm not going anywhere, so best you get used to seeing me around town with Greer." *With Greer* had its own implications, and the deliverance was done with intent. It implied she'd be seeing Greer and I *together*, which wasn't likely to happen, but, in that moment, it was exactly what I wanted her to think. If she wanted to show up unannounced with her claws on show, I could certainly unsheathe claws of my own.

Maisy opened her mouth and closed it again right before spinning on her heel, and walking out. As soon as she was gone, my shoulders sagged in relief, and I slipped my hand from Greer's arm.

"Good morning to you, too," I murmured under my breath. Greer shook his head, a small smile on his face.

"Glad to see you still have your backbone," he said quietly.

I glanced at him, and replied, "That was child's play compared to what I had to deal with in New York."

He hummed and stepped away.

"Your lunch is in the refrigerator," I reminded him. "There's enough for you and Kyle."

I tilted his chin. "Thanks. I was thinking of taking you to Nanna's cabin, and getting that list finalized so we can get to ordering."

"I'm ready to go when you are," I replied. "How about you take me to the cabin and we do one more run through? Then we can head to the diner and talk about it?"

Chapter 7

Della

I looked at the plans in front of me while Kyle—who'd decided to join us for a late breakfast—and Greer spoke about supplies and where to source them. Kyle, rather than Greer, had walked me through the cabin and showed me where the repairs were most needed. Hole in the living room aside, the roof in the kitchen had been weakened by the weight of the tree that had landed on the cabin and would likely need to be replaced.

A young waitress came over with our coffee and our food, so I slid the plans aside to make some space. Kyle dug into his food with gusto while my mind whirred about how long it would take before I could move out of Greer's place. I pushed my food around my plate, looking over the blueprints for my cabin.

"We'll have to remove the old roof completely," Kyle said, drawing my eyes up to him. "And then lay a new one. I found a place a few towns over that have the logs we use, and they can deliver as early as tomorrow."

I had a list in front of me detailing the cost of it all, including labor, and it was the one thing I wasn't worried about. I had enough money for the repairs and then some.

"It'll take about a week to get it sorted," Greer added around a mouthful of food.

I hummed. "How long would it take to remodel the whole cabin?" I'd seen some stunning ideas on Pinterest last week and decided that if I was going to live here, I might as well make some changes. "I mean, if you have the time for a remodel that is?"

Greer and Kyle exchanged a look before Greer said, "We've finished up with the emergency ones. Yours was the last one before we got back to our usual roster."

"We can definitely work on a remodel. I would love that. What did you have in mind?" Kyle asked.

I pulled my phone out of my pocket and opened the reference images I'd found. I slid the phone across to them, and their heads bent forward. Kyle whistled as they flipped through the images.

"I'll pay for it, obviously," I told them. "But if you're taking the roof off, we may as well do a redesign while you're at it."

"It'll take longer," Greer said, looking up at me. I interpreted his inference as *you'd have to stay with me for longer*. And maybe he didn't want that.

"I can move into the inn if it's too much," I told him. "I won't be in your hair for the duration of the remodel if that's what you're getting at." There was a frustrated bite to my tone. I wouldn't overstay my welcome when putting me up already seemed like an issue. He frowned.

"That's not what I meant, Della."

I was about to reply when Daisy-May floated over to our booth, coffee pot in hand. She was dressed in a fuchsia pink tracksuit, and white and gold Nike high-top sneakers. Her red hair was braided over her shoulder.

She poured us more coffee without us having to ask, and when she didn't walk away immediately, I looked up at her.

"Della, sweetheart, you're in the event planning business, aren't you?" I *was*, but I didn't tell her that. Besides, she didn't give me the opportunity to say so before she spoke again. "We have our annual Christmas Market as you know, beginning of next month, and Maisy usually plans it, but she opted out this morning looking rather..." Daisy-May licked her lips and looked down at me, "...*annoyed*, and said she wouldn't be able to plan it this year. I was wondering if you'd be able to help."

I remembered the annual Christmas market. People in town set up stalls in the town square and sold a variety of things. It brought a lot of tourism to Kipsty, and outside of Christmas and New Year, it was one of the biggest events of the year. Nanna had a stall every year and sold sherpa blankets, homemade quilts with a fleece interior, knitted beanies, and mittens. I sucked my lips between my teeth, mulling it over. I didn't have anything better to do with my time right now, and it was hardly the same as planning a high society event like a gala or a celebrity wedding.

"Sure," I replied, giving her a wide smile.

"Wonderful." She smiled appreciatively. "It's a bit last minute, with less than three weeks to go. We should get started as soon as possible, so while the boys do whatever they're doing, I'll bring over the list of this year's participants, and you can come up with the rest."

I opened my mouth, but she was gliding away before I could say anything.

Kyle chuckled. "You've gone and hopped yourself into something now, Della Marie." He shook his head, a smile on his face. "But I have a feeling you'll do a better job than Maisy did. Last year's was a near disaster, and if we can make it better this year, maybe we can get some newcomers visiting the town."

Greer cleared his throat but didn't tell Kyle that Maisy had paid us a visit earlier, and that was probably why she'd been so *annoyed* when she came to the diner. I sat back.

"So..." I hedged, "...can you make the changes I want to the cabin?" I was hoping they could. It was dated, and I wanted to make it my own as much as I loved it for several reasons. And I knew Nanna would want the same.

Kyle scratched his head and took the pencil from behind his ear. He made some notes on the blueprints before explaining, "I'll have to draw up new plans, but I'm pretty sure we can do it."

"Great," I sighed. "I'll go pack up and move to the inn until you're done redoing the cabin."

I noticed Greer's glower but didn't comment on it. Kyle finished his breakfast and slid out of the booth. He knew breakfast was my treat. "I'll get a start on this..." he said, looking between Greer and me, "...and get back to you as soon as I have new plans. See you later?" he asked Greer.

Greer nodded, and we watched Kyle leave just as Daisy-May walked over, a file thick with papers in her hands. She dumped them in front of me with an audible exhale. "Applications have already been approved for each stall," she explained. "But that's as far as Maisy got. We don't have a theme, or decor ideas, or anything else."

"I'll figure it out," I assured her. "Do you have the layout of the town square in here, too?"

"It's all there," she replied. "You're a lifesaver, Della." She winked, and I called for the check a few minutes later. I left some cash and a tip and then left the diner with Greer.

He was quiet as we walked towards his Jeep, and then he stopped so abruptly I walked into him with an *oof.*

He spun to face me on the sidewalk outside the diner. "Why do you want to remodel the cabin?"

My brows furrowed. "Because I need it updated," I replied simply.

"So you can leave again?" He sounded angry, and his conclusion flummoxed me.

"Wha—" I shook my head and blinked. "How'd you come to that conclusion, Greer?"

"It would make sense," he replied harshly. It was a sharp juxtaposition to his mood earlier that morning. "Fix it up, sell it for a profit, and then leave."

I exhaled through my nose and pursed my lips. "I'd like to remodel it because, like I said, it's dated and in need of a facelift. But not so I can sell it. I'd like to *live* in it." When he didn't respond immediately, I added, "I'm not leaving, Greer." He glared, and I glared back. I knew he didn't believe me, but did I need him to? The scary answer was that I wasn't sure. "I don't owe you an explanation—"

"Yes," he snapped. "You do. You waltz back into town like nothing ever happened like you didn't leave, and now you're pretending like it never happened." Suddenly, I knew where this little fit was coming from. I thought we'd made the slightest bit of headway this past few weeks, but clearly, I was wrong.

I stepped into his space, looked up into his blazing eyes, and in a low voice, said, "I remember *everything*, Greer. And I regretted it for months, *for months,* before I made peace with my decision because I knew I'd done what was right for *me*." I looked around, aware that we weren't alone, before looking back at Greer. "You're angry, and to some extent, I understand it, but it was *eleven years* ago, and I've let it go. Have *you?*"

His nostrils flared, and he scowled, but rather than answer me, he tossed his house keys at me and muttered, "Don't wait up for me." I watched him climb into his Jeep and drive away in the direction of my cabin. He was most likely meeting Kyle there later, but either way, he was angry, and it was because of me.

Before heading back to his cabin, I passed by the Inn, only for my plan to be tossed out of the window. There would be a corporate retreat in two days and they'd booked out the entire place for two weeks, and after that, another wedding party. I didn't ask if there'd be room after, already reading the receptionist's face. With Christmas coming up, they were probably booked up until the new year.

Just my luck. I have nowhere to go.

It was a bit of a walk to Greer's cabin, and by the time I got to his cabin, I was panting. I wasn't out of shape by any stretch of the imagination, but it was the altitude.

I unlocked the front door and went straight to the spacious dining area, dumping the file Daisy-May had given me on the rectangular dining room table. Greer could spend the day sulking if he wanted to, but I wasn't going to linger on the past and beat myself up over it all over again.

I'd done that already.

However, if Greer wanted more of an explanation as to why I left all those years ago, then he needed to man up and come right out and say it. I wasn't going to grovel, and considering I was stuck here for the next month or two, there was no point in wallowing in guilt for that long. I took a moment to calm myself down since I'd spent the walk up here mulling over Greer's frustration with me and not having alternative accommodation.

After a quick flip-through of the file, I realized I was going to need a few things from my former office. I sent a text to my ex-assistant and asked her to send what I needed to my new address, then I started searching online at stores in the nearby town that would have what I was looking for. Last year's theme was Winter Wonderland, and all I could do was roll my eyes. Maisy wasn't the most original. Never mind. I'd make sure this year's market was the best the town ever had. And I'd deal with Greer later.

I started by searching on Pinterest, much like I had for cabin remodel ideas, and made notes. I lost myself in my task, like I had with prior events, but rather than be filled with anxiety or dread over a particular event, I was excited about it. Excited to do something that was a tradition in Kipsty. Once I'd settled on a theme, I made a list of what I would need and started looking at where I could find it. It'd mean a drive into Denver, and maybe that's what I needed. It would put a little distance between Greer and me, and I wasn't sure that was a bad thing.

Chapter 8

Greer

"You're grumpier than usual," Kyle remarked as we unloaded the lumber we'd gotten in Boulder for Della's cabin. Kyle had amended the plans, and three days later, we were ready to start remodeling.

After Kyle showed me the pictures he'd received from Della after breakfast, I could admit Della had an eye for design, and what she had in mind for her cabin was quite stunning. Not that I could admit that to her after my outburst. Pretty sure she wasn't going to be speaking to me after that. But hell, I sat in that diner, my mind reeling with memory after memory of us being there together, and suddenly, I had this unsolicited anger boiling behind my sternum.

I wanted to know right then and there why she left. And not why she left *Kipsty Little Town*, but why she left *me*. I thought I'd made my own peace with it, had lived with the knowledge that I may never know the truth for years, but the simplicity of just being near Della again brought it all back. And now I had to know. Admittedly, she didn't deserve my outburst, but the anger in my veins was because of her, and directing it *at* her felt justified. To me, at least.

"She getting to you?" he asked when I didn't reply. I looked up at him, hands on my hips. "I mean..." he continued, "...I was shocked when you told me she's staying with you and wondered how long it would take before you snapped. Have you snapped?"

I adjusted the gloves on my hands and lifted a log onto my shoulder. "I might have lost it after breakfast the other day," I admitted begrudgingly. "After you left. Been giving her the cold shoulder for the past three days." I carefully climbed the ladder and slid the log between two others that were still part of the original roof structure. Because it was flat, we'd replace one log at a time, starting with the roof. I twisted at the hips and gestured for Kyle to hand me the next one. We'd already removed the damaged logs, and if we worked efficiently, the entire roof would be done by the time we called it a day.

"Don't blame you," Kyle said after handing me the last log. He leaned against the ladder. "Has to be hard having her in your house, too."

I was still getting used to it. I lived with Maisy for three years, two of which we were married, but having her in my space never left me restless or uneasy. Like my skin was shifting over my muscles, over bone. Nearly a month of feeling this way had left my system out of whack.

"She's pretending like nothing happened," I told him, if only out of irritation. "Breezes into town and expects everything to just be *normal* like she didn't leave me at all."

Kyle let out a puff of air. "Why don't you just talk to her?"

Good question. Why *hadn't* I just asked her, in a civilized manner as opposed to snapping at her, why she left *me*? I knew why she left Kipsty, even if I didn't understand it, but she never said why it was *me* she chose to leave. Kipsty wasn't enough for her back then, but did that mean I wasn't enough either? The more I thought about it, the angrier I got.

I climbed the rest of the way up the ladder and positioned the logs before grabbing the drill. I took my anger out on the wood, pressing the drill harder than necessary, but it was better than talking about my goddamn *feelings*. Kyle climbed up behind me and checked my work, making sure nothing was loose.

"Looks good," he remarked. "I have a new blueprint for her remodel, and I actually like what she's going for." I only caught a glimpse of the pictures before we drove here, but if Kyle said it looked good, I believed him.

It was well past five when we were done. I helped Kyle load his pickup and then headed home. The lights were on when I arrived, and when I walked in, it was quiet. Della had chosen to set up camp in the dining room, papers and files strewn about with a whiteboard full of her scribblings in front of it. I had found her here the past few days, but she was nowhere to be found today.

As I approached the staircase, I heard her singing, and it was coming from her room. It took me back to when she used to sing in the shower and also reminded me of the showers we often took together without Nanna knowing. Though I was sure she knew, just like she knew we were having sex. There was always a box of condoms in Della's bedside drawer, and I knew she didn't buy them.

I was dragged from the recollection by a shrill scream, and without thought, I stormed into Della's room and blew into her bathroom. She was staring in the corner of the large shower, on the opposite side of the shower head.

She turned as soon as she saw me. "S-spider," she sputtered, pointing to the corner of the floor. I froze for a moment, taking in her womanly shape. She didn't think to cover her front in her state, and I was blessed with a good look at the woman she'd become. Perky, fleshy breasts, her pink nipples erect from the slight chill to the air. She had a soft belly with a slight curve at her waist. A look at her well-trimmed pussy drove blood straight to my core. My cock twitching drew me out of staring at her.

I couldn't remove it or even look at it if Della was naked, so I grabbed a towel, wrapped it around her, and picked her up. I moved her out of the shower and then shut the water off. In the corner was what looked a whole lot like a Wolf spider. They were common in these parts and harmless but scary looking because they resembled a Tarantula. I coaxed it into my hand and let it out the bathroom window.

Della was still shaking when I faced her, and I remembered she had arachnophobia, and for her, the fear was debilitating. She shook, eyes wide.

"You okay?" I asked gently. Without thinking about it too hard, I approached her and started rubbing my hands up and down her arms.

"S-sorry," she murmured, looking up at me, her wet hair still sudsy from her shampoo. "C-can you m-make sure there isn't a-another o-one, p-please?" Her lips trembled, and her eyes grew wet. I licked my lips and forced myself to keep my gaze trained on Della's face and not look lower. I checked to make sure there were no more spiders and closed the window in case another one wandered in from the cold outside.

"You're safe," I told her. "All gone."

She nodded but didn't make a move to step back into the shower. "You should finish up," I told her, gentling my tone despite how rankled I was earlier. I caught sight of her long, tan legs and swallowed when images of what I had seen higher flashed in my mind.

"Can you leave?" She squeaked out. I stared at her a beat and then nodded. I tried the door handle, but to no avail. I yanked and pulled, but the door had closed while I was taking care of the spider and now it was stuck.

"Fuck," I muttered under my breath, trying again.

I rested my forehead against the door as Della quietly asked, "What's wrong?"

I almost didn't want to tell her. Not only did she have arachnophobia, but she was also horribly claustrophobic.

"Door's stuck," I mumbled, looking at her from over my shoulder.

"Try again," she said, her eyes darting between my face and the door handle. I tried again, but it still wouldn't budge.

"You have to be kidding," she said, her voice turning shrill. "This can't be happening, Greer." Her panic rose. "Get it open."

"Della, I need you to breathe. I can get it fixed, okay?" My third and fourth attempts proved just as fruitless as my first and second, and I knew Della was watching.

"Are we stuck?" she asked, panicked more now than she was ten minutes ago. "Greer, we can't, we can't—" Her breathing grew labored, and past experience told me she was having a panic attack. She shook her head vigorously, her breathing choppy, and her eyes widened. So, I did what I thought would calm her down the fastest and closed the gap between us before pressing my lips to hers.

My hand cupped the back of her head, and I held my breath, hoping the kiss would distract her. I'd used it in the past, and it worked because it made Della hold her breath which stopped the panic attack. However, it backfired because the feel of her mouth on mine distracted *me*. She relaxed into me, and though her breathing evened out, we didn't pull apart. I didn't stop kissing her, and she didn't stop kissing me.

Chapter 9

Della

I hated two things more than anything else in this world. Besides my ex. Spiders and being trapped in a small space. But I was less focused on those two things and more focused on the feel of Greer's mouth on mine. His lips were soft and pliable, and I liked the feel. It distracted me from everything else.

I expected him to pull away when my panic receded, but he didn't. I could have, but now that he had his mouth on mine, I didn't want him to pull back. I flicked my tongue to the seam of his mouth and felt his lips part. Tentatively, I slid my tongue into his mouth, and every nerve ending and cell in my body came alive when his tongue slid against mine. I sighed into his mouth and stepped towards him, feeling the length of his tall, hard body against mine.

I clutched my towel against me with one hand and used the other to grip the nape of Greer's neck. My fingers tussled his hair. He moaned into my mouth, and it lit my body up from the inside. He slanted his head, changing the angle of our kiss, and licked the inside of my mouth with fervor. Something about it felt angry, but I soaked it up anyway, injecting my own anger into how I pulled at his hair.

Our teeth clashed, but that didn't deter us. I startled when his hand landed on my hip and moved around my back, his palm flat as he pushed me closer. It was like a trip back in time, kissing

Greer, except his once boyish hands were replaced by those of a man, and his once unsure movements were replaced by confidence and willfulness. He was taking and giving and I was giving and taking, a familiar, but also new, exchange.

In an uncharacteristic display of courage, I dropped the towel between us, hearing it *thud* on the floor. Greer pushed me until my back hit the wall, and then lifted me, my legs going around his waist.

"Jesus," he muttered into my mouth. "Della." I was breathless, but this time it wasn't because of a panic attack. I whimpered when I felt the seam of Greer's denim between my legs, and the hardness behind his zipper. It was tantalizing, all the sensations happening all at once and my heart hammered away in my chest like it was staging a jailbreak.

Greer's phone started ringing, and we both froze, his forehead on mine.

"Fuck," he muttered, rolling his forehead on mine. Keeping me pinned to the wall, he reached into his pocket and frowned. "It's Kyle," he said, his voice hoarse. "If the door's stuck, I'm going to need his help." His eyes met mine, and I hoped the moment was on pause and not over. Slowly, Greer lowered me to the ground but kept his arm around my bare back.

So much for being upset with him.

"Kyle, hey," he answered, his dark eyes on me. I could hear Kyle's voice on the other end, but what he was saying was indiscernible. "Yeah, can you come to the house? Della and I are, uh, locked in the bathroom attached to my old bedroom. Door is jammed shut." Kyle said something, and Greer shook his head, a small smile playing at his lips. "Shut up, asshole, and just get here, okay?" He hung up and bent to grab the towel. He wrapped it around me, his eyes taking in my naked body. I didn't mind, and I wasn't shy. Greer had seen me naked more times than anyone else, even if we were teenagers. He looked at the door, and then at me.

"About the other day..." he started, "...I shouldn't have lost it like that with you." If he was trying to distract me, this was a pretty effective way to do it. God only knew how long Kyle would take to get here, so we may as well talk. I licked my lips and almost dropped my towel when I touched my mouth with my fingers. They were puffy and a little swollen, which spoke to the heat of our kiss. My brows knitted.

"I never meant for you to feel like I left you, but I understand why you did," I said, a slight tremor to my voice. I was starting to get cold and still needed to finish my shower. And that wasn't happening while Greer was trapped in the bathroom with me.

"I thought I wasn't enough," he started, still looking down at me. He touched my cheek, and I shivered, my skin breaking out in goosebumps. "I thought it was me, Della." I was shaking my head before he finished his sentence.

"It had less to do with you, and more to do with what I wanted and couldn't find here. But I knew leaving Kipsty meant leaving you, and trust me, it wasn't an easy decision." I'd cried myself to sleep many a night because even though I was chasing a bigger life than Kipsty could offer, I missed Greer fiercely. He wiped my cheek, and I realized I'd started crying. For him. For me. For us. For the time we lost.

"I regret leaving *you*," I whispered. "Every day. But leaving Kipsty was what I needed, Greer." I let out a breath. "Kipsty was too small, and I felt trapped here, but when I was with *you*, I always felt like I could fly. And then you left for college, and I was stuck here. You came home on weekends, and I knew college was important to you, but you were gone more than you were here, and most days, I felt like I was losing my mind being here alone. Can you see that? After all this time, can you try and understand?"

He opened his mouth but was cut off by a sharp knock on the door. That was fast. Then again, because Kipsty was so small, Kyle could be here in less than ten minutes, regardless of where he was coming from. For all I knew, Kyle was on his way over anyway.

"You guys okay in there? All decent?" His voice was more amused than concerned. "I'm going to jimmy the lock with a screwdriver, see if that works, okay?"

Greer looked at the door. "Okay," he replied gruffly. He positioned himself in front of me, and after a bit of noise, and effort on Kyle's part, the lock clicked, and the door sprung open. He stuck his head in.

"All fixed." He grinned when I peered around Greer. "You'll need to replace the lock," he explained, holding it in his hands. "Until then, you won't be able to close the door."

"Thanks, man," Greer replied, keeping me behind him. When Kyle didn't make a move to leave, Greer cleared his throat. "You mind?"

"Sure." Kyle chuckled. When he was gone, Greer turned. "Finish up in here. I'll leave the bathroom door open, but close your bedroom door, okay?"

I nodded, and he placed a kiss on my forehead before walking out. I heard the shut of my bedroom door and sagged against the wall. I played our kiss over and over again in my head, even while I showered and changed into my pajamas. When I made my way downstairs, Kyle was gone, and Greer was leaning against the window in the living room.

"Hey."

His head snapped in my direction. "Hey. Feeling better? Kyle dropped off some dinner too. It was his but he insisted we had it." Because I had the kiss playing in my head on a loop, I wasn't hungry. Not for food anyway. My body was still vibrating with unspent desire, and it all started with a kiss. Well, not just any kiss. It was because Greer kissed me. And it held both promise and precious memories from our youth.

I knew Greer as a young man, someone who, like me, was finding his way. But I wanted to know him as a man, as who he was *now*. And I found myself wanting him to know this version of me.

"I'm not hungry...for food," I said, something within me snapping. My entire body was still vibrating.

The tension between us tightened for a second before he pushed off the windowsill and approached until he stopped in front of me. I looked up and felt my pulse skitter beneath my skin.

"I'm sorry," I murmured. "For ever making you feel like you weren't enough. Because you were, you always have been, Greer." He took in a sharp breath, and then his mouth was on mine. We were rushed and uncoordinated. Greer picked me up. I threw my pajama top off en-route to his bedroom and unbuttoned his shirt, leaving it on the floor.

He walked into his bedroom, and the entire space smelled like him. I didn't even bother looking around. My mouth fused to Greer's. He laid me on the bed and, without any finesse at all, removed my pajama pants and white lace panties.

Should have come down in a towel? Would have been faster.

I pressed my knees together while Greer removed his denims and boxer briefs and watched as he spread my legs. He leaned over me to the bedside table and grabbed a condom, tearing it open with his teeth. And *then* I looked. His cock was hard and thick, a vein running on the underside that stood out as it wound its way to the head.

Greer slid the condom on with ease and flicked his gaze to me while rubbing hot hands against the outside of my thighs. I squeezed a breast in my hand, primed for him. There was no time for foreplay. We needed this—now!

Inhaling a stuttered breath, my eyes traced his chest, his perfectly shaped pecs, his staggered abdominal muscles, and the pronounced V that led to his shaft. I licked my lips and squeezed my insides. I let out a squeak when Greer pulled me closer and roughly flung my legs to the side. He took his cock in his hand, sliding his hand up and down before pressing the head through the lips of my sex, over my swollen clit. I shivered when I felt him press himself to my entrance and knew, from the gleam in his eye, that this was going to be hard and fast, and that's what he needed, what I needed too.

Lifting my hips, he slid in just an inch, and slid out before snapping his hips forward. My back bowed off the bed as he filled me, and I let out a soundless mewl, my mouth hanging open as I adjusted to his size. He muttered curses under his breath, using a finger to rub my clit. I sighed out a heavy breath as my body lowered to the bed, and when I looked up, he was looking down at where he filled me. I lifted my hips, and he slid out the slightest bit but slid back in when I moved my hips down again. He crouched over me, stealing a kiss before he started thrusting. I grabbed the bedding until my knuckles were white and inhaled our sounds while Greer set a punishing pace.

"Oooh," I moaned into his mouth, grabbing hold of his neck with one hand. "Please," I begged, already close to that glorious precipice. Greer grabbed my butt cheeks and held me still as he snapped his hips faster and harder. My toes curled, and I cried out when he sucked a pebbled nipple into his mouth.

"Yes, yes, y-yes," I chanted, and then gritted out a, "Fuck." He wasn't slowing down, and I was fast approaching the cliff, anticipating the fall.

"Come with me," I breathed. His gaze flicked up, and he moved from my nipple to my mouth.

"Mine," he murmured before sliding his tongue into my mouth. He thrust his hips and stayed still as we crashed over the edge into an oblivion of stars and explosions. My body felt warm all over as I shook, arching my back and letting my legs fall to the side. Greer gripped my throat and grunted into my mouth. He panted, his body vibrating with his release, inadvertently giving me a second orgasm.

My heart felt too big for my body, my lungs working overtime for air. I slid my hands into Greer's hair and pulled, closing the small space between us until I could feel his heartbeat against my chest.

317

That was an angry fuck. No two ways about it.

The thought, however, made me smile against his lips.

"Feel better?" I teased, breathless. He grinned, knowing I'd caught him out, and nodded.

"I don't remember it being like that," he replied, gaze probing.

A burst of laughter came from deep in my chest, and I replied, "We know what we're doing this time." And it was the truth. We fumbled *a lot* when we experimented as teenagers.

"The question is..." I added quietly, a challenge in my tone, "...whether your stamina is the same." Greer was insatiable when we were dating, and so was I. But there was something to be said for time and experience, and the opportunity to mature.

Greer kissed the side of my neck and sucked, leaving a mark. He'd always done it, and I was secretly thrilled he still did. "Let's find out," he replied, reaching for the bedside table and rolling us so that I straddled him.

Game on.

Chapter 10

Greer

Della had her bare leg thrown over mine, her head on my chest as I trailed my hand down her spine, counting the bumps in my head. My floor-to-ceiling windows gave us a spectacular view of the snow falling steadily outside and the big, fat moon in the sky. She sighed, her warm breath fanning over my chest. I turned my head and kissed her forehead, enjoying the feel of her tucked against me and in my arm. She slanted her head to look up at me and gave me the sweetest smile before looking back out the window.

"Tell me about New York," I murmured. "About your business." It seemed a safe topic now that we'd used each other's bodies to get out the pent-up frustration and dormant anger and regret.

"The city is beautiful," she replied softly, nuzzling closer. Any closer and she'd end up under my skin. Not that I'd mind. It felt as though she'd been living there for years, even when were apart. It was the reason Maisy and I never worked out. Because she wanted a place that belonged to Della, and I was a fool to think it could ever belong to anyone else. "It's a hive of activity, and it's true that it's the city that never sleeps. The energy is addictive and loud, and I loved it."

I heard her take a breath before inhaling my own, savoring the scent of her and me mixed together. Sweat and sex and something sweet. "I loved the pace of it all and feeling small compared to everything around me." I tried to picture her there, and the truth was, I could because I'd seen her.

"I saw you once," I admitted in the quiet of my bedroom. I felt her gaze on me but didn't meet her eyes. "I wanted to see you," I sighed. "See for myself that you were happy, and the day I saw you, you were walking down Fifth Avenue with a friend, I think, and you were laughing and smiling, and then I knew I had to let you go. It was about a year after you'd left." I begged Nanna Delia for weeks to tell me where Della lived, where she worked, anything. And at first, she wouldn't tell me. Eventually, she caved in. "Nanna Delia told me that you liked to go get a mid-morning coffee at Bluestone Lane's Upper East Side Café every day of the week before going back to work. I caught the first flight after that."

"Why'd you never say hello?" she asked. Her tone wasn't accusatory. Just curious, if not a little surprised.

I sighed. "Because I could see you were happy, Della. You were with a few people and seemed to be in your element. And I wasn't going to ruin it by showing up out of the blue." I relaxed when I felt her head drop back to my chest. "As long as you were happy, I could cope, you know?"

"I was happy," she admitted. "The people you saw me with were other interns I worked with. It was my first job at an event coordinating firm, and as hard work as it was, I fell in love with my work." She rubbed my chest, and my skin broke out in goosebumps. But I loved the feel of her hand on my skin.

"Three years later, I decided to go out on my own and start my own firm. I took those same friends with me, and one of them became my assistant." I felt rather than saw her smile. "We planned some of the most extravagant events, Greer. Galas and fundraisers for the city's elite, and that's how I built my business. I networked with all the right people, who referred me to more people, and soon I was planning birthday parties for the children of famous athletes and celebrities." She shifted and rested her chin on my chest, her arm around my ribs.

The moon caught her eyes, and they looked icy blue in the light. Her blonde hair was a mess, but she looked beautiful. Ethereal, really. Otherworldly. And I was a mere mortal, soaking up her essence. Her brows knitted then, and I lifted a hand to smooth the frown away with my thumb.

"I'm not sure when I stopped loving it," she said. "It started taking more and more out of me, and at some point, it stopped feeding my soul. I started feeling restless and unsettled. Ungrounded, I guess. And when Nanna died..." she exhaled, "...I asked myself if it was what I still wanted. If being in New York was still what I wanted." I felt the lift of her delicate shoulder. "I got engaged shortly after Nanna died, but that also felt wrong. I thought it was because it was just such a big step to commit to someone for the rest of my life when it was someone else I'd always envisioned my future with."

My heart stuttered in my ribcage.

"I could never admit Alex wasn't the one..." she continued, "...but it felt like it was the *right time*, the *next step*, so I went with it, thinking those feelings would pass." She sucked her lips. "Then he cheated, and as much as that hurt me, I wasn't nearly as upset as I should have been. So, I took it as a sign, and decided I was done with all that. I sold my business and apartment and packed it all up to return to Kipsty."

She tilted her head, laying her cheek on my pec.

"It was the first decision in a really long time that felt right. I *knew* it was what I needed, but I also knew it wouldn't be temporary." She huffed out a laugh. "The last time I saw Nanna before she died, I was so unhappy, and no longer had a clue what I was doing, and she said to me it would be over soon enough because Kipsty was calling." She shook her head. "I only figured out what she meant when I ended up in a damn ditch ten minutes from town."

Her hand rested on my stomach, and Della started playing with my fingers when I said, "You're the reason Maisy and I never worked out."

She frowned, and this time I didn't wipe it away. "What do you mean?"

I shrugged. "She wanted to fill a space that was yours, and when she started talking about having a family, I switched off. I'd only ever imagined having a family with one person my whole life, and that was you. She tried to trap me a few times, did some crazy things, but when she never fell pregnant, we started fighting more until I couldn't take it anymore. I filed for divorce and ended it."

Della swallowed, the shadow of her throat moving. "I'm sorry, Greer. That must have been hard on you."

"Not any harder than being cheated on," I replied. She leaned forward and pressed her lips to mine. It wasn't seductive, or a segue to something more. She was kissing me to make it better. I cupped the back of her head, and held the kiss a little longer, just because I could.

I relaxed back into the mattress, and then asked, "Did you make any decisions about the Christmas market?" I wanted to change the subject, but I wasn't ready to sleep yet. I wanted to keep talking to Della, regardless of what we were speaking about. I wanted to make up for lost time.

She smiled and nodded excitedly. "I was thinking about having Santa's Village as the theme, like the North Pole. My former assistant is sending some things over, and I'm taking a drive to Boulder tomorrow to see what I can find. I'm looking for those big, plastic candy canes, and I was thinking of a petting zoo type set-up where kids can pet some reindeers, maybe some llamas too, I'm still figuring that out, and I want a few stalls where kids can learn to make their own Christmas candy, some Christmas tree ornaments and hot chocolate with chocolate bath bombs. Maybe have a treasure hunt? I'm not sure about all the details yet." The lilt in her tone revealed her excitement, and I had to admit her idea was better than good. And it was different.

"You need to borrow the Jeep for all that? Can't imagine you'll fit much in your Lexus." I was also less worried about damage to my car.

"I'll let you know in the morning," she replied, hiding a yawn behind her hand. "What did you think about my idea for the cabin remodel?"

I quirked a brow. "You want to turn it into a luxury cabin, Della."

"Of course, I do," she laughed. "Nanna lived in that cabin her whole life, so did my mom and I. I think it's time for an upgrade, don't you?"

I chuckled. "Sure, but once everyone sees it, they'll want theirs remodeled too, and you know it's just me and Kyle."

"Would it hurt getting some help? Wouldn't be a bad thing to expand your own business, you know. Besides, it'd be good for tourism if Kipsty became known for luxury cabins. Like yours but on a smaller scale."

"You have a good point." It was my turn to yawn.

"We should get some sleep," Della murmured. She moved to get up, but I pulled her back by her arm.

"Where are you going?"

"Uh..." she blinked, "...to my room?"

I shook my head. "Not happening, Della Marie." I chuckled when she gave me *the* look. She hated being called Della Marie, and I knew it. "You're staying right here, where you've always belonged." I tucked her close to my side again and grabbed the duvet we'd kicked off at some point. I covered us both, made sure she was comfortable, and tucked my nose in her hair.

It didn't take long for her breathing to even out first, and for a while, all I did was listen to the steady cadence of her breath. I looked and saw her lashes fanned across her cheeks, remembering just how many times we'd fallen asleep like this. A small part of me was worried she'd get tired of Kipsty and leave again, but something about her seemed far more settled now than the day she left.

Something in me felt more settled too, and perhaps it was the knowledge that it wasn't me who wasn't enough. Della left because she felt stuck in a small town and needed to experience the world. And I came to the realization that I had expected her to just wait for me when I knew she wanted out. College wasn't something she wanted either, and at the time, I was happy to go to class Monday through Friday and come home for the weekend. But *I* was happy, and at the time, I'd failed to see that Della wasn't. So instead of supporting her the way I should have, I took it personally.

Maybe if I'd supported her the way I could have, she could have left, and we'd have made it work somehow. But I couldn't see anything past my own life then, and I assumed Della would always be there. What I knew now at 30 that I didn't know then was that the first time Della left, I had it in me to just let things be instead of trying to manipulate the situation to suit my needs at the expense of Della's.

A kernel of hope nudged its way into my chest, and I felt grounded in the knowledge that Della wasn't going to leave again. I believed her when she said she wasn't going anywhere. I couldn't ignore the way we'd gravitated towards each other as soon as she arrived, though, and when I looked at her, even now, my heart beat out the word *home*. Because Della *was* my home, and I'd just been waiting for her to come back. Even if I didn't know it, my heart did.

I rolled over, giving the big, fat moon and the floor-to-ceiling windows my back, and slid my hand around Della's waist to push her deeper into my chest and tangle our legs together. And if I had it my way, we'd stay like that. My mind flashed forward in time, a vision just like this playing out, and I liked what I saw.

Chapter 11

Della

Three weeks later

I stumbled through Greer's front door, arms laden with brown paper bags from the Christmas market. It had been one of the most successful markets the town had had in years, and I was damn proud to have pulled it off. Though, if I was honest, I'd pulled off bigger events under more pressure and in less time, too, so a Christmas Market in three weeks was nothing to me.

I may have sold my business and quit the industry, but I still thrived under pressure and made it work. Greer appeared at the top of the staircase and walked down, helping me take the bags to the kitchen. He peered into a few and shook his head.

"You didn't tell me you were a shopaholic," he teased, his mouth tilted to one side. I blew an errant strand of hair from my face, and smiled.

"I couldn't help myself. They had some really nice things on sale this year, and I figured we could use some new decorations for our Christmas tree. Had to get the good stuff on day one." A tree Greer hadn't put up since he divorced Maisy. I'd put it up the day before, and after my little shopping spree today, I'd have wrapped gifts surrounding the tree in no time.

I walked over to Greer, and wrapped my arms around his waist, looking up at him. "How did you and Kyle get on with the cabin today?"

After that first night with Greer, we had a lengthy chat about Nanna's cabin, and what I really wanted to do with it. Greer nixed my idea to move in there, and insisted I just stay with him. On the other hand, I didn't want to let the cabin go so we've spoken about renting it out. And as expected, as soon as people in town started noticing the updated renovations, they started asking Greer and Kyle to renovate their cabins too. Greer was in the process of hiring more hands, but that meant getting people from the next town over. He didn't have much of a choice, though. His business was growing, and he'd have to grow with it to keep up. It was all a series of *fortunate* events, I guess, since I arrived, and I couldn't be more pleased. And I hadn't felt more settled in years.

"Got a lot done, actually," he replied, locking his hands in the hollow of my back. "We should be done in a few weeks, and then we'll start on the next one." I stretched onto the balls of my feet and kissed him. "That's good news. Daisy-May is beside herself with all the patrons at the diner because the Christmas Market started so well today and will be so successful, so I guess that's another win."

Greer hummed and lowered his head, brushing his lips across mine. "Missed you today." We'd been inseparable, for the most part, since the first night I slept in his bed, and rather than feel panicky about it, like I thought I would, I felt calm, and completely at ease with how everything was turning out between us. I tried imagining a different outcome, but every one included Greer, and this was by far my favorite.

There was no talk of me leaving again, and that seemed to negate any worries either of us might've had on the subject. We were in a good place, and I soaked it like a sponge.

"Missed you more," I replied against his mouth. His eyes were ablaze with desire and delirium, and I was sure my eyes reflected the same.

"Have you eaten?" he asked, brushing my hair from my face and removing my beanie and my scarf.

"Grabbed something at the market," I told him. I had a feeling I knew where he was going with this, and I liked it. "You?"

"Grabbed something with Kyle at the diner," he replied. "Told him I had plans tonight."

I quirked a brow. "Plans?"

"Plans," he repeated before sealing his mouth over mine. Oh, so it was *those* kinds of plans.

I giggled against his mouth and pulled away. "You had me this morning," I teased, though I wasn't about to deny him a damn thing right now.

He grinned, showing off his straight white teeth. "And I'm about to have you again. I've got a decade worth of time to make up for." This time, when he kissed me, we didn't pull away. He lifted me with ease, and while he devoured my mouth and I devoured his, he carried me upstairs to our room. Things had happened so fast, but part of me wondered if the universe was just waiting for me to come back so it could all finally fall into place the way it should have.

I stripped out of my parka and lifted my long-sleeve Henley over my head. I shook my hair out and went back to kissing Greer. He dropped me on the bed, making me laugh, and I watched with greed as he removed his shirt and his jeans. I pushed my jeans down my legs and giggled when Greer grabbed a leg and haphazardly flung it over his shoulder. He watched as I got rid of my panties and my bra and then removed his boxer briefs before grabbing a condom from his bedside table. I sat, and as soon as he crawled onto the bed, and laid on his back, I straddled his hips and slid the condom on.

We'd had sex in many positions, and often too, but this was probably my favorite. On my knees, I took his hard shaft in my hand and pushed the head through the lips of my sex, shivering when I applied a bit of pressure over my clit and at my entrance.

Greer gripped my hips and murmured, "Go slow." But I had

other plans in mind. I toyed with myself a little, hearing Greer breathe out heavily while his eyes tracked my movements. I'd very quickly learned he liked watching his cock fill me, like watching my body taking him in. I swallowed and blew out a harsh breath before dropping down until he was buried to the hilt.

"Christ," he cursed, gripping my hips hard enough that he was sure to leave marks. Not that I minded. I leaned my body forward, pressing my lips to Greer's while my fingers dove into his hair. I teased him with my tongue, felt his hands slide around to my butt, and then I sat up, leaning my hands on his thighs. Ever so methodically, I lifted my hips, giving him a front-row seat to the view of him sliding in and out, in and out. He gritted his teeth, a muscle popping in his jaw as a growl surfaced from deep in his chest.

I knew he liked it, but I also knew I'd drive us both insane if I didn't pick up the pace. I threw my head back and bit my lip, sniffling a whimper. It was a true testament to my patience, and Greer's determination, because seconds later, I sat upright and held onto Greer's forearms while he started lifting me up and down.

I fell forward, resting my hands on his chest, and started moving faster. The room filled with the sound of skin-to-skin contact, my whimpers, his grunts and it made for an erotic, if not lewd, symphony. Without warning, Greer flipped us, and started thrusting in earnest.

"Oh God," I cried, my hands slipping over his damp skin. "Harder. Greer." I swallowed, and let out a mewl, feeling the heat start to pool low in my belly. It was my turn to lick my lips and grit my teeth because the bang of the headboard joined the symphony of our chaos.

Breathing hard and fast, Greer sucked my lip into his mouth, and bit. The way he took me and the way I gave myself to him was so feral.

Hearts pounding, bodies colliding, I gave him a wide-eyed look to warn him I was close.

"Greer," I whispered, begging for him to get me there. I was desperate to crash over that cliff, but like always, I wanted him there with me. His eyes were crazed, and when he thrust harder but slower, I knew he was chasing the flames that would incinerate us both alive soon enough.

I lifted a trembling hand, and gripped his nape, digging my nails into his flesh. I held on to him like that when we finally lit up like a wildfire and flew over that delicious and decadent cliff, shaking and quivering helplessly until we floated down.

His hot breath fanned the skin on my neck, and I could feel his pulse dancing as erratically as my own.

When he'd somewhat slowed his breathing, he lowered himself on top of me, still buried between my legs, and I parted my thighs to make room for his waist. He wiped my sweaty forehead and gave me a sex-lazy smile.

"Gets better every time, doesn't it?"

I smiled because he was right. Every time with him felt new and exciting. "I hope it never changes."

A while later, after we'd showered and made something to eat, we sat on the sofa, my head on his lap, watching the snow outside the large floor-to-ceiling windows.

"Do you believe in fate?" he asked, his voice low. I looked up and found he was watching me.

"Sometimes," I replied. "But I also believe we make our own fate. Losing your parents wasn't fate, and having my mother drop me on Nanna's porch before leaving for good wasn't fate, but those things haven't defined us." His hand rested on my chest, and I threaded our fingers together. "But I believe I was meant to come back," I added quietly. "In my own time, I guess."

"Did you think about me when you decided to come back?" His voice was low but laced with curiosity.

I nibbled the side of my mouth, deliberating how much to tell him. Eventually, I decided to just be honest.

"Every day between the time I left New York to when I got to Kipsty," I admitted on an exhale. "I was terrified you'd be married and have kids because I'd always thought that was *our* future, you know? I mean, we were young when we were together, but even then, my future, every which way I looked at it, included you. It's why leaving you tore me up inside. It felt as though I was sacrificing the love of my life to live a life I fell in love with, and that didn't even feel fair. So, of course, I wondered about you over the years. Every time I called Nanna, I had to stop myself from asking about you in case you'd moved on. I wanted you to be happy, but..." I shook my head a little, "...I struggled with the idea of you loving someone else the way you loved me. And I knew I'd never love someone the way I loved you. It was impossible, Greer. I resigned myself to the fact that I'd have to *settle* because I'd left most of my heart here with you."

I blew out a breath, and only then realized I had tears pooling in my eyes. I looked away, but Greer shifted so he could settle me on his lap. His strong, capable hands cupped my cheeks, his thumbs wiping the tears sliding down my face. "I don't regret leaving," I told him. "I needed to grow and find my own way, but you were never far." I lifted his hand and placed it over my heart. "I carried you with me for eleven years."

I sucked in a breath and waited, tracing Greer's masculine features with my eyes. He was beautiful and so divine. I saw my whole life flashing in his eyes, and that made my heart flutter in the confines of my ribcage.

He swallowed audibly, breathing out through his nose when he replied, "I tried falling in love again, Della." The admission stung, but I had no right to feel jealous, so I did my best to quash the feeling in my chest. "But no one ever came close to you. I chose you when I was sixteen. I just didn't realize back then it was for keeps. And I didn't think you'd ever come back..." he trailed off, and it felt as though I could read his mind. He was scared I'd never come back but also tried hard to move on, only to be left disappointed when the me-shaped hole in his heart wouldn't fit anyone else. Little did he know, it was the same for me.

"I never stopped loving you, Greer," I shivered, my voice trembling. "I still do, and it scares me because it was so all-consuming the first time, and now it feels so much bigger."

"Because it is." He rested his forehead against mine. "I never stopped loving you either. I didn't know how so I just stopped trying."

I held onto his wrists, brushing the underside with my thumbs. "How about now?" I asked. "We can't go back in time, but maybe we can start again?" I wanted that, more than he knew. And then he smiled.

"I started again the moment I saw you standing in Nanna's cabin, looking a little lost, and I wanted nothing more than to find you again."

I sighed, the sound a burst of relief and pure affection for this man. "I'm glad you found me," I whispered. "I didn't realize it, but I was waiting for you to find me."

Epilogue

Greer

One year later

I never imagined what my wedding day would look like, just that it would be Della meeting me at the altar; Maisy and I had had a court wedding, and looking back now, I had been adamant about that. I watched her careful steps as Kyle escorted her down the aisle and closer to me. The small church was filled to capacity with our friends and loved ones sitting in the rows of pews.

The officiant smiled down at me and then looked at Kyle. "Who gives this woman away?"

"I do," Kyle replied, reaching for my hand to shake. Della and I spoke about this part at length when we started planning our wedding, and it seemed fitting to have Kyle give her away. He'd never admit to anyone that he got teary-eyed the day we asked him, but he did. He kissed Della on the cheek and helped her up the steps until she faced me. She took my breath away, her white gown flowing around her on the floor. Her shoulders were bare, her blonde hair falling around her in curls. Her blue eyes shined, and her smile was happy.

Once Kyle took his seat, I took Della's hands in mine and felt them tremble. Or maybe it was my hands that were trembling.

"Friends, family, loved ones..." the officiant started, "...we are gathered here today to celebrate the love between Della and Greer and the life they will share together." He made a speech about forever and love, but I was only half-listening. I was too busy staring at Della to pay much attention. Until he cleared his throat. I blinked and looked at him.

"Pardon?" I asked, feeling my cheeks warm when my question caused our guests to laugh.

"Your vows," the officiant said. "Must I repeat them?"

I grinned, and Della giggled. "Please."

He smiled. "Do you Greer, take this woman to be your lawfully wedded wife, to live together in matrimony, to love her, comfort her, honor and keep her, in sickness and in health, in sorrow and in joy, to have and to hold from this day forward, as long as you both shall live?"

I licked my lips, still smiling. "I do."

He looked at Della.

"Do you, Della, take this man to be your lawfully wedded husband, to live together in matrimony, to love him, comfort him, honor and keep him, in sickness and in health, in sorrow and in joy, to have and to hold from this day forward, as long as you both shall live?"

Della's smile was iridescent. "With everything I am," she replied. "I do."

"Rings?" the officiant asked.

Kyle stood from his spot in front and handed both Della and I our rings. I held her ring over her finger.

"With this ring..." I started, "...I promise to love you with everything I am. I promise to stand by you through the hard times, the best times, and everything in between. I promise to be the best husband, the best partner, and, someday, the best father to our children. You are my beginning, my middle, and my end, and everything in between. I vow to love you until my last breath, Della. Every day, all day. Until the sun sets for the very last time." My hand shook as I slid her ring into her finger, and when I looked up, Della had tears coming down her cheeks. She held my ring over my finger and swallowed.

"With his ring..." she started, "...I promise to be your best friend, to love you every day through the good and the bad times, and whatever happens in between. I promise to cherish your heart as long as I breathe and to love you for as long as I'm alive. You are my world, my heart, my soul, my best friend and..." she licked her lips and sighed, "...the father of my child."

The church went still but only for a few seconds, long enough for me to catch what Della had said.

"What?"

She laughed and nodded, tears falling. She quietly slipped my ring on, and then I had my hands around her face. "We're pregnant?" I asked. The church filled with sound, cheers, and claps, and I pressed my mouth to Della's, feeling my heart balloon in my chest.

"We're not at this part yet," the officiant whispered, loud enough to garner some laughter from our guests. But I didn't care. I slipped my hand around Della's back, and held her to me, a vision in my head of her belly growing with our first child. God. I loved this woman more than life itself, and now we were going to have a baby, part of me and part of Della. I couldn't contain my own tears, allowing them to fall freely. I broke our kiss, and wiped Della's cheeks.

"Are you happy?" she asked quietly. I nodded, my gaze flitting between her eyes.

"Completely," I murmured, going in for another kiss, this one longer and far too inappropriate for a church. At some point, the officiant gave in and pronounced us husband and wife to another round of cheers and laughter.

Me? I was wrapped up in my *wife* and the mother of my child. Della squealed when I picked her up and swung her around, her laughter a gentle sound. I put her down and again cupped her face. "Really?" It all felt so surreal.

"Really," she replied. "I wanted to tell you this morning, before the ceremony, but..." She shrugged. "Surprise."

I laughed with pure joy and replied, "You're perfect."

"Give it a few months," she teased. "When I'm round, with swollen ankles and super cranky. Then I won't be so perfect."

I shook my head. "You'll always be perfect, Della. My kind of perfect."

~ THE END OF THE SERIES ~

If you enjoyed the *Mountain Man Daddy Series*, take a look at a sneak peek of the first book of Hadsan Cove Series: *Flames and Forget-Me-Nots*.

Prologue
Clark

Seven years ago

"Do you want to carve the turkey, Clark?" Dad asked me in a vain attempt to drown out my brother's droning through the window. I was craning my neck to see them on the porch. Poor Isla looked devastated. I could see her trembling, although it was cold, and neither of them had worn their jackets.

"Brady said he wanted to do it," I said flatly.

"I don't think he's coming back," Dad said pointedly. He even held out the carving knife across the table for me to take.

Brady caused some drama like this every holiday season. He was always the center of attention, always ready to put on a morbid Christmas show against our will. It was even snowing this year, and it would've been romantic if he was trying to patch things up. We couldn't keep letting him get away with it.

"It'll get cold," my mother added hopefully, but I had lost interest in the meal already. It was always better warmed up the next day, anyway.

To make matters worse, the next song on the playlist started, and I heard Paul Young crooning the opening lines of "Do They Know It's Christmas?" Evidently, they did not.

That was enough for me, and to the tuts of my parents, I left the dining table and crept over to the front door, where I could see their silhouettes clearly through the fogged glass. Their voices were much clearer now.

"You still haven't explained to me why you keep going back to

Mary-Anne," Isla said to Brady with a sigh. Even through the glass, I could see her stiffen, and her voice became sharper.

"I don't know."

"When was the last time?"

"November."

"Just the once?"

"Twice."

"Can't you see she just wants to use you? She never loved you. You were always her backup plan."

This made Brady scowl. It was a fair comment.

"There's no need to be mean," he whined.

"Mean?! You've just admitted to cheating on me, again, with Mary-Anne, again, and you think what I said to you is mean?"

"Yes, you always do this." Brady huffed.

"I always do this? You slept with her last Christmas, right when we started seeing each other. You said our relationship was new and didn't think it would last. You said you came clean about it because you wanted to take things seriously."

"Look, Isla, can we not make a scene? You did this last year, too. We're supposed to be having Christmas dinner with my family."

"Why did you bring it up then?"

"OK. Alright. I'm sorry I mentioned it. Are you happy now?"

"No! And you can try to pretend you mean it. You always sound so cavalier. Why would you do this at your parents' house? Am I supposed to go back there now and pretend everything is fine?"

"If that's what you want to do, but I'd rather you just take off to save me the trouble of having to get through the evening with you," Brady said, venom in his tone, just as Simon Le Bon sang 'There's a world outside your window, and it's a world of dread and fear.'

That was enough for me. I grabbed their coats on the coat rack by the front door, opened the door, and the sound of the latch was enough to burst their bubble. Both of them were immediately silent when I stepped out onto the porch, like I was a schoolteacher catching two of my pupils being mischievous. They both crossed their arms, and before Isla turned away from me, I saw the tears welling in her eyes.

"It's freezing outside. Bundle up," I said, looking between them as I handed them their coats. Isla took hers without looking at me, while Brady practically snatched his, giving an ungrateful scoff. Any other time, I would have torn him a new one for being disrespectful, but the look on Isla's face had been enough to mellow me out.

I heard Isla stifling a sniffle. Poor girl. She deserved better than Brady. I don't know why she kept going back to him. She could do so much better, and could have been with any number of guys who wouldn't have done what he did so callously, so remorselessly. There really was no need for her to keep going through this song and dance over and over.

She was right, too: he wasn't really sorry. He still preferred Mary-Anne, and he always had. They'd been high school sweethearts, though if you ask me, there was nothing sweet about their relationship. Brady had always been wrapped around her little finger, and for the life of me, I couldn't understand how he didn't see right through her. So when Mary-Anne broke up with Brady on their high school graduation day, he'd been devastated. In fact, I'm sure he only started seeing Isla initially to see if it would make her jealous enough to take him back, but when it didn't work, he was stuck with Isla. Whenever Mary-Anne came calling, he would go running back, and I was sure she often did so only to see if he still would.

"Let's take a walk, Brady," I said curtly to him, tapping him on the shoulder and nodding at the driveway.

"Alright. Seeing as it looks like I won't be staying anymore, I will need a hotel, anyway. I parked at the bottom of the hill 'cause of the ice. You can walk me to my car."

"Alright, just hang on one second," I told him, then showed Isla inside. Isla gave Brady a forlorn look before walking through the door frame. But Brady pulled at his coat impatiently, puffing out cold breath. He rubbed his hands, looking towards the bottom of the hill.

Annoyance boiled in me. I'd be having words with him on our way down.

"Is she alright, Clark?" Mom asked.

"Yes, she's fine. I'm just going to sit with her in the living room. I'll come back in a minute."

I took Isla into the living room next to the dining room. It was cozy, with a shag carpet and newly polished wooden furnishings. It was small, but big enough for the two of us to fit inside comfortably. There was a fireplace and a small couch. She walked straight over to the couch and lay down, facing away from me. She was still cradling herself.

"Do you want me to carve you some turkey? I can bring your plate in here for you," I asked her as I took a blanket out from a nearby basket where my mother liked to pack away extra blankets and pillows, and shook it out for her.

She didn't respond. I felt awful for her. She was curled up in the fetal position, wiping her face with her hands. I threw the blanket over her and tucked her in.

"Thank you," she whispered.

"Do you want the fire on?"

"Yes, please," squeaked the reply. I got on my knees at the fireplace and threw a log in. I hadn't done this in years and almost forgot to add a firestarter, which was in one of the drawers of the console table next to the couch. I felt her eyes on me as I passed her, then searched frantically through each drawer from top to bottom. My heart raced when I saw her watching me through my periphery. I couldn't believe the power she had over me, even in the vulnerable state she was in.

I remembered last Christmas when Brady had done the same

thing to her. She'd been dismayed. I couldn't believe, after all that, he had the gall to do it all over again.

Once I got the fire going after what felt like an age, I returned to her, proud of myself.

"Thank you," she whispered, settling down now as the tears started to subside. As I looked down at her amid the flickering flames, I could see her face was still wet. I subconsciously stroked her hair, which calmed her even more and then leaned towards her to kiss her on the forehead.

But as I did so, she turned towards me and reached out, catching my cheek as our noses were close to touching. I froze, unsure of what to do or what she thought as she looked up at me. Her damp eyes sparkled in the firelight, and her dark hair was sprawled out over the couch like an inviting blanket. I noticed a tiny mole on her lower cheek, which made her look like Marilyn Monroe.

It felt so intimate being that close. The crackling of the wood behind me sounded like whatever was being ignited within me by her touch and in receiving her gaze. It washed over us with its warmth.

I had tried to suppress it for so long, ever since she'd started seeing Brady, but my heart was racing now. She placed her other palm on my chest with such a delicate curiosity. She could feel my heart reaching a crescendo, anticipating something forbidden happening between us, and there was no hiding it. There was only the unspoken truth.

She looked at my chest, and back at me. She didn't recoil or protest. She was waiting for what I was going to do next. Welcoming it, even.

I wondered how she would taste if I kissed her now, and how her damp, excited tongue would feel running over mine. Her perfume was so sweet, it was intoxicating, and now all I could think about was feeling her pressed against me with her legs wrapped tightly around my waist.

I was so close. It would be so easy, but the door leading to the hallway was still ajar, just barely out of my reach. My brother was waiting for me outside. My parents could hear from the dining room.

Isla was stunningly beautiful, and she had changed so much in the last year or so since she'd gotten together with Brady. She had just turned eighteen then, both of them in the first year of college a town over from Hadsan Cove. She had much more confidence now. Her touch was so pure as I felt the firm tip of her fingernail on my temple, and her thumb under my chin. She was guiding me to her, and I was utterly powerless to stop her as I hungered for her. I felt that nonexistent gap between us shrinking as she exhaled, and I breathed in her breath that beckoned me to the source just as Band Aid started to sing 'feed the woooorld' next door in their final climax.

Will Isla and Clark find their way back to each other? What happens when a blast from the past returns wanting to make amends? Will Clark prove to Isla that he is the man for her? Will Isla finally put herself first?

Book 1 is now available!